Home Grown

Home Grown

NINIE HAMMON

Bay Forest Books

Home Grown

Copyright © 2011
Ninie Hammon

Cover illustration by Mona Roman Advertising
Interior Design by Bookcovers.com

Published by Bay Forest Books
An Imprint of Kingstone Media Group
4420 Bay Forest Lane
Fruitland Park, FL 34731
www.bayforestbooks.com

Printed in the United States of America by
Bay Forest Books

Library of Congress Cataloguing-in-Publication Data

CIP data applied for

ISBN 978-0-9799035-6-4

Prologue

As he fumbled in his pocket for the keys to lock the office door, Jim Bingham sensed rather than heard someone step out of the shadows behind him. When he turned and saw the man's face, the 69-year-old career journalist's heart began to bang away in his skinny chest like a cook whapping a metal spoon inside a pot to call the hands to supper.

Jim recognized the sudden copper taste of terror in his mouth. The *Callison County Tribune* editor had felt that airless, hole-in-the-belly sensation before, too—the day he took pictures of the writhing black twister as it roared up Chicken Run Hollow, and all those dark nights with bombs exploding around him in London.

A wet-behind-the-ears war correspondent, Jim had covered the Battle of Britain, watched tracers light up the sky from the window of a closet-sized office in a building across from Westminster Abbey. The considerably-larger office he now occupied was in a building across from the Hair Affair Beauty Parlor and next door to the State Farm Insurance Agency. And the story he'd just hammered out, hunkered over his worn-out Royal Electric typewriter, was about the winner of the Brewster Elementary School spelling bee.

But the contrast was what made the big story he was working on so delicious! The irony was half the fun—a shot at a Pulitzer Prize for investigative journalism as an old man. Not some young buck, but a *senior citizen* at the tail-end of his career. And here! While he was running a weekly newspaper in a little five-traffic-light Kentucky town that didn't have a McDonalds, a Wal-Mart, a movie theater or an open-24-hours *anything*. In Brewster, a community where everybody waved, whether they knew you or not, where you could pass along the juiciest tidbit of gossip with a clear conscience as long as you called it a prayer request, where you shoveled your neighbor's sidewalk along with your own and he spanked your kids for you if they needed a backside-tanning and you weren't around to do it yourself.

Who'd ever have guessed he'd unearth a national story this big right here in Callison County?

When he picked up his hat and stepped out into the muggy darkness, he'd been thinking about his daughter. He'd tried to call her, wanted to talk to her about the big story, but she wasn't home so he'd left her a message.

It was probably best he didn't talk to her, though. She'd have been worried about him, scared for him, the way he was now—so scared it tasted like his whole mouth was full of pennies.

Jim never saw the gun in the man's hand, just the smile on his face, a cold smile that never reached his dead, shark eyes. He heard the thundering bang, though, and felt the .45 caliber slug tear into his chest and rip open his heart. Felt it for one agonizing moment before everything began to fade. Then his world dimmed, grayed out and went black.

Chapter 1

CALLISON COUNTY, KENTUCKY
July 1, 1988

Bubba Jamison reached down and scratched Daisy under the chin, just above the scar on her neck where he'd slit her throat when she was a puppy. Most dogs didn't survive, maybe one out of a whole litter. But those that did became the perfect weapon—with slit larynxes, they couldn't bark. Bubba didn't want anybody to hear his guard dog coming.

A drip of the perspiration beaded on the big man's forehead skated down the ridge of his hawk nose to the end and hung there, dangling off the tip. Bubba shook his head like Daisy climbing out of the river and splattered a spray of sweat on the sumac and crepe myrtle leaves he was hiding behind.

Even the chainsaw-cry of the cicadas in the nearby sugar maple trees seemed turned down a notch, like maybe the sweltering heat had sucked all the energy out of the bugs, too. And it wasn't even noon yet.

'Course, he could have been sitting in air-conditioned comfort right now instead of roasting out here in the woods with chiggers chewing on his ankles. He could have gotten all dressed up and gone to the funeral home in Brewster where Jim Bingham was laid out for visitation.

Bubba made a *humph* sound in his throat. Yeah, right. He and the newspaper editor hadn't exactly been on friendly terms the last time they—

He suddenly froze, stopped breathing. The panting Rottweiler at his feet had stiffened. The dog rose slowly, would have growled, too, if she could have. The hair on her shoulders bristled; she bared her teeth in a silent snarl.

There was a rustle of leaves; a branch snapped. Somebody was out there.

His shotgun cradled like a toy in his muscular arms, Bubba peered out through an opening in the brush and strained to hear through the throbbing hum of the cicadas in his ears.

A twig broke, and then he heard the sound of shoes scuffling on rocks. Somebody was coming all right, somebody who was making no effort at all to conceal himself. The idiot was actually whistling the theme song of *The Andy Griffith Show!*

Rival dopers intent on stealing or destroying his crop wouldn't come waltzing into the woods announcing their presence to every critter between here and the Tennessee line.

Neither would the law.

A squirrel hunter. Had to be. Illegal, too; the season didn't open for another month. Bubba heard the distinctive pop of a .22 rifle and a mumbled expletive to his left and down the slope. Another shot. Another expletive. Obviously, the fool couldn't hit the broad side of a tobacco barn, either—some "outdoorsman" wannabe down from Louisville or Cincinnati trying out his brand new Father's Day rifle. Probably had a copy of *Field and Stream* stuck in his hip pocket open to the page titled "Squirrel Hunting For Clowns."

The intruder switched tunes, started belting out *High Noon* loud as a train whistle coming into a station. Bubba shook his head. Did the idiot think squirrels were deaf? That the furry little buggers were all gonna line up on tree limbs with "Shoot Me" signs dangling 'round their necks? That moron'd given enough warning so's ever squirrel in the county had time to build a fort out of acorns to hide in.

Pop!

The shot was a little farther away this time. The hunter was angling along the bottom of the hill where Bubba sat on a hollow log concealed by bushes. He'd hit the dry creek bed in another 50 yards or so, below the spot where there was a small waterfall when it rained, which it hadn't in a month. The rock outcrop there prevented access to the hill, so he'd be forced to follow the creek bed down toward the road. If Bubba just kept still, he'd be gone in 10 minutes.

Bubba and his dope were safe. The fool didn't trip over it; had no idea it was there. He'd get into his car in a couple of hours, might even bag a squirrel, too, if one had a heart attack and dropped dead at his feet. Then he'd drive home without ever knowing he'd wandered within 75 yards of half a million dollars worth of marijuana on the hoof.

But he'd be back. Next weekend or next month. Might bring some friends.

Bubba leaned over the Rottweiler and whispered into her ear.

"Git 'im!"

The black dog tore out of the bushes and down the hillside. She didn't make a sound.

• • • • •

The smell of roses, gardenias, gladiolas and mums combined to form a single cloying fragrance, the signature aroma of every funeral home in America.

Elizabeth Bingham had always hated that smell, but today it wasn't just an anonymous assault on her senses. It was personal. The shiny silver casket beside her held the body of her father.

She'd been in Singapore when she learned he'd been murdered and had only stopped briefly in Los Angeles to pick up Ben before flying to Louisville. Now, she was perched on the edge of an uncomfortable chair—*Why did the furniture in these places always look like it came from a French Chateau?*—in a big, windowless room at Beddingfield's Funeral Home. The funeral director waited at the other end of it for her signal to open the double doors so the people lined up outside could come in for the viewing.

And Elizabeth absolutely did *not* want to see all those people. She'd never met most of them and wouldn't likely remember the ones she had. She didn't want to make nice with a horde of strangers right now, not jetlagged and exhausted, and with a headache she was trying desperately to pretend wasn't jack-hammering a hole in the back of her skull.

As if he could read her mind, Ben patted her reassuringly on the shoulder. It was such a tender gesture from a 16-year-old boy she was afraid she was going to burst into tears again. Instead, she took a deep, shaky breath and nodded to the funeral director. He turned and opened the doors and the dressed-in-Sunday-best crowd surged quietly forward to pay their final respects to the man who'd been a fixture in their community for more than half a century. And to get a look at the daughter Jim Bingham was forever bragging about.

The next three hours were a blur of faces and mumbled condolences. At one point, Elizabeth wondered in semi-hysteria if the people leaving were actually just going out one door, changing clothes and then coming back in the other.

Aunt Clara and her tribe of children and grandchildren arrived late and set up shop in the receiving line on the other side of the casket. Elizabeth had come to the funeral home straight from Standiford Field and hadn't yet spoken to any of her relatives. She searched the crowd of adult cousins frozen in her memory as children, looking for one face, for eyes that gleamed with a sparkle mere years couldn't possibly have dimmed. But she recognized no one.

And after shaking hands with dozens of other equally unrecognizable people, Elizabeth checked out, went on autopilot. Her mind recorded short movie clips, though, a minute or two here and there. One day, the clips would be precious beyond measure to her. The images on them would breathe life into the words from her favorite

Jim Bingham column, the one she'd framed two Christmases ago so he could hang it on his office wall.

"Life in the big city? Naa, I think I'll pass. I'll take a small town any day, a community as close knit as steel wool where lifetimes of shared experiences have so marked people's faces most everybody looks like family. A place where you can count on your neighbors to show up at the significant events in your life and to look for you at the significant events in theirs."

The turtle man was sure to be on one of the clips. Short, round, bald, long neck, hooked nose, no chin, dressed in a dark green jacket and brown pants. He cocked his head to the side in slow motion when he stopped in front of her, and gazed at her with eyes that appeared to have no lids at all.

"Make no mistake 'bout it, Miss Sarabeth," he said in an emotionless monotone, "your daddy's with the Lord."

"Well, actually it's *Elizabeth*, and I know—"

"It's still hard, though, ain't it." The man patted her arm with fingers as long and thin as flippers. "When the good Lord sends you tribulations, you got no choice but to tribulate."

Hard to argue that.

Behind the turtle man was an enormous woman wearing a flowered dress that looked like it was made of upholstery fabric.

"My gracious but you shore do favor your daddy, Sarabeth. He was so proud of you!"

"Uh, it's *Elizabeth,* and I'm the one who's proud!"

And she was, too, fiercely proud of her father. For 51 years, Jim Bingham had described and transcribed the life of Callison County, told his readers what was happening around them and then helped them figure out who they were in the context of those events. Her father had been her hero. Now he lay in a shiny silver casket a few feet away. Elizabeth felt the chill of grief work its way down through her body the way cold water sinks because it's heavier.

She gripped the arms of the chair and struggled for control, scrambled for something to say to keep from crying.

"Did you live next door to us when I was little?"

"Oh, no Sugar, I was your third-grade teacher," the woman gushed. "You're thinking 'bout Edna." She looked up and beckoned a slightly smaller woman wearing an equally-ugly flowered-upholstery-fabric dress. When the pair stood side-by-side, they looked like a couch and matching loveseat. "Edna, say hello to Sarabeth Bingham."

"It's *Elizabeth*."

After a dozen "it's *Elizabeth's*," she finally gave up. The byline on her column in the *LA Times* notwithstanding, here in Callison County, she wasn't Elizabeth Bingham; she was Sarabeth, her father's daughter, the little red-haired girl who grew up in Brewster. After she got used to the sound of the name again, it felt normal. And ... real, *comforting* in a way she was too upset to analyze.

Her mind filmed the line of law enforcement officers, too, all of them with their hats respectfully removed. Gray-uniformed Kentucky State Police troopers. Blue-uniformed Brewster Police Department officers. Brown-uniformed Callison County Sheriff's deputies.

A stocky, bulldog of a man with a kind face and a big badge on his brown shirt shook her hand, offered his condolences and then said gently that he'd like to talk to her about her father's case later, somewhere more appropriate.

"Right here and right now are fine with me," Elizabeth told him resolutely. "If this is about my father's murder, I want to hear it."

Callison County Sheriff Sonny Tackett nodded, an acknowledgement that Jim Bingham's daughter had obviously inherited his salt.

"I just wanted you to know that we've made an arrest, Ma'am. The man's name is Joe Fogerty."

"What makes you think this Fogerty guy did it?" Ben fired the words in a tone that aimed for strong and mature but came to rest a little south of rude and abrasive. Elizabeth reached up and patted his hand resting on her shoulder.

Home Grown

The sheriff looked Ben square in the eye. "Joe Fogerty's a mean, foul-mouthed drunk who went off on Jim about a week ago in the clerk's office in the courthouse." He answered the boy's question respectfully, didn't treat him like a kid. "Jim had published Fogerty's DUI arrest in the *Trib*'s court news and Joe was ticked." Tackett shook his head. "Don't know why in the world he'd care; it's not like he had a reputation to damage. Still, I had to escort him to the street to keep him from taking a swing at Jim. He was the first person I went looking for after Jim was shot."

Elizabeth winced at the word *shot*. As a journalism professor, she taught her students that pussyfooting around reality was usually harder on victims' families than just telling it straight out. But she'd never been a victim before.

"The morning after the shooting, dispatch got a call saying Joe was lying next to the dumpster behind the Esso station on Phelps Road. I found him there in a blackout, didn't even know his name. He had a .45 caliber pistol in his pocket. We'll have the ballistics test results on the gun from the state police lab by the end of the week, and ... "

He stopped. Unexpected pain was etched in the creases around his eyes and in the firm set of his mouth. Though some of his sorrow had settled, it was plain what he was about to say was stirring it all back up again.

"And what?" Elizabeth prompted.

"It wasn't just the gun. We also found your father's hat."

"My father never wore a hat."

Tackett smiled, a wide smile that revealed toothpaste-commercial white teeth. When Elizabeth remembered this conversation later, she would recall the fondness for her father she saw now on the sheriff's face.

"Oh, yes he did! The ugliest hat I ever saw. It was a straw thing he won at the ring-toss booth at the county fair last summer, had this big green parrot feather in the band. Soon's your daddy realized how much everybody hated it, he wore that hat everywhere he went just to be ornery."

The good humor drained out of the sheriff's voice. "Joe Fogerty was wearing that hat when I found him lying by the dumpster."

Elizabeth felt like somebody had punched her in the belly. She bit her lip hard, determined not to burst into loud, sloppy tears. Her father would have wanted her to be strong.

"Will you excuse me, please," she managed to whisper before she turned and bolted out of the room.

Chapter 2

Billy Joe didn't know why he'd stopped. He passed this spot two or three times a week. What was different about today? Probably just wanted to put off going to the funeral home. Or maybe he wanted to take in the scenery before the day heated up. Yeah, that was all it was, just wanted to enjoy the view. Nothing wrong with that.

He pulled his big Chevy Silverado pickup truck off Glen Cove Road onto the shoulder, climbed down and walked around to the front. He leaned his lanky frame back against the warm hood and gazed up into an achingly green hollow so perfect it seemed brand new, and so ancient it felt like time itself had let out its breath there in a slow, sweet sigh centuries ago and had never breathed back in.

Though the real mountains of Eastern Kentucky were next door neighbors, Callison County was not in Appalachia. But it did lie in a belt of almost-a-mountain hills that swung down out of Indiana and made a U turn in central Kentucky about 100 miles west of the Cumberlands. The massive hills the locals called "knobs" created a network of picturesque valleys, deep, secluded hollows and sheltered meadows tucked away from view, all linked together by a web of narrow, winding roads that meandered lazily among the giant hills in no particular hurry to take anybody anywhere.

The knobs that stood sentinel in Callison County set it apart from surrounding counties where thoroughbred colts played tag in paddocks guarded by miles of pristine white fences. That's what the tourists came to see; that's how the world pictured The Bluegrass State. But Billy Joe knew the real heart of Kentucky beat in its center, right here in Callison County. And he felt genuinely sorry for the rubber-neckers who missed it, who drove down the interstates gawking at horse farms and blew right by the take-your-breath-away beauty just a few miles away, snuggled up next to country lanes like Glen Cove Road.

A tattered wisp of morning mist lingered just above the trees on top of the knob high above Billy Joe's head. Glen Cove Hollow spread out before him like a just-completed oil painting with the brush strokes sparkling wet in the morning sun. He felt a sudden lump in his throat and an ache of inexplicable longing—for what, he couldn't say.

A sea of oak, sumac, hickory, maple, dogwood and redbud trees lapped up the sides of the valley, their varying green hues a dappled mosaic in the morning breeze. A picture frame of chocolate-brown, just-tilled earth bordered two fields of burley tobacco that had ripened early, with broad leaves so bright lemon-yellow they were almost florescent. Dense, tangled soybeans cuddled up beside corn stalks standing at attention in rows of military precision. Spotted Holstein dairy cattle grazed in one pasture; sheep stood out like white polka dots in another.

Meandering down Glen Cove like a lazy snake, the north fork of the Rolling Fork River was wide and deep here, spanned by a walking bridge near the road. Wooden steps, sun-bleached a shiny gray, led up 15 feet to a landing where a narrow, slat bridge with rope handrails hung swaying in the wind.

Billy Joe's daughter, Kelsey, had walked from their trailer house on the far side of the river across that bridge every day to wait for the school bus that pulled off the road to pick her up just about where he was now standing.

The trailer wasn't there anymore, of course. After they moved out five years ago, it had sat empty for a long time. Then he drove by one day and it was gone. Apparently, someone had stolen it. Billy Joe figured if they wanted the thing bad enough to haul it two miles downstream to the gravel bar to get it across the river, they were more than welcome to it.

He'd bought it used right after he and Becky got married 15 years ago, snagged it at an auction in Bowling Green. Two tiny bedrooms, a combination kitchen/dining room/living room, and a single bath—with running water. The Callison County Water District lines hadn't come this far out, but there was a spring on the back of the property. The RECC, Rural Electric Cooperative Corporation, had provided electricity, but they didn't own a television set. No phone, either. South Central Bell had quoted them a price to run a line from their nearest neighbor on the other side of the knob, but the figure was far more than they could pay. There had been no sewer system, either. They couldn't afford to dig a proper septic tank, so Billy Joe had laid a pipe from the trailer that emptied into the river downstream.

Billy Joe squeezed his eyes shut for a moment to ease the strain of squinting into the morning sun and the images were just as vivid in his mind as out there in the real world. But with his eyes closed, the trailer house was still there on the other side of the walking bridge, a flower garden out front and a vegetable garden out back with a nearby clothes line where Becky always left a pair of his old overalls hanging to flap in the wind. She said it helped keep the birds and the deer out of the garden.

He could see Becky, too, washing dishes beneath the window with red chintz curtains the night he came home from the tavern in Crawford after his first meeting with Bubba Jamison. She was singing along with Dolly Parton on the radio, "I-I-I will always love you-oo-oo," her belly so big with Bethany she couldn't get close enough to the sink to keep from dribbling a trail of water with every dish she handed him to dry.

Becky was a beautiful woman, wholesome, like her picture belonged on the front of a cereal box. Short, honey blond hair that curled around the pink "chipmunk cheeks" she hated, big brown eyes framed by lashes so long and thick they looked artificial, and a small, slender, delicate body—well, most of the time it was small. And when she was pregnant, there was a glow about Becky that took Billy Joe's breath away. In fact, he'd been staring at that glow as he wiped plates with the red checkered dish towel, drying each dish slowly while he tried to figure out how to tell her what had happened to him that night.

"What?" Becky had cocked her head to one side. "What're you staring at? You got the funniest look on your face, Billy Joe. Is somethin' wrong?"

"I'm staring at you 'cause you're so da-gone pretty, that's what." He leaned over and kissed the tip of her nose. "There's nothing wrong." A heartbeat pause. "But ... " Then he took a deep breath and launched into the story.

He'd stopped in Crawford at the tavern for a beer after he got off work from his part-time job stocking groceries at Brewster Market. Crawford was a town of 500 to 600 people about six miles from their trailer. The tavern there had a hard-earned and well-deserved reputation for being the roughest bar in the county. Brawls were a fairly regular occurrence. Squire Boone's customers were tough men who worked and drank hard, smoked, spit, and didn't fancy strangers.

Billy Joe had gone there a couple of times with his daddy when he was a boy and the place had changed little in the 20 years since.

Same 10-point buck trophy hanging behind the bar, its cloudy marble eyes staring at everything and nothing, its rack knit together with a fine lace of dusty spider webs.

Same lame jokes about the trophy: "That buck sure musta been movin' when it hit that wall!"

Same quarter-sawn, white oak bar, worn smooth by four generations of elbows; same bar stools with seats worn shiny by an equal number of backsides.

The sturdy-as-an-anvil wooden tables and mismatched chairs had survived decades of mayhem to rest on a floor where food and beer had been spilled every night for more than a century. Boone maintained that one of these days he aimed to pry up a piece of that floor, take it home to Martha and get her to put it in a big pot of hot water and make soup.

Boone's family had owned and operated the tavern since it opened sometime in the late 1800s. Though the family wasn't related in any way to the famous Kentucky frontiersman, Boone's parents had named him Squire, after Daniel Boone's father.

A stout, ruddy man whose fiery red hair had gone pure white, Boone's claim to fame was a glass eye—courtesy of a broken-beer-bottle fight—that he pretended to gouge out and then pop into his mouth like a breath mint whenever strangers happened into his establishment. His only son had been killed in Vietnam when the Bardstown National Guard Unit lost 45 men in a firefight on June 9, 1969. He proudly displayed the boy's picture in uniform on the wall by the pot-bellied wood stove.

"Evenin', Squire," Billy Joe said as he stepped up to the bar and politely removed his University of Kentucky cap. Billy Joe bled Wildcat blue. "Guess I'll have me a Bud."

The inn-keeper reached for a mug. "Martha was serving at St. Dominic's fish fry Thursday and we seen you and Becky. That girl looks like she's 'bout ready to pop."

Billy Joe's smile planted dimples in his cheeks so deep you could have scooped grits out of them. "It'll be another couple of weeks yet. We're hoping for a boy this time."

Somebody plunked a quarter into the juke box and selected Alabama's latest hit. "Oh, play me some mountain music, like grandma and grandpa used to play ... " wailed from the machine in the corner as he paid for his beer.

Billy Joe made his way through the haze of cigarette smoke toward the back of the bar where the music wasn't so loud and took a seat just as the conversation about movies ended with the comment, "My wife dragged me to Bardstown to see that movie, *E.T.* Now don't you laugh, but when them kids on bicycles started flying, I's so surprised I liked to a'wet my pants."

Then the group of men around the table started talking about dope. Marijuana was a topic of endless discussion in Callison County. Almost everybody knew somebody who was involved in it. Or pretended they were involved. Or pretended they weren't.

"A fellow got busted last week for growing dope on the back of my brother Roy's farm," said a beer-bellied man wearing a greasy John Deere cap. He lifted the cold mug of beer to his lips with his good left hand. The right had been mangled so badly by a threshing machine when he was a teenager that it hung limp and useless from his wrist. "Scared the bejeebers out of Roy. He figures the law's bound to come knockin' on his door any day now, but he didn't know nothin' 'bout that dope being there."

"Or he made out like he didn't know," said a little man in a red-and-black checked shirt who was always angling for a fight.

"It's a big farm. A fella can't keep track of ever inch of it."

"'Pears to me," drawled an old man with white hair and big ears, in a Georgia accent as thick as it had been the day he left Macon for Kentucky sometime during the Eisenhower administration, "that the dopers is gettin' thicker 'round heah than ticks on a hound dog."

"Ya think?" sneered the man in the checked shirt.

"I seen in the paper where the sheriff found a whole field of dope, more'n two acres of it!" the man in the John Deere cap continued. "Said the deputies cut it down by hand—musta took 'em a couple of days—and hauled the whole lot of it to the landfill and burned it."

"Bet half the teenagers in Callison County was standin' down wind." Billy Joe said.

There was a beat of silence before the old man brayed a donkey laugh that spewed beer out his nose and mouth all over the hostile little man's face and checked shirt. He jumped up, so livid he was dancing in place, spitting cuss words the way a welding torch spits sparks. The others burst out laughing at his response and pretty soon everybody on that side of the room was roaring right along with them.

When the laughter finally died down, the conversation heated up.

"I'm here to tell you, those boys raising dope are making so much money they're out burying suitcases full of $20 bills in the woods 'cause they can't spend it all," a fat, blowhard townie from Brewster said. The Crawford boys wondered how come he drove all the way to Boone's two or three times a week just to have a beer, but Billy Joe had figured out why. He'd met the man's wife; that woman had a face would curdle new milk.

"With pot selling for what it does on the street in Louisville these days"—the townie had no idea what pot sold for in Louisville, but he fancied himself an expert on everything—"they don't have to grow a whole lot of it to make a killing. Ain't no police goin' to find every single plant."

"I don't see what all the fuss is about," Billy Joe said. He was addressing the men seated at his table but the tavern was crowded that night and the dope conversation had drawn the attention of just about everybody there. "Dope money spends the same as your money and my money, don't it? I haven't seen any businesses turning it down. Have you?"

The men shook their heads. No, they hadn't seen anybody in the county turn down dope money, no matter who was spending it or what they were buying with it.

"From where I'm sittin', with a baby on the way and last year's tobacco crop gone to black shank, making some easy money don't exactly sound like a sharp stick in the eye." Billy Joe took a sip of his beer and smiled his dimpled smile. "Shoot, I'd do it if I had the chance."

"Now, don't you be talking like that, B.J.!" the man in the John Deere cap snapped. He'd been a friend of Billy Joe's father. "Blowing smoke about dopers and growing marijuana's all well and good, but it's something else again to talk about joining 'em! This here's dangerous bidness. If the law don't git you, some other doper will. I don't reckon any of them boys is likely to die of old age."

The conversation washed back and forth after that. By the end of the evening, most of the men had argued both for and against the county's burgeoning marijuana industry. Billy Joe'd decided a long time ago he didn't see any harm in it. His daddy hadn't owned a still, but in his day he'd certainly bought more than his share of white lightening from those who did. The government was all the time trying to tell people how to live their lives, making first one thing and then another *illegal.* Growing marijuana was no different from making moonshine; you couldn't blame a man for doing what never should have been against the law in the first place.

Billy Joe finally stood and set down his empty mug. He'd been nursing the same beer all evening; couldn't be drinking up his paycheck with a baby coming. He said his goodbyes and stepped out into the warm night, hoping he wouldn't have to go back in and get somebody with booster cables to jump-start the engine on his pickup. The truck needed a new alternator, but until he sold this year's tobacco, he couldn't afford one.

"You mean what you said in there, Billy Joe?"

The voice came out of the darkness. Billy Joe was so startled he whirled around ready for a fight. Heart pounding, he watched as a huge man moved out of the shadows next to the building and into the puddle of light cast by a lone bulb hanging high on a pole above the gravel parking lot.

If even half the stories about him were true, Bubba Jamison was one of the biggest dopers in the county. Billy Joe had never so much as exchanged a howdy-and-shake with the man and was surprised Bubba knew his name. He was even more surprised at Bubba's size. Dressed in clean overalls and scuffed work boots, he was taller, broader and—well, *meaner looking*—than when Billy Joe had seen him at a distance.

"What I said about what?" B.J. stammered.

Bubba reached into the pocket of his chambray work shirt, pulled out a plug of Red Man chewing tobacco and bit off a hunk. The stillness around the big man gathered and settled. The air thickened, like the breath of a storm before the rain hits.

18

"I need men like you." Bubba's deep voice rumbled in his broad chest like it was bouncing around in an oil drum. He cocked his head toward the tavern. "There's not a one of them farmers in there could pour water out of a boot if the instructions was on the heel. You're a smart man. I'm looking for smart men."

Billy Joe didn't know what to say so he just kept his mouth shut. What had he ever done that had caught the attention, that had *impressed* someone like Bubba Jamison?

"Here's what I'm offerin'. I teach you how it's done so you raise good weed and don't get caught. I'll pay $500 a week starting out, more as we go along. End of the summer, you get a cut of whatever makes it to market. Anytime you want out, say the word and we're quits."

Bubba stepped up to him. Billy Joe was 6'1", but Bubba towered over him. The huge man leaned so close Billy Joe could smell the wet Red Man on his breath. "I can make you a rich man, son. Richer'n your wildest dreams."

Without another word, Bubba turned on his heel and crunched heavily across the gravel toward his custom Ford XLT Lariat pickup parked in a dark corner of the lot.

"You think on it and let me know when you make up your mind," he tossed over his shoulder as he walked. Then he stopped and turned around, his face lit by the solitary light high up on the pole. "You don't want the money, Billy Joe, I'll find me somebody else who does. It don't matter to me one way or the other. What you need to understand is that I can make a fortune with your help. And I can a fortune without it."

Billy Joe got into his ancient Chevy pickup truck, sank down in the hole in the seat and banged the door shut three times before it caught. Then he sat in the silence that followed, trying to get his mind around Bubba's proposition and what it could mean to his family's future.

Billy Joe had not been born poor. He'd had college and career plans before he found himself with a wife and baby to support at age 18. With no marketable skills, he'd become a farmer. It was all he knew. He'd certainly never intended to spend his life barely eking out a living, but every year, his finances were worse than the year before and Billy Joe could see no way to dig himself out of the hole.

He let out a big, shaky sigh and smiled a little. Ever since he was a kid, he'd heard folks talk about once-in-a-lifetime opportunities, but he'd never personally run across one. Until five minutes ago. With his heart hammering like a lunatic woodpecker in his chest, it was all he could do to grab hold of his excitement and rein it in so he could drive home at a reasonable speed. The tires on his truck were bald as a newborn baby's butt; wouldn't do to have a blow-out. Not tonight!

As he told Becky the tale, he studied her face, but he couldn't read her reaction. When he finished, she just looked at him, then reached out wordlessly, took the towel he was holding and dried her hands with it.

"What do you think?" he blurted out. "Five hundred dollars a week! That's dang near more'n I make in a month."

"No."

That was all, just that one word hanging out there in the still air between them.

Not a soul who knew her would have described Becky Reynolds as a strong woman. She'd been 16 when she got pregnant and she and Billy Joe'd "had to get married." She'd never spent a moment of her life standing on her own or thinking for herself. She hated confrontation and had only one time in their nine years of marriage failed to sail right along with whatever Billy Joe wanted to do. When he'd suggested they move to Louisville or Cincinnati or Nashville so he could get a factory job that paid better than farming, she'd been absolutely adamant. Callison County was home! Period.

Becky's lower lip began to tremble and words tumbled out. "Billy Joe, I don't want you to do this. Please tell me you'll say no, that you'll tell Bubba Jamison to go find somebody else to turn into a criminal and leave you and your family alone!"

She ended with a sniffle right before her voice broke. She didn't cry though, and Billy Joe was glad. He hated it when she cried.

"Now, Honey ... "

"Billy Joe Reynolds, we don't need that man's money! We don't need nobody's money. We're doin' just fine. Oh, we don't have some things maybe we wish we did, but someday—"

"Becky, listen to yourself. We don't *need* his money? We're *fine?* If you didn't can vegetables from the garden every summer, we wouldn't have enough to eat! We can't pay for Kelsey's school lunch so she has to be in that federal program, the one for *poor* people. My truck's dying, Becky. Every time I turn the key, I pray it'll start just one more time. We can't afford to fix it. What are we gonna do when it's gone—walk?"

He hadn't meant to raise his voice, but he was close to shouting. Becky stood in front of him trembling, a little mouse in the cold. She wasn't crying, but her face was slick with tears. He shouldn't have upset her, not with her pregnant and all.

"We'll be Ok—you'll see," she said, her voice thick and tear-clotted. "We've made it this far. We'll be all right."

There was about Becky a little-girl quality that was at once endearing and maddening. Sometimes, she just flat refused to see life the way it really was. She'd been raised in a big, gregarious Catholic family, the tenth of 12 children, grew up eating beans and grits and wearing triple hand-me-down clothes. She had never had much and was content—no, *happy*—with very little. Her world was simple and uncomplicated, and Billy Joe had done his dead level best all these years to protect her innocence, to shield her. But how much longer could he shore up their crumbling lives before reality crashed down on both of them?

"You get all tangled up in this marijuana business, you're gonna get caught. What'll Kelsey and I do then—huh? And the baby—what about the *baby?*"

He watched the realization that she could be left to raise two children on her own send Becky over the edge and she burst into tears. She threw her arms around his neck, pulled as close to him as the melon in her belly would allow and cried, shoving her face into his chest to muffle the sound so Kelsey wouldn't hear from her bedroom.

"Please don't, Billy Joe," she begged between hitching sobs. "Please, Baby, tell me you won't do this. *Please!*"

Billy Joe caved in. He was no match for her tears.

"Ok, I won't. I'll tell him no. Now stop crying. I'll say no—you listening to me? Hush now. Shhhhhh." He patted her back until she stopped sniffling. "You get yourself all worked up and that baby's gonna come early."

He pulled out of her arms, took the dish towel back and wiped the tears off her round cheeks with it. "Can't have that bun coming out of the oven 'fore it's brown on both sides, now can we?"

That got a smile out of her, though her bottom lip was still trembling slightly when she patted her round belly. "This bun'll stay right here 'til it's done all the way through. A little crying's not gonna to change that."

Becky leaned up on tiptoes and kissed his cheek.

"I love you," she breathed in his ear, and somehow managed to sound sexy even with her face all wet and a belly full of baby. "Now, you go put Kelsey to bed while I finish these dishes." She shoved him toward the little girl's bedroom. "And say her prayers with her."

Billy Joe went into the tiny bedroom where his 9-year-old daughter's pixie face was buried in a book. The little girl's thick braids hung down her back all the way to her waist, so flaxen blond they were almost white. Her eyes were a clear, startling, ice blue, a stark, arresting color that gave the child's slightest glance a penetrating quality, "like she's looking right through you and out the other side," Becky often said.

"Time for bed, Kells. Go brush your tooth so it don't fall out and come say your prayers."

Kelsey heaved a long-suffering sigh. "You know I got more than one tooth, Daddy." She rolled her pretty blue eyes, then closed the book reluctantly and laid it on the bedside table. When she returned from the bathroom, she knelt, folded her hands together on the bed, squeezed her eyes shut tight and began a sing-song litany of God-blesses.

"God bless Mommy and God bless Daddy and God bless the baby and please make it a girl and God bless … "

But Billy Joe wasn't listening to Kelsey's prayer anymore. When he knelt beside her, his knee had landed on her shoes. Now, he held them in front of him, turning them over in his hands. There was a quarter-sized hole in the sole of the left shoe and one bigger than a fifty-cent piece in the sole of the right. Becky had placed cut-out pieces of heavy cardboard inside the shoes that fit as perfectly as store-bought insoles.

The little girl finished with an amen flourish and hopped into bed. Billy Joe kissed her goodnight and turned out the lamp. But even in the dark, he could see the shoes with their pieces of cardboard.

He could see the shoes still. As he stood on the roadside with his face turned toward the empty spot on the riverbank where the trailer house once stood, he could see the shoes in his mind as clearly as if he were holding them in his hand.

A wave of emotion swept over Billy Joe so powerful he was stunned by its intensity. Hot tears filled his eyes and streamed down his face. He couldn't identify the feeling; had no idea what it was. So he just stood there looking up into Glen Cove, crying silently.

Chapter 3

With the bathroom stall door locked firmly behind her, Elizabeth Bingham collapsed on the closed toilet lid and cried, great heaving sobs that left her breathless and aching. Though her sorrow was too sharp, too jagged for anything as simple and cleansing as tears, after awhile she felt better, exhausted and hollow, but better.

She didn't feel good enough to go out there and face all those people again, though. Not yet. When she opened the bathroom door, she spotted another door marked "Family Lounge" at the end of the hallway. She could hear voices coming from the room, but when she stepped inside, she was surprised to find only one person there. He had his back to her, talking on the telephone, making enough noise for several people.

"Let's just say he ain't the quickest bunny in the forest," the tall, willowy young man was saying into the receiver, laughter in his voice. "He's 'bout as sharp as a marble."

Then he turned and saw her. Recognition registered in his eyes and his face was lit by the sunny smile she remembered, the dimpled smile that'd break your heart.

"Sarabeth!" he cried.

He blurted "Gottagobye!" into the telephone receiver and dropped it on the cradle, then bounded across the room and enveloped her in a long-armed bear hug—not a plastic, greeting hug, but a real hug, tight. He rocked her back and forth and patted her on the back, crooning, "Sarabeth, Sarabeth."

Yeah, it was Billy Joe alright.

He finally released her, stepped back, took both her hands in his and smiled down on her.

"When did you get in?" he asked.

"Seems like a hundred years ago, but it was just this morning, I think. I'm still on Singapore time and I'm not really certain what day it is."

"I'm sure sorry 'bout your daddy." His voice caught in his throat and tears welled in his eyes. "Uncle Jim was as fine a man as I ever hope to meet." He reached out and put his arm around her shoulders. "But it's so good to see you, Bessie."

Bessie. Nobody on the planet except Billy Joe had ever called her that. When they were kids, Billy Joe was forever giving people silly pet names, and her initials, Sarah Elizabeth Bingham, spelled backwards, were BES. And she had called him Bije, rhymed with siege. Billy Joe. B.J. Bije.

Though they'd become Christmas-card relatives as grownups, Bessie and Bije had been inseparable as children, hanging out together on their grandparents' farm near Crawford. They'd climbed trees, built snow forts, chased chickens, went fishing—even sneaked up into the steeple at St. Simon's one Sunday morning and rang the bell during services.

Billy Joe was the youngest of Aunt Clara and Uncle Frank's five children. The others were girls, much older than Elizabeth. Even if they'd been her age, Billy Joe would still have been her best friend. His sisters didn't have his special magic. Energy, enthusiasm and good humor crackled in the air around Billy Joe like sparks off a blown transformer. And there was something about his eyes. Elizabeth had struggled for years to put a name to it, but the best she was able to do sounded like some goofy song lyric. It was true, though—Billy Joe's eyes *twinkled.*

"You're way more beautiful than I remember, Sarabeth," he told her, and his dimpled smile was so sincere it put a lump in her throat. But Billy Joe was looking at her with his heart or he'd have seen a much-too-thin woman with eyes sunk in circles as dark as cigarette burns in her pale, gaunt face.

Even when life was normal, before all that had happened to her in the past six months, Elizabeth had not been beautiful. She had never been beautiful. Her features were too large and expressive for traditional beauty. Striking-looking was a better description. A high forehead, almond-shaped hazel eyes, and a wide mouth with full, Sophia Loren lips that made her face sensual and arresting. At 5'10", she was big-boned like her father. But now, she was as hollow-cheeked and emaciated as a refugee. She had purposefully selected a shapeless black dress that camouflaged, as much as possible, her skinny frame.

Her great saving grace, however, was her hair. It always had been. Long, thick, natural curls the color of rust cradled her thin face and tumbled down around her shoulders.

"Well, you haven't changed a bit," she told Billy Joe and she meant it. He'd gotten bigger, tall and slender with sandy brown hair falling into his eyes, but he still looked like a boy even at 32. She smiled in spite of all her pain, just because Bije always made her feel like smiling.

All of a sudden, the door burst open and in fluttered Billy Joe's mother. Elizabeth had always believed her Aunt Clara was proof positive that the incidence of gypsies switching babies was a whole lot more prevalent than most folks believed. That this tiny, twittering, bird of a woman could be related to her father, who'd been so sturdy, strong and unflappable, was one of the great mysteries of Elizabeth's life.

"Why, there you are, Billy Joe!" She was talking as she opened the door, her voice high and squeaky, her salt-and-pepper hair falling into her eyes just like her son's. "I was wondering where you were. Can you go get a casserole out of Gladys Jackson's car and put it in mine?" She gestured toward the door that opened on the parking lot. "It's in the floorboard of the big blue Chrysler parked under the oak tree. And use the hot pads 'cause she just got it out of the oven."

When she noticed that someone was standing next to her son, curiosity played across her face before the wires connected.

"Why, Sarabeth honey," she squealed, and rushed over to grasp her niece in a remarkably tight hug. "I thought I saw you out front, Sweetie, but with all those people, I couldn't ... Oh, I'm so glad you're here. It's been so hard!" Tears filled her eyes and her lip began to tremble.

Oh, please don't cry! Don't get me started again.

Elizabeth felt sorry for her dithered aunt. Her brother's murder must have been a terrible blow. Clara's husband, Frank, had died soon after Elizabeth's mother swept her off to California. For awhile, the brother and sister had needed each other. But for years now, the need had been one-sided.

Aunt Clara didn't cry, though. She pulled herself together, cleared her throat and shifted gears.

"Where's Becky and the girls?" she asked Billy Joe.

Billy Joe took a beat too long to answer. Even in her current state of mush brain, Elizabeth picked up on it.

"Becky's not ... feeling well, Mama, so she ... Kelsey's home with her. She and Bethany, they're looking after their mother."

Aunt Clara blew past the answer as if she'd never even asked the question. But a pained, defeated look skittered across her face before she continued.

"Those hot pads, get 'em on good and tight 'fore you pick up that dish or you'll burn your hands. I'm parked on the street down from—"

Ben appeared at the door.

"You Ok?" he asked Elizabeth.

She gave him a weak smile and nodded.

Billy Joe looked from Ben to Elizabeth and back to Ben.

"Well, you sure enough got your mama's hair, boy—that's a lead-pipe cinch!" He gave Ben a big welcoming smile, then stepped over, grabbed the boy's hand and pumped it up and down like he was trying to draw water. He turned to Elizabeth. "I didn't know you had a son, Bessie. Uncle Jim told me about what happened, 'bout how you … "

He stopped, confused at the look of fresh, raw pain on Elizabeth's face.

Actually, Billy Joe was right. Ben did have hair just like his mother. Just like *their* mother.

"I'm Elizabeth's brother, Ben," the boy said when it was obvious Elizabeth was in no condition to respond. The self-introduction begged a bigger explanation, of course, but it was much too complicated to get into now.

The teenager had whispered into Elizabeth's ear earlier, during the interminable visitation. "I should have made myself a nametag: 'Hi, I'm Ben Malone and you've never met me so stop giving yourself a brain freeze trying to remember who I am.'"

She'd smiled for an instant and whispered back, "That's not a nametag; that's a bumper sticker."

Elizabeth was proud of Ben. He looked so clean-cut, so—what was the word? preppy—standing there in his Oxford cloth shirt and cuffed khakis. More than that, he seemed so grown up, had just stepped right in and taken over. She wanted to tell him that, but now she couldn't seem to find the air to speak. She was tired, so very tired.

It was probably Ben; the boy was as quick as a cat. But it could have been Billy Joe; he was closer. Elizabeth wasn't sure which one of them caught her before she smashed into the floor.

• • • • •

The squirrel hunter never saw Daisy coming. The big, black Rottweiler leapt on his back and used her 75 pounds of pure muscle to topple him face-first into the dirt. Then she went for his forearm, bit down hard and began to tear at it.

Home Grown

The initial shock of the dog's attack knocked the breath out of the 57-year-old pharmacist from Cincinnati. When she bit into his arm, he screamed, rolled over on his back and tried to throw her off. She let go of his arm and he scrambled to crawl away. Then she went for his leg. He tried to scoot backward in the dirt while the monster dog, its face smeared with his blood, mauled his leg. *Without making a sound!*

Bubba could hear Daisy at work from where he sat, could hear the sounds of the struggle, the man flopping around, probably hitting at her, kicking, trying to shove her away, and all the time howling in terror and pain.

He smiled. Good girl, Daisy. Good girl!

Bubba would have liked to have watched the attack. He'd have enjoyed seeing her rip the man's arm off. But he stayed where he was, hidden from view, and listened to the man scream as Daisy bit into his face, tearing out his right cheek and exposing his teeth.

The man began to cry then; the sound of sobbing mingled with his shrieks. Reluctantly, Bubba pulled the silent dog whistle out of his pocket and put it to his lips. Daisy froze, a piece of the pharmacist's flesh in her mouth, her muzzle gory with his blood. Then she leapt off him, bounded up the hill and vanished.

The injured man staggered to his feet and began to stumble away in the opposite direction. He made it down the hillside, across the meadow, over the fence and all the way to the car he'd left sitting on the side of the road. He fumbled the keys out of his pocket, sobbing, managed to unlock the car, leapt in, slammed the door shut behind him and then just sat there crying hysterically. It took him awhile to pull himself together. Then he started the engine and roared away, leaving a cloud of dust behind, to settle out of the air around Bubba's feet.

He'd followed along down the hill, far enough behind that the man couldn't see him, not that the idiot could have seen him 10 feet away if Bubba didn't want to be seen.

Bubba had to make sure the fool made it to his car. What good would it do for him to let Daisy rip the man apart if the guy didn't live to tell about it? About the black dog that came at him silently through the woods and almost killed him.

The big man looked around, picked up a fallen tree branch and used it as a broom, methodically swiping it back and forth across the ground until every trace that a car had ever been parked there was gone. He piled a mound of brush on the spot where the man had staggered out of the woods. There was a thick stand of Queen Anne's lace right beside the road and Bubba pulled all the plants up by the roots and threw the remains into the woods. He kept the city boy's precious new .22 rifle that he'd left behind in the dirt, though; Bubba loved guns.

Standing back, Bubba surveyed his work. It didn't look much different from before, but different enough. Tucker's Ridge was criss-crossed by dirt roads. This one wound through the knobs for 15 miles, twisting and turning like a drunk snake. There were probably 50 different places along it to pull a car off on the side of the road and park.

Why, it was out there on Tucker's Ridge, that urban idiot would tell the doctors and nurses, and eventually, the game warden and the sheriff.

Reckon they're gonna cite him for huntin' out of season?

Bubba grinned.

They'd bring him out here to show them where it had happened, but the man would never be able to lead them to the spot. Even if he managed to find the right dirt road, he'd been too traumatized to remember much about it, and this place looked just different enough now that it wouldn't match whatever picture he had of it in his head.

Meanwhile, his story would spread, getting bigger with every telling. Inside 24 hours, there wouldn't be a man, woman or child in the whole county who hadn't heard about the pack of rabid monster dogs prowling the hollows on Tucker's Ridge looking for prey.

And the squirrel hunter wouldn't be back next weekend.

Bubba turned with a smile, beckoned Daisy, and the two slipped silently back into the trees.

• • • • •

The four-man work crew assigned to unload barrel wagons outside the Double Springs Distillery warehouse called Citation pulled up in front of it as Seth McAllister hurried out of his office across the road and headed toward his vintage 1965 Mustang in the parking lot.

Brodie Jenkins, one of the crew men, spotted Seth and waved a greeting; the distillery owner lifted his hand in an absent-minded response. A tall, muscular man with hair as black as the night sky and eyes the color of a Hershey bar, Seth was distracted and running late. He wanted to stop by Beddingfield's Funeral Home for Jim Bingham's visitation before his one o'clock meeting at the cooperage and if he got stuck behind some farmer pulling a hay wagon on the road, he'd never make it.

The truck driver on the barrel crew eased the trailer into position in front of the warehouse. He parked it with the back end inclined at a steep angle down hill so gravity could propel the six 500-pound whiskey barrels lying on their sides in the trailer down guide rails behind it once the gate was removed and the retaining chock was knocked away from behind the back barrel.

A worker lifted the trailer gate off and tossed it into the grass just before the lunch buzzer sounded inside a nearby building. He and the others hopped down off the barrel wagon and headed for the break room.

But Brodie lingered behind, struggling with a fitting on the end of the first guide rail.

"I'll be right with ya," he mumbled under his breath. "Just gotta get this dad-gum catch ... "

He suddenly screamed, shrieked a chilling, heart-stopping wail of pain and terror! The back barrel had come loose, crushing his whole right arm as it rolled toward the end of the chest-high trailer. Worse, he was trapped! The five other barrels behind the one pinning his arm were loose now, too. Gravity was tugging them, dragging them down the slanted floor of the trailer. With no guide rails attached, all six barrels would topple off the end—right on top of Brodie!

He screamed again, a breathless cry of agony that ended in a strangled sob.

Out of nowhere, Seth appeared behind him and grabbed the hoop rings on both ends of the barrel a heartbeat before it tipped over the edge.

Brodie moaned, staring wide-eyed at his smashed arm. Then his knees buckled and he passed out, collapsed but couldn't fall, merely dangled by his pinned arm off the back of the trailer.

Seth planted his feet, locked his elbows, shifted all his weight into his shoulders and arms, then shoved the barrel with all his strength. His knuckles turned white, his face red; black spots appeared in front of his eyes. But his feet were sliding! He could hear the barrel scraping against the rough oak side of the next barrel in line as it inched relentlessly forward.

When he was 10 years old, Seth had wormed his way through a group of workers crowded around something, and before his father could drag him away, he'd seen the man lying in a pool of blood, crushed by a barrel. The man had looked like road kill.

Come on, somebody! he screamed inside his head, but had no air to cry for help.

The barrel inched forward. Seth couldn't hold it! Any second now …

Voices. The sound of running feet. A man appeared on either side of him, grabbed the barrel and started pushing.

"Here, Seth, we got it now," the carrot-haired man on his right grunted, but Seth wouldn't stop shoving until the barrel had been rolled all the way back into the trailer and the gate set in place behind it and fastened securely.

Once Brodie's arm was freed, he'd collapsed in a heap in the dirt. As soon as the trailer gate was reattached, Seth collapsed beside him, sweat-soaked and panting. A crowd had materialized out of nowhere and everybody was talking at once. Seth couldn't distinguish any one voice so he ignored them all, just lay there on his back for a moment looking at the blue sky, sucking in the smell of his own fear sweatmingled with the scent of warm grass and wildflowers.

Someone had rolled Brodie over face-up and Seth got to his knees beside him. The short, bald man's arm was swelling like a water balloon on the end of a hose. It hung at an odd angle from his shoulder, too, and a lump showed through the skin there. Blood squirted in bursts from the compound fracture of his wrist where his right hand had been crushed backward onto the top of his forearm.

Seth shook his head to clear it.

Think!

"Somebody get me a belt, a rope. I need to make a tourniquet." He was surprised that his voice was shaking, then he looked down and saw that his hands were, too.

A round-bellied man quickly unsnapped his suspenders. "These work?"

Seth wrapped one of the straps around Brodie's arm just above the wound, picked up a stick off the ground, tied the other end around the stick and twisted the stick tight. The spurts of blood from Brodie's wrist shrank to a trickle.

"Has anybody told Martha to call an ambul—?" Seth stopped. "No, wait." Yesterday, he'd seen the Callison County Rescue Squad truck parked at Joe Denny's house less than a mile away. "My radio's in my jeep. Will somebody get it for me?"

Seth turned to the man who'd given him the suspenders. "That toolbox over there, scoot it up under Brodie's feet, and get something to cover him up." He sat back on his heels, ticking off a mental list. If only his hands would stop shaking! He looked up at the men crowded around him. "Anybody know what happened here?"

Everybody replied at once.

"You know them barrels couldn't have started to roll 'less the chock was out."

"Maybe the chock come loose."

"How could a chock come loose with a barrel sittin' on it?"

"It coulda slipped."

"Brodie just got careless, that's all," someone said, not accusing, just stating a fact. "Nobody in his right mind'd stand behind a barrel wagon 'thout the rails attached."

A worker rushed up with the radio out of Seth's jeep along with the quilt off the rocker in the Visitor's Center. As two men stretched the covering out over Brodie, Seth flicked the switch on the small hand-held device, producing an instant of static. He held his breath. The distillery was notorious for bad radio reception. Then he pushed the button to transmit.

"Joe Denny! This is Seth. You there?"

Static buzzed out of the radio again for a couple of seconds and Seth repeated the message into the mouth piece. When he released the transmit button, the radio hummed.

"What are we gonna do with you, Seth boy?" A twangy, Tennessee accent spoke out of the box. "We're gonna bounce you out of this squad one of these days if you don't learn to use call letters and 'over' and 'clear' and—"

"Brodie Jenkins is hurt, barrel got him."

"Bad?" The bantering tone was gone.

"He's bleeding, compound fracture of the wrist, cut the artery. I had to put a tourniquet on it, but he lost a lot of blood and he's in shock. His shoulder's dislocated, too, I think. Is the truck still parked at your place? Will it run?"

"It'll run; fixed it yesterday. My partner's here, too. We'll be there in five minutes." There was a pause. "KWO 376 clear!"

Seth smiled a little at that, then switched off his radio.

But as he sat in the dirt waiting for the truck, the familiar knot formed in the pit of his stomach. It struck him that he'd just experienced a perfect metaphor—a whiskey barrel about to topple down on top of him as the whole distillery was poised to tumble down around him. He had to admit though, being scared he was going to die had at least temporarily trumped being scared he was going to lose the distillery that had been in his family for five generations.

Chapter 4

Seth stood at his office window and watched the late afternoon shadow of the knob stretch out across the meadow toward the distillery.

The shader's a'comin'.

His toothless grandmother would stop picking tomatoes or shucking corn or drawing water from the well and stand stock still, looking up as the sun dropped below the mountains that cradled her little Eastern Kentucky valley.

When it's yore time to cross over, the shader'll come for ye.

Granny Walker had died when he was 14, drew her last breath one afternoon a moment after the shadow of the mountain reached out its dark finger and touched the roof of her clapboard shack.

"So, how did it go?"

Seth had heard Martha come in but pretended he hadn't, bought himself another few seconds before he had to face her.

Martha Gregory stood 5-foot-nothing and was somewhere between 50 and 200 years old. She'd worked for Seth's father, Joseph Caleb McAllister III, the dashing young distillery owner who'd swept Granny Walker's only daughter off her feet and carried her away from the mountains. Martha had been Joe McAllister's assistant, his "right arm," and since Joe's death, she'd done her best to keep his son from making a mess of everything Joe'd worked for.

"Well?" She tapped her foot.

"It was awful."

He tossed a file folder onto the pile of papers on his desk and sat down hard in the big, high-backed chair. "I suppose it could have been worse, but that would have involved incendiary devices and dead bodies and—"

"Don't be cute with me, Seth," she interrupted. Only it didn't sound like a reprimand from his third-grade teacher. He looked into her eyes and saw compassion. That was harder.

"Ok, screw cute. Anderson Bertrand is a piranha and he smelled blood in the water."

"*Bertrand* was there?" Martha sank into the chair in front of his desk, like maybe her knees couldn't hold her up anymore. Seth had seen men go dead white when they saw Bertrand file into a divorce hearing beside their soon-to-be ex-wives. He was the lawyer who took the criminal cases nobody else wanted, soaked his clients for every dime they had, and then somehow managed to get most of them off, even when they were guilty as sin. No, *especially* when they were guilty as sin. Bertrand went for the jugular every time.

Seth's meeting had been held in the board room of the cooperage just outside Brewster that had provided employment for generations of tough, strong men. At one end of the building, teams of workers operated huge band saws, slicing virgin white oak lumber into thin strips called barrel staves. Further down the line, a crozier machine fit the staves together, bent them into a barrel shape and attached metal hoops. Then the barrels, open at both ends, rolled down a conveyor belt toward the dragons—at least, that's what Seth thought they were when he was a little boy.

The first time he went to the cooperage with his father and older brother, he'd taken one look at the gigantic flame-throwers shooting fire through the open-ended barrels, and bolted for the car. The unique, American whiskey called bourbon was developed in the early 1800s when a distiller in Bourbon County, Kentucky, discovered that a charred, white oak barrel gave whiskey aged inside it a distinctive color and taste. Since then, bourbon had become America's most popular whiskey.

"Sam Abernathy and his accountant were there, too, of course, but you can guess who did most of the talking."

The men in three-piece suits had made nice for awhile. Seth's altercation with the whiskey barrel had made him too late to make the visitation, but Abernathy and Bertrand had come to the meeting from the funeral home. They all talked about Jim Bingham's murder. It was the buzz of the community. Then they switched to the Callison County High School Wildcats' abysmal showing in the Sweet Sixteen Basketball Tournament in the spring and the football team's chances in the fall.

Seth had taken the offered seat at the head of the conference table where everybody who wanted to take shots at him would have a clear line of fire. He said very little during the small-talk stage. Then the nasal-voiced, bespectacled little accountant, who was the CFO of the cooperage, cleared his throat and picked up a file folder in front of him.

"I'm sure you're aware of the size of the overdue balance on your account," he said to Seth. "We're here to discuss the options available to Abernathy Bourbon Cooperage, Inc. to recoup the losses we have incurred re your distillery."

"Look, I think I can save all of us a lot of time by not doing some kind of dance here," Seth said. "I know what the numbers are. So do you. I owe you roughly $375,000 and change, right?"

"Not counting interest and late fees," Bertrand added.

Bertrand was a bookish, tweedy-looking man with a long, narrow face and pale blue eyes behind thick glasses. "I'm sure you're aware that the contract you signed allows my client to charge 10 percent interest on any amount in arrears more than 30 days."

Seth didn't miss the "my client" part and knew he wasn't supposed to.

"And to assess late fees on any account more than 60 days past due." Bertrand shoved a paper with yet more numbers across the big oak table toward Seth, "I have here the amount owed if the debt were to be settled in full today, which I take it you didn't come here to do."

Seth glanced down at the number and the knot in his stomach cinched tighter: $421,120.76.

"I am correct, am I not? You are not here to make payment in full, are you Mr. McAllister?"

"Cut the *Mr. McAllister* crap, Andy. I knew you when you had zits the size of hominy. I didn't come here to make payment in full, but I didn't come here to play games either."

"I can assure you, *Seth*," Bertrand purred as his pale eyes narrowed in rage, "that the only game we're here to play is hardball."

"Fair enough." Seth turned to face Sam Abernathy, whose shaggy gray eyebrows looked like dead wooly-worms over his eyes. "You pitch." He turned to the accountant. "You catch." His gaze returned to Bertrand. "And I'll see if I can hit one out of the park."

"I have here," Bertrand said, "a copy of a motion I plan to file Monday morning in Callison County Circuit Court seeking—"

"Whoa!" Seth said, glaring at Abernathy. "Since when did we start dragging *courts* into our business affairs?" Maybe it was time to eat a little crow. "Sam, I think you know what's going on here, that what's happened to Double Springs is my doing."

Sam and Joe McAllister had been good friends. If Seth had accrued any emotional capital from his father's relationship with Abernathy, now was the time to spend it.

"I'm sure Daddy told you about the changes I wanted to make." Seth winced at the memory of the look on his father's face when he'd shared his plans. "You know how he was, wanted the Springs run the old way." He struggled for an aw-shucks grin but couldn't pull it off. "Classic story—clash of the generations."

It had been more than that, of course. It had been the prodigal son story, too, except the father hadn't greeted the boy with open arms. It had also been a ghost story, with his dead older brother sitting in as the invisible third party in every conversation.

"When Daddy died, I wasn't prepared ... You know nobody ever dreamed ... " Joe McAllister had suffered a massive coronary at the Fourth of July picnic two years before, was, the EMT later told Seth "dead before he hit the ground."

"And all at once I was in charge." Seth paused. "I was an idiot."

No one offered any argument.

"I made some business decisions that I can see now were neither wise nor prudent."

Like refusing to lay off employees. The bourbon industry had hit the skids hard and every other distillery had cut its workforce and tightened its belt. Not Double Springs. When Martha had confronted Seth about it, he'd lashed out at her.

"If you want me to throw 18 people overboard, then you get to decide who," he'd said. "Tatum? Joel starts to law school in the fall. Or Rebecca? She's pregnant, you know. Or…"

Seth had kept right on bottling bourbon even though it wasn't selling.

"My business plan wasn't—"

"We could sit here all day and listen to you sing *mea culpa*," Bertrand interrupted. "But we're not here to discuss your poor business judgment. It is totally immaterial to my client why you incurred the debt to Abernathy Cooperage. He's only interested in collecting it."

"Good, because I'm here to talk about paying it."

That wasn't what any of the men at the table expected to hear. It was now clear why they'd been gathered in the room all stiff and formal and awkward. They hadn't come to badger, browbeat, or cajole Seth. They planned to get a judgment against the distillery and attach its assets. They were going to shut him down.

Seth opened the briefcase Martha'd gotten him for Christmas. It still smelled new. Taking out a document, he slid it across to Sam Abernathy. He had only one copy; he didn't know there'd be a party. Let them fight over it.

As the men huddled around Abernathy to get a look at the document, Seth continued.

"That's the payment schedule. Spells it all out—for the original $375,000." He waited for Abernathy to lift his eyes from the paper, then grabbed his gaze and held it. "I'm not paying any penalties or interest. If you expect a dime more than what I owe you for the whiskey barrels you sold me, then you *are* going to have to drag this into court and let a bunch of strangers settle it."

He figured Abernathy had sense enough to take a bird in the hand when he saw one. If he had to pay Bertrand's legal fees, collecting the penalties and interest could end up costing the cooperage more than Abernathy would get back if he won.

Bertrand barely glanced at the document, just said to Abernathy. "*Don't* take this offer. Our lawsuit will demand payment of the *full* amount owed."

"Any barrels you purchase between now and when the balance is paid in full would be cash-and-carry," the accountant put in quickly. "That would have to be part of the agreement."

"Of course," Seth said evenly.

"Now wait a minute." Bertrand shot a dirty look at the accountant, then turned to Abernathy.

"Where are you going to get this kind of money, Seth?" Abernathy asked. No challenge, simple curiosity.

Seth just stared at him with his dark eyes, long enough for the look to become uncomfortable. Then he rose to his feet. "Do we have a deal?"

"A deal? Absolutely not!" Bertrand sneered. "My client isn't interested in any deal that—"

"We have a deal," Abernathy cut him off and nodded.

"Then I don't see that we have anything further to discuss."

Bertrand rolled his eyes and slumped back in his chair, the accountant pored over the payment schedule document and Sam Abernathy studied Seth, a quizzical expression on his face.

"Good day, gentlemen." Seth couldn't manage a smile, even a small one. It just wasn't there. He simply turned and strode out the door. He walked to his car without looking back, got in, drove out of the parking lot and turned west on KY 44. He managed to make it out of sight of the cooperage before he had to pull off on the side of the road. He opened the door of the little red Mustang, leaned out and threw up.

He didn't tell Martha that part. When he did stop talking, he waited for a barrage of questions that didn't come. She didn't ask him where he was going to get the money. She just stared at him with a look he couldn't read, then got up, stepped behind the desk and put her arm around his shoulder. Such a display of affection from Martha Gregory was staggering.

"You do what you have to do," she whispered fiercely. "You make your daddy proud."

After she left, Seth stared at the spot where the sun was setting, making a hole in the sky for the night. Hours passed. The full moon rose over the knob. Still he sat, wondering if what he was about to do would make his daddy proud.

• • • • •

On the other side of Callison County, that same big, yellow moon cast a checkerboard shadow on Elizabeth Bingham's front porch where it shone through the lattice of the honeysuckle trellis. The soft *eech-eech, eech-eech* sound the swing made as she glided back and forth in it was a soothing melody. The Kentucky night seemed gentler, somehow, than evenings on their deck in California. Maybe it was the honeysuckle smell, or the aroma of the jonquils and gladiolas that lined the porch steps. Or the scent of the giant rose bushes under the widow, so laden with blossoms the stems bent all the way to the ground.

Or maybe it was just the little breeze that made Elizabeth appreciate the patchwork quilt Ben had brought out and wrapped around her shoulders.

The boy sat opposite her in an ancient spindle rocking chair that "walked." When you rocked, the chair moved all over the porch. But Elizabeth didn't tell him; Ben should be allowed to discover that for himself.

It was odd how at home the boy seemed in this town and this house he'd heard about but never seen. His mother certainly hadn't felt at home here. Years into what Jim Bingham assumed would be a permanent bachelorhood, he'd met a starry-eyed flight attendant 15 years his junior on a plane bound for Los Angeles and the American Press Association Convention. After a whirlwind romance that culminated in a not-well-thought-out marriage, he'd brought his bride home to the county seat of Callison County, Kentucky. To Brewster, population 8,000, counting the dogs and chickens, a sleepy southern town of tree-lined streets where large Catholic families raised broods of rowdy kids in big old houses with wrap-around porches. And where a collection of clapboard shacks out by the fairgrounds housed filthy, barefoot children who played in dirt yards littered with the carcasses of dead appliances and dismembered automobiles.

Oh, the good citizens of Brewster pretended those people didn't exist, of course. And Allison felt like she didn't exist either in a town where relationships dated back generations. She hadn't been there a week before she hated everything about it. If she hadn't gotten pregnant, Allison wouldn't have lasted six months in Callison County; for her daughter's sake, she stuck it out for 12 years. But when Elizabeth was in the seventh grade, her mother finally threw in the towel, filed for divorce and took Elizabeth back home with her to Los Angeles, to the big city with its culture, art, music, fine dining, and stores that stayed open past five o'clock in the afternoon.

In short order, Allison met and married Craig Malone, the defensive line coach for the USC Trojans, and Elizabeth grew up at Los Angeles Memorial Coliseum. But she spent every summer in Kentucky with her father. Jim took her hunting, fishing and hiking in the knobs. She tagged along with him when his police scanner sent him dashing out in the middle of the night to cover a fire, a flood or a wreck. He taught her how to develop film, print pictures, design and lay out a weekly newspaper, imparting to his only child his fierce love of journalism. He didn't have to teach his daughter to love Callison County, though. She enjoyed California; but Brewster, Kentucky, owned her heart.

One day toward the end of Elizabeth's senior year in high school, Allison had sent her to the store for chocolate ice cream, then casually added, "And bring back some pickles, too, the big sour kind."

"Pickles and ice cream, yuk!" Elizabeth teased, "You sound like you're pregnant."

"Well, as a matter of fact, I am."

The 18-year-old stared at her mother wide-eyed, then blurted out the first thought that came into her head. "You have sex at *your* age?"

Like many late-in-life babies, Ben had been an absolute delight. Doted on by his parents and big sister, he grew to be a bright, winsome young man with his father's athletic skill and his mother's freckles and flaming red hair.

But when Ben was 10 years old, Craig and Allison were killed in a five-car pile-up on the freeway. Elizabeth folded the shattered, frightened child into her arms, her heart and her life. Oh, they'd had their moments in the past six years, but they were remarkably close.

It was the closeness that planted such concern on the boy's face now, the pinched look that was becoming a permanent visage. Elizabeth sighed. She couldn't do anything about that, had no control over any of the events that had turned her life and her world wrong side out.

"You want some iced tea?" he asked. Ben was intrigued by the sweet tea of the South. *Did they put a whole cup of sugar in there?* "Or something to eat?"

The kitchen in her father's rambling, two-story house was jammed with food, the aroma of it drifting out to the porch, luring, tempting, enticing—if you could stand the thought of food, that is. The neighbors had been bringing in covered dishes all day like ants storing up provisions for winter, more food than the two of them could eat in a month.

"Sit still, Ben. This afternoon was a fluke. I'm fine." Of course, she wasn't fine. On any level. Three days ago, she'd found out her father had been murdered. And three weeks ago she'd found out she had MS.

Multiple Sclerosis. The mystery disease. The pull-the-arm-on-the-MS-slot-machine-and-see-what-symptoms-line-up-today disease. The migraine headache, dizziness, weird pain, can't walk, debilitating fatigue disease. The doctor she saw in Singapore who'd confirmed the MS diagnosis had been worth the trip if for nothing other than his candor. MS doesn't have a cause. It doesn't have a cure. We can't treat it and we don't know what it will do to you. You could lead a normal life; you could be bedridden in six months, so crippled you never get out of a wheelchair again.

Industrial-strength honesty, truth in a hospital gown with the strings undone.

The symptoms that sent her seeking medical help had been all over the map, just like the symptoms of everybody else with the disease, she was finding out. She'd spent six months in agony. A dagger-in-the-eardrum pain stalked her night and day. Doctors couldn't find a thing wrong with her ears. Her fingers went numb, the rest of her body tingled. Doctors said her neurological system was perfectly normal. She couldn't see properly. It was like she was looking at the world through Saran Wrap. Her ophthalmologist informed her it wasn't Saran Wrap that was distorting her vision, it was her imagination. By the time the best medical minds in California finally started batting around the MS diagnosis, Elizabeth was beyond caring.

Call it whatever you want; just tell me what's wrong with me and what I can do about it.

She finally got half of what she wanted.

Then, right before her trip to Singapore, the symptoms vanished as surely as if they'd never been there at all. Well, not all of them. But, by then, the Saran-Wrap vision had become so normal Elizabeth would have been surprised to see the world any other way.

Doctors told her there was no such thing as a "remission" in the disease that attacked the lining around the nerves. But it was not uncommon for patients to go months, sometimes years, with only a few mild symptoms.

Hey, if it looks like a remission and quacks like a remission …

There was no way to predict how long her "not-remission" would last, of course. A week? A decade? She had been trying to get her arms around the uncertainty of all that when the phone rang and she heard Aunt Clara's bird-squeak voice sobbing on the other end of the line.

"Sis, I've been wondering about something." Ben was rocking back and forth, lost in thought. He hadn't yet noticed that his chair was about to fall off the porch steps. "Maybe this isn't the best time to bring it up, but we're here now and we'll be leaving in a couple of days, so I just thought …"

When he'd cowered at the end of the high diving board at age 7, trying to work up the nerve to jump off, his face had looked a lot like it looked right now.

"Spit it out, Ben."

"What are you going to do about your job?"

Oh yes, her teaching job at USC, where she'd used up all her sick leave and vacation time, and where she'd have to go in sometime soon and inform the dean of the School of Journalism that she couldn't guarantee from one day to the next whether or not she'd be well enough to work. That would be just the excuse the ugly old troll had been waiting for; he'd fire her on the spot.

"You know what the doctor told you about stress."

"Yeah—don't!" Stress brought on MS symptoms when they weren't there and made symptoms worse when they were.

"Don't you think you'd do better with a slower-paced lifestyle, working fewer hours?"

"Well, sure, but I don't see what that has to do with—" All of a sudden, it hit her where Ben was going with all this.

"Here?" she looked at him incredulously. "You think Brewster would be, that I'd be better off if—"

"I think it's something you ought to think about. I can finish high school anywhere. It doesn't matter at all to me."

Yes, it did! Ben was the star wide receiver on the Monterey High School football team and he'd be a senior this fall. He had friends, a life. It had to matter to him.

"Your father's newspaper, it's yours now, isn't it? You inherited it, didn't you?"

Until that moment, Elizabeth hadn't given so much as a nanosecond of thought to *The Callison County Tribune*. But Ben was right. It was hers now.

"Running a weekly newspaper in a small town would be a lot less stress than working for Darth Vader."

That was Ben's nickname for the dean, partly because the old man had a raspy, breathy voice, but mostly because he was the heartless enforcer for the Evil Empire of academia that ran the journalism school. Without tenure, Elizabeth was the man's helpless slave and he never missed an opportunity to treat her like one.

"If you're the boss, who can complain if sometimes you don't show up for work?"

"Aren't you forgetting one little bitty detail? I've never run a newspaper, never even worked at one except as a college intern. And there's a reason for that. Those who—"

"I know, I know." Then Ben mimicked in a sing-song whine, "'Those who can't *do, teach.*' But how do you know you can't do it? You've never tried."

Elizabeth didn't have the energy to argue with him. She was too tired. She didn't know if her debilitating exhaustion was jetlag and no sleep for three days or an MS relapse. At this point, it didn't matter much one way or the other. "I just can't think about that right now, Ben. Maybe tomorrow ... "

Tomorrow was her father's funeral. Her father, who'd been murdered. She put her head in her hands and Ben got up from the rocker, crossed the porch and sat down in the swing beside her. She knew her little brother understood what she was going through; he'd lost his own father. And Ben was grieving for her father, too. Jim Bingham had been like a grandfather to the boy whenever he visited them in California.

Ben put his arm wordlessly around Elizabeth's shoulders and held her while she cried.

Chapter 5

I t was the tail end of August, almost two months after Jim Bingham's funeral, with the sun blazing overhead so hot it bleached
the blue right out of the sky.

Billy Joe climbed to the top section of rails in the front of an old
tobacco barn and carefully inspected the roof to see if it needed
patching. The barn was located on the back side of a farm that had
been in foreclosure for more than a year, though the land looked
like it hadn't been farmed in a decade. The fields had grown up in
weeds, brambles had reclaimed the fence line and the two remaining out-buildings, a tool shed with a hole in the roof and this tobacco barn, lay hidden behind overgrown bushes and brush.

Billy Joe'd had a hard time finding the barn, but the road was
good enough once you located it. He wouldn't have any trouble
getting trucks back in here.

Yep, this looked like a real good place to house this year's marijuana crop.

Billy Joe smiled when he thought about his high school English teacher, a clueless Yankee who'd maintained haughtily that
"house" was a noun, not a verb.

"You cannot *house* (rhymed with mouse) tobacco!" she'd said.

Of course you could, too, *house* tobacco. Happened every summer in barns all over Kentucky, Tennessee, West Virginia and the
Carolinas. To house tobacco meant to hang it up in a barn to dry.

Home Grown

In tobacco-growing states, farmers usually hauled their ripe burley tobacco into the barn on poles in late August, the huge leaves bright yellow and malleable. After a couple of months in the barn, the leaves dried and turned brown and the farmers stripped them off the stems by hand and bailed the leaves to be sold at auction.

Kentucky'd shot to the top of the domestic marijuana production industry in large part because growing dope was so much like growing tobacco. Just about every farmer in the state knew how, had the right kind of equipment to plant and harvest it and proper barns to hang it in to dry.

Billy Joe was out looking for a new barn because he liked to switch sites as often as he could. The first few years he grew dope, he'd mixed it in with his own tobacco to dry. But that was dangerous business. You could claim you didn't know somebody was raising dope on your farm, way on the back side where you couldn't see it. But it was a sight harder to convince a jury you didn't know there was marijuana hanging in your barn right alongside your own burley.

Billy Joe climbed down from the top rail and got on his hands and knees in the dirt on the barn floor, checking for any sign that there'd ever been dope here. It wouldn't do to decide to hang his crop in the same barn some other doper had already staked out to hang his.

He'd already had trouble with other dopers and the problems were escalating. Every year, it got worse as more farmers tried to cash in on the easy money, men Billy Joe called "five-plant dopers" who couldn't tell sinsemilla from crabgrass. They didn't know how to grow good weed so they were always out in the woods looking to come across quality stuff somebody else was raising. They'd steal it if they could, destroy it if they couldn't steal it, or set the police on the location with an "anonymous tip" just for spite.

Violence was commonplace. Bubba shot a man he caught in his dope field last summer, shot him dead! At least that's what Billy Joe heard, that Bubba'd buried the guy up a hollow somewhere

49

wouldn't nobody ever find his body. Gave Billy Joe the heebie-jeebies just thinking about it.

A lot of amateurs ended up getting caught, which was both the good news and the bad news. Good news because while the DEA, the federal Drug Task Force, the Kentucky State Police and the Callison County Sheriff's Department were chasing those guys, they were too busy to look for Billy Joe. And busting a herd of amateur dopers every summer made the law think they were actually getting somewhere in their war against the marijuana industry.

The bad news was that every bust drew more attention to Callison County and the spotlight shone brighter every year.

Billy Joe walked to the far end of the barn to check out the high rails there. Last spring, he'd been in a barn near Cade's Crossing showing some of Bubba's nubies the ropes when an old beam broke and almost spilled him down 20 feet to the barn floor.

He still found it hard to believe Bubba wanted him to talk out loud in front of strangers about how to grow dope. Who were those guys, anyway? But you didn't tell Bubba Jamison you didn't want to do whatever it was he'd told you to do. Not if you valued your front teeth.

Though Bubba maintained Billy Joe raised the best weed in Kentucky, there'd been a red-faced, pot-bellied man in the barn that day who didn't seem much impressed by his expertise. The others had come to learn but that fool kept butting in.

"In a whole lot of ways dope's easier to grow than burley," Billy Joe had started out. He was nervous and fidgety and hoped they couldn't see it. "Dope's a weed. It'll just about grow in spite of you. You can plant seeds, or you can plant the seeds in grow-boxes and transplant the seedlings, somewhere they can get a minimum of eight hours of sun a day. The plants need to be at least 3 feet apart, in different spots up against a fence line, or in between row crops. They just need to be random, so the color green doesn't look like a pattern from above."

"I thought you could rig a tobacco setter so's you could plant dope with it," the fool said.

A tobacco setter was a farm implement pulled behind a tractor that was used to plant burley. A man—two if it was a double setter—sat facing backwards on the machine only a couple of feet off the ground, feeding seedlings into the conveyor that dropped them into holes in the soil.

"Well, you *could* do that," Billy Joe'd responded with a smile, trying real hard not to sound annoyed. "But I don't know anybody 'round here plannin' to grow a whole field of dope. When I started out, you could grow an acre maybe, here and there up in the hollows. Now, the Drug Task Force choppers would spot a whole field of weed before they lifted off the tarmac in Frankfort."

"You could do it though, use a setter I mean, if you was plannin' to grow a field of it?"

Billy Joe had allowed that yes siree, you surely could, if you didn't mind spending the next 20 years as a guest of the state.

The fat man wouldn't last a season, Billy Joe had thought. But he got paid whether that fool was busted or not. Got paid very well.

B.J.'d worked for Bubba for five years now, and he honestly didn't know how much money he'd made. Hundreds and hundreds of thousands of dollars. He didn't keep records. What for, so the IRS could confiscate them? All he knew was that Bubba had made good on his promise; he'd made Billy Joe rich beyond his wildest dreams.

After he laundered enough money so he could pay taxes like a legitimate farmer, Billy Joe paid cash for everything—groceries, clothes, cars, dental bills, piano lessons—everything. He'd built a huge, rambling ranch house and purchased every nail, board, brick, door, couch, lamp, toilet and the swimming pool on the back deck with stacks of bills, used twenties and hundreds, not in numerical sequence, impossible to trace.

He looked at his watch and realized it was time to go by his mother's and pick up Bethany. He smiled as the image of his youngest daughter bloomed in his mind—honey gold curls and round cheeks like her mother, dimples like her father. His little princess!

Sometimes it scared him how much he loved that child. She was all he had now.

$$\bullet \ \bullet \ \bullet \ \bullet \ \bullet$$

Jim Bingham's daughter sat on edge of her bed, buttoning her blouse and yelling at herself. Not out loud. In her mind.

What were you thinking?

She'd been nuts even to consider Ben's crazy idea. But she hadn't stopped at considering! She'd quit her job and moved half way across the country, actually believed she could just pick up the reins of her father's newspaper, yell giddy-up, and go riding off into the sunset. What had possessed her?

Oh, make no mistake about it, the thin woman with curly red hair had always admired her father. She just had sense enough to grasp she could never hope to be like him. Jim Bingham had been strong, out-going and confident; his only daughter was quiet, self-effacing and reserved.

Ben's knock interrupted her mental tirade.

"Come on in," she called out, "but don't bring your sword because right now I'm looking for one to fall on." Fumbling with the last button, she realized her hands were shaking. Not from MS; from SS—Scared Silly.

The boy entered the room laughing. "You're not nervous are you, Eliza ... I mean *Sarabeth*?"

They'd talked about her name as they drove across the Arizona desert. Sarah Elizabeth Bingham had been dubbed Sarabeth as soon as she hit first grade, courtesy of the southern penchant for double names. Her mother had switched it back to Elizabeth when they moved to California.

"But in Callison County I feel like ... no, I *am* Sarabeth Bingham," she'd told Ben, and he'd shrugged and said, "Sarabeth it is then."

She'd tried during that long drive to tack words onto her feelings about returning to her hometown. Not about the newspaper job; they'd steered clear of that conversation. But about Callison County and what it meant to her.

"There's something profoundly ... *good* about Callison County," she'd said. "No matter where I've lived, it always felt like home—that place you look back at and know you just fit there."

Ben looked at his sister now, sitting on the edge of her bed. "What are you nervous about?"

"Let's discuss what I'm *not* nervous about. The list is shorter."

He laughed again, a gentle encouraging laugh. "You're going to be fine, just fine."

Someone else had said those same words to her, ten days ago at Joe Fogerty's sentencing hearing.

Sarabeth wouldn't let Ben go with her, told him it was something she needed to do by herself. The truth was she didn't know how she'd respond to being in the same room with the man who had murdered her father and she didn't want Ben to be there if she lost it.

The hearing was held in the small, district courtroom on the ground floor of the courthouse. She'd slipped into the back of the room shortly before the bailiff called out: "All rise. Callison County Circuit Court is now in session. The Honorable Earl S. Compton presiding."

The robed man who entered and took his seat in the black chair behind the bench looked like a judge. In his early 50s, he had dark hair with prominent gray at the temples and a thin face. He wore black-rimmed glasses and looked out over the top of them when he surveyed the courtroom. His gaze fell on Sarabeth and lit there for a moment before it moved on, as if he knew who she was. Maybe he did.

As everyone was seated, the bailiff announced: "The case of the Commonwealth of Kentucky versus Joseph Edward Fogerty." Sarabeth gasped and that's when she felt a hand on her shoulder. She looked up and there stood Billy Joe.

He slipped in beside her, took her hand and squeezed it as her eyes filled with tears. "Mama couldn't stand to come, but I knew you'd be here," he whispered. "You don't need to be doing this all by yourself, Bessie."

The family had been notified that Fogerty had agreed to plead guilty to second degree murder, though he maintained he had no memory of the crime or of anything else that happened that day after he started drinking.

Sarabeth was grateful there'd be no trial. What was the point? Fogerty had been found with the murder weapon in his pocket and her father's hat on his head.

As soon as a sheriff's deputy led the handcuffed man with shaggy gray hair into the room, Sarabeth began to cry softly and Billy Joe put his arm protectively around her shoulders. Through the sudden roaring in her ears, she heard the judge ask, "How do you plead?" and barely caught the man's one-word response, "guilty," before the judge slapped his gavel down and gave him 25 years in the Kentucky State Penitentiary in Eddyville. For an old man like Joe Fogerty, that was a life sentence.

One frozen moment from the morning stuck with Sarabeth, like a snapshot captured in the glare of a flashbulb. When the deputy took his arm to escort the prisoner back to jail, he had turned and spotted her sitting in the almost empty courtroom. For a heartbeat or two, the two of them made eye contact. In that moment, and in the days since, Sarabeth had wanted to hate Joe Fogerty. Oh, how she had wanted to hate him! But it just wasn't there. Truth was, he was a pathetic old drunk with a bloated face and rheumy eyes who'd killed her father in a blackout because the editor had published his DUI arrest in the court news. And he didn't even remember the crime! Jim Bingham would have been just as needlessly dead if he'd fallen under a bus. All she felt was unutterably sad that such a circumstance had stolen her father from her.

When Fogerty turned away, she'd collapsed in Billy Joe's arms, sobbing. He'd held her tight, rocked back and forth crooning in her ear, "Shhhh, now. Hush. You're going to be fine, Bessie. Just fine."

Ben crossed quickly from the doorway to the bed when he saw his sister's eyes fill with tears.

"Hey, I'm sorry. I didn't mean—"

She waved her hand and forced a smile. "No, it's Ok. I was just … thinking about Daddy." She reached up and wiped away a tear that had escaped down her cheek. Then she took a deep breath and repeated softly. "I'm going to be just fine."

• • • • •

The day went south on Sarabeth as soon as the farmer showed up with the potato.

She'd gone into the office early because she knew that walking in the front door of *The Callison County Tribune* would be the hardest part. Her father had been shot in the recessed doorway, had died there, and a part of her thought there ought to be some sign of that, like the ornate, gold and silver historic markers scattered all over town.

A National Historic Landmark sign near the Brewster Depot designated the spot where rogue Confederate General John Hunt Morgan's youngest brother, Tom, was killed in battle during Morgan's daring raid through Union lines across Kentucky and into Ohio in 1863. Another sign marked the house where the general himself rode his horse up the porch steps and into the parlor. The horse's hoof prints were still visible on the porch—or so the owners said.

Allison Bingham had felt trapped in a little "been-nowhere, going-nowhere" town. Sarabeth didn't see Brewster that way at all. She loved its history and heritage and admired its spunk. Though every retail business was located on the five blocks of Main Street, the community had scraped together funds to build an industrial park just outside town. No industries had located there yet, but it was a start.

Though the elementary, junior high and high school buildings were old, they were well maintained. Kids' test scores were higher than the state average and the drop-out rate was lower.

A major state road, KY 55, crossed Main Street at the traffic light by the post office and passed Callison County Hospital, renovated in 1986, and the new nursing home built last year. The town boasted a small park with two tennis courts, a baseball field and a children's playground, and a nine-hole golf course out by the cemetery.

Sarabeth thought that, all things considered, Brewster, Kentucky, seemed like a really good place to raise a family.

The newspaper office was a block south of the courthouse in a two-story, red-brick structure with large picture windows on both sides of the front door. The building was probably 100 years old and had served as a hospital in the early 1900s and a flop house for much of the 1930s. *The Tribune* had just taken up residence there when Jim Bingham was hired as a reporter/typesetter/ad salesman/janitor a year to the day before Hitler marched into Poland.

The downstairs office space had tall ceilings with fans in every room. Her father's office—*her* office—was large and comfortable, with a snuggly old sofa she suspected her father slept on most nights, two overstuffed chairs and a 5-foot-tall antique roll-top desk that might very well have been worth more than the whole rest of the building.

By the time her employees arrived at eight o'clock, Sarabeth was ready with a smile on her face and a sign to tape on the front door: "Sorry, we're closed. We'll re-open at nine o'clock."

The five-person newspaper staff arranged themselves around the long table in the break room. Advertising manager Jonas Haskins, a grumpy old man with close-cropped hair the color of a gun barrel, sat frowning beside receptionist Harmony Pruitt, a pretty girl in her early 20s who was either several sandwiches shy of a full picnic or was running a good bluff. Wanda Lee, the circulation manager, eased her bad back carefully into a chair beside the composition manager, Beverly Thompson. If there was a living soul in Callison County Wanda didn't know—and Sarabeth sincerely doubted that such a person existed—then you could bet Beverly did. The two middle-aged women had been friends since high school.

Wanda had brought a plate of brownies for everyone to share at lunch, and she smacked Bobby Wilson's hand when he reached for one. Wilson was the part-time reporter who also covered sports, a gifted writer who could have had a real future in journalism if he hadn't been so unashamedly lazy.

When everyone was seated, Sarabeth launched into a short speech that was designed to sound totally extemporaneous. She'd worked on it for hours. She didn't stand when she spoke, kept her hands in her lap so no one could see how badly they were shaking.

After thanking everybody for their years of faithful service to her father, she told them how grateful she was that they had kept the newspaper running after his death. She said she planned to make no major changes in the newspaper operation in the foreseeable future and announced they'd each find a bonus in their paychecks at the end of the week.

The bonus part was the first thing that got a rise out of anybody. The women smiled and nodded; Bobby turned to Jonas and gave him a high-five.

"Any questions?" she asked.

Harmony had only ventured out of Kentucky one time, on a 4H trip to Cincinnati, and wanted to hear about what Sarabeth had done after she left Brewster.

Sarabeth's pulse kicked into a gallop. She didn't want to be dishonest, but it wouldn't exactly inspire confidence in her leadership for her staff to know how precious little experience she had at real newspapering.

So she told them that after she'd earned a Masters Degree in Journalism from Stanford, she'd worked for the *LA Times,* that she'd gained quite a reputation there for writing kick-butt editorials. What she didn't tell them was that as a "Contributing Writer" for a big-city newspaper, she'd ranted and raved about everything from Jerry Falwell's defamation lawsuit against *Hustler Magazine* to the kidnapping of Terry Waite in Beirut and never once had to look a flesh-and-blood reader in the eye afterwards.

She told them about guest-lecturing on topics such as general and spot news writing, news and feature photography and front page design. She didn't tell them she'd never actually *done* any of those things except as a college student.

She described teaching classes in newspaper management, but didn't point out that she'd never been anybody's boss until today.

"Are you gonna cover Elsie Bingo in Bear Claw?" Bobby wanted to know. "It's always the first Saturday in September and that's this weekend."

"You bet. I'm all over it." She had no idea what Elsie Bingo might be.

"And the trials Monday morning?"

"What trials?"

"Dope trials. Three of them on the docket. Circuit court starts at nine o'clock." He caught Jonas' eye and grinned. "So you'll be out before lunchtime."

"Three drug dealers can be tried in one morning?"

Sarabeth had spent two semesters monitoring the judicial system for a college court-reporting class, watched murder, burglary, assault and drug trials. The drug cases sometimes took weeks to try.

"Not *dealers*, Honey, *growers*," Wanda said with a nervous, twittering laugh. She was a small, compact woman whose little spurts of movement reminded Sarabeth of a squirrel.

Dealers, growers, whatever. That's still major swift justice!

Someone banged on the office door and Sarabeth glanced at her watch—nine o'clock.

"Today's the classified ad deadline," Harmony said. "Everybody wants to get their yard sale in the paper." She and the others rose to go back to work.

But the person at the door wasn't looking to purchase a classified ad. From her office, Sarabeth could hear the conversation at the front counter.

"No, you gotta hold it like this here. Look. Now do you see?"

"Kind of," Harmony said, and it was obvious she didn't.

"Chin's right there and his nose—you got eyes, girl? If you did, you'd see it your own self right there, plain as day."

"Oh yeah, now I see!" Harmony actually squealed with delight, a high pitched *eeeeeeh* that set Sarabeth's teeth on edge. "Jonas, come here, you *have* to come see this. This potato looks just like that profile of Alfred Hitchcock."

No. Surely not.

Harmony appeared in the doorway of Sarabeth's office holding a big, lumpy potato.

"Look at this!" The girl was as excited as a 5-year-old, which Sarabeth was beginning to suspect might be her mental age. "Look at this and tell me what you see?"

Sarabeth got up and peered at the potato, and in truth she could sort of pick out facial features.

"Come on, what do you see?"

Sarabeth sighed. "Alfred Hitchcock."

"Didn't I tell ya!" the farmer bellowed in triumph. Dressed in dirty bib overalls and a Massey Ferguson cap, the man looked— and smelled—like he hadn't had a bath since shortly after the earth cooled off. He stepped to the swinging half-door in the middle of the counter and looked at Sarabeth. "Where's yore camera?"

He couldn't actually believe she was going to put a picture of his potato in the newspaper!

"I don't think this looks as much like Alfred Hitchcock as that other one, the one that looked like Abraham Lincoln," Wanda put in. She turned to Sarabeth. "Your daddy put a front and a side view of that one on the back of the A section."

"It wasn't Abraham Lincoln," Haskins grumbled from across the room. "It was Lyndon Johnson."

"No, you're thinking 'bout the tomato last summer," Wanda said. "Mrs. Rutherford from Black Gnat brought it in and she gave us all sacks of fresh tomatoes out of her garden, too, remember?"

"I grew me a tomato onct looked just like the Pope," the farmer said.

Sarabeth bit the inside of her lip so hard she drew blood in an effort not to burst into giggles. If this was the kind of news her father covered, what in the world had he meant by the cryptic message he'd left for her the night he died? Sarabeth had played it over and over just to hear his voice. And not just his voice, but his voice so *alive.* He was energized like she hadn't heard him in years. Excited and enthusiastic.

She could recite the message from memory.

"Hold onto your hat, Baby Girl, 'cause your daddy's got big news. I've wanted to tell you about this a dozen times, but I had to be *sure* first. I've been working on a story that's going to make *national* headlines! Just have to keep my mouth shut for another week or so. Only a couple more i's to dot and t's to cross and then I'll break this story wide open. When I do, the national press is going to be all over Callison County! Call me as soon as you get this message and I'll tell you about it. I love you, Honey. Bye."

But what big story could possibly come out of a newspaper that published potato look-alike pictures?

Late that afternoon, as she pulled the final page of her introductory column out of the old Royal Electric typewriter, she looked up to see a young man dressed in a t-shirt and acid-washed jeans standing in the doorway of her office. He was tall and skinny, with an unruly shock of chocolate-colored hair that was either styled in a bad mullet or the kid seriously needed a haircut. He had a big nose and Alfred E. Newman ears, but he was spared homeliness by clear blue eyes and a white-toothed grin so endearing it almost seemed to rearrange the features on his face.

"Excuse me, Miss Bingham. I'm here to work in the darkroom. If you want help, that is."

There was nothing in the world Sarabeth wanted more right then than help.

"For a couple of years now, I been coming in once a week to do whatever your father didn't want to do. It's one of my part-time jobs. He was teaching me how to process film and print pictures when he got ... before he died." He reached out his hand to her. "I'm Gabe Lee, Wanda's son."

"No way! You can't be *Gabe.*" Sarabeth looked him up and down. "Oh, my goodness, you *are.* Tell me, do you still bang your head on the floor and scream when you don't get your way?"

Gabe's brow wrinkled in confusion.

"The last time I saw you, you were maybe 2 years old. You were lying right there," she pointed to a stretch of worn hardwood floor just outside her office, "throwing a Category Five temper tantrum because your mother wouldn't let you play with her typewriter."

The boy smiled. "You've got me confused with my little brother, Jesse. I had way more style. I'd hold my breath until I passed out to get what I wanted." He sucked in a huge breath and squeaked out, "You *are* gonna let me work for you, right?" Then he filled his cheeks with air and squeezed his eyes shut, and within seconds his face was the color of a fire truck.

"I give! I give!" Sarabeth surrendered to her own laughter, too.

The boy sighed the breath back out. "Works every time."

"Son, you have just become my new best friend. I hate the dark-room. Let's go see how much you already know."

For the next two hours, Sarabeth taught Gabe as her father had taught her, enjoying the boy's non-stop chatter as they worked. The darkroom was hardly bigger than a closet, with a shelf for a big metal enlarger and three trays. One for developer, one for water, and the third for fixer. There was a safe for photographic paper, a small sink, and under the shelf were bottles of chemicals.

"My girlfriend and I saw *Who Framed Roger Rabbit?* in Bardstown the other night," Gabe said. "You seen it? And I'm taking her to the Kentucky State Fair in Louisville on Sunday afternoon," He held the metal canister upright and methodically swished the chemicals around the rolls of film inside it while counting one-two-three-four-five under his breath. "I'm prepared this time, though. Got me one of those airplane puke bags to put in my hip pocket. Last summer, she chucked her chili dog on the Tilt a' Whirl."

"My brother Ben's about your age. What are you, 16, 17?"

"Eighteen, Ma'am. I'm a senior, though. Mama wouldn't let me and Jesse start school 'til we were 7."

"Save the Ma'am for your grandmother. Sarabeth'll do." She snipped the film that was already dry into six-frame strips and slid them into paper holders.

"Your brother play ball?"

"Ben was a starting halfback last year."

"No, I mean *ball.* Round ball, the orange one that actually bounces, the big B. I got a nothing-but-net three-point shot's gonna pay my way through college, if I don't blow out a knee or tear up a shoulder."

Sarabeth fit one of the negatives into the slot in the enlarger and turned on its light.

"I may not be Division One good, but Murray State, EKU, Morehead."

"What do you want to study?" She focused the negative image on the enlarger pad, then switched the light back off. "Hand me a piece of paper out of the safe. And make sure you close it back tight. It sticks sometimes."

"I'll tell you, but if you laugh, I'll open the door and expose all your paper."

"I won't laugh. What?"

"Pre-med."

"Good for you!"

"What, no lecture on how I'll never be able to afford medical school?"

Sarabeth turned on the timer and the image appeared on the photographic paper for seven seconds. "Here," she said, gesturing to the paper and stepped back to let Gabe complete the process. The boy picked up the exposed paper and dropped it into the developer. They both watched in silence as the image began to form. Then Gabe snatched it out of the developer a second before Sarabeth could tell him to, swished it through the water to stop the development and plopped it into the tray filled with fixer.

"I've worked my butt off at part-time jobs during the school year and farm work in the summertime for years," Gabe continued. "I'm gonna put my savings together with scholarships and fellowships. And finish it all off with the grants I'll get for a four and no shoes."

"'A four and no shoes?'"

Gabe's teeth gleamed in the green glow of the safe light. "With a 4.0 GPA, I can become some socially conscious, East Coast med school's token deer-and-a-beer, barefoot hillbilly. There's all kind of education funding out there for 'underprivileged' kids from Appalachia. I figure Callison County's close enough to the mountains in Eastern Kentucky they'll never know the difference."

Sarabeth smiled. This kid had a lot more on the ball than a three-point shot.

When all the prints were hanging by clothespins from the dark-room line to dry, Sarabeth put up her hand and gave Gabe a high-five. "One more afternoon of lessons and you'll be flying this dark-room solo!"

"Now you're talking! I'll see you next week."

But Gabe didn't return the next week. The engaging teenager who worried that his girlfriend would throw up on the Tilt a' Whirl and dreamed of becoming a doctor never came back to the news-paper office again.

Chapter 6

Bubba turned his custom, dual-wheeled Ford Bronco off Lowery Road onto a nameless tree-lined lane. Except for the numbered brick mailbox beside the road, there was no sign anyone lived anywhere near.

Most people didn't know Bubba owned the whole hollow where his house was nestled in the woods a mile off the highway. His Louisville attorneys had purchased the land plot by plot for a development company that was a front for many of Bubba's business dealings. The hollow lay on the opposite side of Ballard Ridge from Double Springs Distillery, about three miles as the crow flies, 11 by the road around the base of the knob. In the wintertime, when there were no leaves on the trees, there were a couple of places on Bubba's property where you could see the distinctive cedar shake roof of the bottling house on the top of the knob. Bubba liked that view, felt connected to the history the distillery represented.

Once he'd acquired all the land in the hollow, Bubba had systematically destroyed every building on it. He tore down all the deer stands in the woods, too, and posted No Hunting, Private Property and Keep Out signs. A 9-foot-tall, 220-volt electrified fence with strands of barbed wire stretching up another 3 feet encircled his house and outbuildings. It was hidden back in the trees behind a tall hedge though, because Darlene hadn't wanted the place to look like a concentration camp.

Home Grown

An electric gate that opened with a key-punch code interrupted the fence at the bottom of the driveway. Inside the gate, a Rottweiler named Daisy, a pit bull named Target, and a German Shepherd named Lucky patrolled the perimeter relentlessly. Only Daisy had been silenced. The others let out a raucous cry if anyone came near. Nobody could get past those dogs. There was also a small gate in the fence in the trees behind the house. Visitors who didn't want to be seen came and went through it, and Bubba used it to go hunting, or to turn the dogs loose in the woods.

The driveway wound from the gate to the house around a five-acre, man-made pond. Bubba had bulldozed it himself, re-routed a stream to fill it and stocked it with catfish. He smiled when he thought about the fish. They'd certainly gotten huge; must have been feeding well on something. His 15-year-old daughter, Jennifer, would maintain they'd gotten far too big, of course, and his smile broadened at the memory of the day he and his son, Jake, had been summoned to the back deck by the sound of Jennifer shrieking. They feared she'd come upon a rattlesnake, or that somehow a cottonmouth had gotten into the pond. But she had merely pointed to a line of baby ducks swimming like beads on a string behind their mother. Without warning, an open-mouthed catfish had surfaced like *JAWS* behind the duckling at the end of the line. In one mighty gulp, the fish swallowed the little bird whole.

Bubba almost wet himself laughing.

Jennifer had failed to see the humor in it. Of course, she was always taking care of strays, dogs or cats she found abandoned on the roadside, injured birds. Anything that couldn't look after itself. Just like her mama. She looked like Darlene, too, had a full, buxom figure like her mama. Some folks'd say she could stand to lose 30 pounds, but they'd said that about Darlene, too.

Bubba didn't think about the kids' mother very often. She had disappeared, vanished in a puff of smoke when Jake was 9 and Jennifer was 7. Nobody ever did find out what happened to her.

He parked the truck in front of the first bay of the four-bay garage. The space for Jake's Jeep Wrangler sat empty. The bay on the end of the garage was a woodshop with several saws, a router, lathe, electric sander and all manner of smaller tools. Jake liked to work with his hands. He'd started out building bird feeders and picnic tables; but last year for Christmas, he'd made a walnut gun rack for Bubba and a cedar chest for Jennifer that looked like he'd bought them in a furniture store.

Bubba had another pickup truck, a beat-up old Chevy with a broken grill that he kept out by the storage shed behind the house. He'd had it for years, since the time in his life when he could afford nothing better, and he never replaced it because it was as comfortable as an old house shoe, and because it kept him close to his roots. He maintained that pickup's old engine so it hummed along smooth as a Singer sewing machine.

Going through the back door into the house, Bubba sat on the bench in the mudroom and removed his boots, pausing to claw furiously at the chigger bites on his ankles, courtesy of spending so much time in the woods. He could have hired guards for his dope crops, of course. But he liked standing watch, enjoyed lying in wait for prey, like sitting in a deer stand ready to shoot whatever buck or doe happened by.

The bench where he sat had been reinforced to make it sturdy, as had all the furniture in the house, but it still groaned under his 300 pounds of pure muscle. Bubba stood 6 feet, 7 inches tall, with legs like tree trunks, knee caps the size of saucers and forearms so thick he had to have watchbands custom made.

He'd weighed almost 12 pounds at birth, dang near killed his mama. His daddy had often cocked his head toward his hulking son and pointed out that here, at least, was one youngster who'd never lay claim to being a descendant of the lanky 16th President of the United States, as much of the population of the little county next door to Callison County did. Abraham Lincoln had been born just a few miles from where Bubba had sicked Daisy on the squirrel hunter in the woods. Honest Abe's Uncle Mordecai settled nearby, where his houseful of children multiplied like fruit flies, breeding a drop of Lincoln ancestry into just about anybody in the county who wanted to trace his roots back far enough.

Bubba had never looked up his family tree. He'd learned all he cared to know about his heritage from Grampa Jamison, who'd lived to be 91 in spite of the bullet he carried in his left side from a revenue-er's ambush. Grampa Jamison had been big, too, but not as big as Bubba. He was about Jake's size, and quick like the boy, too. Jake used his quickness as the quarterback for the Callison County High School Wildcats. Grampa Jamison had used his speed to avoid getting caught working the half dozen stills he'd hidden in secluded places all over the knobs. For half a century, the Jamison Clan's brew was the gold standard for moonshine, the finest quality free-range whiskey available anywhere between the Ohio River and the Tennessee border.

Bubba noticed his fingers were wet, covered with blood from where he'd clawed into his itching ankles. He yanked his socks up over the bleeding wounds, stood and padded toward the kitchen to wash his hands.

The house was large and spacious, built like a log cabin with a high vaulted ceiling in the living room and a homey den that opened onto a deck overlooking the pond. It was a nice house—no expense had been spared—but it wasn't a mansion, it wasn't a castle like those other idiots built. They were just asking for trouble with their showy houses and cars, daring the law to come after them.

As he dried his hands on the red-checked dish towel, he heard the voice of Reba McEntire belting out *Only In My Mind* from his daughter's room. Jennifer had a voice like that, deep and husky. His Jenny. She was a good girl, a *good* girl. He wondered why she wasn't singing along.

• • • • •

She didn't like mirrors. Sometimes there were things in them, hidden in the shadows, that maybe you didn't want to get a good look at. But after Jennifer got out of the shower, she wiped the steam off the mirror and stared briefly at her own reflection.

She certainly was no beauty, though she could have been. Her long, black hair fell to her shoulders, thick and shiny. Ignoring the popular "big hair" styles, she wore it straight, parted in the middle, and when she turned her head, it was a waterfall of black moving with her. Her eyes were a striking shade of pale green and her lips were full. But her skin was sallow, her face covered in pimples, and she never wore makeup. Then there was her bubble butt and her thunder thighs. Oh, call it what it was: fat. She was *fat*. Not that it mattered. Not that she cared.

The radio switched from Reba McIntire's husky voice to Michael Jackson's high falsetto, singing about *The Man in the Mirror*. He didn't much like what he saw there either.

Jennifer turned and studied her closet for something to put on. All her clothes were ugly—shapeless dresses in black or drab colors, oversize blouses and baggy pants. She often wore men's shirts and overalls, and hats she pulled down low over her eyes.

Selecting an old chambray shirt and a pair of size 16 jeans, she dressed, wondering idly if she should snort a line of coke to make her head stop hurting, or smoke a joint so she just wouldn't care.

Jennifer Jamison was insane; she understood that. She just wasn't sure why.

Maybe the craziness was a result of all the drugs she'd taken, and there probably didn't exist a pharmaceutical compound other than Geritol or Pepto-Bismol she hadn't abused at one time or another.

But deep down she knew it wasn't that. She knew what it was. She had watched the disintegration of her mind and soul with the detachment of a spectator for years, the spiraling down, down, down into darkness.

The fundamental difference between Jennifer and normal people was that she wasn't a whole human being. She was a collection of pieces put together so they looked like they worked, but they didn't.

The older Jennifer got, the harder it was to hold the pieces of her psyche together so they appeared normal and functioning. And the effort required to keep the mechanism of her sanity from disintegrating altogether was absolutely exhausting.

Pieces had already fallen off, big pieces.

Music had been the great balm of her existence. She had a remarkable alto voice, deep and husky, with the pure, resonating tone of a gong on a cold morning. When she sang, the beauty of the sound took her far away and a feeling welled up inside her she had no name for. It was joy.

Then one morning, she couldn't sing. That piece was gone. In its place was a vast, empty cavern in her soul where music had been. She'd gone there once, stood on the edge of the eerie abyss and listened. The wind whistling through it made a sound like dying birds.

Jennifer couldn't see colors anymore, either. The color piece had fallen off, left a vacant space. And she went back to it again and again, like your tongue constantly seeks out the ragged hole in your mouth where a tooth's been pulled. But there was no cavern where color had been, no sound. Just profound darkness.

Now, she could distinguish only black, white and shades of gray. She ached to experience green grass and a blue sky and a purple sunset—just one more time.

Every day, the blacks were darker, the shadows deeper. How long before the light piece was gone, too? She lived in fear that some essential piece would fall off and she wouldn't be able to function. Then what would she do?

She pulled open the night stand drawer, took out a bag of dope and some papers and began to roll herself a joint.

• • • • •

It was the Saturday after Gabe worked at the newspaper, and he was thinking about printing pictures when he heard something outside, like a car door slam. It was hard to tell, though, with Jesse's old transistor radio blaring *She's Like the Wind* from *Dirty Dancing* along with intermittent bursts of static. He stopped, stood very still and listened. If he'd been on a ship, Gabe would have been the guy in the crow's nest, up on top so he could spot trouble coming. But there were no windows in the tobacco barn where he stood on the top rail, 25 feet above the concrete floor, waiting for his younger brother, Jesse, to start the next stick of marijuana up the line.

"You ain't day dreamin' up there are you, Gabe?" The boy on the bottom rail jeered. He was hollow-chested, with thick glasses and acne so severe the skin on his face looked like ground meat. Gabe always cut the boy slack, figured living his life probably wasn't an easy job.

On the barn floor with another teenager, Jesse handed a stick loaded with marijuana up through three other workers to Gabe. Using the long arms that fired off perfect three-point shots on the basketball court, Gabe positioned the stick on the rail that stretched across the barn above his head so the marijuana plant could hang down from it to dry.

He had almost filled the top rail on that end of the barn. Another couple of sticks and all the boys would shift down one rail.

"Don't you be thinkin' 'bout Shelly now, hear?" The pimply-faced boy sent the remark up to Gabe along with another stick loaded with dope. "All the blood drains out of your head into your pants, you'll get dizzy and fall smack down on top of us."

Gabe ignored the remark and concentrated hard, trying to hear through the walls. Nothing. He wiped the sweat out of his eyes on the back of his arm. It was at least 20 degrees hotter up in the top of the barn than it was outside, which meant it had to be 100-110 degrees where he stood—and it wasn't even noon yet.

They'd started early, as soon as there was enough sunshine to see what they were doing in the unlighted barn, and they'd worked straight through, no breaks. Everybody wanted to get the job done and get out of there.

Jesse wobbled with the dope-laden stick he was passing up the line. Though just 14 months younger than Gabe, Jesse was six inches shorter and 50 pounds lighter, and marijuana was harder to work with than tobacco. He picked up a plant that had fallen off the stick and the other boy on the floor helped him fit it back in place so they could pass the stick up the line. Gabe reached down and grasped the end of it when it got to him. As he raised it above his head, the long, willowy plants slid over his shirtless, sweating back, laying down a swath of itchiness he couldn't reach to scratch.

"You ever get nicotine poisoning?" he asked the black man on the tier below him. In his early 30s, he was the oldest worker in the barn.

"Nope, but my uncle did once and he was sick as a dog!"

Nicotine poisoning was a little known malady that afflicted tobacco workers, particularly when they were housing burley at the end of the season. Working in the heat, sweating, the pores of their skin open as the leaves dragged across their shoulders, some men absorbed so much nicotine that they passed out or suffered violent nausea and diarrhea.

"Maybe you could get dope poisoning the same way," Gabe wondered aloud as he lowered the stick to the rail and began to scoot it into place.

He had never smoked a joint, never used drugs of any kind and never intended to. He'd watched the lives of too many friends go up in dope smoke, watched them stop caring about their grades or their families or their futures. Gabe was focused. He knew where he was going and smoking dope wouldn't get him there.

But what if this made him high? Wouldn't that be a kick?

There was a thump against the side of the barn, loud enough they all heard it. So did the team of six boys working at the other end of the barn. Everybody froze, stopped breathing. Then they heard voices outside, loud, angry voices.

The man who'd hired them had shown them the sentries posted out in the woods all around the barn. Wouldn't nothing get past those guys, he'd said. So what was happening?

All of a sudden, the doors on both ends of the barn slammed inward at once; Kentucky State Police troopers swarmed inside, their guns drawn.

Gabe's heart began to hammer in his chest, banging away like it did when he was 7 and the black widow spider appeared on the log he'd picked up off the woodpile. When it crawled onto his hand, he couldn't breathe, couldn't even scream, just watched it—*felt it!*—creep on tiny, tickling legs up his arm, across his bare shoulder, around his neck, down his chest and belly onto his jeans and off onto the ground. He hadn't even stomped it or smashed it with the log in his hand. He'd just watched it crawl in slow motion back into the woodpile and disappear.

The gray-uniformed men below him were moving in slow motion, too, like spiders swarming over the barn floor. Then one of them, a big officer wearing one of those ridiculous, flat-brimmed KSP trooper hats, looked up, pointed a gun at him, and started yelling.

Gabe's heart was pounding so loud he honestly couldn't hear what the officer was shouting.

He'd had nightmares about getting caught. This was the third summer he'd housed marijuana. He knew lots of guys who did it every summer just like he did and it didn't seem to bother them a bit. They'd show up at school in the fall, showing off the clothes and stereo systems and other junk they'd bought. You could make $500 a day, tax free, in a dope barn, more in a couple of long week-ends than he made the whole rest of the summer sacking groceries at Brewster Market. He saved just about everything he earned, had stashed away quite a little nest-egg.

But he understood the risks; the penalties were unthinkable. Get busted and you weren't looking at simple possession. They'd get you for marijuana cultivation for sure, maybe even trafficking. Cultivation was one to five years; trafficking was five to 10 years. And if you were 17, they tried you as an adult. Gabe was 18; Jesse had turned 17 four days ago.

A felony conviction would stay on your record the rest of your life. No medical school would admit a criminal.

"I said, get your hands out where I can see 'em," the officer shouted at him. "Do you hear me, out where I can see 'em. Now!"

All the sounds were magnified, echoed like the barn was an empty rain barrel. Jesse was sobbing. He'd clasped his hands behind his head like the cops said and a trooper grabbed them one at a time, twisted them behind his back and handcuffed him.

All the other workers were on the ground now. The officers handcuffed them as well, while Gabe stood frozen like a hood ornament way up on the top rail.

His pants were suddenly wet. It was sweat, had to be sweat soaking through.

Another trooper joined the one who had his gun trained on Gabe.

"He won't move," the first officer said.

"Get those hands out where I can see 'em, son" the second officer called out menacingly as he pulled his gun from his holster and pointed it with both hands at Gabe. "You don't want me to have to come up there after you."

Finally, Gabe's body responded to the commands from his brain. Like he'd been poked with a cattle prod, he threw his hands into the air above his head, so high he bumped the stick he'd been setting in place when the barn doors burst open and the world exploded. The end of the stick laden with marijuana slid off the rail and dropped on top of him.

Gabe tried to maintain his balance, but there was nothing to grab, nothing to hold onto. He felt himself falling backwards, reaching out frantically for something, anything, listening to the wail of his own scream mixed with the song that was now blaring out of the radio as he plummeted 25 feet down to the barn floor.

The song was the new Bobby McFerrin hit *Don't Worry, Be Happy.*

Gabe actually heard the crack when the back of his head struck the concrete, heard his skull fracture, then he didn't hear anything else at all.

Chapter 7

"You sure that wasn't the turn?" Ben asked.

Sarabeth looked over her shoulder at the road they had just passed. "I don't think so. I think it's up ahead. I was here a couple of times with Daddy but it's hard to remember turns when you're not driving."

She'd started the day with her mind muddled, hazy like the knobs looked on summer mornings when it was going to be hot. When she'd awakened before dawn, it was like she could hear a faint buzz, a dial tone, somewhere deep in her skull. The Saran Wrap on her eyes seemed triple thickness and there was a too-tight girdle pulled up snug around the base of her skull.

So she'd asked Ben, "Wanna drive me to Elsie Bingo after lunch?" Like a 16-year-old boy didn't have better things to do on a Saturday afternoon.

And he'd said, "Sure."

Truth was, he hadn't made any friends yet and really didn't have anything better to do.

She stared at his profile, the lush Kentucky woodlands a green blur behind him. He looked so much like their mother. And since she did, too, it wasn't surprising people thought he was her son. Though he wasn't, he had helped fill the gaping hollowness inside her when her own child was ripped out of her arms and carried away.

Ben interrupted her thoughts. "There, look. Is that the blue bridge you were telling me about?"

Up ahead lay a metal bridge, painted bright blue and as broken out with campaign signs and bumper stickers as a teenager with zits. If volume was any indication, Michael Dukakis was a shoe-in in Callison County. His "New Season, New Leader" slogans outnumbered the Bush/Gore "Kinder, Gentler Nation" stickers 3-to1.

"That's it. It's just a little way past the bridge."

"That thing's only wide enough for one car. What happens if two cars going opposite directions get to it at the same time?"

Sarabeth shrugged. "Play chicken, I guess. The school's down from that church on the left. I think that's where the festival is." When she pointed, her finger shook. Ben saw it and shot her a concerned look. She was grateful he didn't say anything.

People had parked in the church lot and a small army of men, women and little kids streamed past the pickups, cars and farm trucks lining both sides of the road all the way to the school. Fifty yards from the entrance, a bright red pickup pulled out just as they arrived and Ben snapped up the parking place. Sarabeth was profoundly grateful. Her legs felt rubbery. She didn't know how far she'd be able to walk, and it was already hot.

"You're not going to tell me, are you?" Ben asked as she shoved her car door shut.

She fit her camera bag strap around her neck and held out her hand. "Keys."

"Aw, come on—"

"You'll lose them. Keys."

He dropped the car keys into her palm and she deposited them in the side pocket of her bag.

"I told you everything I know about it. This festival is an annual fund-raiser. The fire departments and rescue squads in these little communities are manned by volunteers, and Bear Claw uses the proceeds from booth rentals and food sales to pay for their equipment. But I don't have any idea what Elsie Bingo might be."

She slipped her arm through his. "What do you say we go find out? You solve the mystery first, I'll split it with you."

"Split what?"

"The mega-bucks I get paid for investigative journalism." Her brother didn't appear to notice that she leaned on him slightly as they walked away from the car.

The festival had set up shop behind the school building, on the ball fields and in the parking lot. By the time they made their way around the side of the gymnasium, the feeling had returned to Sarabeth's legs and she dropped Ben's arm and plunged headlong into the crowd of at least 5,000 people.

It was a scorcher, maybe 95 degrees. Sarabeth wondered if the heat would bring on MS symptoms. Sometimes it did; sometimes it didn't.

Welcome to my crap-shoot life.

The awnings attached to canvas-covered booths afforded the only available shade. Set in rows with mini "streets" between them, they formed a village in the parking lot, offering hand-made wares of every imaginable sort from Christmas ornaments to statues carved out of coal.

Sarabeth had been struggling to regain the 20 pounds she'd lost in the past eight months because of daily, low-grade nausea, probably caused by the megatron doses of vitamins and mineral supplements the doctor in Singapore had recommended. But when the wind wafted her way the combined aroma of smoky grilled hotdogs, buttery pop corn, fluffy pink cotton candy and hot funnel cakes topped with powdered sugar, she was struck by a sudden, ravenous hunger. She followed the most appealing scent like a hound dog tracking a rabbit and soon stood beside a huge grill where two dozen chickens slathered in sweet bourbon barbecue sauce dripped juice onto a bed of red-hot charcoal.

"You look like you haven't had anything to eat since the last time there was a Democrat in the White House." A tall man with black hair and matching eyes reached out his meat fork and turned a whole row of chicken carcasses, one after another, with the expert skill of a career short-order cook. "Can I interest you in one of these? Or half a dozen?"

"If they taste as good as they smell!"

Ben stepped up behind her and made sniffing sounds in her ear. "I smell pizza!" he said. "Meet you ... " He looked around and spotted a make-shift stage sitting at home plate on the baseball field. "... in front of the stage in fifteen minutes." He turned and vanished into the crowd.

Sarabeth's sudden appetite vanished just as quickly and she wondered idly if people with MS ever starved to death.

She looked up into the smiling face of the tall cook and shook her head sadly. "No, thanks," she said, then turned and walked away.

Ben joined her at the stage just as an old man with a deeply lined bloodhound face hobbled with a cane out onto the stage. He was wearing a scraggly straw hat and coveralls so worn it was hard to tell their original color. The man stepped up to the microphone, smiled a toothless grin, dropped his cane and put a beat-up fiddle under his chin. He raked the bow across the strings a time or two, making a raucous, set-your-teeth-on-edge sound. He stomped his foot four times as a lead-in, then began to belt out *Cotton-Eyed Joe*.

As the crowd stood in stunned silence, the fiddle sang, wailed, barked and cried. The listeners began to sway with the music. They clapped their hands to the beat and exploded in thunderous applause when he finished.

Sarabeth fired away with her father's old metal Nikon, the sweat in her eyes making it hard to focus sometimes. She froze the blur of the bow at a thousandth of a second, captured the old fellow's knobby, callused fingers and his eyes buried in a spider web of smile wrinkles.

Turkey in the Straw followed. And when the fiddler ripped out *The Devil Went Down to Georgia*, Ben jumped up and down beside her cheering.

She left her brother at the fiddling contest and wandered around shooting other events, planning out the section front she'd fill with photos, imagining that she might even use color if she could get Beverly to show her how to make color separations.

She even shot the tobacco-spitting contest, froze it "on the fly" so to speak.

Note to self: Next year, wear closed-toe shoes.

So far, the only heat symptom Sarabeth felt was sweat, dripping down her flushed face. She should have worn sunscreen. In fact, as the day wore on, she felt more and more like her old self. Her appetite returned and she wolfed down two hot dogs, fries and half a funnel cake before a voice squealed and squawked through the PA system.

"It's time for the *maaaaaain* event, folks. Make your way to the center pen. We'll be starting Elsie Bingo in 10 minutes."

The two followed the crowd to a fenced-in area on the far side of the baseball diamond. Sarabeth climbed up and sat on the top rail and had just gotten settled when somebody pinched her—square on the butt! She turned in a rage, ready to cold cock whoever it was, only to find a grinning Billy Joe!

"You varmit! That *hurt!*"

"Awww. Poor baby. Payback, Bessie, my love. Payback! The time you tripped me, remember? Dumped me face-first into a cow patty." His twin dimples were deep enough to eat pudding out of. "I think 'bout that every year at Elsie Bingo."

Ben recognized his sister's cousin from the funeral home. "Ok, I give. Will you *please* tell me what Elsie Bingo is?"

A teenage girl stepped out from behind Billy Joe. "It's a dumb game, that's what it is. Totally stupid." She turned to her father. "Do we have to stay here? Can't we go now?"

Billy Joe pushed his UK cap back on his head and put his arm around the girl's shoulders. "My daughter, Kelsey," he said to Sarabeth, then turned back to the girl. "You've heard me talk about my cousin, haven't you Kells?"

"Don't. Call. Me. *Kells!*"

"And this is her brother Ben ..."

"*Malone.*" Ben put in.

"My baby girl's all grown up now. Last time you saw her was when you were here right after graduation and she was a little bitty thing."

Sarabeth figured it was a safe bet Ben had picked up on the "all grown up" part, given the "little bitty thing" the teenage girl was wearing: a skimpy, low-cut tank top and a tight spandex mini-skirt. Bracelets, both bangles and jellies, extended from her wrists half way up both arms and she wore a white-lace, fingerless Madonna glove on her left hand.

My mother would have thrown a bathrobe over me if I'd ever tried to leave the house dressed like that!

Kelsey's electric-blue eyes glared sullenly at the world through layered black eye-liner and thick mascara. Two huge *rocks* hung from her ears, sparkling pendant earrings at least three carats each if they'd been real diamonds. The overall effect was less an outfit than a costume.

After a grunted, monosyllabic greeting, the girl fell silent, but her gloom was instantly eclipsed by the exuberant cheeriness of the little girl who appeared out of nowhere and crashed into Billy Joe like a runner sliding into home plate.

"Daddy, gimme some money, *quick!*" The child was out of breath and her words whistled through a wide gap in the front of her mouth where she was missing key teeth. "I wanna win a teddy bear and I gotta have a quarter, lotsa quarters, 'cause all's you have to do is get a ring over some milk bottles and they give you a teddy bear!"

She had golden curls and dimples even deeper than her father's.

"Bethy, honey, I want you to meet Sarabeth and Ben."

"Gladtomeetcha." She fired a smile Sarabeth's way and Sarabeth felt Billy Joe's spark in the child.

I bet her eyes twinkle.

"Give me a whole buncha quarters, Daddy, so I can win!"

"Bethany, those games are rigged," Kelsey told her. "They'll just take your money and you won't win anything. You can get a teddy bear in the Bardstown Wal-Mart twice the size of those scrawny things." She cocked her head toward her father and sneered. "Just ask Daddy, he'll *buy you* ..." She stopped, like she was finished, then completed the sentence. " ... anything you want."

Billy Joe began to dig around for change in his pockets, not looking at Sarabeth. "Let's see how many quarters I got, Sweet Pea."

"You both got hair the same color." Bethany was looking from Ben to Sarabeth, squinting up into the sun. "Did your mommy give you your red hair? My mommy gived me my hair. It's *golden.*"

"It sure is, Sweetheart." Sarabeth noticed that even Kelsey was smiling.

A loud squeak split the air, followed by several seconds of static before a voice intoned, *"It's tiiime for Elllsie Bingo."*

"Come on, *somebody*," Ben pleaded. "Tell me! What's Elsie Bingo?"

"See those marks spray-painted on the ground?" Kelsey pointed to a checkerboard of lines on the grass inside the pen, 10 across and 10 down. Then she indicated a big sign set by the fence. A design of the grid was drawn on it with each of the squares numbered. "It's real simple. You buy a number, like placing a bet."

"Ok, but what am I betting on?"

Kelsey gestured toward the gate in the far end of the pen where a small cow was tied to the fence just outside. "In a minute, they're gonna put that heifer into the pen. You win $100 if she craps on your square."

"You're *kidding!*"

"Am not, am I Daddy?"

The look on Ben's face was unreadable. "All these people are betting on where a cow takes a sh—" He caught himself in time. "Dump?" Then he threw his head back and laughed, a merry, musical sound that warmed Sarabeth's heart and won Billy Joe as an instant, lifetime friend. "Not a soul I know in California will believe this happened." He turned to Sarabeth. "You gotta take pictures, Sis, lots of pictures." He whirled toward Kelsey. "Where do I go to buy a square? Show me!"

She turned wordlessly and led him away to the booth.

"Daddy! The quarters?"

Her father dumped out a pocketful of change into Bethany's outstretched hand and she was gone. Sarabeth watched her go, and a sudden lump formed in her throat so big she was afraid to try to talk around it.

"Your girls are gorgeous, Billy Joe." Her voice was ragged. She looked away so he couldn't see the tears that had instantly welled in her eyes. "You're a lucky man!"

"I am, aren't I. Sometimes I forget that. A teenage girl ..." he shrugged and glanced toward the spot where Kelsey had disappeared into the crowd.

Sarabeth blinked like she'd gotten something in her eye and wiped the tears away quickly. Billy Joe didn't pick up on it. "It's just adolescence, Bije. Give her a few years. Whatever issues she's got, she'll grow out of them. They always do."

Bethany crashed into her father again. Did the child ever just walk?

"I forgot. I want cotton candy, too, Daddy, and you didn't give me enough moneys for that. Will you get me some cotton candy?"

"I gotta go feed the beast," Billy Joe said to Sarabeth.

She'd had time to regain her composure, time to shove the pain back down into the dark where it lived in its own little world, so her response was warm and sincere. "We need to get together, B.J. We didn't have a chance to talk the last time ..." She didn't finish, didn't want to mention the hearing. "I'd love to get caught up on your life. You and Becky and the girls need to come over for a bowl of my famous Hamburger Helper homemade soup."

She saw him wince when she said Becky's name. She'd been about to ask where his wife was, but thought better of it.

"That'd be great. Sometime. I'll give you a call."

He let Bethany drag him away as the announcer instructed the cow's handlers to, "Let that heifer loose and leeeet's plaaaay Ellllsie Biiiingo!"

Sarabeth did as Ben had instructed, took lots of pictures, though there was precious little to shoot. How many pictures can you use of a cow wandering aimlessly around a pen?

The fellow standing beside Sarabeth told his wife, "They fed her some high octane alfalfa a little while ago and it's gonna work through her real fast. She'll start going any minute now."

With no Elsie action to speak of, Sarabeth focused on the faces of the crowd cheering the cow on, yelling when she came near the square they'd bet on, moaning when she walked away.

When the beast finally bingoed, it came all in a rush. Elsie made a grunting sound and a brown, viscous substance streamed out at a 90-degree angle from her backside.

Somewhere in the crowd, a woman squealed, "That's my number, that's my number!" and ran toward the betting booth with a ticket stub.

But Elsie wasn't finished. She continued the deposit non-stop, in something like a spray now, splattering on numbers in a wide arc around where she stood, causing an eruption of "No, it's on *my* square—see!" from no fewer than a dozen ticket-buyers.

Out of nowhere, Ben appeared beside Sarabeth.

"She get anywhere near your number, Ben?"

"Nope. There weren't many squares left by the time I got there. Mine's waaay over in the corner. That cow couldn't have hit it if she'd been aiming at it." He took the number, tore it in half and pitched it on the ground.

"Where's Kelsey?" Sarabeth asked.

"Don't know." Ben looked puzzled. "Turned around and she was gone."

"Sarabeth! Oh, Sarabeth, Honey!" Harmony Pruitt's voice was shrill. She raced up and grabbed Sarabeth's hand. "You don't know, do you? Oh, it's so awful."

"Know what?"

"About Gabe. Gabe Lee. He's been … hurt. They had to Stat Flight him to Louisville. A head injury."

● ● ● ● ●

While Ben was concentrating on the number board, Kelsey slipped away into the crowd. She didn't like ditching him like that. Truth was, he seemed nice. Wholesome. Not like the boys she knew. But she needed to get away. *Had to* get away.

Half a dozen white Port-A-Potties were lined up on the far side of the baseball diamond and she hurried to one with a green "vacant" sign showing above the sliding latch. The stench hit her 50 feet away. When she opened the door, the rank, heat-intensified sewer smell, overlaid by a sweet chemical stink made her gag. She felt vomit rise in the back of her throat but she swallowed it down, stepped inside, latched the door and immediately shoved the toilet lid down. That helped a little with the smell, but there was nothing to be done about the heat. Had to be 110 degrees in here.

She sat down on the closed lid and from the inner zipper pocket of her purse, she removed a paper towel folded to the size of a playing card and laid it in her lap. Lifting each of the folds carefully, she revealed the object in the center. A shiny new single-edge razor blade lying on a pile of Band Aids.

Kelsey heaved a huge, trembling sigh; relief flooded over her as refreshing as a spring rain. Pent-up tension, squeezing tighter and tighter, had been building all day and just the sight of the blade began to release it.

Somebody tried the latch on the door and Kelsey jumped, almost dropped the paper towel and blade on the filthy floor.

"Can't you read? It says 'occupied,' moron!" she cried out, and ignored the mumbled words outside the door as she removed the bracelets from her left arm. Beneath them were dozens of thin, white lines.

With a trembling hand, Kelsey placed the sharp edge of the blade against the soft skin there. She pushed slightly and grimaced when the blade sank in. Then she slowly drew it across her arm. She threw her head back, squeezed her eyes shut and held her breath to keep from crying out as a red trail of warm blood chased the razor's shallow wound.

Two inches across and she stopped, panting, from the heat, which had drenched her in a full-body sweat, and from relief so pure it sang like the perfect *ping* of a crystal glass struck with a fork.

Kelsey had been a cutter since right after she turned 13. For over a year now, she'd been slicing into her inner arms and thighs to let off the pressure that often felt like it was about to blow off the top of her head. Only cutting brought sweet relief.

Every now and then she wondered how she'd gotten here, to this, and she'd try to trace it back, to find the very last time things had been good, normal and real. Then she searched for the point where life first felt hollow and empty and scary. And looked between them, to find the spot in the middle where it all had changed. She wanted to examine that place, the in-between place, the railroad-switch place that routed a train from one track onto an entirely different track going in the opposite direction.

She never could find the in-between place, of course, and finally came to understand there wasn't one, that the good/normal/real life just naturally transformed into the hollow/empty/scary life. Like a caterpillar into a butterfly. That's what happened to everybody. It was called growing up.

Careful not to let the blood drip onto her shoes, Kelsey sliced slowly across her arm again, crying softly from the pain. Her tears mingled with sweat and black eye makeup to form a dark sludge that oozed slowly down her cheeks.

It *hurt!*

But that was the point. She did it *because* it hurt. In the pain, Kelsey Reynolds felt alive. The rest of the time, she felt numb.

• • • • •

A large man approached the minister, who was still wet from the waist down from the baptisms he'd just performed in the river.

84

"Yo, Preach," he said. "'Bout time for the circle, don't you think?"

The man was breathing hard. The early afternoon heat had slathered him in sweat, sticking to his considerable belly and wide chest the white Sunday shirt he'd worn to services that morning. It was now so transparent he looked like a contestant in a wet t-shirt contest.

The little girl standing next to the minister looked up at the man and asked, "Didja go fwimmin'?"

"Did I what, Sugar?"

Gracie's tongue was so enlarged most people had trouble understanding her. And every now and then, that was a good thing!

"Why don't you go get everybody gathered up under the willow tree," the minister said to the man, then turned to distract his daughter. "Would you put my Bible in the car for me, on the front seat where it won't get lost?"

He handed the 9-year-old the worn *New Testament* out of his shirt pocket and watched her make her way across the field, past the kids digging rounded spoonfuls of watermelon out of the rind, around the handful of old men playing horseshoes, and behind the gaggle of women cleaning up after the meal. The child headed as unerringly as a bird dog on point to the brown Ford Tempo parked in front of the three neat rows of vehicles, probably two dozen of them. It wasn't a big congregation. But if it had been, they could have afforded a full-time minister and Sonny wouldn't have had a flock. Things worked out the way they were supposed to.

As the minister passed by the food table on his way to the crowd gathering under the willow, Brodie Jenkins fell into step beside him. His whole right arm was encased in a massive cast that stretched from his collar bone out past his fingertips. His face was thin and gaunt; the ordeal of the injury and the three surgeries that followed had been hard on him.

"You heard about the Lee boys?" he asked.

Sonny nodded. He'd heard.

"Don't s'pose there's anything you can do 'bout it." It wasn't even a question. Brodie already knew the answer, but it was just hard not to grasp at straws. Brodie had played ball with the Lee brothers' daddy in high school, had been a groomsman at his wedding and a pall bearer at his funeral.

The preacher shrugged. "Barn where they got busted was in Landry Hollow, Baker County side," he said.

"Dang shame. She's good people, that Wanda is. Worked hard to raise them boys right all by herself."

The men had reached the gathering of the congregation under the swaying branches of the willow tree that grew along the riverbank. Sonny looked around for Gracie. She often wandered off, got lost. Then he spotted her talking to her grandmother.

A tall, black man stepped out to greet Sonny.

"Hear Gabe's got a closed-head injury," he said, picking up the thread of the conversation. "Could kill him or leave him paralyzed. They say he might not ever wake up."

"And 'course they got Jesse locked up … " Brodie paused, then spit out the next three words in a harsh whisper. " … in Baker County!"

The talk died right there. Baker County prosecuted dopers to the fullest extent of the law.

Sonny took advantage of the sudden silence to redirect the group focus. He smiled at the two newest members of the congregation, the young couple he'd just baptized in the river.

"We're not a real formal church, as I'm sure you've seen by now," he began.

"You probably picked up on that when we passed 'round that hubcap to take up the collection," Brodie said and everybody laughed. He'd always been a joker. Since his accident, though, his humor seemed forced. It was obvious he was still suffering a lot of pain, but he wasn't the kind of man to complain.

"And we have this little tradition," Sonny continued. "It's our way of letting you know that you're family now."

The 50 or so people stood when Sonny nodded, stepped forward to form a circle around the young couple whose hair was still wet with river water.

"Why don't you start," Sonny said to the tall, gawky man standing to his left.

"I'm Will Dunlap," he said. "This here's my wife, Margie. Two of my three girls are here, but Shelly ... "

Shelly was Gabe Lee's girlfriend. Everybody knew she was at the hospital in Louisville. "I drive a school bus for a living but I'm real handy with engines. I can fix most anything runs on gasoline. So if you ever need help, your car won't start or your muffler comes loose or anything like that, just give me a call and I'll see what I can do."

Then Will stepped forward and handed the couple an envelope. Inside it was a card, like a Christmas card, with a little-kid-drawn picture of a car on the front. The elementary-age Sunday School class had supplied cards for the whole congregation. Will's name, address and phone number were printed in large block letters on the inside.

And so it went around the circle.

"I work at GE in Louisville, but I'm a fair enough plumber," said a middle-aged man with a narrow face and bushy eyebrows. "So if you ever get a clogged sink, or your toilet's overflowing ... "

"I teach piano lessons ... " said an elderly woman with her white hair in a bun.

"I'm unemployed right now," said a tall, broad-shouldered man. "But I'm strong's an ox. You need to move sumpin'—a piano or a frigerator or a chifferobe... "

Sonny stood back from the circle and watched the newly-wed couple, whose eyes were wide with wonder. He loved the old church's traditions, especially this one. In some ways, it felt as profound as the baptism itself. The young man and woman had come up out of the water clean new creations, members of God's family in Heaven. Sitting here together, holding hands and smiling, they were being welcomed as new members of the Church, God's family on earth.

"Ya'll know me and what I do," Sonny stepped forward after the person to his right finished speaking. "I wear a couple of hats

87

that seem real different to some people. But they're not different at all, at least not as I see it." He smiled, reached into the same shirt pocket where he'd kept his *New Testament* and pulled out an envelope. "If you're ever in trouble, this is how to reach me."

He handed the young man a card like the others, with his name, address and phone number on the inside. A child's drawing of a cross and a star decorated the front. "I'll help you any way I can. That's my calling as 'Preach.' He turned to grin at Brodie and Will, who'd given him the nickname years ago. "'Course it's also my job, which is the calling I get paid for."

He reached into his other shirt pocket, opposite the one where he carried his *New Testament*, took out a badge and pinned it to the front of his shirt. It was a gold star emblazoned with the words: "Callison County Sheriff Sonny Tackett."

Chapter 8

Jimmy Dan Puckett figured to walk out of the courthouse this morning a free man, and it was about danged time, too! He hadn't been able to make bail so he'd been sitting over there in a jail cell for four months, ever since they busted him where he'd camped out on the creek bank to look out for the weed he and his partners had planted in the edge of a meadow about 50 yards away.

He'd been at the campsite for a couple days to make sure the two dozen plants they'd pulled up out of another doper's seedling bed had taken root.

He'd been sleeping in his pickup truck, had just got up and stretched, built a fire and made a pot of coffee. He was about to pour himself a cup and smoke a cigarette when he heard them coming, but it was too late by then. The sheriff came stomping out of the woods with two deputies and some real pale guy in a suit.

J.D.'d dropped the coffee cup, turned and bolted around the side of his truck and into the woods by the creek. He didn't know if they saw him or not so he just kept running until his side hurt so bad he couldn't run any more, and he looked back and didn't see anybody. So he sat where he'd collapsed in the weeds under a sumac, panting, and tried to think.

What was he going to do? All the sheriff had to do was kick back and wait. Jimmy Dan's truck was right there, and sooner or later he'd have to go back for it. Or leave it where it was and have them check out the license plate and come looking for him later. Either way, they had him. He stuck his hand in his overalls pocket hoping to snag a cigarette, though he knew he'd left them on the ground by the coffee pot, and pulled out a bunch of lint, a quarter, a safety pin, a nut, bolt and washer off his bathroom sink, and a 6-foot length of fishing line.

Then he sat there in the weeds for a long time figuring out what he was going to do.

• • • • •

Sarabeth saw the sheriff pass by on the wide expanse of marble-floored hallway outside the courtroom where she'd stopped off to watch a few minutes of the Monday morning proceedings in district court. She slipped out and caught him as he was heading up the nearest of the two sets of stone stairs at each end of the courthouse.

"Sheriff Tackett."

Sonny stopped and turned toward her. He was taller than she remembered but just as tough-looking. Built like a professional wrestler, he had huge, muscular arms and a head that almost seemed to rest on his shoulders, with no neck at all.

"Could I ask you a few questions? I'm trying to understand—"

"I'm due in court in five minutes and you can't ask me enough questions in five minutes to understand anything you really need to know," he said, cutting her off before she could go any further. "You going upstairs for circuit court?" District court was for misdemeanors; felonies were tried in circuit court.

"That's the plan. Drug trials, right?"

"Dope cases. There are three on the docket and I'm only testifying in one of them, the first one. If you'd like to wait, I can talk to you after that."

His voice was deep and rumbling, but kind, the way she remembered. He'd liked her father, she remembered that, too. And she was willing to bet her father had liked him.

When they got to the top of the stairs, Sonny indicated a door at the end of the hallway, past the big double doors leading into the courtroom. "I have to wait in the witness room until I testify, so I can't decide what I'm going to say based on what somebody else says on the stand. When I'm finished, I'll translate for you, explain what's going on. Sit in the back so Judge Compton doesn't ask the sheriff to escort us out for talking." He took a couple of steps, then turned back to her. "Oh, wait. I *am* the sheriff." He grinned. "Sit in the back anyway."

Sarabeth shoved open one of the big oak doors. It moved on its hinge as smooth and silent as skis on fresh snow. The first-floor courtroom had obviously been renovated. It still had tall, recessed windows and a high ceiling, but the rest of the décor was modern. The circuit courtroom was another thing entirely. It looked like it had been shipped to the spot directly from the set of *To Kill a Mockingbird.*

The historic building had survived the courthouse-burning spree of General John Hunt Morgan's raiders during the Civil War, and the third floor courtroom sat beneath the building's dome that rose into shadows at least 50 feet above the cold marble floor. Six 18-foot windows lined each side of the room, forming wide sills in the 2-foot-thick stone walls. The bench towered five steps off the floor, a huge cherry edifice with hand-carved lattice trim. Attached to its side was the witness box, enclosed in the same battlement of shiny cherry. The jury box was on the left behind an ornate 3-foot railing and there was a huge oak door, with a knob in the middle, in the back wall behind it where the jurors could file out into the jury room for deliberation. A matching door on the other side lead to the judge's chambers.

Two tables, each big enough to seat a dozen people, sat in front of the bench, one for the prosecution, the other for the defense. High above Sarabeth's head, a gallery stretched in a semicircle around the seating area below it, accessed by an oak staircase with elaborately carved handrails, stained dark like the doors, window casings and crown moldings. The stairs rose along the back wall

91

over the entry doors, but a velvet rope hung across the first step at the bottom, barring access.

Only a handful of people sat on the wooden benches in the audience. Two men were seated at the defense table, one at the prosecution and a stenographer sat at a small desk in front of the bench. They all jumped up when a sheriff's deputy/bailiff stepped out the door of the judge's chambers and called out, "All rise. Callison County Circuit Court is now in session. The Honorable Earl S. Compton presiding."

The words sent Sarabeth's mind reeling back to Joe Fogerty's sentencing hearing earlier that month and a shiver ran down her spine. His plea bargain had spared Jim Bingham's family the ordeal of a trial in this huge courtroom. Hard as that would have been, she suspected there'd have been something profoundly satisfying about it, too. A deeper sense of closure, perhaps.

Jury selection in the dope trial was already complete, so at a nod from the judge, another deputy opened the door behind the jury box and 12 people filed in to sit behind the wooden railing.

"Is the prosecution ready?" the judge asked the white-haired man seated alone at a table on the right side of the room.

Simon Henry rose to his feet. "We are, your Honor." The Commonwealth's Attorney was a small, narrow-shouldered man with a surprisingly-loud orator's voice. Sarabeth liked his air of self-possessed confidence. He didn't seem cocky, just competent.

The judge asked the defense the same question and then called for opening statements. The prosecutor spoke only briefly to the jury, outlining in simple terms the case against the defendant, James Daniel Puckett, seated in a suit and tie beside his lawyer at the defense table. He said that the prosecution would prove that on the fifth day of May, 1988, Puckett had been arrested while guarding his field of marijuana.

The defense attorney who had risen and faced the jury looked like a college professor addressing his students. She searched for his name on the docket sheet. Anderson Bertrand. "The defense needs no opening statement, your Honor," he said and smiled at the jury, a predatory smile, Sarabeth thought, that couldn't possibly have endeared him to anybody. Then the judge instructed the prosecution to call its first witness.

"The prosecution calls Callison County Sheriff Sonny Tackett." A deputy went to fetch him and the big room was as quiet as a dead rooster until his footsteps clacked down the marble center aisle. He sat in the witness chair, raised his right hand, put his left on the proffered Bible and was sworn in.

"State your full name for the record, please," Henry said.

"Andrew Jackson Tackett, III."

"What is your occupation, sir?"

"I am the sheriff of Callison County, Kentucky."

"And where were you at eight o'clock in the morning on May 5, 1988?"

"I was in the woods in Clark Hollow."

"Were you alone?"

"No sir. My deputies Ross Parker and Jude Tyler, and Kentucky State Police Detective Darrell Hayes were with me."

"What were you doing there?"

"We had received an anonymous tip that there was marijuana growing in that location, and we went to check it out."

"Did you find any marijuana?"

"Objection." The defense attorney's voice was raspy, grating, like something metal dragged across creek rock. "Your Honor, we have not yet defined what location we're talking about here. Clark Hollow is 3 miles long and 2 miles wide."

"Let me re-phrase the question. Would you just tell the court in your own words, Sheriff Tackett, what you and the other officers observed—"

"Objection. The witness can only testify to what *he* observed."

"Sustained."

"What *you* observed that morning in the woods."

The sheriff looked directly at the jury and told his story.

"We were approximately three-quarters of a mile west of the dirt road that hits Fern Creek Lane just south of mile marker 18." He cast a glance at the defense attorney. "A creek runs through the woods there beside an open meadow about half an acre wide."

He said he had come upon a campsite on the creek bank, with a fire burning and a pot of hot coffee. There was a 1981 Ford pickup truck parked nearby. A foot trail, worn in the dirt and weeds, led from the campsite to the meadow, 50 yards east, where he found 27 marijuana plants, approximately 8 inches tall, and from the condition of the dirt around them, they appeared to have been recently transplanted.

"Did you see anyone at the campsite?"

"No sir, I did not. I heard what I thought was somebody running in the woods by the creek, but I couldn't find anybody."

"Did you take pictures of what you have just described?"

"Yes sir, I did."

"Do you have those pictures with you today?"

"Yes sir, I do." Tackett lifted a manila envelope out of his lap and handed it to the prosecutor.

"We'd like to enter these photographs into evidence as people's exhibits A through J." Henry handed the envelope to the judge. "We have furnished copies of these photographs to the defense." The judge glanced at Bertrand, who nodded.

"I hereby enter these into evidence." The judge gave the envelope to the bailiff, who stamped the back of each of the 10 pictures, stepped up to the jury box and handed the photographs to the jury.

As Tackett continued to testify, the jurors passed the photos from one person to the next.

"I used my radio to call in the registration on the truck just to be sure, but I knew it was Jimmy Dan's because I—"

"Objection, the sheriff's history with the defendant is not relevant to these proceedings."

"Sustained. Confine your testimony to the day in question, Sheriff Tackett."

So Sonny described sitting at the campsite waiting for whoever had driven the truck to come back for it. And around noon, Puckett had emerged from the woods, was arrested and charged with trafficking in marijuana. The plants had been confiscated, photographed and then destroyed, he said.

"What was the value of the marijuana growing in that field?"

"Somewhere between $90,000 and $320,000."

"Thank you Sheriff Tackett, no further questions."

Bertrand fairly leapt to his feet.

"Do you expect this court to believe that two dozen marijuana seedlings would sell for $320,000?"

"He didn't ask me what they'd sell for." Tackett was calm, like he'd expected the question. "He asked me what they were *worth*. Now you could go out anywhere in Callison County and buy a newborn colt for a couple hundred dollars. But you'd pay $500,000, maybe more, for a thoroughbred colt, and the difference is potential. That little horse's bloodlines, what it's going to grow up to be someday makes it worth—"

"We're not interested in you equine analogies, Sheriff Tackett," Bertrand cut in. "Your Honor, please instruct the witness to confine his testimony to—"

"Objection! It has been established that the value of marijuana growing in—"

"Gentlemen!" Both attorneys fell silent. The judge turned to Sonny. "Sheriff Tackett, how much marijuana could you get from a mature sensemilla plant?"

"Two, two-and-a-half pounds."

"What's the street value of a pound of marijuana—as far as you know?"

"An ounce bag'll sell for $75 on up to $350. Depends on the quality. That's $1,200 to $5,600 a pound."

"So the marijuana from 27 mature sensemilla plants would sell for … do the math for me, Sheriff."

"At two-and-a-half pounds a plant, that comes out roughly $80,000 to $320,000."

"And seedlings? What do they sell for?"

"I don't know … The cost of the seeds, maybe $250. Could be a lot more, though. Again, depends on the quality." Sonny smiled. "The bloodlines."

The judge turned back to the attorneys, who both stood fuming. "Now, we'll let the jury decide for themselves the value of the marijuana in question. Mr. Bertrand, you may continue your cross-examination."

"The truth is, you were not totally forthcoming with this jury when you described the arrest of my client, now were you, Sheriff Tackett?" He didn't wait for Sonny to respond. "You left out part of the story, didn't you?"

The sheriff said nothing, just looked at the defense attorney with barely disguised contempt.

"Sheriff, will you tell these fine people," he gestured toward the 12 jurors, "what my client was carrying with him when he walked out of the woods the day you and your posse arrested him?"

"Turtles," the sheriff said.

"I'm sorry, I didn't catch that, could you speak a little louder, please."

"I said, *turtles*."

"How many turtles?"

"Three."

"What kind of turtles were they?"

"Regular snapping turtles."

"The kind you make turtle soup out of?"

"I can't answer that question, sir. I've never made turtle soup."

"And how was Mr. Puckett carrying the turtles?"

"They were tied by their heads to the end of a stick with a length of fishing line."

"Excuse me, with what?"

"With fishing line."

"Thank you Sheriff Tackett, you've been most helpful. No further questions."

The sheriff stepped down out of the witness box and walked up the center aisle toward the back of the courtroom, passing Deputy Jude Tyler, who had been called to take the stand next.

Slipping in beside Sarabeth, the sheriff whispered, "You might as well leave now. It's over."

"Over?" She looked at him quizzically.

"We lost. He walks. But no, stay. Sit here and watch. It'll be educational."

All the police officers who had been at the scene of the crime testified and all said the same thing. They'd come on the camp-site with an abandoned truck, a fire and a coffee pot, there was a trail leading from the site to a field where they found 27 marijuana plants. And Jimmy Dan Puckett had come walking out of the woods two hours later, carrying three turtles.

The prosecution rested; Bertrand called his only witness.

"I call the defendant, James Daniel Puckett." After he was sworn in, the small, wiry young man with his hair freshly cut in a McGiver mullet gave his version of what had happened on the morning of May 5, 1988.

"Will you tell the jury, Mr. Puckett, why you were camped out in Clark's Hollow that day."

"I was goin' turtle fishing." Jimmy Dan reached up unconsciously and pulled on the square knot holding his pin-striped tie too tight around his skinny neck. "I went out and made me a camp the night before, so I could get out right after dawn. Turtles is easiest to catch early in the morning, 'cause when it gets up in the heat of the day, they stay hid out under rocks and logs where it's cool and you can't get at 'em."

He described getting up, making coffee and then going off into the woods. And how he'd been surprised when he returned to find "the whole place broke out with cops."

"They said I was under arrest for growing dope, that there was a trail through the woods to the place where the dope was planted. Shoot, I didn't see no trail. I got there after dark and went out fishing just after sunrise. How was I s'posed to see a trail? I was just there to go turtle fishin'."

Sarabeth sat back in her chair with a sigh. The sheriff was right. The accused was going to walk. The sheriff noticed that she had disengaged, leaned over and whispered. "Want a cup of coffee?"

"Might as well. This guy's so sincere, *I* believe him."

They filed quietly out of the courtroom as James Daniel Puckett recited for the jury his favorite recipe for turtle soup.

● ● ● ● ●

The Sheriff's Department was at the other end of the courthouse on the second floor. Sonny spoke to a handful of people—one of whom addressed him "Yo, Preach"—as he led Sarabeth through the outer office to his private, inner sanctum overlooking Main Street.

He gestured toward an overstuffed armchair beside his desk. "Have a seat," then pointed toward a pot filled with a dark, sinister-looking substance. "Coffee?"

Sarabeth eased down into the chair. Her whole right foot felt tingly. Tiny needles were stabbing it like she'd been sitting on it and it had been "asleep." Only she hadn't been sitting on it.

"You sure that's coffee? Looks more like slime from the wreck of the Exxon Valdez."

He really looked at the pot then and smiled. "Right. You could trot a mouse across the top of that stuff. I'll get Jana to make a fresh pot." He stepped to the door and spoke to his secretary seated at a desk just outside.

His office was small, but neat as a pin. Spit and polish, military neat, Sarabeth thought. Other than three phone message notes—which managed to look urgent because they were so bright pink—the desktop was empty. A picture rested on the adjoining credenza of a younger Sonny with a pretty blond woman and a little girl, maybe 3 or 4 years old, with Down Syndrome.

"Your family?"

Sonny followed her gaze and smiled. "Yeah, that's Gracie and me, and my late wife, Mary. I'm a widower. You married? Got any kids?"

The sheriff's openness was disarming, but Sarabeth couldn't go there. Ok, *wouldn't* go there. It amounted to the same thing. "My brother, Ben, lives with me. His parents were killed. My mother … *our* mother, different fathers … it's a little complicated. Ben's 16."

"Don't worry, I'm not flirting with you," Sonny said.

"I didn't think you *were*—" Heat flooded her face and colored her cheeks.

"That's not to say I won't someday." He grinned. "But not to-day. Today's a day to make things clear, not muddy the water. You look like a woman who needs some clarity. Like a woman with lots of questions." He sat down in the big leather chair behind the desk and swiveled to face her. "Fire away."

Sarabeth struggled for composure. She pointed at the ceiling, toward the third floor where the trial was still going on. "Was what happened up there typical?"

"Well, the verdict will be typical, but the defense … " He offered a tired smile. "I gotta hand it to Jimmy Dan, credit where credit's due. Coming out of the woods with those turtles, that was pure genius. I knew as soon as I saw him that we'd lost, but I don't get paid to decide who goes to trial. I get paid to bust dopers."

"What's your conviction rate on dope busts?"

When he looked surprised, she was thrown totally off her game. Maybe she shouldn't have asked that. She'd taught her students to be direct, to ask the "hard questions," but it had never occurred to her that the hard part was the asking. She instantly tried to back-pedal.

"Oh, I know you probably don't keep exact statistics. But gener-ally speaking, a ballpark guess."

"Ten percent. On a good day. When the jury's full of Baptists."

Sarabeth was so caught off guard she burst into a coughing fit.

"You Ok? Can I get you a drink of—?"

"You're joking!" she sputtered. "You *are* joking, aren't you? It can't be one out of 10!"

"You're right. It's probably more like one out of a dozen." As

Sarabeth continued to cough, Sonny got up and met his secretary at the door, carrying a tray with fresh coffee.

"You take cream? Sugar?"

Sarabeth shook her head yes to the cream and no to the sugar, as she struggled to get her breathing under control. Sometimes she had trouble swallowing and that was part of the problem. Of course, she didn't tell him that. She hadn't gotten her own arms around her illness yet; she wasn't ready to share it.

But the rhythm of swallowing soothed her and the choking sensation eased off.

"I'm sorry. I just got strangled," she said.

"Don't get this part confused," Sonny continued as if there'd been no interruption. "This isn't about whether marijuana *should* or *shouldn't* be illegal It *is* illegal. And as long as it is, it's my job to bust the people who grow it." He sighed. "And it's the court's job to let them go. That's the rhythm of my professional life."

"I don't get it."

Sonny took a big gulp of his own coffee—black—sat down in the chair and leaned back in it. "Let me see if I can make this simple. It's the 'there-but-for-the-grace-of-God' principle, with a good portion of 'we-look-after-our-own' thrown in for seasoning. Every time I put a doper on trial, he's facing at least one juror who's raising dope, or has raised dope or has thought about raising dope, or who's brother/father/uncle/cousin or next-door-neighbor is, has or is thinking about it."

Sarabeth was flabbergasted. "How in the world … ? Juries are selected randomly from voter-registration lists, right?"

Sonny nodded.

"Callison County's population is about 16,000 people, so there are what, maybe 6,000 registered voters?"

"Seven thousand, four hundred and eleven as of the May Primary Election."

"So a computer randomly selects—?"

Sonny shook his head. "No computer. Every voter's name is typed on a piece of paper. Each paper is put into an individual clear plastic cylinder, and then the cylinders are loaded into a huge drum. It's in the basement, locked up with padlocks that require three keys—mine, the circuit judge's and the commonwealth's attorney's. Every January, we add in the new voters, roll the drum around to mix up the cylinders, and then select 300 of them, toss out the names of people who've died or moved out of the county and that's the year's jury pool."

"And you're telling me that out of those 300 people, you can't pick 12 jurors without getting at least one who's either raising dope or knows somebody who is?"

"I'd wager the percentage is even higher than that." The look on Sonny's face said it was true, whether she believed it or not.

"I don't get it," she said. "There was nothing like that going on when I grew up here."

"The last time you were home was ... ?"

"Almost 14 years ago."

Sonny made a *humph* sound in his throat. "A lot can change in 14 years."

She hadn't stayed away from Brewster on purpose. She'd just been chained to her job. With the tenure monkey on her back, she felt compelled to teach every summer semester and tutor during holiday breaks. Jim Bingham loved to travel, and he'd used visiting Sarabeth as an excuse to shake the dust of Kentucky off his feet for awhile.

"But Daddy never said a word to me about marijuana."

"I suspect Jim didn't talk about what was going on at first because he didn't want to admit it was happening. None of us did. And later ... " Sonny looked uncomfortable. "He probably didn't want you to worry about him."

"Why would I have worried?" A twinge of dread raised the hair on her arms.

"There were a couple of incidents. Somebody threw a brick through the front window of the newspaper after Jim started publishing the dope arrests in the court news. Tires slashed, prank calls, that kind of thing."

If her father had been in some sort of danger, why hadn't he said something? Why had he kept as tight-lipped about that as he'd been about the big story he was working on? Sarabeth felt the dread settle cold as a stone into her belly. Were the two related?

"What happened here?" she asked, a plaintive note to her voice. This was *not* the Callison County she remembered.

"If you really want to know, there are any number of ways you can find out. You could study sociology and criminal pathology— a good history course might be a plan, too. Or I can give you the random rambling of one man with a shiny gold star."

"I'll take Door Number Two," she said, tried to smile but couldn't quite manage it.

"You do know they used to grow industrial hemp in Kentucky, right?"

"I do now."

"Industrial hemp's used to make rope, but it's a form of cannabis—marijuana—with a real low concentration of the chemical that gets you high." Sonny drained his coffee cup and set it down beside the sugar bowl and creamer packets on the tray. "There were a lot of Callison County boys went to Vietnam." He paused. "Bunch of them never came home, and the ones who did come home weren't the same boys they were when they left." He stopped, cleared his throat and continued in a stronger voice. "And our boys in 'Nam tramped through the jungles next to soldiers who were smoking the same stuff that was growing wild out behind grandma's barn back home—smoking it and paying *big* money for it."

He leaned toward her. "We're talking *farm* boys here. A few of them …" He paused again and Sarabeth suspected he could name exactly who those few farm boys were. "…came back to Callison County with seeds to grow a crop that wasn't on the US Department of Agriculture's list of approved produce."

"And it didn't matter to them that growing marijuana was against the law?"

"So was making moonshine, but that never stopped their granddaddies from brewing it. Callison County produced the best hooch in the state. Same principle, different day."

Sonny got up and walked to the window, drew the curtain back and looked down on the street. "It was the easy money. Raise a dope crop for a couple of years and you're driving a big car and living in a fancy house, and folks thought, 'What's the harm in that?' Pretty soon, everybody wanted some of the action."

He turned back to face her.

"See, dope itself isn't the problem. It never was. The problem is the outrageous fortune you can make growing it. That kind of money breeds evil like a fly breeds maggots. Big money, easy made, attracts bad people. And charms good people into making bad decisions. Disastrous combination."

"Sounds like there wouldn't *be* a problem if they'd just legalize—"

"No sense in going there!" Sonny interrupted. He'd obviously heard that line before. "It is what it is. Growing dope's against the law. Period. Just like brewing whiskey was against the law during Prohibition. And the millions made on illegal booze birthed organized crime, the Mafia. Look how many good people *they've* hurt over the years."

Sarabeth thought about the engaging young man who'd been working in a dope barn to make some of that 'big money' to finance a medical school education.

"You know Wanda Lee? She works for me. Her sons, Gabe and Jesse—"

"I know Gabe. Coached him in Little League before he shot up tall and started playing round ball." He dropped the curtain and leaned back against the window sill. "A good boy. What happened to him ..." He couldn't finish. "And Gabe Lee's not the first. He won't be the last, either."

Sarabeth was suddenly afraid if she didn't change the subject, she might cry. "Taxes, what about taxes?" So emotional, she was just so emotional lately. "Can't you catch dopers like they caught Al Capone?"

"Dopers have figured out ways to scrub their money cleaner than shoving quarters in a washer at the laundromat." Sonny seemed grateful for the change of subject, too. "Everything from investment schemes to music festivals."

"Music festivals?"

"Yeah, they hire a bunch of top-name bands and set up expensive sound equipment in an open field. Tickets, booze, concessions— all cash, of course—and no matter what happens, they win. If it rains and everybody stays home, they claim huge business losses. If there's a full moon and a warm breeze, they claim that 10-20 times more people showed up than actually did. How you going to count a bunch of drunk teenagers in the dark? And now they've got legal income to report."

Sonny's face darkened. "Plus, there are businesses all over this county—*legitimate* businesses—propped up by marijuana money. Businesses that are sailing on down the pike, good times or bad, because somebody's pouring dope money into them and cooking the books so you can't see it."

He stepped back to his desk and sat down slowly in the chair.

"It's not just the little guys like Jimmy Dan. There are powerful men out there, *bad* men." He turned and looked her full in the eye. "And the money is so huge …"

"You think it's going to get violent, don't you."

"It's already gotten violent!" Sonny's voice was tight with suppressed anger. "I'm saying it's going to get *worse*. Sarabeth, these people are only a generation or two and a couple hundred miles removed from the Hatfields and the McCoys."

Jana stuck her head into the office and caught the sheriff's attention. "The jury just came in with a verdict upstairs," she said and shook her head. "Not guilty."

Chapter 9

That afternoon, after her staff had gone home, Sarabeth climbed the stairs into the attic of the newspaper office and brought down two huge books marked 1987 and 1988. Each contained back issues of the *Callison County Tribune*.

She sat down at the big table in the break room and began to flip through the bound volumes, looking at front pages starting in January of the preceding year. There was no marijuana news in any of the 1987 newspapers until springtime.

But when she turned to the April 24 issue, a headline leapt off the page at her. *Crawford man found dead in pot field.*

The story said an anonymous tip had sent the Kentucky State Police to Blackburn Ridge. They found a 24-year-old Callison County man shot in the back of the head, his blood soaking into the ground around two dozen 5-inch-tall marijuana plants.

He was survived by his wife, who was "expecting their first child."

Six weeks later, the June 5 issue proclaimed six columns across the top of the page: *Dopers beat, torture local couple in their home.*

The subhead read: *Three children hear parents' screams.*

Sarabeth's hands began to tremble as she read the bizarre story of mistaken identity. Three men had broken into the house they thought belonged to a man who'd reported their dope crop to police. They locked the couple's children in a closet and tortured the man and his wife for hours.

"They would have killed us," the woman said from her hospital bed. "But they found John's driver's license when they were going through his wallet. He wasn't who they thought he was, so they left."

After Sarabeth read that story, it was as if every dope-related event in the huge books was colored florescent red. The words, a headline here, a few sentences in a story there, jumped out at her, page after page.

The man accused of injuring four men in a hail of gunfire outside a bar last Friday night claimed three of them had stolen marijuana out of his barn. The fourth was a bystander.

Police believe the arson fire that destroyed a home on Keynes Lane Monday night was retaliation in a feud between rival dope-growers.

Shots were fired at a Drug Task Force helicopter last week.

The marijuana news tapered off during the winter months and bloomed with the crocuses the following spring. There were raids on dope fields, four separate incidents of shootings in the woods; one of the victims would remain paralyzed for life. A state police trooper was stabbed while arresting a dope grower, and of course, the recurring melody of "found not guilty" haunted the songs of marijuana trials.

Sarabeth stopped at the July 8 issue, the newspaper published the week after her father's funeral. A headline there read: *Killer dog mauls Cincinnati man*. The story said police believed the animal was guarding a marijuana crop.

Sarabeth didn't go into the office the next day. Instead, she walked up and down Main Street in Brewster asking questions. She did the same thing every day for the rest of the week, wandered the streets in all the smaller communities in the county. She figured it was time she found out how the residents of Callison County felt about dope.

She stopped young mothers pushing strollers and old men pushing walkers. She talked to mail carriers, bank tellers, rescue squad members, store clerks and one semi-comatose man slumped on a bench in the back of a pool hall. Even talked to the jailer and the janitor at the high school. Not in-depth interviews. More what her grandfather called "howdy-and-shake" conversations, though she didn't do much of the talking. Just asked questions about marijuana-growing and listened. To what the people said, and more importantly, to what they didn't say.

• • • • •

When Sarabeth opened her eyes Saturday morning, the amber glow of autumn sunshine filled her bedroom with light so bright it hurt her eyes, so pure it left sparkling flakes like fairy dust on every surface it touched. Birds sang a haunting melody outside her bedroom window, and the aroma coming from downstairs was irresistible. Ben had made coffee, fried bacon, too. She could smell them both! She reached up to throw back the covers and—

She couldn't move.

She could feel her body, her arms and legs stretched out under the sheet and the hand-made quilt, as unresponsive as a crash dummy. Like it wasn't even *her* body. She struggled, tried to lift her leg or wiggle her finger. Nothing.

Panic welled up in her chest, hot lava from a crack in the earth's core. She was paralyzed. *Paralyzed!* Overnight, the MS had taken it all, her world, her life, everything.

Sarabeth screamed, wailed, her voice a high-pitched shriek she didn't recognize.

"Nooooo!"

She sat bolt upright in the midnight dark, the sweat-soaked sheets so tangled around her they felt like wet straps binding her— *mental hospital restraints*—and she fought them in silent hysteria, praying she hadn't really cried out.

"Sis! What's wrong?"

Ben stood in the doorway, a shadow backlit by the spill of illumination from the hallway nightlight.

"I'm all right," she gasped. When she saw him fumble for the light switch on the wall, she begged, "Please don't turn on the light. A nightmare, I just had a nightmare."

Ben flipped the switch on the lamp on the chest of drawers by the door, padded across the room in his bare feet and sat down beside her on the bed, his red hair an unruly tangle that any other time would have made her smile.

She forced herself to take a deep breath and exhaled slowly.

"Ben, you need to go back to bed. I just had a bad dream. I'm fine."

"No you're not."

"Yes, I—"

"No you're not! Your hands shake sometimes and you limp. Sometimes, your vision is all screwed up. You're not fine. Don't pretend you are, that none of this is happening. Don't *protect* me. Let me in."

She fought back tears.

"Ok. I'm not fine, but I'm doing the best I can and it's not awful."

When he started to protest, she raised her hand. "Really. It's not bad, at least not as bad as it could be. But I'll tell you. If it gets worse, I'll tell you."

"Promise?"

"Promise." She paused. "You haven't told anyone have you?"

"Of course not! You said it was private."

After the initial shock, Sarabeth was certain she could eventually come to terms with MS, figure out how to live with it. She was equally certain she would never be able to live with other people's sympathy. She couldn't countenance hanging her disease around her neck like an albatross.

"This job, it's more stress than you thought it'd be, isn't it? It's making the MS worse. Maybe we shouldn't have moved here."

"No! Remember the rule…" Then the two of them chanted in unison: "No looking back." Sarabeth reached up and shoved her bedhead hair out of her eyes. "Moving here was the right decision, Ben."

Home Grown

She'd been surprised by how quickly Ben had adapted. He'd taken to life in a small town like a duck to quacking. And she felt so deliciously free here, released from bondage to the Academia Troll.

"Give it some time. I just need to get the hang of actually doing all those things I taught." But it looked like she'd have to forgo the luxury of gradually getting her feet wet. A few weeks as a practicing journalist wasn't nearly enough preparation, but it was all she had.

"I need to be here right now," she said quietly. "It matters." She reached up and tousled his unruly hair. "Now, go back to bed."

She lay back and tried to sleep, flopped around like a guppy on a table top for what seemed like hours. Then she got up, quietly so as not to wake Ben, pulled on a pair of sweatpants and a t-shirt and drove the three blocks from the house to her office in the pre-dawn darkness.

She sat in front of the typewriter for a long time, thinking about her father, conjuring up his image. Finally she spoke aloud to his presence in the room. "Daddy, I don't get it. Why didn't you write about this?" In her search through the back issues, she'd found lots of news stories about pot, but the silence from the editorial page had been deafening. And there was nothing her father loved more than a good rant. "Why didn't you stand up to the dopers?"

The only response was silence.

"Surely, you don't expect *me* to. I can't!" But, of course, she could, too. Fact was, few people were better qualified. Editorial-writing was her one great gift as a journalist. Still ...

She pleaded with the silence to let her off the hook. "It's so engrained now if I shoot the flea, I could end up killing the whole dog."

Then she heard the memory echo of her father's voice in her head. At age 6 or 7, she'd asked him what he did at the newspaper. She never forgot his response: "My job is to tell as much of the truth as I can in the space I've got."

Marijuana-growing was hurting people, *killing* people in Callison County, in the little community that would forever define "home."

That was *truth*. Whether she felt qualified and prepared or not, she had to take up where her father had left off. It was her job to connect the dots for people, just like Jim Bingham had done for 51 years.

She took a deep, trembling breath and began to type. The words of her first editorial for *The Callison County Tribune* lined up on the page neat as rows of staples in a box.

> *On my first day in the office, I told the staff of my father's newspaper that I hadn't come back home to Kentucky with some grand plan to change the way the paper operated or what we covered, that I didn't intend to turn The Callison County Tribune into the LA Times.*
>
> *I said that my only plan, such as it was, would cast me as the prophet Jeremiah. One of my favorite characters from the Old Testament, Jeremiah had an important job to do— rebuild the wall around Jerusalem. But before he started, he determined to step back and study. He took time to survey the wall.*
>
> *That's what I've been doing, surveying the wall in Callison County. I've read old newspapers and talked to so many people I've lost count. Here's what I learned. If you haven't looked at Callison County, really looked at it in awhile, what I'm about to describe may shock you. But ask yourself, are you really surprised?*

Then she laid it out. All of it. She tacked words onto what everybody knew but nobody was willing to say out loud.

She described farmers who *haven't hit a lick at a snake in five years but live like kings*. And businesses willing to take *mildew-smelling bills—like maybe the money's been buried*, in payment for everything from groceries to dentures.

She chronicled the crimes—the shootings, the stabbing, the beatings, the murder, and described the marijuana trials, the hung juries, the acquittals, the never-been-to-court-at-alls.

She wrote about kids like Gabe ruined for life, and about federal Drug Task Force choppers—thwack, thwack, thwacking, low over the knobs, scanning the wind-whipped vegetation below for a particular shade of "marijuana green."

Callison County, you've been pretending the emperor has clothes on long enough!

There is a mammoth marijuana-growing industry in this county, folks, and don't tell me you don't know it. You've seen it lurking in the shadows for years. Trouble is, you may not have figured out that marijuana's easy money has bred greed and evil, and one of these days it's going to land on you with both feet.

But you don't have to wait until some doper breaks your door down in the middle of the night and brutalizes your family, or your son gets busted in a dope barn in another county and vanishes into a 20-year prison sentence, or your uncle gets shot in a parking lot or you get attacked in the woods by a savage Rottweiler. You can fight back now. Right now!

The dopers in Callison County think they're 10 feet tall and bullet proof. Don't you think it's time somebody showed them different?

Look around you. Call the sheriff and report what you see. Testify in court. Indict. Convict! Stand up to the dopers and tell them you want your community back.

The Tribune hit the racks and landed in the mailboxes or on the doorsteps of the county the following Friday morning. And by noon, Sarabeth was hosting the sheriff and a man she recognized from Jimmy Dan's Puckett's marijuana trial. Kentucky State Police Detective Darrell Hayes was tall and thin. When she saw him testify that day, Sarabeth had thought he was an albino, with his pink skin and wispy flaxen hair. But up close, she could see that the man's eyes, set inside almost-invisible blond eyelashes and eyebrows, were gray. Gun-metal gray eyes behind wire-rimmed glasses, in the angular face of a department store mannequin.

"I'm pleased to meet you, Detective Hayes," she said and gestured for him to have a seat in one of her father's comfortable chairs. "What can I do for you gentlemen today?" As if she didn't know.

"Well, I certainly don't question your chutzpah," the detective said.

Sarabeth cringed. She could have loaded her lifetime supply of chutzpah into a girdle and still had room for a fat woman. Oh, it was easy enough to write a fire-breathing editorial. She'd done that dozens of times. But actually facing the readers' response, that was another thing altogether.

Hayes leaned forward and rested his forearms on his knees, put the tips of the fingers of both his hands together in a here's-the-church-here's-the-steeple fashion and tapped them as he spoke. "I'm just not sure I'd have declared war without checking with the troops first."

"I guess you've got a point there," she said.

Sarabeth glanced at Sonny, seated beside him, and discovered the sheriff was smiling.

"I was just thinking about your father," he said. "About how many times I've sat in this same chair delivering this same message after he'd gone off about something—strip mining, unsafe roads, whatever."

The mention of her father broke her heart along old fault lines that were just beginning to heal. "What I can't understand is why Daddy didn't write this same editorial a long time ago."

"In the past year, Jim was uncharacteristically quiet," Sonny said. "And busy. He was working on something, I think." He looked a question at Hayes.

The detective shrugged. "He could have been chasing some story, I guess."

"He was," Sarabeth said, and told them about the last message her father had left for her, pointing out that he'd said he needed to "keep his mouth shut" about the story for a little while longer. Hayes immediately perked up.

"Do you know what the story was about?" He was totally focused on her response. "Did he tell you?"

Sarabeth shook her head. "But I bet it had something to do with dope." She didn't even realize she'd reached that conclusion until the words dropped out of her mouth.

"Not necessarily," said Hayes. "Your father was big into environmental issues, too. Did stories on that hazardous materials dumpsite on the county line and on polluted groundwater—a lot of gasoline storage tanks have been in the ground so long they've started to leak. Your father had his finger in a lot of pies."

The detective sat back in his chair and refocused. "You're busy and we're busy, so here it is, straight out. Dopers are like those bugs you find under rocks, roly-poly bugs. They operate best in the dark where nobody can see them and anytime you get near them, they roll up behind hard shells to protect themselves. But if you lift up that rock and let the sunshine in, they *will* come after you."

"It could be as civilized as getting a bunch of your advertisers to cancel their ads," Sonny said. "Or all of a sudden the chamber of commerce is all over you for giving the community a bad name, so it's your fault if a jockey shorts factory decides not to build a plant here and out-of-work folks can't find jobs."

"Or it could be as uncivilized as a brick through the window." The pale detective paused. "Your daddy tell you about that, about the brick through the window?"

"No, but Sonny did."

"Dopers don't care about bad publicity," Hayes continued. "If their reputations mattered to them, they'd probably be in a different line of work. But if the folks in this county take your advice—if they report dopers instead of covering up for them, convict them when they're on trial and indict the big boys—then those roly-poly bugs are gonna grow fangs and come out from under that rock and bite you. And keep on biting 'til you drop the rock and leave them be."

"Point made; warning taken." She kept her voice level, but her insides were quivering like Jell-o hit with a fork. There was no big-city anonymity to cower behind here; Callison County offered nowhere to hide.

"Dope's seasonal; most of it's in barns now and we can't go looking for it without a warrant." Sonny sighed. "There'll be no way to tell if your editorial has built a fire under the good citizens of Callison County until marijuana-planting season next spring."

And that would have been a natural place for the men to get up and leave. But they just sat there.

"There's something else we need to talk about," Hayes said. "If you're planning on taking the gloves off with dopers, you need to know who you might be swinging at." He looked at Sonny, tossed him the conversational ball.

"I could make you a list right now of a dozen people I *know* are raising dope," Sonny said, "people I've been trying to catch for years, but I can't prove a thing." He paused for a beat, and in that moment Sarabeth knew. She didn't know how, but she knew.

After the officers left, Sarabeth sat in her office with the door closed, examining memories that suddenly felt as fragile as crystal Christmas ornaments.

The little boy who dangled his feet in the creek with her, chased fireflies in the backyard with her, and didn't tell anybody when she accidentally shot him in the back of the head with a BB gun. *You'll shoot your eye out.*

The boy who killed a snake with a rock before it could bite her. It had turned out to be a blacksnake, totally harmless, but neither one of them knew that at the time, so the act of courage counted.

The kind soul who'd held her hand while a judge passed sentence on her father's murderer.

" … sorry, Sarabeth, but your cousin, Billy Joe Reynolds, his name's right up at the top of that list."

• • • • •

Jake Jamison sat on the back deck that overlooked the pond behind his house and shoved his size 13D feet into a pair of new

Nikes. It was early Saturday morning, just about time to leave for football practice in town. The first and second offensive teams were scheduled to scrimmage the junior varsity squad today.

He stood up and looked out over the pond. Three swans slid silently across the glassy surface—they'd gotten bigger birds after the catfish ate the baby ducks. The trees mirrored in the water were just beginning to turn, the edges of their leaves outlined in red and gold. He stopped to listen to the dogs. Target and Lucky were chasing something through the woods. Daisy was probably with them but she'd run down whatever they were after and kill it without making a sound. It was likely just a rabbit. Hopefully, not a porcupine! He'd had to take Target to the vet last week after he lost a battle with a porcupine and came home with a snout full of quills. And please, Lord, don't let it be a skunk!

The boy loved animals. And that made a good excuse to get out of going hunting with his father. The real reason he didn't want to go was more sinister. He just couldn't stand his father's cruelty. Bubba never killed anything straight out; he always figured out a way to make his prey suffer so he could watch.

"The best part's seeing it in their eyes," his father told him once as they stood over the helpless body of a wounded doe. "When they know they're going to die but they can't do a thing about it."

A lot of Vietnam veterans refused to talk about the war but Bubba loved to. The day they'd shot the doe, he told Jake about the time his company had been questioning suspected Viet Cong sympathizers when two C119 Flying Boxcars laid down a wall of napalm on the hillside above the village.

"We had four gooks tied to posts at the bottom of the hill and all at once there were rivers of fire flowing down, coming right at them. It was like lava from a volcano. Seeing death come for you, that's worse suffering than dying. Watching it, and there's nothing you can do but scream."

Jake would never forget the look that had been on his father's face. It had been a hungry look, a profoundly evil look. Jake shuddered at the memory, turned to go into the house and there stood Bubba.

"Daddy!" Jake gasped. For a huge man, his father moved as silently as a mouse on a cotton ball. Out of nowhere, he was just there, behind you or beside you. It was more than just unnerving; it was spooky. It was calculated, Jake knew, designed to un-settle. And it worked every time.

Bubba had been standing behind Jake, studying the boy, for a full minute before he'd turned around. The big man didn't often have mixed feelings. He knew what he liked, what he didn't, what he wanted and how to get it. But he had mixed feelings about his only son.

The boy was a mystery to him, a profound paradox, one he thought about often, turned over and over in his head the way you worried a lemon drop with your tongue in your mouth. Bubba understood that his son was fundamentally different from his father in just about every way possible. Oh, he'd gotten his father's size. At a thick, muscular 6 feet 4 inches tall, he was big for a 17-year-old. And he looked more like Bubba than Jennifer did. Jennifer was the image of her mother. But Jake had his father's hawk nose, dark hair and eyes and square chin. He had Bubba's voice, too, or would someday, deep and booming. It had been comical to listen to it slide up and down the scale when the boy was 13 and turning into a man.

But in all the ways that mattered in a human being, Jake was not his father's son. Oh, he was tough. You didn't want to fight him; he'd put you on the ground in a heartbeat. Mess with his little sister and he'd break your arm, had actually dislocated the shoulder of a boy on the school bus who put gum in her hair when she was in elementary school. Jake didn't enjoy fighting, though; he wasn't belligerent and aggressive like his father. He had an easy smile that lit up his eyes, he laughed a lot, had tons of friends. He was a good student, too, on his way to college after he graduated. Bubba had never completed high school and few people guessed how brilliant and clever he actually was, which was fine with him. What other people thought was of colossal unimportance to Bubba Jamison.

"I need you to do something for me, son," Bubba said.

"Sure thing," Jake said. "What can I help you with?"

"I want you to make friends with Ben Malone."

It was such a totally bizarre request that Jake was afraid he hadn't understood it properly. Ben Malone was the red-headed California kid who'd moved to town right before school started. He'd come out for football, but since he hadn't been around for summer practice, Coach had pretty much written him off. You didn't sweat with the team in the summer, you didn't play with the team in the fall. Ben had ridden the bench the first two games, though it was not going unnoticed that when the California kid was running sprints, he was a rocket. Jake didn't know him; didn't like or dislike him. But how did his father know Ben? And why would he want Jake to become his friend?"

"You want me to ... ?"

"You know who he is, don't you?" Bubba rumbled.

"Yeah, I know," Jake said, *but how do you?*

"Then you do what I said. Get to know him. Be his friend. I want you two to become buddies."

Jake had been around the block often enough not to ask any questions. His father wouldn't answer him if he did, and with Bubba's hair-trigger temper, Jake could very easily get decked for asking.

"Ok," he said, and shrugged his shoulders. "Whatever you say."

"Good. Go on now, you'll be late for practice."

Jake turned and headed out the door.

Bubba went out on the deck where he could hear the dogs getting all over some critter in the woods. He pulled the folded-up copy of *The Callison County Tribune* out of his hip pocket, sat down in the chair Jake had just vacated, and opened it to the editorial page where a headline read: *And the wall came a'tumblin' down.*

Bubba sat back and read it again.

Chapter 10

Ben had already left for football practice when Sarabeth looked at her watch. Squinted. Moved her arm closer to her face, then farther away. Still blurry. She'd just have to get a watch with bigger numbers on it, that's all. The clock on the dresser confirmed she needed to get moving if she was going to get the house clean and the laundry done before her one o'clock interview.

She'd set it up after she saw the front page of the Kentucky section of Thursday's issue of the Louisville *Courier-Journal.* A story there under the headline "On the Rocks" described how the state's bourbon industry was tanking, with sales at their lowest point in almost 30 years. Stiffer drunk-driving laws, new federal excise taxes, people out jogging instead of sitting home drinking had combined to send the industry into a tailspin, causing huge losses at Jim Beam, Barton and Heaven Hill.

It was one sentence at the end of the story that caught her attention, though. Seems Double Springs Distillery in Callison County appeared not to be experiencing the same financial difficulties as the others. It was bottling whiskey just like it had two years ago without a single layoff. One distillery chugging along like *The Little Engine That Could*.

She figured she'd go out to Double Springs and shake a few trees and see if anything fell out. And there was the niggling little itch in her mind she couldn't scratch. Double Springs distributed bourbon all over America. Maybe Daddy's *national* story had something to do with the distillery.

As the sun moved westward past noon, Sarabeth pulled her car off the road and parked in a shaded gravel lot beside one of the few remaining covered bridges in Kentucky. She slipped the strap of her camera around her neck, fit a 20 mm lens on its nose and stepped out to shoot a couple of wide-angle shots of the collection of ancient, blue-shuttered buildings scattered like a child's toys over the top of Ballard Ridge knob high above the Rolling Fork River. Even the full-color brochure she'd picked up at the chamber of commerce office didn't do justice to the grandeur of the distillery so untouched by the years it had been named a National Historic Landmark.

"Double Springs—where the making of fine, Kentucky bourbon is more an art than a business." At least that's what the brochure said.

Sarabeth fired five or six quick shots, then slowly lowered her camera, shaded her eyes with her hand and stood staring up the hill. There was something about this place, something almost mystical. She'd been here a couple of times with her father when she was a kid and she'd felt it then, too. But whatever the special *it* was, she knew she hadn't tacked its image spread-eagled to the film inside the camera dangling from a strap around her neck.

The Double Springs office building sat at the top of the hill across the road from five ancient, funeral-black whiskey barrel warehouses—not the distillery's only warehouses, but the oldest, the grandfathers of all the others. Double rows of lush red begonias lined the sidewalks in front of the office and flowed in profusion from two blue window boxes by the front door. A small, gray-haired woman who looked like she might have commanded a battalion of Panzers in another life ushered Sarabeth into a paneled office where a dark-haired man in a gray suit, his dress shirt open at the neck, sat behind an enormous desk. When he rose to greet her, she realized why the desk was big. So was he—6 feet 6 inches at least. Maybe taller.

"Seth McAllister," he said, stepped to the side of the desk and extended his hand. "Can I get you anything? A cup of coffee? A soft drink? A barbecued chicken, maybe?"

"Excuse me?" She must have heard him wrong.

His face was more rugged than handsome, with a wide forehead and a Kirk Douglas cleft in his chin. But his eyes were penetrating, so dark brown you couldn't see the pupils. He didn't just make eye contact; he grabbed it and held on.

"Just thought maybe you'd regained your appetite."

"The chicken man!"

"No, you're thinking of the old guy, white hair, white suit, goatee—Colonel Harlan Sanders. People get us confused all the time."

"Elsie Bingo. I remember now. You were in the food booth flipping chickens. I'd have sworn you were a career short-order cook."

"Considered it as a life's work, but gave it up for making bourbon. Chicken tastes better, but you don't have to pluck a whiskey bottle. So tell me, to what do I owe the pleasure of a visit from the editor of *The Callison County Tribune*?"

Sarabeth smiled and sat down in the leather chair in front of an acre of cherry desktop; he settled his big frame into the one beside it.

"Like I said on the telephone, I'd like to do a story on Double Springs, how it's been affected by what's going on in the rest of the industry."

"Twenty column-inches of See Dick and Jane Make Joy Juice?"

"Something like that. Are you nervous about being interviewed?"

"Not nervous," he said. "Honored."

Careful, girl. This guy could charm the shine off a doorknob.

The tour of the grounds started beside the office building at the stone fence, where a trickle of liquid flowed a couple of inches deep over mossy rocks.

"The water in this creek is run-off from Ballard Ridge." Seth pointed to the hillside behind the buildings. "We pipe water to run the distillery from a spring-fed lake. First words out of the mouths of our tour guides—"Doubles Springs bourbon is *not* made from this creek water!"

"You personally write the script for your tour guides?"

"No, but I know what they say. I used to be one." He gestured with one long arm, a sweeping motion that took in the whole distillery. "I've done every job here at one time or another. Summers as a kid, I rotated barrels in the warehouses, worked the line in the bottling room and did any other idiot job my father could find, including tour guide. When I came to work here full-time, I started at the bottom." He paused. "Well, not rock bottom. Rock bottom is handing out souvenirs in the Quart House."

"And that would be ... ?"

"That building down there."

Seth nodded toward a small stone structure, the only building at the bottom of the hill, separated from the Rolling Fork by the 6-foot rock fence that encircled the property. The building rested directly below the five old warehouses whose shadows pointed toward it like fingers.

"The Quart House might just be the oldest package liquor store in America."

"Got a drive-through window?"

"I know you're joking, but it probably had something very like that years ago."

Seth explained that when the distillery had been built by his great, great, great-grandfather in 1865, the building down by the river was already on the property. Early moonshiners had used it to sell their wares to farmers, who brought their own jars there to be filled with whiskey dipped directly out of a barrel.

"Made a good cover for the Underground Railroad, too."

"That building was part of it?"

"There's a secret cellar under it where they used to hide runaway slaves and then sneak them out and downriver at night. Roll-

121

ing Fork hits the Kentucky River, Kentucky River empties into the Ohio. Plaque on the wall by the door tells all about it."

Then she remembered. Her fifth-grade class in elementary school had taken a field trip to different spots around the county when they were studying the Civil War. She remembered stopping at the Quart House, remembered her teacher talking about the brave people who'd operated the Underground Railroad there, who'd sacrificed and died to spirit run-away slaves to freedom.

Sarabeth looked out past Seth, gazing at the immense oak trees with just a hint of autumn color and the worn stonework. There was an order in this place older than the rest of the world that hurried by outside the creek-rock fences. The years had been gentled here. Mellowed. Time hadn't halted altogether, but it had paused, sighed and then left behind the ghost of another age when it moved on.

"Now, the Quart House is a gift shop, has a big picture window cut in the front wall to show off the view, flower beds and stonework all around, and a couple of barrels of bourbon in it plus souvenirs. If you want to go down and get a keychain or a shot glass, we can."

"Thanks, but I think I'll pass." She looked furtively to the left and right and then whispered, "Would the ground open up and swallow me whole if I confessed that I don't drink. I've never been able to stand the taste of alcohol."

"Bite thy tongue, small woman," Seth intoned in the booming voice of a Pentecostal preacher, "lest lightening strike ye dead on the spot!" He paused. "Actually, your secret's safe with me. I think mint juleps taste like paint stripper."

The mystical quality Sarabeth had sensed earlier became both more evident and more elusive during the next two hours. Seth took her to the print shop where bottle labels were printed on hand-operated presses. He showed her how his father had modified the covered bridge with native grown oak to accommodate the weight and girth of Double Springs' tractor-trailer trucks. Then to the still house, where grain and corn were combined with yeast to ferment in an ancient cypress vat before distillation into the clear liquid deposited in the barrels for aging.

As the afternoon wore on, Sarabeth relaxed and let herself enjoy Seth's company. She responded to the warmth in his dark eyes and loved the sound of his easy laugh. Their conversation had eased into the pleasant banter of old friends until they got to the bottling house.

Seth explained that most of his employees were concentrated in that one area, and were working on Saturday because of a water main break the day before.

"We bottle miniatures like you get on an airplane, pints, flasks, fifths and gallon jugs."

"You say you've got 68 people working for you altogether?"

"Sixty-six full-time, then there's two high school kids who work after school in the Quart House and on the grounds."

"How many employees did you have two years ago?"

"Sixty-eight."

"Are you selling bourbon like you did two years ago?"

Seth didn't answer.

"Beam is down 30 percent. Barton is closer to 35. What's your secret?"

He still didn't answer.

Sarabeth felt her face flush. She *hated* this! Hated prying, putting people on the spot. Why had her father so loved his job? Her father. His memory shoved steel into her backbone. She didn't want to ask the next question, but the degree to which she didn't told her exactly how badly she needed to ask it. "You got extra capital coming in that they don't?"

Seth's voice was as cold as a stone in the night. "Double Springs is the finest bourbon whiskey in the world. We're a small distillery because we choose to remain small, to make bourbon the old way, the right way, with the emphasis on quality. The only extra capital we've seen lately is in sales."

"You're telling me that everybody in this room's still got a job because your sales are *up?*"

Sarabeth looked deep into his eyes. He returned the stare. Maybe he should have stayed with his original calling. He was good at chicken, *playing* chicken. He never blinked.

"That's what I'm telling you," he said.

And she believed him. Trouble was, if she'd been on that jury, she'd have believed Jimmy Dan Puckett, too.

All at once she was tired. No, more than tired. Exhausted.

"Thank you so much for your time," she said. "I think I've got everything I need."

"You can't go yet. You haven't seen the Family Five." He must have spotted the sudden fatigue on her face because he gestured back the way they'd come. "It's no farther, just by the office, where your car's parked."

As they walked back across the grounds, Seth pointed to the woods behind the distillery where she could see the front two of eight huge barrel warehouses nestled in the trees. Then he told her about the five original warehouses, the first one built in 1900. She had to concentrate hard to catch what he was saying. Energy had whooshed out of her like water sucked down a sump pump.

" ... great, great grandfather was born on Derby Day, 1900. His father built the first big warehouse then and named it Lieutenant Gibson, for the horse that won the roses that day at Churchill Downs."

As they approached the five big, black warehouses, arranged like the dots on a number 5 dice, Sarabeth could see ornate signs with names over the doors on each one.

"That started the tradition. My father was born in 1924 and that year's Kentucky Derby winner was Black Gold." He pointed to the warehouse behind Lieutenant Gibson. "Uncle Jonas was in 1925—Flying Ebony. That one's the biggest, the one in the middle. My brother Caleb was born in 1948—Citation. And mine's over there behind his—Black Star, 1953."

"Your brother Caleb, does he work here?"

"Killed in Vietnam."

It was clear by the way he said it that he didn't want to talk about it.

"Barrels full of bourbon—50 to 55 gallons in each—are aged for five to seven years and they're rotated on a regular basis." They walked along the side of the Citation warehouse to the massive door on Black Star behind it. Seth shoved. It opened with amazing ease and Sarabeth stepped past him and into the building. "The barrels start out on the top, where it's hotter and wind up down here on the bottom row."

The ancient oak door closed slowly behind them. It was dim in the huge warehouse, quiet and still. The light filtered in through rows of narrow, barred widows high above their heads, slanting down in bright strips on the floor. Flakes of dust danced in the golden shafts of sunlight and vanished in the shadows.

The sudden quiet was intimidating. Like standing alone in an empty cathedral. Even a whisper would disturb the silent audience of whiskey barrels stacked rack upon rack, higher and higher until they melted into ghostly, shadowy figures in the gloom of the ceiling seven floors above.

The silence lengthened.

Seth reached out in the shadows and took Sarabeth's hand. His touch was like a low-power electric current that sent shock waves all through her. She discovered that she was powerless to remove her fingers from his grasp, even if she'd wanted to, and she didn't want to.

"Come here," he said, his voice hushed. "I want to show you something."

He led her like a child down the center aisle between the mammoth racks of barrels, down the whole length of the warehouse to the far end where there was a space about 3 feet wide on both sides of the aisle between the racks of barrels and the back wall of the building. Turning sideways, Seth edged between the barrels and the wall, along the open space until he came to the back corner of the building.

It was cramped and musty, the air heavy with the weight of uncounted years. Hazy light filtered down from high above where sunshine spilled off barrels 50 feet over their heads. Seth turned in the cramped space to face Sarabeth, his back against the side wall of the warehouse, with the barrel rack on one side and the back wall of the warehouse on the other.

"There," he said simply, pointing to a spot on the rough oak board of the barrel racks stretching from the floor up into the gloom above. At first, Sarabeth saw nothing. Then her eyes made out crude letters carved in the wood about even with her elbow. She bent to examine them.

"When I was a kid, this was my hiding place," Seth said.

"J.S.M.," she read out.

"Jordan Seth McAllister. Carved it one afternoon after Martha gave me a Category Five backside tanning for Super-Gluing Caleb's butt cheeks together."

"You *didn't!*"

"Did, too! I can't remember why anymore. I must have figured he'd earned it, but I don't know what he did that made me mad enough to select that particular method of payback. I just know I decided to run away from home afterwards and this is as far as I got. It became my special place. My sanctuary. Even made a ladder so I could climb up to the top rack from back here and peek out the high window at the world. You can see the Quart House at the bottom of the hill and the whole rest of the valley."

Seth pointed to odd-sized pieces of wood nailed in 2-foot intervals all the way up the beam into the twilight. Sarabeth impulsively reached out, grabbed the piece above her head and pulled herself upward, feeling around with her foot for the rung nearest the floor. She took another step, and another, but the fourth piece of wood came loose when she put her weight on it. Off balance, she twisted toward Seth, reached out and he caught her as she tumbled, pulled her tight against his chest and let her slide down his body to the floor. Then he made no movement to let her go. She stood with his arms around her as one emotion slammed into another inside her like cars rear-ending each other in a freeway pile-up. Time suspended, elongated as she stood unmoving, reveling in his nearness.

"It's stuffy in here," she finally gasped, and stepped back. "I need to get some *air!* " She whirled around, made her way quickly to the center aisle and practically ran out of the warehouse, her shoes click, click, clicking on the ancient wood floor in the heavy silence.

She made it out the door, then leaned up against the side of the building, trying to regain her equilibrium. She was dizzy, disoriented and a little sick.

All of a sudden, Seth was standing in front of her. His big shadow enveloped her and blocked out the late afternoon sun.

"I know what it is," he said quietly.

She looked up, startled. "You know what *what* is?"

"Hunger. You didn't have any lunch, did you?"

"Nothing since this morning's breakfast of champions." She sighed out the words. Relief she couldn't explain made her almost giddy.

"That I can fix. Have dinner with me."

Don't do it! Tell him you're busy. Tell him you're sick. Tell him it's raining frogs and you're getting ready for the Second Coming. Just say no!

"Yes. Dinner sounds wonderful. I'm starved."

Seth smiled and pointed to a white house at the top of the hill. "I live right up there and I'm sure I can rustle up a meal and have it on the table in less than an hour."

"You're making dinner?"

Seth tilted his head back and laughed out loud, a deliciously free, joyful sound.

"No, I meant I'd get my housekeeper to whip something up." Then he grinned. "Though I did try my hand in the kitchen once." He paused for effect. "My cooking was so awful the flies took up a collection to patch the hole in the screen door."

• • • • •

The center snapped the ball; the quarterback faked to the right and handed the ball off to Ben. He made it three steps. The offensive lineman missed his block and Ben got nailed by a linebacker. The force of the broadside impact squirted the ball out of Ben's hands like a bar of wet soap. The nose guard caught it on the first bounce and was high-tailing it toward the opposite goal line before Ben even hit the ground.

Whistles shrieked all over the field. The coach was spitting bullets.

"You got pig grease on your fingers, boy?" he screamed.

Ben jogged over to stand by himself on the sidelines.

"Coach is so tough they say his spit'll raise a blister on boot leather." Ben looked up to see the big quarterback, Jake Jamison, standing beside him. "His problem is he'd rather yell at you than tell you what you did wrong. I saw what happened out there."

Then Jake pointed out that Ben had been holding the ball too far from his body, and with one hand. Ben had grown up on the USC sidelines watching his father coach, had started playing peewee football when he was 8 years old. He knew how to hold a ball! But obviously he hadn't done what he knew to do.

The coach yelled, "Ok, run the same play again."

Jake handed the ball off and Ben grabbed it with both hands this time, spun off around the linebacker, sidestepped another tackle and was flying toward the end zone like a missile, leaving the defense grasping for air.

Ben ran the ball three more times before the scrimmage was over; he ran two of those possessions in for touchdowns.

In the locker room afterwards, Ben was something of a celebrity. Nobody had made much effort to get to know him before; now, everybody wanted to be his friend. But he sought out Jake, who was standing in front of his locker buttoning his shirt.

"I never got a chance to say thank you," Ben said. "What you said, it helped a lot. I just wasn't thinking."

Jake shook his head. "Obviously, I wasn't telling you anything you didn't already know. You were awesome out there."

Ben blew by the compliment. "I missed summer practice this year and it's hard to play good ball if you haven't run a play in 10 months. I'm sure not up to speed with the rest of you guys."

"God help the defense when you *do* get up to speed!"

A short, chunky, blond boy hollered at Jake. "You driving?"

"Yeah, I'm driving," he called back, then turned to Ben. "We're going out for a burger. Wanna come?"

"Sure." Ben grinned. "I'll get my jacket and be right back."

When Ben came around the corner, Jake actually looked at the jacket for the first time. It was a red-and-white letter jacket with *three* letters on it.

"You were playing with the varsity as a *freshman*, weren't you?"

Ben nodded.

"We're gonna have to get you a new jacket, bud." Jake beamed. "One in black and gold."

● ● ● ● ●

His belly full, a hot cup of black coffee resting beside a half-eaten piece of extra-gooey Derby pie on the table before him, Seth sat back and tried not to stare at the red-headed woman seated across from him. He hadn't said much. For all his charm and charisma, he was at his core a quiet man, a listener, an observer.

And his housekeeper, Mrs. Hannibal, had kept the conversational ball bouncing just fine without him. The stout, buxom woman had begun peppering Sarabeth with questions about her travels as soon as she found out the newspaper editor actually had a passport. He watched expressions play across Sarabeth's face as she described the time she'd attempted to order a sausage biscuit at a McDonalds in London.

"A biscuit in England is a *cookie?* Well, I never!" Mrs. Hannibal squealed.

Seth studied Sarabeth without appearing to, a maneuver he managed to pull off by not looking directly at her. It had been a roll of the dice, of course, homey meal, table right in the kitchen, not every woman would have responded to that, but Sarabeth fit right in.

As she was speaking, a glass of water unexpectedly slipped out of Sarabeth's hand, tumbled to the floor and exploded like a hand grenade on the stone tiles.

"I'm so sorry! I—"

"Now, don't you never mind a thing!" Mrs. Hannibal clucked.

Sarabeth quickly scooted her chair back as the big woman dropped a dishtowel and a couple of napkins on the puddle of water at her feet.

"Let me help." Sarabeth reached for her own napkin, but her hand was trembling. She balled it quickly into a fist around the napkin, but Seth saw. And he saw something else, too. Her other hand was steady.

"Why don't we get out from under foot," Seth suggested. He stood, stepped to the back door and pushed open the screen for Sarabeth. "Is the squeak of a screen door the same in British English as in American English?"

"I never saw any screen doors in England." She got up and stepped around the puddle of water. "Or screens on the windows either. Guess they just like bugs."

He followed her out onto the porch that wrapped all the way around the old house.

"Wait just a second," he said, then turned, walked quickly to the front corner of the house, looked around it and came back smiling. "Come here, I want to show you something."

He didn't realize that he'd said the same words, or that there was the same hushed quality in his voice earlier that afternoon in the barrel warehouse.

The tree frogs in the pin oak trees had taken up their *eech-eech, eech-eech* to add to the symphony of crickets and the deeper *rub-buph, rubbuph* of the pond frogs as Seth and Sarabeth stepped out onto the part of the porch that swept across the whole front side of the house.

Home Grown

An enormous full moon had just cleared the horizon and was sitting like a scoop of orange sherbet atop the knob on the other side of the valley from Double Springs. It spilled bright liquid gold down to shimmer on the night-blackened river and honey-glaze the mist hanging in the hollows and drifting up off creeks in the distance. Fireflies by the thousand glittered green-gold in the meadow below the house, sparkling the night with a mystical, other-world magic. The distillery, with lights twinkling in buildings here and there looked like a fairytale kingdom. Somewhere in the woods a solitary nightingale sang its lonely song.

Sarabeth walked to the porch railing and looked out over the valley. Seth came and stood beside her, drinking in the night.

"Oh, Seth!" Her voice was an awed whisper. "Have you ever in your life seen anything more beautiful?"

It was out of his mouth before he could catch it. "The moonlight in that red hair of yours ... it's close." In for a penny, in for a pound. "And in case you were wondering, yes, I'm hitting on you."

Her response surprised him. She said nothing for such a long time, he began to feel awkward. He started to—

"Don't." Only the one word.

"*Don't ...?*"

"Hit on me. Just don't."

"If it's about the story, you know, what you're writing ... " He was sorry the moment the words passed his lips. Why in the world had he brought up *that*? He saw her stiffen.

She turned and looked full into his face. "I guess I found out everything I can, right? Everything you're willing to tell me."

He sighed. Heard the psychic slamming of all the doors that had opened between them. "I've told you everything you need to know," he said.

Chapter 11

Jimmy Dan Puckett and Donnie Scruggs were dead set on it and they'd agreed when they started this that the three of them were in it together. Lester Burkett thought it was a bad idea, though. A colossally bad idea. Oh, they'd voted and he'd lost and there it was. But he still thought it was a bad idea.

Donnie was checking out the building while Lester—his friends called him Doodlebug—and Jimmy Dan waited in the woods with the money in a canvas gym bag, $35,000, divided equally into used twenties, fifties and hundred-dollar bills. Perfect for spending. Of course, they weren't going to spend it, not right now anyway. That's why they were out here in the woods with it; that's what they'd agreed to.

Now wasn't the time to run the whole thing back up the flagpole. Wasn't nobody going to salute a new plan now. Still, the fat man couldn't keep his mouth shut.

"It ain't too late to chuck this idea and do somethin' different, you know," Doodlebug whispered. He and Jimmy Dan were in the shadows behind a big oak tree with a stand of brush in front of them. Doodlebug didn't know why he was whispering, who it was he thought could hear them, but the magnitude of the occasion seemed to call for it.

The building Donnie was investigating was about 50 yards away, a dilapidated shed that might be close to 100 years old. It had last been used to store fertilizer, weed killer and insecticide. You could still smell the chemicals that had been spilled over the years on the dirt floor. But clearly it hadn't been used for anything in a long time. The briars, brush and brambles had grown up around it so high it was almost invisible.

A lot of buildings as old or older than this one dotted Callison and neighboring counties, their wood a shiny silver from the graying of the elements, some of them leaning badly, their roofs riddled with holes. This one was better than most, about 12 feet by 15 feet with a pitched roof and a slanted-ceiling loft. It probably had been built as a tool shed. Maybe there'd been a house nearby, though there was not even the stubble of a foundation left anymore. There were big cracks between the timbers of the walls, but it was in good shape, good enough for what they needed. The door even fastened, and you could have put a padlock on it, too, but doing that was like announcing, "Hey, there's something so important in here it had to be locked up." That was just inviting somebody to snoop, least that's what Jimmy Dan said.

Doodlebug wiped his runny nose on his beefy arm encased in a tight sweatshirt and pulled the hood up to cover his ears. It had turned cold Halloween Night. All the little kids had worn coats over their costumes when they'd come knocking on his door and he'd handed out pieces of candy to put in their sacks.

Jimmy Dan didn't seem to notice the icy breeze. He wasn't paying any attention to Doodlebug, either. Not surprising. He and Donnie'd been on the same side as soon as they'd come up with the idea, sitting in the tiny living room of Donnie's cracker box house near the Callison County Fairgrounds.

Doodlebug was short, but Jimmy Dan was even shorter, a little guy with no butt—none whatsoever—which meant he had to reach down about every six seconds and pull up his pants or they'd slide off his backside into the dirt. He reminded Doodlebug of a Jack Russell terrier, sort of prancing around, always angling for a fight. That night, Jimmy Dan had been sitting on the floor lovingly counting the bills lying in a pile in front of him. He set them in neat stacks in a cardboard box on the floor beside the coffee table as he counted them, and jotted down totals on a notepad he kept in his front shirt pocket.

"So, we just go out there and spend it like there's no tomorrow and you don't think Bubba's gonna catch on?" Jimmy Dan had said. He may be as mean as a snake, but when you look in them eyes, you can tell he's smart, too."

Doodlebug was sitting on the sofa, sunk down in the cushion where the springs were broken, patiently rolling a joint from the contents of a sandwich bag. He'd gotten interested in dope in high school when somebody told him smoking it would make food taste better. He'd probably put on 50 pounds smoking weed and cutting classes until he finally quit school altogether and went to work for his uncle as a mechanic at the Burkett Brothers Garage.

Donnie returned from the kitchen with beers all around. He was blond and really did look a little like Don Johnson on *Miami Vice*, except his broad shoulders weren't shoulder pads. He worked on the crozier machine at the cooperage. The self-professed ladies' man of the group, Donnie had a sex drive you couldn't rein in with a choke chain. If you believed half the tales he told about his exploits with women, he must have been the daddy of half the illegitimate children in Callison County.

"You guys still arguing about what we're going to do with the money?" he asked. "Shoot, I thought you'd have it all figured out by now." He handed a beer to Jimmy Dan, who set it down on the coffee table next to the box and kept counting bills. Doodlebug set his beer beside J.D.'s while he continued rolling the joint. Donnie turned his up and drank half the bottle in one long gulp.

"If you ask me, I think Bubba Jamison's all hat and no cattle," Doodlebug said, then carefully licked the edge of the filmy paper, stuck it down and twisted the ends. "Just 'cause he's so big and scary lookin' he's got everybody buffaloed. I don't believe all those stories I've heard. I bet Bubba made 'em up."

He put one end of the joint into his mouth and lit the other with a butane lighter, sending the cloying, sweet scent of marijuana into the room. He inhaled deeply, held his breath and passed the joint on to Donnie.

"You been smokin' more'n dope if you don't think that man'd strangle his own grandmother for the gold in her teeth," Jimmy Dan said. When Donnie tried to pass him the joint, he shook his head and kept counting bills. "If he ever figures out what we've done, he'll cut us up and feed us to his dogs."

"He didn't figure out about them seedlings, did he?" Doodlebug challenged. "You was so scared you about wet yourself when you got busted in the spring, afraid Bubba was gonna put it together that we stole them plants out of his seedling bed. Well, he didn't catch on to that and he ain't gonna figure out the rest of it neither."

The three men had worked for Bubba off and on for years, knew his whole operation, and two years ago, they'd come up with what Donnie'd called a "long-range plan" to make themselves some serious money. True, the starting-their-own-organization piece had gone up in smoke when the police burned their whole first crop. But the rest—well, proof of its success was laying right there in stacks in the box.

For two summers, each of them had stolen small amounts of dope from every one of Bubba's barns they worked in, not enough so's anybody'd notice. They were smart, careful, didn't get greedy, just kept stashing it away a little at a time. They'd been sharp enough to sell the stockpile the same way—a little here, a little there—to different buyers who'd never heard of Bubba Jamison, and made sure to get paid in used tens and twenties so it couldn't be traced when they spent it.

Only now, J.D.'d got his jockey shorts in a wad about not spending it at all!

"You really don't think Bubba'd notice if we suddenly showed up in Brewster with all kinda money? If we started buying fancy clothes?" He turned and looked at Donnie. "Or motorcycles?" He shifted his gaze to Doodlebug. Both men knew Doodlebug had his eye on one of those Harley Davidson choppers sitting in the window of the dealership in Bardstown. "You don't think he's gonna start wondering where we come up with that kind of money? He knows what he pays us and it ain't *that* much. We don't lay low for awhile, we're gonna disappear just like that wife of his done. And Roger Furman—ain't nobody seen or heard from him since he went out looking for dope on Blackburn Ridge."

Doodlebug was still holding his breath after his toke on the joint. When he sighed it out, he breathed words out with the smoke. "His wife run off with some other man, you know she did. Can you imagine being married to that gorilla? And Furman's gonna turn up any day now with some story about falling off the wagon and waking up in Syracuse."

Jimmy Dan had completed the money count. In the box were 35 stacks of bills with 25 bills in each stack. When Doodlebug passed him the joint, he took it, drew a big lung full of smoke and held it as long as he could. As soon as he released it, he started in on Doodlebug again.

Donnie finished off his beer and announced with a loud burp that he had to go pee. He walked back into the room a few minutes later, put both fingers into his mouth and blew. The loud whistle produced instant silence.

"That's enough!" he said. "We can argue about this all night. I say we vote. How many thinks we ought to divide up the money— J.D., what's the total?"

"Exactly $35,250."

"Ok, that we split the $35,250 three ways and do whatever we want with it?"

Doodlebug raised his hand high in the air, looked hopefully at the other two, then dropped it in his lap in resignation.

"And how many thinks we sit on it until next summer, say June first, long enough that Bubba will figure we musta made money doing something else during the winter, long enough so he don't connect the dots?"

Jimmy Dan and Donnie raised their hands.

Disgusted, Doodlebug got to his feet and lumbered toward the bathroom. As he stepped around Donnie, he bumped the coffee table and knocked the two full cans of beer into the box with the money.

That had ended all discussion. From that point on, they'd been frantically drying it off, running around cussing and stumbling into each other, spreading it all over the house quick so the bills wouldn't stick together. The next morning when the money was dry, they'd gathered it all up and put it in the canvas gym bag.

Once they'd decided they weren't going to spend it, they had to find someplace to hide it. Donnie was only renting and he had two or three on-again, off-again live-in girlfriends who sniffed around him like coon dogs all the time to make sure he wasn't cheating on them. Jimmy Dan had been sleeping on the couch at his brother's since he got out of jail. Doodlebug was the only one who had his own place, but it was a trailer and didn't offer an obvious spot to stash that much cash.

Then, Donnie'd remembered the old tool shed he'd come upon once when he was tracking a wounded doe. It had sounded good, so they had come out to take a look.

Jimmy Dan turned his attention away from Donnie's inspection of the building and looked at Doodlebug. "Naw, it ain't too late for us to decide to do somethin' different, but unless you got some sort of plan we ain't heard about yet, then we're stickin'."

Doodlebug said nothing. He had no better plan; he just didn't like this one.

Donnie waved the two of them out of the woods. They were careful to move the Kudzu vine that had wrapped around the shed door so they could put it back when they left. Inside, the shack was dark and cold and smelled like bug spray. Though it had no windows, shafts of sunlight spilled in all around through cracks in the walls. But not a speck of light shown through the ceiling. No leaks; the roof was sound.

"I was thinking we ought to put the money in that half loft up there, scoot it back in the corner and, you know, maybe cover it up with ... " Donnie looked around. An ancient burlap bag hung on a nail on the wall. "Put this old bag on top of it. It's not like we got to worry about hidin' it. Don't nobody ever come here, you can see that."

He stopped and thought for a moment. "And we can't come nosing around here neither, checking on it all the time. We do that and somebody's gonna notice. I say we put the money here and agree to leave it be until June first."

Doodlebug didn't like that one bit, and this time Jimmy Dan was on his side. The three men instantly started yelling at each other.

Finally, Donnie made a point the others couldn't argue.

"If we buried the money in a hole, would you dig it back up every few weeks just to make sure it was still there?" No response. "Well, if you don't think putting it here is just as safe as burying it, then maybe that's what we ought to do, just go dig us a hole—"

"We ain't gonna bury it!" Jimmy Dan said. There was a wild look in his eye. "We already been all through that."

Neither of the other men was surprised by Jimmy Dan's reaction. The little man had been so dead set that the money wasn't going into a hole in the ground that he'd threatened to take his share and spend it right then if that's what the others planned to do. He never would say why he was so against it, but Doodlebug figured it had something to do with Jimmy Dan's old man. His daddy beat those kids something fierce, and done other things, worse things Jimmy Dan wouldn't talk about. Doodlebug had seen his back; J.D. had scars from Christmas to Easter. So whenever the little man got weird—about the dark or graves or being in tight places—Doodlebug always suspected that was why.

"I'm with Donnie," Jimmy Dan said. "I say we come back for the money on June first and not before. Agreed?"

They turned to look at Doodlebug and the fat man just shrugged. He didn't think leaving the money here was a good idea, period. But they were partners and they had to stick together.

It would never have occurred to any of them to fear betrayal. What they shared was deeper than trust. Their bond was a common understanding of the nature of reality. If one of the group went back and claimed all the money for himself, what would he do with it? Where would he go? Callison County was the known universe and it afforded nowhere to hide.

Donnie got a big rock and shoved it up against the door. With it open wide, the interior of the shed was lit well enough to see a ladder on the wall. As the smallest, Jimmy Dan was dispatched to the loft with the money bag, which he shoved up against the back wall and covered with the dusty burlap sack.

But when he turned toward the ladder to climb down, a hunk of ancient timber under his left foot gave way, dumping him on the floor with his leg dangling through a hole above Doodlebug's head.

Donnie and Doodlebug burst out laughing, then Donnie realized Jimmy Dan didn't think it was funny.

"Aw, come on, J.D., don't be like that," he said. "It's good you made a hole right there, ain't it, Doodlebug? Now, nobody can get to the back wall of that loft where the money is."

And he was right, nobody could get to the money bag. But as it turned out, nobody had to; the money came down out of the loft all by itself.

● ● ● ● ●

On her way to cover the Andersonville Christmas parade on a freezing December morning, Sarabeth spotted it. A little white building set back from the road with a steeple that dwarfed the rest of the structure and a scattering of tombstones in a fenced-in area beside it. Sonny's church.

He'd told her about it the Friday before Election Day when he'd taken her to lunch, an oft-repeated but seldom accepted invitation. Sonny had never actually asked her out, but he'd come perilously close a time or two. Though she'd managed to sidestep his advances, he'd joked once that "dating isn't a disease, you know." No, she'd thought, but Multiple Sclerosis is.

They had been seated across from each other in one of the booths that lined the back wall of the Jiffy Shop next door to the county jail. Dukakis and Bush were probably sweating bullets, coming down to the wire neck and neck the way they were, but Sonny Tackett was totally relaxed. He was running unopposed.

They'd been discussing politics when he'd suddenly shifted gears so quickly Sarabeth was left standing on the tracks as his train of thought pulled out of the station without her. Happened a lot with Sonny. He was … random. A man you could envision mounting his horse and riding madly off in all directions.

"Well, don't look at me like you just discovered a new species!" Sonny laughed. "I said I was a preacher, not a proctologist. And I'm not Jimmy Swaggert!"

It had been all over the news that the televangelist had been caught in New Orleans with a prostitute.

"You don't see it as odd—that you've got a gun in your hand on Saturday night and a *Bible* in your hand on Sunday morning?"

"Right and wrong, good and evil, they're just different sides of the same coin," Sonny had said. "I try to help people focus on the most important part—the good guys win in the end."

Ben had begged off the Christmas parade shoot. He and Jake were headed to Louisville to round out their Christmas shopping in a mall.

Her shopping was almost done. Ben had been easy. He'd grown up in California. Didn't own a winter coat or a single wool sweater. Now Jake was another matter. She still hadn't come up with a gift idea for the young man who had become such a fixture around their house she had taken to calling the boys Thing One and Thing Two. She'd even threatened Jake that she was going to claim him as a dependent on her income taxes. Of course, that had been before Sonny had whispered in her ear at the homecoming football game.

"You remember that list I told you about the first day I came to your office?"

"I remember."

"Well, the very first name on it, in all caps, is Jake Jamison's father, Bubba."

Sarabeth had managed to wall that information away from her relationship with Jake. He was a good boy, deeply troubled, but kind and thoughtful. She refused to visit the sins of the father on this particular son.

Rounding a corner, she saw Andersonville up ahead. The highway went right through the center of the little town, up a steep hill to a traffic light and down the other side.

She pulled into a parking space in front of the Andersonville Mercantile Store. The parade was scheduled for noon and it was only 11:30. She hoped to get something hot to drink before it started. The temperature beneath the clear blue sky was probably only a couple of degrees above zero.

She climbed the wooden steps to the porch in front of the store and noticed an old man in a rocker. Wearing nothing but a ragged denium jacket, he was carving something out of wood.

"Excuse me, could I get a cup of—?"

"Can't hear ye." He looked her up and down, his eyes clouded with cataracts, and motioned toward the store. "Go on in and git what ye came fer. Price's marked on ever'thing. Cigar box's on the counter, but there ain't change in it for nothin' bigger'n a $20." Then he turned his attention back to the carving.

She opened the squeaky door and stepped inside, onto an oiled, hardwood floor so dark and worn smooth it could have been marble but for the slat marks.

"Well, hello there!" came a voice from the shadows to her left.

Seth!

Sarabeth's heart began to hammer in her chest like a fist on a door. She'd only seen him once since she'd interviewed him that day at Double Springs. There'd been a three-car pile-up on Springhurst Road in October and when she got there, Seth and two other rescue squad members were using the Jaws of Life to get one of the victims out of the wreckage. They'd barely had time to say hello, but she'd been profoundly unsettled by her response to his presence. She'd felt as shy as a tongue-tied teenager.

She felt pretty much the same right now.

"What brings you to Andersonville today?" she said.

The big man stepped nearer. She caught a faint whiff of English Leather, her favorite aftershave, and her laboring heart continued to slug away in her chest.

Grow up! You're acting like a school girl with a crush!

"The parade, of course. You do know this parade is a legend in these parts."

"What for?"

"Because nobody watches it."

Sarabeth looked confused.

"There's nobody left in Andersonville to watch the parade because just about every man, woman and child in town is *in* it." He smiled a hundred-watt smile. "You see anybody out there on the street?"

She shook her head.

"I rest my case."

When he just stood there smiling at her, she felt color rise into her cheeks and he seemed to notice her discomfort. "Truth is, I brought a barrel wagon over for the Methodist church to build a float on." He looked around. "You want a cup of coffee?"

She eagerly accepted his offer and managed to get her emotional ducks beak-to-tail-feathers by the time he returned with it. Then they sat in two of the chairs pulled up close to the wood stove in the corner of the room and talked. It amazed her how quickly she felt at ease around him, though she couldn't look directly into his eyes for long. They were so dark and deep she felt like she was drowning. He was wearing a pale blue wool sweater under a light jacket, but sitting so close to the fire, he soon had to shed both and she marveled at his grace. Most big men were a little clumsy, but his movements were as lithe as a cat.

Their conversation flowed effortlessly and she found herself laughing often and talking much more than usual. Seth asked lots of questions and was an interested, engaged listener.

"Got all your Christmas shopping done?" she asked.

"I'm always finished before Thanksgiving." He laughed at her grimace. "I don't have many people to shop for. Christmas for me is midnight Mass at Gethsemane Monastery near Bardstown and serving Christmas dinner at a homeless shelter in Louisville."

"You don't go to a family gathering?"

"You're looking at the whole McAllister family."

The words formed and leapt out her mouth before she even had time to think the thought.

"Then you have to come to Christmas dinner with *my family!*" As soon as she realized what she was asking, she hurried ahead before she lost her nerve. "I'm serious. There's a big family blow-out, a famstravaganza—Billy Joe's word, not mine—at Aunt Clara's house. More food than Attila the Hun and a teeming horde of bar-barians could eat in a week. Kids everywhere. Neighbors dropping in. I was there at Thanksgiving and it was a grand time."

He hesitated.

"Please!"

"Ok, count me in."

"Wonderful!" Her voice betrayed just how wonderful she thought it was. "Here's the drill: no presents. But each adult selects another adult for a gag gift. You have to make it yourself and you can't spend more than $5."

There was a sudden, loud *whoop-whoop-whoop* sound from a fire truck at the top of the hill, signaling the beginning of the parade.

Sarabeth grabbed her camera bag and stood.

"I have to shoot this. I'll call you with specifics about Christmas. Thanks for the coffee!" Then she turned and bolted, left him sitting there looking a little surprised by her abrupt departure. She wasn't really in that big a hurry to take pictures, but she had to get out of the glare of the big man's attention. It was like sitting alone in a spotlight on a bare stage.

She knew she'd be sorry later for what she'd just done. As soon as she came to her senses, all the reasons why it was a bad idea to invite Seth McAllister to Christmas dinner with her family would crash down on her like Galliger's mallet on a ripe watermelon.

But right this minute, Sarabeth was supremely glad.

She got a particularly good shot of Sonny on a black horse, leading a mounted unit of deputies near the end of the parade. Gracie was seated in front of him in the saddle. The little girl had mastered the weathervane wave and she looked like a queen reviewing her troops. Sarabeth would use that shot as the lead picture on the front page.

Chapter 12

Ben grabbed Jake from behind, wrapped his arms around him and jerked his body sideways, pulling him away from the boy Jake had just knocked to the ground.

"That's enough, Jake," Ben hissed. Jake struggled to shake Ben off his back, but Ben held on. "You've made your point. It was just a lame joke. Leave him alone!"

Jake stopped struggling. "Ok," he said. "I'm done. Let me go." Jake was so strong that if he'd really wanted to break Ben's hold on him, he could have shrugged him off and kept at the kid.

Stepping back, he stared down at the boy lying on the sidewalk in front of him. The boy's lip was cut, his nose was likely broken, and he probably had some loose teeth. And Jake had only hit him once; the boy'd never landed a single blow.

With a threat clearly meant for all the other teenagers gathered around, Jake told him menacingly, "Don't you *ever* say anything like that about my sister again. Do you hear me? If I find out you've even spoken her name, I'll kick you into the middle of next week."

Jake leaned over, picked up his ball cap off the ground and stormed away through the crowd. He got to his Jeep, banged his fist on the roof and then leaned over and rested his forehead on the door frame. Ben came up behind him.

"You can't go around smashing that fist of yours into just anything, you know," Ben said pleasantly. "We may have lost in the playoffs, but that hand of yours is still a national treasure. You tossing 'em, me catching 'em—badda boom, badda bing—six points!"

"You think I really hurt him?"

"Yeah, you really hurt him!" Jake spun around in surprise and Ben continued. "You hurt his pride, might have been a mortal blow, hard to tell without X-rays and a CAT scan. His swagger, too, which is in intensive care but not expected to live. And I figure his reputation's deader than a possum run over by a school bus."

Jake smiled in spite of himself.

"Get in," he said, shaking his head. "We got Christmas shopping to do."

As they headed out of town toward Louisville and the mall, Jake thought about the four months he and Ben had been friends. It seemed like a lot longer. One of the many things he'd come to cherish about his freckle-faced sidekick was Ben's knack for draining the pressure out of tense situations and difficult conversations. The two of them had been in several of both.

The first one had been only a couple of weeks after they'd met. Ben had just asked Jake straight out, "I hear your father's a doper—is he? Because if he's not, I'm going to have to start decking some people."

They'd been on their way to a homecoming party when Ben said it and Jake had almost run off the road.

Ben had watched an incredible mixture of emotions wash over Jake's face, and thought he probably should have waited for a more opportune time to spring such a question. But he'd needed to know. It hadn't been important to him whether or not Jake's father was a doper, but it had mattered huge how Jake felt about it if he was.

"The Turtle Creek overlook is just up ahead," Ben said quietly. "Let's pull over and talk."

They never made it to the party.

"Does everybody think that? Do they talk about it? Is it *common knowledge*?"

Ben was surprised Jake didn't know what people said. But maybe he didn't know because he didn't want to know. "I just moved here, and I know. If I know, everybody knows. Or thinks they know. Maybe everybody's wrong. People get reputations they don't deserve. I'll trust whatever you tell me. Is it true?"

"My father has all sorts of business dealings, he buys and sells land, he finances construction projects, shopping centers and stuff like that. He makes boatloads of money in ways people never see."

Jake's voice was just a little shaky. Ben sat quietly and watched his friend wrestle with it.

"People say things because they're jealous. It's hard to see somebody making a whole lot of money when you're barely getting by. I can see why people say stuff about him, but he works hard and ... "

Jake stopped talking in mid-sentence, like a wind-up toy that had run out of juice. He stared at the valleys, hills and meadows dressed in fiery red, gold and orange autumn plumage spread out below the overlook. His eyes were moist.

"Yeah," his voice was soft, barely above a whisper. "My daddy grows dope." He was silent for a time, staring straight ahead. When he continued, it was more like he was thinking aloud, not actually directing the words to anybody in particular.

"Marijuana really shouldn't be illegal anyway. It's no worse than alcohol. Shoot, it's better than alcohol. Smoke weed and you don't get aggressive, you just get mellow. And hungry. There shouldn't be a law against it, let people decide for themselves if they want to smoke, just like they decide if they want to have a beer."

Then he turned to Ben. "I've said all that stuff in my head for years, and a part of me believes it. Marijuana really shouldn't be illegal. It doesn't hurt anybody." He dropped eye contact and looked out the windshield again. "But it *is* illegal. And if Daddy gets caught growing it, he'll go to prison, for a long, long time."

He turned back to Ben and spoke in a low growl. "And I hope he *does* get caught! Ever since I was old enough to know what he

147

was doing was against the law, I've dreamed that the police would show up at the door one day and put handcuffs on him and drag him away."

Choked-back tears thickened Jake's voice. " ... and put him behind bars where he couldn't ever get near me or Jennifer again."

"Does he hurt you?" Ben blurted out, immediately sickened. "You and your sister? Does he abuse ... ?"

"*Abuse?* Grow up, Ben! You mean beat the crap out of us?" Jake made a *humph* sound in his throat. "'Abuse' defines our daily existence; it is the putrid stench of reality in the Jamison household." The sarcasm drained out of his voice and he reverted to the odd, almost-talking-to-himself tone, staring out the windshield at nothing. "Tiptoeing around, trying to be quiet so you won't attract his attention, 'cause the last thing in the world you want is for Daddy to notice you. My best-of-all-possible-days is to make it out of bed in the morning and back between the sheets at night without the awareness of my existence ever making it to the higher centers of my father's brain. Even before Mama left—"

He turned and looked Ben in the eye. "And I don't blame her, by the way. Not one bit! I'm proud she got away, and I hope wherever she is, she's happy!"

He turned back toward the view. "But even when she was there, she couldn't stop him. When he un-fastened his belt, pulled it out of his pants and started slapping his hand with it, nobody could ... And when she tried, he just went after her with it."

"Why didn't you tell somebody?"

"Oh, come on—tell *who?* Who in this county's going to stand up to Bubba Jamison? Some minimum-wage social worker from Child Protective Services? Yeah, right. But we learned. Jenny and I were quick studies. We figured out real fast that as long as you didn't cross him, most of the time he'd leave you be and you could just go on with your life."

"But if you did cross him?"

For just a moment, Ben saw raw terror skitter across his friend's face. Then Jake slammed all the doors shut and sat with a haunted look in his eyes. "He'd beat the crap out of us, that's all. Like I said."

Ben knew there was more, but he didn't push it. He wasn't at all sure he wanted to know what it was. He wondered if Jake had any contact with his mother. How could she just walk out and leave her children alone with that monster?

Jake leaned his head back on the headrest and the two were quiet for a time.

"So everybody knows about Daddy?"

"Yeah, pretty much everybody."

"Don't know why I'm surprised. Everybody knows about Joe Kessler's daddy, and Sarah and Bob Fisher's daddy. And Kelsey Reynolds' daddy. So why not mine? Guess I just thought my father was smarter than theirs, did a better job of hiding it."

"Kelsey's father's a doper? Billy Joe Reynolds is my sister's cousin. He's a doper?"

"Yep. Works for Daddy. At least I've seen him around the house a time or two, and it's not like my father has any *friends*. But the way Kelsey's daddy flashes cash, anybody could figure it out. Gives her more money than she could possibly spend, though I bet he doesn't know she's spending it on drugs."

"Do you … use drugs? Smoke dope or do other stuff?" Ben didn't, never had, never intended to. It was a decision he'd made at age 13 when he'd watched some friends drop acid. One of them decided he could fly and before the others could stop him, he climbed up onto the roof of the garage and jumped off. He'd be in a wheelchair the rest of his life.

"I've tried it. But no, I don't smoke dope, or do the hard stuff." Jake downshifted into rage so quickly Ben actually jumped. "'Cause I'm *not* my father! I'm not anything like him. I don't want to have anything to do with him or his world. I *hate* him!"

Jake looked shocked, like he was surprised he'd actually said the words out loud. Then all the air whooshed out of him and he

149

settled back against the seat, stared up at the ceiling and blinked back tears.

Ben wanted to put his arm around his friend, comfort him somehow, but it felt awkward. So he just sat with him in silence, remembering his own father and mother, how much he'd loved them. Losing them both had been a staggering blow. But he'd had Sarabeth. Without her, he'd have been lost.

And at that moment, Ben made a commitment to Jake. The big, dark-haired boy needed a family, a real family. Ben's wasn't much, but such as it was he determined to share it with Jake. Though he'd only been around Jake's father a handful of times, at football games or briefly at Jake's house, Ben hadn't been surprised by anything Jake said about the man. Bubba Jamison's eyes held a cruelty as old as time.

"I've got less than a year left on my sentence in hell," Jake said. "Soon as I graduate, I'm outa here. Daddy knows I'm going away to college, but what he doesn't know is I'm *never coming back.*"

Then Jake spoke so softly Ben barely caught his words. "I'm scared of him, though. He can hurt you, in ways you can't imagine."

Jake turned and looked deep into Ben's eyes. "It's an awful thing, to know something like this. But I do, I know it—like you know there'll be sunrise on Easter Sunday morning."

"What? What do you know?"

"If I ever defied Daddy—truly *defied* him—he'd kill me."

● ● ● ● ●

Christmas Day dawned cold and sunny. Sarabeth and Ben had opened their gifts to each other the night before, sitting in front of the small Christmas tree in their den. They'd kept it simple; it was Sarabeth's first Christmas without her father and every time she stumbled into the jagged hole of his absence the pain took her breath away.

Aunt Clara's house lay at the end of a winding, tree-lined dirt road about a mile off KY 28 six miles south of Crawford. The old farm house had been Sarabeth's grandparents' home when she was growing up. It was three stories tall, with a wide staircase leading from the parlor to the bedrooms upstairs, and a dark, spooky back staircase that snaked down from the attic to the back wall of the kitchen. Sarabeth and Billy Joe used the back stairs to sneak out on their dishwashing chores when they were children.

Ben hopped out to unload the food as soon as Sarabeth parked under the leafless oak tree just outside the picket fence around the yard. They'd brought a deep-dish apple crumble pie, a plate of gooey chocolate brownies and Sarabeth's back-by-popular-request white salad—cherries, pineapple and bananas in a fluffy mixture of Cool Whip, cream cheese and sour cream.

As Ben hauled in plates, and gifts for the children, Sarabeth sat for a moment listening to the latest news report about the crash a few days before of a Pan Am jet over Lockerbie, Scotland that killed 270 people, including 11 people on the ground.

Shaking her head sadly, she thought about the people who'd been going about their daily lives when out of nowhere an airplane dropped out of the sky on their heads! She was so engrossed in the story that she jumped when somebody rapped on the car window. It was Billy Joe.

"You get out of that car right this minute, Miss Bessie Bingham," he commanded, "and give your favorite cousin a Christmas hug!"

She opened the door and stepped into his long arms. He held her tight, the standard Billy Joe embrace. He appeared genuinely glad to see her and she breathed a quiet sigh of relief. After what had happened at Thanksgiving ... well, their relationship could have been strained.

It had been a gray, overcast day, spitting snow, and Sarabeth had been hurrying up the porch steps with her soon-to-be-famous white salad when she'd bumped into Bethany. Or rather, Bethany had bumped into her, more like crashed into her.

"Hi Sarabeth!" The little girl had squealed after the collision, then flung her arms around Sarabeth's waist. "I remember—you were taking pictures at Elsie Bingo."

151

"That's right, and you were trying to win a teddy bear at the ring-toss booth."

"Yeah, but I missed," she said with a disappointed sigh.

"Your daddy bought you that great big panda bear, though. At Wal-Mart. Remember, Sugar?" said a woman standing on the porch smoking a cigarette. The woman wore a white fur jacket Sarabeth suspected might actually be real ermine and had a rock on her finger the size of the Hope Diamond. The little girl nodded but still looked downcast.

When the woman made no effort to greet her, Sarabeth stepped up on the porch and introduced herself.

"Hi, I'm Sarabeth Bingham and you must be Becky, right, Billy Joe's wife? We met once years ago, maybe you don't remember."

Sarabeth remembered. But the teenage girl who'd been holding a wiggling, flaxen-haired infant that day more than a decade ago bore little resemblance to the woman who stood before her now. The girl had had soft golden curls, a round, happy face and a cheerful smile. This woman's hair was a brittle, bleached-blond in a frizzy, Madonna-esque style, and the smile on her thin face was as empty as Al Capone's vault.

"Sarabeth, yes, I've heard Billy Joe speak fondly of you on numerous occasions." She articulated each syllable of the words carefully, like a battery-operated doll: "Hi, I'm Chatty Cathy. Do you want to play with me?"

Becky didn't look at Sarabeth when she spoke, but at a point in space about six inches left of her face. Sarabeth had to fight the urge to move over into the flight path of the woman's gaze.

There was an awkward silence then. Becky just stood with a little half smile, as if she would be content to wait there until somebody came by, picked her up and set her somewhere else.

"Is Billy Joe here?" Sarabeth asked.

"He's in the house."

Again, silence. Becky took a deep drag on her cigarette, sighed smoke out her mouth and nose and continued to stare at a distant nothing.

Bethany reached up and took Sarabeth's hand. "I'll show you," she said quietly. The sadness on the child's face when she looked at her mother broke Sarabeth's heart.

She hadn't meant to mention her encounter with Becky to Billy Joe, but after the huge Thanksgiving feast, she found herself alone with him in the back yard. They'd been pushing Bethany in the tire swing, the same one the two of them had played in as children, when Aunt Clara called out, "Who wants ice cream?" and Bethy hopped out of the swing and bolted into the house.

"You don't want ice cream, Bije?" Sarabeth asked.

"I'm so stuffed if I took one more bite I'd have to put it in my ear." His face brightened. "Remember the home-made ice cream Grandma used to make? She gave Becky and me that old hand-crank freezer and Becky used to make strawberry ice cream in it when Kelsey was little."

"About Becky ..." Sarabeth began. All the light went out of Billy Joe's face. She didn't know if she should continue, but he looked so desolate. "B.J., what's she on?"

He didn't say anything for so long Sarabeth thought she'd gone too far, presumed too much on a childhood relationship. She was about to backtrack when he spoke, said one word so softly she barely heard him.

"Everything." He pulled in a ragged breath. "Started out with coke, but anymore ... I don't even know what she takes now."

Before Sarabeth could stop them, the words leapt out of her mouth. Not in an accusing tone, just sad. "It's about you growing dope, isn't it?"

Billy Joe's head snapped back like she'd slapped him.

"Sarabeth Bingham! Why would you say a thing—?"

"Save it, B.J.," she cut him off gently, reached out and touched his arm. "I know."

He started to protest again, but the look in her eyes stopped him and he just hung his head. He was quiet again for a time and Sarabeth let him be, didn't push.

153

"I lied to her," he finally said, "told her I wouldn't and then did it anyway. I said I was sorry, though, done everything I knew to make it up to her. And I've asked her, *begged* her to get help, but she won't listen." He lifted his head and looked at Sarabeth and there were tears in his eyes. "What she says don't make sense, Bessie. She says all our money makes life worthless, that nothing she does matters 'cause I could pay somebody else to do it better. Says she don't *fit* in this world. Crazy stuff like that." He turned away and ran his hands through his hair. "Becky never had nothing growing up, barely had food on the table, and I swear, sometimes I think she wishes *we* were starving, too. I can afford to give her anything she wants, but she …"

He hung his head again, shook it slowly back and forth. Then his shoulders began to shake. He didn't make a sound, but tears ran down his face.

Sarabeth put her arms around him, pulled him close and patted his back. She didn't know what to say, so she just stood there, holding him, trying not to cry, too.

"Do you hate me, Bessie?" he asked in an anguished whisper.

She did cry then. "Of course not, Billy Joe! I love you. Nothing will ever change that."

And now, as she stood with his arms around her in the bright December sunshine, what she'd said a month ago was true.

"Mama said you invited Seth McAllister to the famstravaganza," he said, stepping back and grinning down at her. "You wouldn't be just a little sweet on the guy, now would you, Bess?"

"Don't start, Bije! Don't even *start*." She closed the car door and they headed into the house together.

Seth showed up a few minutes later, dressed in a forest green cashmere sweater and carrying a small box wrapped in bright red paper with a huge silver bow.

The day was too rowdy and loud to qualify as a Courier and Ives family Christmas. Billy Joe's oldest sister had twin teenage boys who decided to play keep-away with another cousin's UK ball cap and the three landed in a wrestling heap that upset the dessert table, dumping pies, cakes and Sarabeth's salad on the floor.

Kelsey refused to engage with anybody, stood off by herself, her flaxen hair "crimped" and her bangs hanging in her eyes. Becky didn't show up at all; B.J. explained awkwardly that she was "home sick." Ben, Billy Joe, Seth and two of B.J.'s brothers-in-law tossed a football around in the back yard until one of them—there was much dispute about *which* one—chucked it through the glass storm door in the kitchen.

It was a joyous time, though, made even better by Seth's presence. He was charming and gregarious, full of jokes and good humor. And he hovered so near Sarabeth that every time she glanced at Billy Joe, her cousin raised one eyebrow and winked at her.

Right after Christmas dinner, which was scheduled to go on the table at noon but didn't make it until 2:30, a sudden pain jabbed deep into Sarabeth's left ear, like someone had stabbed her with an ice pick. She tried to ignore it, but the jagged ache throbbed in rhythm with her heartbeat, which seemed to grow louder and louder until she couldn't hear out of that ear at all.

By the time everyone settled in the living room for the gag gift exchange, Sarabeth was in so much pain she sat rigid on the couch, her face pale, her lips pressed tight together.

"You Ok?" Seth asked as he lowered his big frame down beside her. "You look—"

"I'm fine." She stopped him, but she knew he could see she wasn't and that made her want to bolt out of the room in tears.

Bethany had been designated the gift distributor, and as she dashed around the room handing out presents, Seth took Sarabeth's hand and squeezed it. She could sense his vigilant attention, feel his concern, and she ground her teeth in frustration at being struck down—like those people in Scotland—totally out of the blue. But her anger made her ear hurt worse; Saran-Wrap vision was settling over her eyesight, too, and the whole left side of her head throbbed like a smashed thumb.

"This is for you," Bethany squealed, her shrill voice shoving a blade of agony into Sarabeth's ear. The child deposited Seth's red box in Sarabeth's lap, then turned to Seth. "And this one says *S. E. T. H.* right there." Bethany handed him a shoebox-sized gift wrapped in newspapers. Ben and Sarabeth had spent all yesterday evening making it, gluing dozens of chicken feathers to a whisky bottle.

Ben squeezed in next to Sarabeth on the other side and leaned close. She'd seen him eying her from the other side of the room. "We need to leave now, don't we," he said quietly. All Sarabeth could do was nod her head.

The boy took her elbow and helped her to her feet, then made as casual an announcement as he could.

"The surprise gag gift Sarabeth just got for Christmas is a migraine," he said, and everyone groaned sympathetically. "So we're going to take that unexpected present and go home. But we had a great time and we'll see all you folks soon."

Of course, everybody clucked over her maddeningly as she tried to get out the door before she collapsed. Billy Joe gave her a gentle hug and a peck on the cheek, seemed to understand better than the others that whatever was going on, it was private. She was glad Seth had taken the arm Ben wasn't holding because she was rapidly losing the feeling in her left leg.

She managed a remarkably sincere fake smile and Ben shooed her relatives out of the way without too much fuss and soon she was down the front porch steps and on the way to her car. Ben opened the door, Seth helped her in, then Ben went back inside to gather up Sarabeth's empty dishes.

"I'm so sorry," she told Seth as he knelt on one knee beside her. "I invite you out here and then I bail out—"

"You have nothing to apologize for," he cut her off. "This has been the best Christmas I've had in years! I just want you to go home and get to feeling better." She hated hearing such concern in his voice. He patted the red-wrapped gift she still clutched in her hand. "I hope you like her. I worked hard to get her just right."

The front door slammed shut behind Ben and Seth started to rise.

"There's just one thing, one Christmas gift I've been hoping for all day," Seth said. "I tried, but I never managed to get you under the mistletoe." He leaned over and brushed his lips gently across hers.

"Merry Christmas, Sarabeth," he said tenderly.

She was in bed for two days, off work for a week. Seth called several times, but Ben was a pit bull of a gatekeeper when she needed him to be. In the quiet solitude of her father's old house, she withdrew, closed and locked doors she'd been foolish to open up to the big man with dark eyes. Her disease had made her limitations painfully clear; she didn't intend to impose her less-than life on anybody else.

Chapter 13

As Sarabeth waited on hold to book a flight for her spring check-up at the USC Medical Center, she picked up the blue Smurfette doll that lived on the shelf by her typewriter, the doll Seth had painstakingly Miss Clairol-ed from a blond into a redhead as her gag gift at Christmas.

She smoothed the doll's fire-truck red curls. The months since Christmas had passed remarkably fast. She'd worked hard at the newspaper and her confidence grew, one small victory at a time. From standing up to the angry mother of a bride whose wedding picture had been misidentified on the social page, to asking the parents of a drowned child for a photograph of the toddler to run with his obituary, Sarabeth was earning her stripes as a journalist.

Ben had been right; she *could* do this.

Life in general had taken on an ordinary-ness as time passed, too, gradually defining itself the natural way a stream finds its own path down a hillside. Perhaps the decrease in her stress level was responsible for the decrease in her MS symptoms. She hadn't had an earache or a migraine in months. Only an occasional tingling in her fingers and Saran Wrap vision. Of course, it could also be that her megatron vitamin supplements had finally taken effect.

The American Airlines reservation agent came back on the line.

"You wish to depart Standiford Field on May 15, is that right?"

"Yes, and return to Louisville May 20."

She'd waited to book a flight until after all the Kentucky Derby fans had gone home. The Derby, Ben's first. It had rained, *poured*, miserable day. Except she'd seen Seth! And what were the odds of *that* happening? More than 150,000 people and he'd bumped into her while she was waiting in line for a chili dog.

"Well, hello there stranger," he'd said, with a wide smile that accentuated the cleft in his chin. He'd stepped back and surveyed her outfit. Everyone dressed to the nines for the Kentucky Derby; no woman would dare show up at Churchill Downs without a hat. Sarabeth was wearing a pale yellow dress with a tiny rosebud design, and a wide-brimmed yellow hat with rosebuds on it. "I do believe you win the prize," he said admiringly. "You are the most beautiful woman at the 1989 Run for the Roses."

Sarabeth's face turned the color of the flowers on her hat.

"You're no slouch yourself," she said.

Seth looked positively dashing in a three-piece suit with a rose boutonnière.

"Do you think I might tempt you with better cuisine than a chili dog? We have tons of food upstairs and the view is amazing from the Double Springs box." He didn't say "on Millionaire's Row," but he didn't have to. Everybody knew there was a section in the stands reserved for the rich and famous. "I'd love for you and Ben to join me. He's here, isn't he?"

"He and Jake are in the infield."

"It's a lake out there; he'll drown!"

"He's 17, you think he cares?"

Seth laughed. She'd forgotten how warm and inviting that sound was. No, she hadn't forgotten. But she had tried to forget. Just like she'd tried to forget how much she enjoyed Seth's company.

"All the distilleries are grouped together in one place." Seth leaned over and continued in a wheedling tone, "They're serving all sorts of different drinks up there and I know how much you *love* bourbon."

Jim Beam, Barton, Heaven Hill. She'd read just the other day how the industry was still struggling, still laying off employees. Which, of course, begged the questions—had Seth reduced his workforce? And if he hadn't, how …?

She didn't want to go there. What was the point? More importantly, she *did* want to go *there*—to the box on Millionaire's Row with Seth, to laugh at his humor and revel in his attention. And the degree to which she wanted to go told her exactly how badly she needed to stay away.

"No, I think I'll pass." She had to force the words out. "But thanks for the invitation."

Seth had looked terribly disappointed. But more than that, he'd looked tired. Worn out. Like maybe he'd even lost weight. He hadn't looked like that when he'd crossed the whole length of the crowded church to say hello to her on Easter Sunday. Or when—

Stop that!

She really had to quit measuring history in terms of Seth sightings. The time in February when they'd stood in the snow together on the post office steps. The flood she'd shot last month when he'd showed up with the Callison County Rescue Squad, the—

The reservation agent clicked on the line, announced, 'Hold, please,' and was gone again. Sarabeth could hear Harmony Pruitt's voice at the reception desk outside her office and she tuned in to listen. Harmony sounded quiet and serious. That was odd. Then Sarabeth turned and there in her office doorway stood Wanda Lee.

Wanda hadn't been at the newspaper more than a handful of times in the past seven months, what with Gabe in the hospital and then in rehab. And Jesse in jail. Sarabeth had told her to stay home, do whatever she needed to do, her paycheck would arrive in the mail every Friday just like it did when she was working. The rest of the staff found out what Sarabeth had done and before she had time to hire somebody to fill in for Wanda, the others quietly took on extra tasks, did their work and Wanda's, too, never put down their overtime hours.

Sarabeth reached over and hung up the telephone.

"I wanted you to hear it from me." Tears filled Wanda's eyes, sunk deep into gray craters in her emaciated face.

Jesse's trial in Baker Circuit Court had started yesterday but was expected to go on for several days since all the boys arrested in the barn that day were being tried together.

"Jury wasn't even out an hour, found them guilty, all of them." Her voice had the vacant, disconnected sound of someone reciting the alphabet. "The original charge was trafficking in marijuana in the first degree. That's a Class C felony. But because they were working in a barn full of it, they said it was 'manufacturing,' and convicted them all of a Class B felony, which is ..." She couldn't finish, but Sarabeth knew the penalty. At least 10 but not more than 20 years—*in prison*. "Sentencing is set for next week."

"Wanda, sit down," Sarabeth said. "Let me get you a glass of water."

Wanda remained standing in the doorway, leaning against the frame for support. "They're kids, just *kids*." In Kentucky, a juvenile could be tried as an adult at age 17. "Jesse only did it because Gabe did. And Gabe—"

"Mama!"

Wanda turned toward the voice.

"Mama, I want to see Sarabeth." The words were slightly slurred.

"Gabe, I told you to wait in the car."

Sarabeth rose from her chair and stepped to the door of her office.

Gabe lurched through the swinging half door in the front counter, dragging his left foot, his left arm dangling useless at his side. He brushed his mother aside and enveloped Sarabeth in a one-armed hug.

"I'm gonna help you make pictures!" His breath was nauseating. Drool dripped off his chapped chin onto the front of her blouse. "I make good pictures, don't I, Sarabeth." He turned back to his

161

mother, but only one eye tracked. The other appeared to be looking at something else entirely. "Tell Mama I make good pictures."

Sarabeth found it unexpectedly hard to speak. "Yes, Gabe, you make very good pictures."

"Can we make pictures now?"

"Sure you can," Wanda told him as she reached over and lifted the boy's arm off Sarabeth's shoulders and started herding him back toward the front counter. "You just go out and sit in the car for a minute, and then you can come back in and make pictures."

"Ok!" He shuffled toward the front door under his own steam. "I'll come back in a little while and we'll make pictures." He got to the door and stopped, stood facing it but made no effort to try to open it.

"He has almost no short-term memory," Wanda told Sarabeth quietly. "In a minute or two, he won't remember any of this."

Sarabeth's eyes filled with tears.

"There's a center in Bardstown that's like daycare for adults. As soon as Frazier Rehab releases him, I'll put Gabe on the waiting list. In a few months, maybe, I'll be able to come in a couple of days a week."

"Wanda, you just take care of Gabe and don't worry about your job. It'll be here when you're ready for it."

"I need to come back to work." Desperation was sheathed in the quiet voice.

Sarabeth couldn't think what to say. "Call me if there's anything I can do."

Wanda nodded. "Let's go home now," she said to Gabe.

He turned toward her and the half of his face that still functioned came to life. "Home. Ok, home."

Wanda opened the door for him and he stumbled through. She followed and closed it behind them.

Sarabeth looked around and realized the whole staff was standing there. Everyone had slipped in from the back shop. Ben was there, too, his mouth set in a thin, tight line. He'd never met Gabe, but he'd taken over the job of processing film and printing pictures in the darkroom after Gabe was injured.

Then Harmony started to cry. Collapsing into her chair, she put her head in her hands and sobbed. Sarabeth walked over and patted the girl on the shoulder, her own cheeks wet with tears.

• • • • •

The boy lay on his belly in the tall weeds on the side of the road, cradling the metal ammo box that contained the detonator for the bomb he was going to use to blow up the KGB headquarters while the rest of his team rescued the Russian scientist.

He looked both ways, gave the secret signal wave and his two teammates appeared out of the bushes to his left and ran across the road to the bushes on the other side. He stayed behind to make sure they weren't being followed. Jim Phelps always stayed behind to make sure they weren't being followed.

Then the sandy-haired 12-year-old bent low and sprinted across the road to where his team was hiding. When he got there he found his sister crying. She was always crying about something.

"What's wrong this time?"

"I don't want to play anymore," Maggie Mae fired back at him. She pulled up the leg of her jeans and showed her brother a red spot on her knee. "I fell down and it *hurt.*"

Adam sighed. That's what happened when you had to drag your little sister with you everywhere you went. She messed up everything. But he had to humor the 8-year-old. If she went running home now, she'd tell Mama they were playing in the woods on the knob and they were never allowed to cross the road.

"Why don't you be Shannon Reed today instead of Casey Randal. Shannon used to be in the Secret Service." He tried to sound encouraging. Those were the only two women on the Mission Impossible force, and Adam figured they were put on the team for the same reason Maggie Mae was tagging along after him—somebody made them do it. He, of course, was Jim Phelps. Eddie, sitting in the grass a few feet away, trying to get the zipper of his jacket unstuck, was Nicolas Black, the master of disguise.

When the remake of the 1960s series had premiered in the fall, *Mission Impossible* instantly became the kids' favorite television show. This week's episode had been about a Russian scientist and his daughter. Eddie had gotten the old ammo box he'd found laying beside the road and Adam had furnished the wind-up clock to make a bomb they were going to plant in the old shed in the woods on the other side of the knob.

Maggie Mae stopped sniffling. "And she even kinda has hair like mine, too." With her red pigtails, Maggie Mae looked like a life-sized Raggedy Ann doll and Shannon hair's was blond. But Adam wasn't going to tell his sister that.

"Are you guys gonna play or not?" Eddie wanted to know. He couldn't manage to get his jacket zipped. It had been an unseasonably warm spring until Derby Day last weekend, when it had turned cool and stormy. Today the wind was downright cold. "Cause if you're not, I'm gonna go home." He was wearing shorts under the light jacket, with scabs riding both knees. "It's freezing out here."

"It'll be warm in the shed," Adam told him and Eddie grinned. Going to the shed always produced the tingling excitement of the forbidden, and they hadn't been there since last fall. Adam had broken his leg Halloween night and it had been in a cast for months.

"Let's move out, team," he commanded in his best Jim Phelps voice. "Keep your heads down and watch out. There could be snipers in these trees."

The three children moved silently through the woods, climbed up to the top of the knob and down the other side to the shed worn shiny silver by a 100 years of rain and sun. They'd discovered the building years ago and sneaked away to play there as often as they dared. It was the one secret Maggie Mae had been able to keep, because she knew they'd get their backsides tanned for crossing the road if she told. The building was their private clubhouse and once you'd been inside for a little while, you hardly noticed the chemical stink.

Eddie moved the thick Kudzu vine back from across the door and dragged it open. He made a hand motion and Maggie Mae and

Adam sprinted from their hiding place behind an oak tree, pushed past him into the building and closed the door behind them.

It was warmer than outside if you left the shed door closed. The dusty, dry smell that unused spaces always had, like the room behind the school where they stored textbooks over the summer, was mixed with the smell of fertilizer and weed killer.

Though there was no window, the interior of the shed wasn't scary dark. Shafts of light pierced the shadows where there were cracks between the wall boards. As soon as their eyes adjusted to the darkness, they'd set the explosive.

Eddie heard the scratching of mice in the loft and jumped. Maggie Mae turned toward him and noticed a pile of something lying in the floor just outside the reach of a shaft of light coming through a crack in the wall. She took two steps, leaned over and picked up a piece of paper just as Adam began giving orders.

She held it out in the dim light. Adam snatched it out of her hand. It was a $20 bill!

"Where'd you get this?"

"Off the floor. It was over there." Adam turned to where she pointed. Eddie reached into the darkness and drew back a piece of paper into the light.

"It's a $10 bill!" he said.

Adam shoved the door open wide and wedged a big rock against it. A shaft of sunlight stretched out through the darkness across the shed floor toward the far wall. In the center of the light was a pile of bills.

"Holy shi—" Adam caught himself before he cussed. Maggie Mae would certainly tell Mama about that! The three children dropped to their knees beside the money and began grabbing handfuls of it.

Eddie burst out laughing. "I bet there's a couple of hundred dollars here."

Maggie Mae tossed a handful of bills into the air. "Wheeee!" she squealed.

With the door open, the wind whistled through the shed. Thick, white dust swirled around, along with some of the bills.

Adam turned to Eddie. "Gimme that ammo box."

He dumped out the clock and started stuffing handfuls of bills into the box. "We gotta gather all this money up and put it in here before it blows away."

The children scrambled around until they'd gathered up every bill on the dirt floor.

"There may be more of it where we can't see," Eddie said, so they got down on their hands and knees and crawled around, feeling into dark corners. The shack was empty, there wasn't really anywhere to hide anything.

"Maybe there's more up there," Adam said, pointing to the loft. "Look, there's a hole in the floor, like somebody was up there."

Eddie ran to the wall and climbed the ladder as nimble as a spider. Adam climbed only high enough to see into the loft while Maggie Mae stayed on the ground, dust filtering out of the loft into her hair.

The powdery dust that was blowing around in a whirlwind in the shed was much thicker in the loft, so thick it was hard to see. There were bigger pieces of stuff in the dust there, too. Edging around the splintered hole in the floor, Eddie stepped toward the back wall and dozens of mice scattered.

"See anything?" Adam asked.

"Yeah," Eddie said. "Mice. And a ton of mouse turds."

When he leaned over and picked up a piece of tattered burlap, mice scurried away toward the corners and startled him. He jumped backward and almost fell through the hole in the floor.

"There ain't no money up here, just mice. It's a regular mouse hotel!"

It was, indeed, a mouse hotel.

The field mice that lived outside during the summer fled the cold of early winter to build warm homes in barns and other buildings all over the county. A whole herd of the little creatures had been enticed into the loft of the old shed in the woods by the smell of beer on the huge pile of paper in a canvas bag. They'd chewed their way into the bag and had been feasting on the beer-flavored bills for months, using the rest, and the remains of the bag, to build warm winter nests.

The only paper that hadn't been converted into mouse turds or confetti was what had fallen out of the loft through the hole in the ancient flooring. The chemicals in the dirt that formed the shed floor kept the mice away. Eddie saw only what was left of their feast, powdery confetti and small pieces of mouse-chewed canvas and burlap.

By the time Eddie had climbed down out of the loft, Adam had a plan.

"We gotta count this and we can't do it in here. It's too dark and the wind's blowing too hard." He was trying to think like Jim Phelps. "So we're gonna take this box to Eddie's barn and spread the bills out in a horse stall and see how much there is."

"Are we gonna tell our folks we found it?" Eddie asked.

"Where did it come from?" Maggie Mae asked. "Whose money is it?"

"It's our money now," Adam said adamantly. "We found it." Then it hit him. They had found the money alright. On somebody else's property! In a place they'd been expressly forbidden to go.

Maybe they could just keep the money and not tell anybody about it, Adam thought, but in his heart he knew that would never fly. Maggie Mae would never keep her mouth shut about something like this.

He looked at her. "Unless you want Mama to bust your butt so hard you won't sit down for a week, you better not tell her we came here. If she finds out we crossed the road, she'll beat us both half to death."

Maggie Mae's eyes were open so wide she looked like a baby owl.

"I won't tell." She made an X on her heart with the index finger of her right hand. "I promise."

Adam believed her. She couldn't be trusted on much, but when a spanking was involved, his little sister could lie with the best of them.

"Ok then, here's the deal. If we tell anybody about this money, and I'm not saying we're going to, but if we do, we didn't find it here. Is that understood?"

"Where did we find it?" Eddie asked.

"In this box," he said, pointing to the ammo case. "We were just walking along on *our* side of the road and we found this box in the weeds by that big maple tree. Got it?"

The others nodded solemnly.

"Now, let's get home and see how much money there is." Adam picked up the box and the three children bolted into the woods, leaving the door of the shed propped open. The biting wind whipped through the cracks in the walls and out the door, carrying with it a swirling cloud of white confetti.

• • • • •

Doodlebug was up under a Chevy pickup about to pull the plug out of the oil pan when he heard it on the eight o'clock morning newscast. He hated rolling up under cars; he was so fat he barely fit. It was a little better under trucks, but not much. The radio sitting on the workbench was turned to the local station, WCAL. It played exclusively country music, and that's what Doodlebug liked, The Gatlin Brothers, Ronnie Milsap, Hank Williams, Jr., George Jones. He was only half listening when he heard something that turned his blood cold.

" ... found cash, fives, tens, twenties near Cade's Crossing ... "

The shed where they'd stashed the money was only three or four miles from Cade's Crossing.

Somebody found the money we stashed in that shed!

He scrambled to get out from under the car.

" ... Karen Davis, the mother of two of the children who found the cash said that unless someone steps forward to claim it, she intends to keep it," the announcer continued.

Of course she does! Doodlebug thought. Any fool'd know it was dope money, and what doper was gonna show up at her front door and ask for it back?

The three men met that night at Doodlebug's place and spent the first half hour yelling at each other, each blaming the others. Jimmy Dan nearly got into it with Doodlebug. The little man was always spoiling for a fight, but Donnie broke them up. He pushed Doodlebug down on the couch, and shoved Jimmy Dan up against the wall and held him there by his shirt collar.

"That's enough, J.D.!" Donnie yelled. "The two of you can beat the crap out of each other but that don't bring our money back."

Donnie leaned on Jimmy Dan, got up in his face and spoke slowly. "Let it go," he hissed. "Just let it go. It don't matter now whose fault it was. We gotta stop yelling and start thinking."

He turned to Doodlebug. "Are you listenin' to me?"

Doodlebug nodded. He hadn't wanted to fight, was just trying to keep Jimmy Dan from taking a swing at him.

Jimmy Dan relaxed in Donnie's grip. "Fine, but I don't see what we got to talk about. Ain't no way to get the money back now."

"When those kids were on TV this evening, their story didn't add up," Donnie said. The WHAS 11 news truck had driven down all the way from Louisville to do a story on the three children.

Doodlebug had been thinking the same thing. Jimmy Dan hadn't seen the kids on television. As soon as Donnie called to tell him what had happened, he had roared out past Cade's Crossing, parked in the woods and sneaked through the trees to the shed. The door was propped open with a rock. There was no gym bag in the loft of that shed, no money, nothing but an old alarm clock laying on the dirt floor by the ladder.

"What didn't add up?" Jimmy Dan asked. "What did they say?"

"They said they found the money in some kind of ammo case by the side of the road," Donnie said.

"And they showed the pile of money on TV and the little kids sitting there with it grinning," Doodlebug said. He and Donnie looked at each other. "The little girl said there was $5,250 in the box."

"Five thousand dollars!" Jimmy Dan roared. "What happened to the other 30 grand?"

"That's what we gotta figure out," Doodlebug said.

They never were able to come up with a plausible explanation for why the kids had said they found the money in a box by the side of the road instead of in the shed. But the other part was easy. Those kids said they found $5,000 because that's all they turned in. They had kept the rest, the remaining $30,000.

"Now all we got to figure out," Donnie said, "is how we're gonna get it back from 'em."

Chapter 14

They knew they were making history. The one with a beard even said so when the five of them stopped to catch their breath in the brush by a fence that ran alongside KY 93.

"You know we're the first ones ever done it," he said, panting. "There's been men tried before, but nobody ever made it out of Eddyville, 'til now."

"Think they're gonna put up a plaque on the wall where we come down the side of the building on them extension cords?" Another one sneered. "Maybe build a statue?"

The biggest one of them sucked in great, heaving gulps of air. Tall, with an enormous beer belly, he was sweating buckets in the mid-July heat, just couldn't seem to catch his breath.

"The only plaque I'm ever gonna see ... " He wheezed in a gulp of air. " ... is the headstone over my dead body." Gasp! "And the inscription'll say, 'Here lies an escaped con too stupid to know when to stay put.'"

"Didn't nobody put a gun to your head and force you to come along," the bearded man said. "And they're gonna be setting that headstone in the dirt pretty dern soon if you don't get the lead out and git moving. I ain't waiting. I say we split up now!"

Without another word, he turned and started running through the brush in the ditch.

In the distance, the rest heard the sirens start to wail, startling the sparrows perched on the razor wire atop the walls of the Kentucky State Penitentiary in Eddyville, the commonwealth's only maximum security prison. They all jumped up and bolted.

The fat con collapsed from a massive coronary in a field three miles from the 6-by-9-foot cage where he'd spent the last 19 years of his life. He died alone among the corn stalks.

The bearded man's taste of freedom lasted less than 24 hours. State police found him hiding in a chicken house on the bank of the Ohio River.

The other two stole a car and made it across the state line. They killed a convenience store clerk and stole $200 and some black hair dye, switched cars and then tried to bluff their way through a Tennessee State Police roadblock. They ended up shooting one trooper before police opened up on them. One made it, the other didn't.

That left only one escapee still at large—Joe Fogerty, the man who'd pleaded guilty to killing Sarabeth Bingham's father.

Sonny went to her office to tell her personally.

"You can't be here about that parking ticket!" She said as soon as he poked his head into her office. She was on tiptoes, getting her father's worn copy of the Associated Press Stylebook off the top shelf of the bookcase. "I've already worked that out with the judge. I swear, the space wasn't marked handicapped."

"I'm here about this morning's escape from Eddyville. You might want to sit down." She didn't, of course. "One of the fugitives is Joe Fogerty."

Then she wanted to sit down.

"He's out?"

"I've called in all my off-duty deputies. Inside an hour Callison County will be crawling with state police troopers. And—"

"Why on earth would Joe Fogerty come here? There's a whole world out there to get lost in. Why would he turn up where people would recognize him?"

"Because he's stupid. But if those guys were smart they wouldn't be in prison in the first place. People who escape from jail or prison or mental hospitals are all the same. Eighty-five percent of them go home. We're expecting Joe. If he makes it this far, we'll be waiting for him."

Four days later, Sarabeth's police scanner went ballistic. Within minutes, she was flying down the road toward Andersonville where the scanner said Joe Fogerty was pinned down behind a fallen tree trunk on a sandbar in the Rolling Fork.

It wasn't hard to find the spot. More Kentucky State Police cruisers than she could count and three Callison County Sheriff's Department cars were parked along the roadside. Sonny spotted Sarabeth and let her through the barricades.

"As far as we know, he's not armed, but we're still going to wait for the KSP canine unit. They'll send the dogs in after him."

Sonny led her down the embankment to the river. She could see the gravel bar where Fogerty was holed up around a bend downstream. Officers were everywhere, behind trees and rocks on both sides of the river. It was an impressive amount of fire power.

"Do you really need this many officers to capture one unarmed fugitive?"

"There's method in the madness. We bring an overwhelming presence of officers to bear on a situation like this—a big boatload of cops—because the sheer magnitude of the opposition is usually enough to get the bad guys to throw in the towel and come out with their hands in the air. And that's a much better outcome than sending out a couple of cruisers and a handful of officers and an armed gunman decides he might just be able to win a shootout."

The sheriff smiled. "I'd rather intimidate a man any day than fight him."

There was nothing to do but wait. Sarabeth got her camera ready, fit its telephoto "Jimmy Durante" lens snug in place so perhaps she could capture the actual arrest. Then she sat down on a log behind a huge rock and stared past the flank of police officers at the distant gravel bar.

Sonny stepped out of the glaring sun into the shade beside her. "You Ok?"

Before she could answer, the world exploded. It was over in seconds. Fogerty suddenly stood up from behind the tree trunk where he'd been cowering and started to run across the sandbar to the river. Half a dozen officers yelled at him, "Stop! Police!"

He paused, lifted the small handgun nobody knew he had, and yelled, "I ain't goin' back there."

"Drop the gun and raise your hands over your head!"

Fogerty wouldn't listen. He turned abruptly and pointed the gun at the nearest officer, a good distance away but only partially hidden behind a tree.

The police opened fire and Fogerty folded up and collapsed in the sand.

It had been a struggle to focus the huge 500 mm lens on a moving target, but just as Fogerty turned toward the cop, Sarabeth captured him. She instantly screamed, "No!" but it was too late. The gunfire drowned out her voice before she could tell the officers what she could see through the telescope of the lens. The fugitive wasn't holding a handgun; he was holding a tree root.

Sarabeth was glad Sonny hadn't been among the officers who'd fired. He'd find out Fogerty had committed suicide by cop soon enough, though. He'd bolted toward the downed man as she sank back onto the log.

She was still fiddling with the catch on the lens, trying to remove the Jimmy Durante nose from her camera when a deputy raced toward her, shouting, "Sheriff Tackett sent me to get you. Hurry!"

The deputy led her through the crowd of officers to Sonny, who was down on his knees beside Fogerty. The old man was still alive.

"Someone give me a t-shirt," Sonny said. "Where are the EMTs with that stretcher?"

A deputy ripped off the shirt of his brown uniform and quickly removed the undershirt beneath. He handed it to Sonny, who wadded it into a ball and pressed it against Fogerty's bloody belly.

The bottom part of the old man's shirt was soaked crimson and there was a bullet hole in the right side of his chest, too. Blood bubbled out of it every time he took a breath.

When Sonny spotted Sarabeth, he motioned for her to kneel beside him and told her bluntly, "You need to hear this. He's saying he didn't do it, that he didn't kill your father."

Sarabeth gasped. The old man's eyes shifted to her at the word "father," and recognition dawned on his face. He remembered her from the sentencing hearing and he struggled to speak, but blood ran out of his mouth every time he tried. She leaned closer. Still, she could barely catch his words.

" ... dying ... know it ... wouldn't lie now ... " he croaked, then coughed out a spray of blood that splattered on Sarabeth's face and clothes. He reached out, like he was trying to grab her hand, but couldn't manage it, so she took his.

He summoned the strength again to speak. "It come back to me. I remember that night, what happened. I didn't shoot nobody!" He said the last part so forcefully it set off a barrage of coughing that spewed blood all over Sarabeth and the sheriff. "He put the gun in my pocket. I seen him ... with the hat." His breathing became hitching gasps for air and his eyes grew wide.

"*Who* put the gun in your pocket?" Sonny demanded. "Joe, who did you see?"

A final breath sighed out, bubbling blood on his lips, and then Joe Fogerty sank back into the sand and was still.

Sarabeth straightened up slowly from where she'd been leaning over the old man and sat back on her heels. A drip of Fogerty's blood ran down her cheek. She looked at Sonny.

"If he didn't kill Daddy ... who did?"

● ● ● ● ●

Doodlebug and Jimmy Dan watched the kids for three months, while Donnie cooled his heels in the Callison County Jail. He'd tied one on a couple of days after the kids found the money, went tearing down KY 55, weaving all over the road, got pulled over and busted for DUI. It was his second offense and the judge gave him 90 days.

The other two took turns tracking the children so they wouldn't be obvious. They watched them with their classmates in the school playground. And after school let out for the summer, they watched them playing with each other in Adam and Maggie Mae's back yard and behind Eddie's house around the barn. They watched Eddie, his mother, step-father, and two little brothers go to church in Cade's Crossing on Sunday. Adam and Maggie Mae's mother didn't take them to church.

They had plenty of time to plan, with Donnie locked up until the middle of August, plenty of time to figure out the very best place to snatch the children. What they were planning wouldn't be kidnapping because they weren't going to keep the kids or ask for a ransom. Donnie'd said if you didn't keep 'em, it didn't count. Besides, those kids were never going to rat out the men who made them return money they hadn't told anybody they had.

The three men had stayed up all night after Donnie and Doodlebug watched the kids on television, discussing what they should do and how. Once they'd calmed down and got to thinking about it, getting the money back didn't look like it was going to be all that hard after all.

"When we get through scaring those kids, they ain't gonna say nothing about us to nobody," Jimmy Dan had said.

"We ain't gonna hurt 'em!" Doodlebug's voice had been low and threatening. It took a lot to get a rise out of the fat man, but he'd have fought Jimmy Dan over that. "I ain't gonna let you hurt them little kids." Doodlebug loved kids.

"We're not gonna hurt anybody," Donnie'd said soothingly. "We'll just make 'em think we're gonna shoot 'em or something and they'll be begging us to take the money back and leave 'em be."

This time, when they came up with a plan, the vote was unanimous. The plan was simple enough. They figured the best time to snatch the children was when they were waiting for the bus in the morning, after school started back up the second week of August. They were all in one place by themselves and close to the road where they'd be easy to grab. And they were always out there for a few minutes before Bus 29 came around the bend in the road. There was plenty of time.

They'd grab all three of them and make one of them go get the money while they kept the other two. Then they'd take 'em into Brewster and let them out behind that old house down from the elementary school. If the kids cooperated quick, they might not even be late for school, and if they were, they'd just have to say they missed the bus.

The men had talked it all through over and over. The plan was foolproof. Even so, when they got together the morning of the snatch, they were nervous. Doodlebug had borrowed the white cargo van with "Burkett Brothers Garage" painted on the side. It didn't have any windows in the back.

Donnie was driving, Jimmy Dan was in the back and Doodlebug was up front, 'cause he was good with kids. When they pulled around the bend in the road, Doodlebug was sort of hoping the kids wouldn't be there. But all three were standing right where they'd been every morning that week, with their books and backpacks.

Donnie pulled off the road just a little past the kids and Doodlebug got out of the front and waddled over to talk to them.

"You kids know anybody wants a puppy?"

"What kinda puppy?" Adam asked.

"I got three of them in the back of the van," Doodlebug said. "Black labs, six weeks old. Cutest things you ever seen. I gotta find a home for 'em or I'm gonna have to take 'em down to the river and drown 'em."

"You can't drown puppies!" Maggie Mae cried.

Eddie loved dogs. "You wouldn't really drown 'em, would you mister?"

"Wouldn't want to but I ain't got no choice!" Doodlebug did a real good job of looking upset about it. "You can take a look at them if you want to. You never seen no cuter puppies. If you can't take 'em, maybe you know somebody who could."

The children followed him to the back of the van like sheep to the slaughter. He opened one of the back doors and climbed in. Jimmy Dan was sitting beside a cardboard box at the far end of the van, up by the front seats, and Doodlebug pointed to it.

"They're in that box," he said and all three kids hopped up into the van to have a look. It was that simple. Doodlebug reached out, grabbed the back door and slammed it shut, and Donnie buried his foot in the accelerator. The van fishtailed in the gravel, shooting dirt and rocks out behind, before it bumped back onto the road and sped away.

• • • • •

When the van lurched forward, it caught all three children off balance and they fell backward into the door and slid down it in a heap on top of each other in the floor.

Maggie Mae started to wail. They weren't crocodile tears, either. Adam knew that cry. Maggie Mae was terrified. So was he.

"You shut up, you hear me?" the skinny guy by the box told her. "Shut up!"

His command did absolutely no good. Maggie Mae kept shrieking in that piercingly high voice she had sometimes that was so shrill it actually hurt your ears.

Eddie's lower lip turned down and tears began streaming down his face, too.

"What do you want with us?" Adam asked. His own voice sounded strange in his ears, all hollow and shaking.

Eddie continued to cry. His nose ran now, too, down his lip and chin, wetting his face along with his tears.

"We want our money back, that's what, and you're going to give it to us or you're never gonna see your mama or daddy again," the skinny man snarled.

Adam's heart froze in his chest. The money they'd found in the shed belonged to these guys!

His mouth was so dry he could barely get the words out. "We don't have the money anymore. We gave it to our parents and they called the police. The police took it away."

By the time they'd counted all the money, laid it out in stacks on the floor of the horse stall in Eddie's barn, Adam had known they were going to have to turn it in. Maggie Mae had been acting like a 3-year-old, hopping up and down, babbling about the Barbie doll house she was going to buy with her share.

Eddie hadn't been much calmer. When they'd gotten up to $1,000 he'd started laughing, giggling like a girl.

There was no way either one of them would be able to act like nothing had happened that day—go home, eat supper, take a bath and go to bed without anybody guessing something was profoundly different about them. Adam figured Maggie Mae would blurt it out as soon as she walked in the door.

So they hadn't even talked about dividing it up and hiding it. They'd just put it all in the box, marched into Eddie's kitchen and set the box down on the table. And then the whole world had turned upside down—policemen and then reporters and even a television news crew! It had been the single most exciting thing that had ever happened to any of them.

The police had explained to the children how long the money would remain in trust, waiting for somebody to claim it before it could be returned to them as "finders keepers." It was something like a year, so far in the future that Adam couldn't manage to stay excited about it. The thought of the money hadn't even entered his head in weeks.

"You need to get her to hush up, now," the fat man said, almost nice.

"If she don't shut up, we're gonna have to hurt her." The skinny guy didn't sound nice at all. He sounded like he meant it.

Adam turned to his little sister, put his arm around her and whispered in her ear. He told her everything would be Ok, that he'd take care of her, that he wouldn't let anybody hurt her. She slowly stopped sobbing, just sat there sniveling and hiccupping, staring with wide, terrified eyes at the two men in the back of the van.

Donnie pulled off the highway onto a gravel road that wound into the woods. He went about 50 yards down it and stopped. They had picked this spot because even though there were houses fairly close by, you couldn't see the van from the highway. And they couldn't go very far. One of those kids was going to have to go to wherever they'd hidden the money and bring it back.

Jimmy Dan cut to the chase. He'd been designated "bad cop." Doodlebug was "good cop."

"I'm not talking about the $5,000 you turned in," he said. "I'm talking about the rest of it, the other $30,000. You got it hidden somewhere and we want it back!"

The children exchanged a confused look.

"I don't know what you're talking about, mister," Adam said. "We found that money in a box by the side of the road and—"

"You didn't find no money in a box," Doodlebug cut him off. "You found it in that shed in the woods. We know, 'cause we put it there. It's our money, not yours, and we want it back. Now, where did you hide the rest of it?"

"There isn't any more," Adam said. He looked at the other two children. "Is there?" They both shook their heads frantically from side to side. "We found the money on the floor in that shed, gathered it up and put it in a box. Then we took it home and counted it and turned it in. That's all there was."

Not once in all their careful planning did it ever occur to the three men that the kids might deny they had the money. That they might try to hold onto it, to keep it. It threw them totally off balance.

Donnie turned around in the driver's seat so he could see and yelled at Adam. "Don't you lie to us, son!"

"There was another $30,000 in that shed," Jimmy Dan snarled. He'd started getting edgy as soon as he got into the back of the van.

He hated cramped places with no windows; the growing menace in his voice was genuine. "What did you do with the rest of the money?"

"I'm not lying," Adam said. "There wasn't any more money."

Eddie spoke up for the first and only time, his voice high and reedy. "We looked."

Listening to those snot-nosed little brats talk back to him made Jimmy Dan's head pound. A sudden, blinding pain pierced his temples like an ice pick, then shot down his neck into his shoulders. There were too many people jammed in here and not enough air! He reached his hand behind him and pulled out a .25 caliber pistol, its broken hand grip held together with a mound of dirty duct tape. When he'd stuck the gun down in his pants, he'd had to cinch his jeans tight with a belt to keep it from falling through.

Doodlebug was just as stunned to see the gun as the kids were.

"Hey, we said there wasn't going to be any rough stuff," Doodlebug began.

"Put that away, J.D.," Donnie said.

Jimmy Dan ignored them both. He pointed the gun at Maggie Mae. "Tell us where that money is or I'm going to put a bullet in you."

Maggie Mae screamed at the top of her lungs. The shrieking, so loud in that small, metal space, set Jimmy Dan's teeth on edge; his eyes darted back and forth between the children, rage building so fast you could see it, like watching blue fire spread across the lighter fluid in a charcoal grill.

Doodlebug knew the gun wasn't loaded, but he didn't think scaring the kids to death was the best way to get them to talk. He reached over and picked Maggie Mae up off the floor and set her in his lap, meaning to calm her down. But the gesture had the opposite effect on the child. She began to kick and scream and fight, so he wrapped his arms around her and put his hand over her mouth to shut her up.

Twisting her head back and forth to get his hand off her face,

Maggie Mae managed to get one of his fingers into her mouth. And she bit down with all the might of a terrified 8-year-old, all the way to the bone. Blood squirted out of the wound and Doodlebug roared in pain.

Adam lunged for the gun, grabbed the barrel and tried to wrench it out of Jimmy Dan's hand. Seeing Maggie Mae fight back, draw blood, he knew she was creating a diversion so Jim Phelps could—

BAM!

The gunshot sounded like the explosion of a cannon in that confined space, reverberating against the metal walls. Stunned, everybody froze in shocked surprise.

Nobody moved, except Maggie Mae. She slumped forward in Doodlebug's arms with a flower of crimson on the front of her dress that grew bigger and bigger and bigger.

Jimmy Dan held the gun out in front of him like a dead fish on a stick, his face white, staring in horror at the child in Doodlebug's arms.

Eddie jumped up, hit the handle and shoved open the back door. He leapt out of the van and started running down the gravel road toward the highway, trailing a wild, eerie wail behind him as he ran.

Jimmy Dan turned and knocked Adam out of the way as he dived out the back door behind Eddie and took off running through the woods.

Donnie fumbled for the key in the ignition and tried to start the van, pumping frantically on the accelerator in panic. Within seconds the motor was flooded. The starter turned it over and over but nothing happened.

Banging his fists on the steering wheel two or three times in terror and frustration, Donnie took a deep sobbing breath, turned and looked into Doodlebug's eyes. He was crying. "The gun was *loaded!*"

After he choked out the words, he opened the van door, leapt to the ground and ran.

Adam had been sprawled on his back on the van floor where Jimmy Dan had knocked him down. He got slowly to his feet, his eyes huge.

"Go get help," Doodlebug whispered. That was as much sound as he was able to make. "Go on now, son. Go get somebody to come help your little sister."

Adam stared at Maggie Mae for a heartbeat longer, turned and jumped out the back door of the van and was gone.

Then it was quiet. Not a sound but the wind in the trees, blowing a handful of dry leaves across the gravel road. Doodlebug sat in the back of the van holding the little red-haired girl in his arms, rocking her gently back and forth as she bled out. It didn't take very long at all.

Chapter 15

Yellow Police Line tape sealed off an area 50 yards wide all around the Burkett Brothers Garage van, parked down a gravel road off Bishop's Lane.

Sarabeth arrived as Sonny was putting Doodlebug into his cruiser. The whole front of the fat man's shirt and pants was soaked in blood, the same color as the bright red Callison County Rescue Squad truck parked beside the sheriff's vehicle. An ambulance, the blue light on top slowly spinning around and around, sat beside the van. If Sarabeth had understood the codes on her police scanner correctly, it was long past too late for the rescue squad or the ambulance.

A crowd of people had gathered on the outside of the perimeter, not gawkers but sympathizers—friends and neighbors. They had not come to revel in suffering; they had come to share it. Most of the women were crying softly. Some of the men were, too.

Sarabeth ducked under the tape and approached the sheriff. His mouth was set in a tight line. She could see he was holding his professional detachment in a white-knuckled grip, which helped her to hold onto hers.

She drew her notepad out of the front pocket of the camera bag that hung on her shoulder and asked him quietly, "What's going on?"

"Killed a little girl, 8 years old." he said through clenched teeth.

"What happened?"

"I don't have all the answers yet. When I do, you can come by my office and I'll tell you the whole story."

"Deal," she said and put away her notepad.

When Sarabeth turned away from Sonny, she spotted Seth, standing beside the big red truck talking quietly with one of the other rescue squad members. He saw her and nodded a greeting. She nodded back and they stood, their eyes locked together in a glance for a few moments before she forcefully broke the connection and wandered over to the ambulance. The back double doors were open and a stretcher sat inside. The sheet was pulled all the way over the small lump in the middle of it. An EMT sat inside the ambulance beside the stretcher, doing nothing, just sitting. He looked absolutely devastated. Sarabeth knew the man. He was Harmony Pruitt's fiancé. She'd met him a time or two in the office and she searched frantically through her mental Rolodex until she finally located his name.

"Rough call, huh, Pete."

He looked up at her with anguished eyes. "There wasn't nothing we could do. She was dead before we got here. Bled to death." Pete put his head in his hands. "Not a thing we could do."

Sarabeth's heart went out to him. She climbed the two steps into the ambulance, sat down on the bench seat beside him and put her arm around his shoulders.

"I know you'd have saved her if you could."

"Such a pretty little girl." His voice was thick. "Just looks like she's asleep."

He reached over and picked up the end of the sheet covering the child, "Looks like at any minute she'll wake up, climb down off this table and go play." Then he pulled the sheet back to show Sarabeth the child's peaceful face.

The sight hit Sarabeth with the force of an 18-wheeler flying down an interstate. She couldn't move or breathe. If she'd been standing, her knees would have buckled out from under her and dumped her in a heap on the ground. She covered her mouth, had to hold the scream inside to keep it from roaring up her throat and out into the world.

The fantasy child Sarabeth had kept alive all these years, the 8-year-old little girl her daughter, Moriah, would have grown to be lay there on the stretcher before her. Moriah's face, yet so pale the freckles stood out on it like ink blots, and her red pigtails clasped at the ends with barrettes.

Sarabeth couldn't speak. She stood on shaking legs, stumbled out of the ambulance and around to the side of it facing the woods, away from the crowd. She leaned against the cool metal, sucked in huge gulps of air to keep from fainting. Her mind understood the little girl wasn't really hers, but her heart knew different. Her heart knew that the child who formed such a small lump under the white sheet on the stretcher was Moriah. The little girl she'd already lost once was now gone again.

Seth came around the ambulance to where she stood.

"Are you all right?" One look answered his question. "What's wrong?"

Tears flowed down her cheeks and she made no effort to wipe them away. She looked into Seth's dark eyes and just blurted it out.

"I had a little girl and she ... died."

He moaned, a groan deep in his throat, then wordlessly wrapped his arms around her and drew her close, held her while she cried silently against his chest.

"My little girl, Moriah, would have been 8 this year." The words came out between hitching sobs. "She was killed ... " She struggled to say more, but couldn't seem to get the words out of her mouth.

"You don't have to talk about it."

"Yes, I *do!*" She pulled back and looked up at him, stunned by the fierce intensity of her own response. Suddenly, she did *have to* talk about it. It was a sorrow she had buried too deep, carried for too long. It had festered in the darkness and the sight of the little girl lying dead on the stretcher had lanced the boil.

He looked tenderly into her face. "I'm listening," he said and folded her gently back into his embrace.

At the sound of his voice, it felt like someone reached out and turned down the volume on the world, hit the dimmer switch, too, so bright reality only existed in a puddle around the two of them—everything beyond was quiet and grayed out.

Once she got started, she was surprised by how easily the words flowed. She had never talked about what happened. It was like she had taken this detour out of her life for two years, met an incredible man, fell in love, got married, had a baby—and then it was all gone, popped with a little sparkle like a soap bubble and vanished.

"The hail hit right before we got to Littlefield, this nowhere little town on the west Texas prairie," her voice was distorted by the effort it took not to cry. "Aaron had wanted to spend the night in Lubbock. You could see the storm brewing in the west, huge, ugly green clouds. But I'd promised Mom we'd be back home in California by Ben's birthday."

She took a shaky breath and her voice sank to a whisper.

"The car skidded into a drainage ditch and we got out and tried to make it to this big pipe, but ... " The image formed so clear in her mind that goose bumps popped out all over her body. "I looked up and just for an instant I could see into the tornado. Greenish black and writhing, lightening dancing and sparking. It smelled like moldy dirt, a cemetery. Like death."

Seth squeezed her tight against him, but she pulled back in his arms so she could look up into his face again. She barely noticed the tears in his eyes.

"I tried to hold onto her!" She dug her fingers into his big biceps, her voice an anguished rasp. "I *tried!* She was only 9 months old." Her voice trailed off as she gazed into a past that she never allowed herself to revisit.

"But she was so little ... I felt her being sucked out of my arms." Sarabeth closed her eyes. "Moriah didn't even cry. She was asleep, wrapped up in a blanket, and all the wind and rain—it didn't even wake her up. I felt her go. Felt my arms empty ... and then." She let out a sigh. "I woke up in the hospital six days later."

She let him pull her back against his chest and she rested there. Time passed—a minute, three days—before sound and color slowly began to return to the world. She felt so warm, so safe in his embrace that it took a wrenching effort to ease out of it. But she did, stepped back and leaned against the side of the ambulance again, surprised that when she spoke, her voice was steady.

"They never found her body. And by the time I came to, they'd already cremated Aaron. They were both just ... gone, like they'd never existed at all."

She took a deep breath, to finish it. To say it all, get it all out.

"So I had this *fantasy* that Moriah was alive, that she'd survived, that she was out there somewhere." She looked up, saw tracks of tears on Seth's face. "I always knew what she looked like—when she was 2 and 4—and 6 with missing teeth. I always knew."

"And at 8 she'd have looked just like that little girl on the stretcher." Seth's voice was thick. "Of course she would—red hair and freckles! She'd have looked like Maggie Mae Davis."

Maggie Mae Davis. Somehow knowing her name completed Sarabeth's transition back to reality, back to the world where Maggie Mae had a mother and a father, maybe brothers and sisters. A real family who were as devastated right now as she had been eight years ago, staggering under the weight of their loss.

"Has anybody told her parents?"

"They radioed the Brewster police chief and he's gone to notify her mother, probably telling her right now. As I understand it, she's a nurse at Callison County Hospital. I don't know about the father, though. I think he's been out of the picture for a long time."

Picture. She should be taking pictures. But she was reluctant to move, to break the spell, to close the doors between her and Seth again. She pulled in a deep breath, let it out, reached up with both hands and wiped the remains of tears from her cheeks.

"Look, Seth, I—"

"Don't," he said quietly. Just the one word.

She had a sense of déjà vu, like they'd already had this conversation.

"Don't thank me. I'm here for you anytime. Anytime at all."

Sarabeth didn't know what else to do, so she just nodded.

"I have to shoot this," she said. Shifting gears was painful. "It's my job."

Taking pictures at a crime or accident scene was a dicey business. As soon as you put a camera around your neck and started firing, you instantly became the focus of everybody's pent-up rage. You ceased to be Sarabeth Bingham and became "the press"—heartless exploiters who used blood-and-gore pictures to sell newspapers. She'd watched police officers, EMTs, people he'd known for years turn on her father at an accident scene, even though he had never once, not in 51 years, published a "body shot" in *The Callison County Tribune.*

"You sure you're Ok?" Seth asked.

The tenderness in his voice made her want to cry again.

"I'm sure."

"Then you need to get to work." Perhaps he tried to smile, but it didn't work. So he looked down at her and stroked her cheek with the backs of his fingers, then turned and headed back toward the rescue squad truck.

Sarabeth took the old metal Nikon out of its bag and slipped the strap around her neck and began to capture images in it. A short time later, the ambulance pulled away, driving slowly down the gravel road and out to the highway. There was no need for haste now and every need for dignity. It wasn't an ambulance anymore; it was a hearse bearing the body of a small murdered child.

Sarabeth was about to put her camera away when she saw a woman running down the gravel road from the highway. One shoe was missing and she paid it no heed. Her hair was wild, her eyes wilder and she wore a nurse's uniform. The image was a powerful, prize-winning news photo, but Sarabeth didn't shoot it.

The crowd of people standing at the yellow Police Line tape parted to let the woman pass.

Sonny saw her, too, and tried to intercept her, but she blew by him and dashed to the van. She threw the back doors open as if she expected to find her little girl there. What she found was her daughter's blood instead. There was a lot of it. She staggered backward from the sight, whirled around and started to scream frantically.

"Maggie Mae! Maggie Mae! Do you hear Mommy? Maggie Mae, you come here to me right this minute, do you hear me! Maggie Mae!"

The sheriff stepped to her, took both her hands in his and got so close he filled all her view, then spoke to her softly. Sarabeth couldn't hear his words. But as she watched him, she understood for the first time the sheriff/minister fit: strength and compassion, two sides of the same coin. Like the other coins of his twin professions: right and wrong, good and evil, life and death.

At one point, the woman jerked back from him, tried to wrench her hands out of his grip, shook her head frantically in denial.

"No, no, no, you're wrong, that wasn't Maggie Mae, you know it wasn't. Now, you tell me it wasn't Maggie Mae!" She begged Sonny to change reality somehow, to make the horror pass her and her precious child by, leave her and her little girl unharmed. Her pleading broke Sarabeth's heart.

As he spoke, Sonny gently eased the woman toward one of the Kentucky State Police cruisers parked near the edge of the woods. The trooper took his cue, stepped up, removed his hat and opened the back door for her. Sonny helped her inside, then turned to the crowd of onlookers.

"Anybody here a neighbor, a friend of Karen's?"

A large woman who had been crying softly stepped forward.

"She lives right down the road from me," she said.

"Can you ride with her into town? She shouldn't be alone right now."

The woman went immediately to the cruiser and got into the back seat with the little girl's mother. The trooper closed the door, got in behind the wheel and slowly drove away.

As Sarabeth made her way through the crowd of onlookers toward her car she overheard a snatch of conversation, " ... found that money in a box by the road right after Derby Day ... "

Sarabeth felt the 18-wheeler slam into her chest again. *Maggie Mae* was Margaret Davis! This little girl was one of the three children who found $5,000 by the side of the road, money everybody knew had to belong to dopers.

Sarabeth had been in California for her checkup when the story broke. Bobby had covered it, had done a pretty good job, though his picture of the children hadn't been terrific. The focus was too soft. And, of course, in the black-and-white photo, you couldn't tell the little girl had red hair.

You couldn't tell she was Moriah.

• • • • •

The fat man in a bloody t-shirt and jeans sat in a straight-back chair at a table in a small room off the sheriff's office. Commonwealth's Attorney Simon Henry reached over and pushed "record" on the tape machine in front of him, said the date and time and identified the people present in the room with them: Sheriff Sonny Tackett and State Police Detective Darrell Hayes.

"Mr. Burkett, you—" Henry began.

"I ain't *Mister* Burkett. Name's Doodlebug."

"All right, *Doodlebug,* you need to know that everything that is said in this room from this point forward is being recorded." Henry waited.

When he realized everyone expected him to respond, Doodlebug grunted. "Recorded, yeah. Ok, I know you're recording this. Is that what I'm s'posted to say?"

Then the Commonwealth's Attorney gave him his Miranda rights and asked if he understood them.

"I understand." His voice was surprisingly quiet. "I understood it when the sheriff said it and when the trooper said it, too. I don't want me no lawyer."

Henry relaxed imperceptibly. Anderson Bertrand would almost certainly end up the defense attorney in the case. Bertrand loved publicity. Henry was profoundly grateful for a chance to question the accused before Bertrand jumped in with both feet and muddied the waters.

"You don't git it. I done what I done and I don't need no slick lawyer to get up and say I didn't. I didn't mean to hurt that little girl! Didn't none of us mean to hurt those kids, we just wanted to scare 'em so they'd give us our money back."

"What money?" Sonny asked.

"The money we hid in that shed," Doodlebug said, and then poured out the tale in one long stream.

By the time he was finished, Doodlebug was sobbing. Tears squirted out of his eyes and down his cheeks. "I wish it'd been me instead of that little girl. I wish I's dead 'stead of her. I didn't have no right to keep on living and breathing with her just laying there limp in my arms."

The three other men looked at each other. Henry's mouth was set in a thin line and Hayes had the detached look he got when he was concentrating hard. But Sonny couldn't help it—he felt sorry for Doodlebug. What a pathetic waste.

Then the men set about unpacking Doodlebug's story, getting specifics, details. Once Detective Hayes got the names, addresses and descriptions of Doodlebug's accomplices, he stepped out of the room to call the information in to the Columbia State Police post for broadcast to every trooper, sheriff and police department in the state.

A short time later, the sheriff stepped out of the room and dispatched Deputy Jude Tyler to an abandoned shed in the woods near Cade's Crossing. The deputy returned before the interrogation was over.

"There was no money in that shed," he told Sonny after the sheriff closed the interrogation room door behind him so Hayes and Henry could continue their questioning. "All I found was this." The officer emptied the contents of a brown grocery sack onto a table—an old alarm clock; a handful of chewed-up pieces of canvas; six metal grommets; a small buckle, like from a belt or a strap; a tattered 18-inch zipper and an envelope containing about a tablespoon of what looked like fuzz, or confetti. "I used a pocket knife to dig this white stuff out of the cracks in the floorboards. And there were mouse droppings all over that loft; I didn't bring any back with me."

The sheriff looked in wonder at what the deputy had laid out for him. He picked up the alarm clock. "What in the world?"

Tyler shrugged his own bewilderment.

Sonny lifted the zipper with frayed, chewed-on edges and held it up to the light.

"If there was a canvas bag in the loft of that shed, all that's left of it is this stuff right here," the deputy said and held up a ragged piece of canvas. "Mice ate the rest of it." He picked up the envelope and poured out the contents into his cupped palm. "And I don't know what this white stuff is, but I think I could make a pretty good guess."

The sheriff shook his head. "Bag that as evidence and send it to the Kentucky State Police lab for analysis."

He looked into the deputy's eyes, still trying to take it all in. *"Mice?"*

Tyler nodded. "Mice."

Chapter 16

J immy Dan got lucky, or at least he thought so at the time. He had run through the woods for what seemed like hours, up into the knobs, just running, seeing the blossom of red on the little girl's dress before him as he ran.

He kept replaying the scene over and over trying to figure out what had happened. None of it made sense. But sense or not, the reality was that he had shot that little girl, probably killed her.

When he couldn't run another step, he collapsed in the tall grass on the side of a field next to the road. Given the general direction he'd been running, he figured the road must be KY 28 between Cade's Crossing and Crawford. A few minutes later, a farmer drove down through the field toward the road pulling a hay wagon behind his tractor. Jimmy Dan stole out of the high grass, jumped on the back of the wagon and covered himself with loose hay.

Wherever the farmer was taking that hay, whether to the next field or to the other side of the county, Jimmy Dan was going with him. That's when he got lucky. The farmer chugged down the highway, not going more the 15 or 20 miles an hour for what seemed like an eternity, before slowing to turn off down a dirt road. Jimmy Dan peeked out of the hay to get his bearings and saw big, black barrel warehouses on top of a distant knob. He slipped off the back of the wagon and hid in the weeds in the ditch until the road was empty. Then he sprinted across it and into the woods on the other side. But he wasn't just running blind anymore. He knew where he was going. Bubba Jamison's house was out there by Double Springs Distillery. It wasn't more than two or three miles as the crow flew from where Jimmy Dan had jumped off the hay wagon.

Donnie caught a ride into town on a milk truck. He told the driver, a guy he used to shoot pool with, that he'd been at some woman's house when her husband came home unexpectedly and he'd had to hightail it out of there. The driver laughed all the way into Brewster about that, trying the whole way to wheedle it out of Donnie who the woman was. Right before they got to town, two sheriff's cars, three Kentucky State Police cruisers and an ambulance blew by them going the other way, and the truck driver joked that he bet that woman's husband figured out what she'd been doing and took his shotgun to her. Donnie tried to grin in agreement, but felt such naked terror at the sight of the police he very nearly wet his pants.

When Donnie got home, he ran inside, slammed the door shut behind him, leaned against it and sobbed.

He tried to calm down, tried to make his heart stop racing and think, but his mind just wouldn't be still. The sound of the gunshot reverberated in his head, and every time he got a thought process going, the gunshot would explode it and he'd have to start all over again.

He did know one thing, though. He couldn't go to prison. He didn't let himself think about the things his uncle had done to him when he was a little boy, but he remembered them well enough to know he'd rather die than be assaulted in prison.

He had to get away to Canada or Mexico. Yeah, Mexico! Where nobody could find him. He grabbed a suitcase, threw ridiculous things into it because he couldn't think—underwear and socks but no shoes, two shirts, pictures of two different girlfriends, a tube of toothpaste and his razor—bolted out to his car and drove away.

Heading west, he aimed for Interstate 65 south toward Nashville. He'd take I40 to Memphis and Little Rock, I30 down to Texarkana and cross the border in Laredo or El Paso.

But he never even made it to the Kentucky state line. He forced himself to drive five miles under the speed limit so as not to draw attention to himself, so when the Kentucky State Police trooper who passed him whipped his cruiser around and turned on his lights, Donnie knew he'd been caught. Panicking, he shoved his foot to the floorboard of his little Ford Taurus and took off down the road.

He was going somewhere close to 90 when he missed the turn, crossed the center line, hit the ditch on the other side and flipped over. Donnie wasn't wearing a seatbelt so he flew halfway out of the car through the windshield when he hit the ditch. The car rolled four times before it finally came to rest upside down in a soybean field. Donnie Scruggs didn't have to worry anymore about going to prison.

If Bubba hadn't been there to call them off, his dogs would have ripped Jimmy Dan to shreds while he was still in the woods outside the fence behind Bubba's house. Early that morning, Bubba had released the dogs through the back gate to chase rabbits. As it was, Daisy sunk her teeth into Jimmy Dan's calf before Bubba had time to whistle. She let go and Jimmy Dan collapsed in the dirt, blood squirting out twin puncture wounds.

"Ain't you got better sense than to come here without calling first?" Bubba spit the words out in contempt and made no effort to help Jimmy Dan to his feet. It was obvious the man was more afraid of whatever he was running from than he was of Bubba and three snarling dogs, which meant he was running from something fierce indeed. Bubba was curious to find out what on earth that could be. "What do you want with me?"

"I need your help, Bubba," Jimmy Dan blubbered, almost crying. "Something terrible has happened and I ain't got nobody to come to but you."

Bubba said nothing, so Jimmy Dan poured out his story. Doodlebug and Donnie had hidden some gambling money in an old shed, he said, and some kids found it and turned in part of it and kept the rest. And when they went to get their money back, they hurt one of the kids. He reached into his belt, pulled out the pistol and tossed it on the ground in front of Bubba, stammering that it had gone off accidentally, all by itself, they hadn't meant for it to, and now he had to get away.

Bubba still said nothing. He stood looking at the bleeding man, mulling it over in his head, trying to make up his mind. He wasn't deciding whether or not he was going to help Jimmy Dan, he was deciding how he was going to kill him.

He'd suspected last summer that those three morons were stealing dope, so he'd nosed around, found four different buyers they'd sold weed to. He couldn't let them get away with that, of course, and had already begun to make plans. Now it looked like the problem had just solved itself.

"Know what I do to a man who steals from me?"

Jimmy Dan's eyes grew huge.

"I let my dogs eat him."

Jimmy Dan shook his head no, but didn't have the breath to form words. Bubba watched him, a half-smile playing across his face. J.D. knew he was going to die and seeing that knowledge on his face sent a thrill all over the big man's body.

"Guard!" Bubba commanded softly, and the dogs instantly surrounded the man on the ground, growling, their dripping fangs bared inches from his face. Bubba lifted his eyes with crocodilian menace and fastened them on Jimmy Dan's.

"How's it feel, huh? Knowing them dogs is gonna *feed* on you?"

The terror in Jimmy Dan's eyes was priceless.

"My dogs is trained to attack if you move, if you so much as blink. So if I's you, I'd sit real, real still."

Bubba saw horror soak all the way through the man at his feet. The big man reveled in that kind of horror, bald and almost smoking, the kind that lay beyond the curtains and furniture of simple, ordinary lives.

He could smell the little man's fear sweat, saw him cut his wide eyes from one snarling dog to the next—without blinking!—and he almost laughed out loud. Jimmy Dan didn't last long, though. Bubba knew he wouldn't. A sudden, odd noise burped out of his throat, the kind of sound an animal caught in a hay baler might make, and then he broke, scooted backwards in the dirt and scrambled to get to his feet to run. The three dogs leapt as one, knocked him to the ground and tore into his flesh, snarling and growling. He screamed, tried to fend them off, flopped around in the dirt kicking and fighting and shrieking in agony and terror. Lucky, the German Shepherd, got to his throat first, sunk sharp canine teeth into the soft flesh and ripped it out. Jimmy Dan stopped screaming abruptly, made a strangled, gurgling sound and went limp, but the dogs continued to attack and tear at him. Bubba let them. He watched for a little while before he called them off.

"Down," he commanded, and all three dogs dropped to the ground, panting. "Stay."

Bubba was a masterful dog trainer. His animals could respond to more than a dozen verbal commands and hand motions. The three dogs would remain on "down/stay" until he released them, wouldn't move an inch to chase a rabbit if it hopped up to one of them and kicked him in the nose. Bubba could come back tomorrow morning and they'd still be right where he left them.

The big man looked around until he spotted a tree with limbs growing out of the trunk chest high about two feet apart. He picked up Jimmy Dan's mauled body as if it were a rag doll and hung it between the limbs, draping the dead man's right arm over one limb and his left over the other. Then he unbuttoned his own shirt, took it off and placed it on the ground beneath the dangling corpse. He unhooked the clasp on the knife sheath on his belt, took out his hunting knife, and in one quick motion, stabbed the knife about an inch deep into the dead man's chest just below the sternum and ripped downward to his pubic bone. When he sliced horizontally at the base of Jimmy Dan's belly from pelvic bone to pelvic bone, most of the dead man's internal organs slid out in a slimy pile on top of Bubba's shirt—just like gutting a deer. After he cut all the organs free of the body, Bubba tied them up in his shirt, leaving one long sleeve dangling. Then he picked up the warm bag and headed back in the direction from which Jimmy Dan had come.

It was easy to back-track Jimmy Dan over the hill and down the other side and Bubba moved quickly for a big man. When he'd gone about half a mile, he found the spot where Jimmy Dan had turned and started up the hill. Jimmy Dan's trail led back west; Bubba set the shirt/sack on the ground on that spot, took hold of the dangling sleeve and headed east, dragging the sack on the ground behind him.

The bag was wet, from body fluids, not blood, and left a slimy snail trail behind on the ground. That would dry in a few minutes and be invisible to the human eye. But not to a bloodhound's nose.

Careful not to leave any footprints, Bubba wound through the woods until he came out of the trees on the bank of the Rolling Fork River. About 100 yards downstream was a walking bridge.

Keeping to the edge of the tree line, Bubba made his way to the bridge. He scanned the riverbank up and down to be sure no one was in sight. Then he dragged the bag up the steps and out on the plank floor to the middle of the bridge, held the make-shift sack out over the river, opened it up, and dumped Jimmy Dan Puckett's guts into the Rolling Fork. He pitched the shirt into the river after them and set off the way he had come, careful to turn back up the hill at the exact spot where he had begun to drag the bag. He stopped there to listen, but the woods were silent.

When Bubba passed by the dogs on his way to his garage, they were sitting where he'd left them next to Jimmy Dan's gutted corpse, hanging amid a buzz of green flies in a tree. He returned a short time later with a shovel and a wheelbarrow. He picked up the gun with the duct-taped handle and shoved it down in his belt and placed the bloody corpse in the wheelbarrow. Then he used the shovel to dig up dirt and toss it on the attack site. He gathered up limbs, leaves and sticks and scattered them around until there was no sign of a struggle or blood anywhere. Then he called his dogs and they padded along beside him as he hauled the gory corpse back past his house to the edge of the pond and tossed it into a rowboat. Loading three concrete blocks and three 4-foot lengths of bailing wire into the boat, he rowed out to the middle of the pond, tied Jimmy Dan to the blocks and tossed him overboard. The water turned red at the site and bubbles rose to the surface as the body sank slowly down in the murky water to the bottom of the pond. Bubba waited until the water was still, then rowed back to shore.

After he hosed down the rowboat, the wheelbarrow and the dogs, he stripped naked and dumped all his clothing, boots and all, into a metal trash drum, poured half a gallon of gasoline into the drum and tossed in a match. When he heard the *whump* sound of the fire taking hold, he went into the house for a long, cool shower. He was sitting on the back deck eating a sandwich a little after noon when he first heard the baying of the hounds. He sat very still and listened, tracked their advance by the sound that grew steadily louder. He could tell by the dogs' sudden silence that they had gotten to the spot at the bottom of the hill where the trail had split and gone in opposite directions, could picture them sniffing frantically around in circles. But the trail leading up the hill was just that, a trail. The one leading east was more like a four-lane divided highway, an interstate, a freeway, the scent so powerful it was irresistible. After only a few moment's hesitation, the blood-hounds began to bay again, the sound no longer getting louder as it approached, but fading away as the dogs dragged their handlers toward the river.

Bubba sat still and quiet until he could no longer hear the dogs, then he relaxed in the deck chair and looked out over the pond smiling.

● ● ● ● ●

Sonny leaned back in his creaky office chair and rubbed his neck, wondering idly as he did if Sarabeth Bingham knew how strikingly beautiful she was. She didn't appear to. As she sat across the desk from him scribbling in her notebook, he looked at her hair, the curls falling around her shoulders, and couldn't imagine that a woman could look like that and not have a line of men standing at her door. Part of it was that there was no flirt in her. But women had a way of telegraphing when they were available even if they didn't flirt. Sarabeth's telegraph wasn't even plugged in.

She looked up from her notes and almost caught him staring at her.

"Daddy always said truth was stranger than fiction, but I never imagined I'd ever write a story as pathetic as this. Mice eat these guys' dope money so they go out and kill a little girl."

"I warned you this was going to get ugly." Sonny let out a long sigh. "Donnie's dead, and I even feel sorry for that stupid Doodle-bug. He's dumb as a box of doorknobs but he'd good-hearted. He ought to be up under somebody's car changing their transmission fluid instead of on a slow walk toward death row."

"You think he'll get the death penalty?"

"There's never been a death penalty handed down in this county, but he could be the first. If you kill somebody with a gun in the commission of a felony, that's a 'special circumstance' that qualifies for the death penalty." The sheriff leaned forward and put his elbows on his desk. "Lot depends on what happens when we catch Jimmy Dan. The two little boys told the same story Doodlebug did, said Jimmy Dan was the trigger man. So, can a defense attorney blame it all on J.D.? Say Doodlebug was an unwilling accomplice? Depends on who defends him. Right now, Doodlebug's still refusing an attorney. He expects the death penalty, says he doesn't want some lawyer to get him off when he deserves to die. He'll change his mind eventually. And Jimmy Dan's still out there."

How Jimmy Dan had escaped was a mystery. The dogs had tracked him from the van in the woods. He'd left a jacket behind so the dogs got a strong, clear scent and they'd followed it to a walking bridge across the Rolling Fork. The hounds had never wavered, never seemed uncertain, but the trail ended in the middle of the bridge. The only possible explanation was that Jimmy Dan had jumped into the river to throw off the dogs, though one of the troopers who knew Jimmy Dan swore he couldn't swim. The canine units had split up then, scouring both sides of the riverbank for three miles downstream and three upstream, but could find no trace of the fugitive leaving the water.

"He's not smart enough to stay undetected for long, though. Eventually, he'll poke his head out of whatever hole he's hiding in and we'll catch him."

Sarabeth shook her head. "Two people dead, one on the way to death row. And for what?"

Sonny told her that the three men had hidden the money in the shed because the dope they'd sold wasn't theirs.

"They stole it from Bubba Jamison,"he said.

Sarabeth felt sick. "Jake's father." How could such a good kid be the son of a monster?

"He and Ben are pretty good friends, aren't they."

"Blood brothers. Twins separated at birth."

"This is going to go down hard, I'm afraid. I've been after Bubba for years. He is a Very. Big. Dog. The biggest dog in the whole junkyard and certainly the meanest. Doodlebug did a chapter and verse for us on Bubba's operation. And he's willing to testify. Simon's going to take it before a special session of the grand jury in the morning."

"What's the hurry?"

"Bubba has managed to stay a couple of steps ahead of the law for years. He doesn't know what's coming down and I don't want to give him time to figure a way out of it."

• • • • •

Sarabeth waited outside the grand jury room on the second floor of the courthouse across the hall from the circuit courtroom with Sonny and Detective Hayes. Both had already testified and Commonwealth's Attorney Simon Henry was still presenting evidence.

Since a grand jury didn't decide guilt or innocence, merely determined if there was enough evidence to warrant a trial, they didn't typically take very long to come to a decision.

It was a busy day at the courthouse. District and circuit court were both in session, the offices for driver's license renewals and land transfers had long lines and the hall was crowded with people. All at once, Sonny nudged Sarabeth and cocked his head toward the stairs.

"Would you look at that," he said. "There he is in the flesh. Bubba Jamison. I think it's right thoughtful of him to show up here today, so I don't have to go find him to slap the cuffs on him."

Sarabeth looked at the big man, and the movie *Princess Bride* popped into her mind. The guy looked like Fezzik, the walking mountain who had caught Buttercup when Wesley tossed her out the window of the castle. But Bubba Jamison's face didn't have the soft, gentle lines of Andre the Giant. His face was dark, with thick, black eyebrows that hung over arresting eyes, like the eyes of a cobra, quick and alert. And absolutely soul-less.

And those eyes were looking at her, sizing her up, taking her measure and taunting her, all at the same time. She stared straight back at him, back into the black pit of his eyes and stood her ground defiantly. It was something she'd never have been able to do a year ago when she'd taken over her father's newspaper. She'd come a long way, Baby.

A man stepped up to talk to Bubba and he dropped his gaze. The connection broke and Sarabeth realized she'd balled her hands into fists at her sides and was holding her breath. She let it out in a sigh that was as much sadness as relief. Thing Two's father. The family resemblance was uncanny, though Jake's face had a sweetness that existed nowhere in his father's countenance.

"You gonna tell me your secret or not?" the farmer asked Bubba with a nervous little laugh.

"Secret for what?" Bubba growled.

"Them catfish," the farmer said. "Your boy tole my boy all 'bout

203

them giant catfish you got in that pond of yours, how they ate duck-lings they was so big. You got some secret feedin' formula?"

A slow smile spread across Bubba's face.

"Matter of fact I do. Now, don't tell nobody, but ever so often, I feed 'em something special—a great big hunk of red meat."

"Naw, really? And they eat that?"

"Shore do. I been doin' it for years. Started back in May of '78." Bubba's smile widened. "I remember exactly 'cause the first time I done it was the day Darlene left me."

The grand jury room door opened and out strode Simon Henry. Sarabeth didn't like the look on his face. Or the two words he spat out when he stopped in front of Sonny.

"No indictment."

Sonny looked stunned.

Henry's booming orator's voice was quiet, as taut and controlled as a bow string. "The grand jury foreman said they returned a no-bill based on the 'lack of credibility of the only witness.' Supposed-ly, Doodlebug was not reliable because he was charged with capital murder and would be willing to say anything that might induce the commonwealth to go easy on him."

"But you didn't offer him a deal," the sheriff sputtered.

"That's the reason they gave, Sonny. Now, you want the truth?" He cut his eyes toward Bubba and they followed his gaze. "You think it's an accident he's here today? He's here to gloat."

"But how did he know … ?" Sarabeth didn't finish the question; she was literally struck speechless by the big, toothy smile Bubba flashed her. He looked just like a barracuda.

The other three followed Sonny down the steps to his office in silence, then sat together choking down his infamous road-tar cof-fee. The men raged, but Sarabeth was quiet.

Finally, she turned to Henry. "And this doesn't happen in the other three counties in this circuit?"

"Nope." His voice was tired. "Oh, I'm not saying nobody's rais-ing dope anywhere but here. But you can get an untainted jury pool in the other counties. You can get a fair trial in the other counties. You can get convictions in the other counties. Not here."

He sighed, then pointed out that another jury pool would be selected in January, just seven months away. Maybe it would be better.

Sarabeth spoke softly, her words velvet-covered hand grenades. "You could go to the U.S. Attorney's office and get federal indictments."

The three men turned with the perfect unison of a chorus line and stared at Sarabeth.

"Twenty-five years ago when black people in the south couldn't get a fair trial, when juries wouldn't convict a white man, federal marshals came in and charged people with violating federal laws and tried them before U.S. District Court juries. We could do that here."

Nobody said a word.

Sonny was the first to reload. "You do realize you're suggesting the judicial equivalent of bringing in the National Guard and declaring martial law."

"You want to turn this county over to the feds?" The pale blond state police detective was incredulous.

Calling in federal marshals was admitting to the world that local law enforcement had failed. Leap-frogging local juries and trying cases in U.S. District Court was announcing that the county was so corrupt, so morally bankrupt that its judicial system could not function.

Sarabeth looked at Sonny with compassion. One reason she'd been reluctant to suggest the idea was that she knew what would happen to Sonny if he supported it. He'd never be re-elected; his career would be over. The commonwealth's attorney and the circuit judge were elected officials, too, but the circuit contained four counties. Henry and Compton would survive. Hayes didn't have a dog in the fight; he worked for the Kentucky State Police. Other than hurt pride, he had less to lose than anybody, yet his was the most vocal opposition.

"You do that, and there's no mercy," the pale detective said. "With the feds' zero tolerance for drugs policy, a conviction means a mandatory 20-year sentence with no possibility of parole. That's a dandy idea for the Bubba Jamisons of this world, but what about those kids who get caught working in dope barns? You want to send some 17-year-old off to federal prison for 20 years?"

"So we just sit back and let the dopers take over the county?" Sarabeth fired back. "The body count's two in the last 24 hours! One of them's an 8-year-old child, lying in a box at Beddingfield's Funeral Home. And some dumb mechanic's facing the death penalty. Just how bad does it have to get?"

Henry waded in then before Hayes could respond. "U.S. District Court is the nuclear option and I'm not willing to push that red button until we've tried everything else."

"What else is there to try?" she asked.

"The circuit judge has the authority to ask that a new jury pool be selected right now, throw out the old one and start over. I've never seen a judge do that, but the law allows it, and I believe I can talk Earl into it. He's as fed up as we are with the lawlessness in this county. We get a new jury pool, a new grand jury, and we take Bubba's case before them. If we can't get an indictment then, I think we're out of options."

"Why do you think 300 other people will be any better than the 300 we've already got?" Sonny obviously didn't like saying it. "If these people won't indict him, what makes you think the next batch will?"

"Maybe because the next batch will be better informed."

They all turned to look at Sarabeth again.

"You've seen Daddy's sign, haven't you, the one that hangs over the typewriter?" They nodded. "I read it every time I went to his office when I was a kid, but it was years before I really understood what it meant."

The plaque was a simple phrase, hand-lettered in her father's bold cursive: *Don't mess with a man who buys ink by the barrel.*

"The next batch of 300 people—and their neighbors, the people who sit beside them in church on Sunday morning and the folks they bump grocery carts with at Brewster Market—are going to understand what's at stake here. I will make it very clear that unless this county is willing to police itself, the federal government will come in here and do it for them."

It had been a long time coming, but at that moment, Sarabeth Bingham finally understood what it meant to be a journalist. She knew her father would have been proud of her.

The room was quiet.

"You've already had your name scratched off the Christmas card lists of every doper in the county," Hayes said. "Now you're about to get the law-abiding citizens all indignant, too."

Sonny was more blunt.

"That's a dangerous thing to do, Sarabeth."

"And it's your job," she looked pointedly at Sonny and Hayes "to see to it that nothing happens to me. If I get killed, I'll never speak to either one of you ever again." It was weak, but it was the best she could do.

Henry stood up and headed for the door. "I'm going to go have a talk with the judge."

Sarabeth stood then, too. "And I've got a story and an editorial to write." She'd have liked to have strode out all macho like Patton off to kick Rommel's butt. It was hard to pull that off, though, with her knees shaking.

Chapter 17

There wasn't a single copy of *The Callison County Tribune* left in any news rack anywhere in the county by noon on Friday, even though Sarabeth had upped the press run by 2,000 copies. The racks in the newspaper office ran out, too, and Jonas had to grab 25 issues and hide them in his desk so he'd have tear sheets—the page a specific advertiser's ad ran on—to send to his customers.

It wasn't surprising that the whole county gobbled up the newspapers. The story about the little girl's murder took up the whole front page above the fold, with sidebars about the men accused in her abduction, along with a story and picture of Jimmy Dan, who was still at large.

There was also a re-fer line—"referring the reader" to the editorial page for an accompanying editorial and column. They were a perfect one-two punch.

In her column, Sarabeth was vulnerable. She actually wrote about losing Moriah, the agony of feeling the wind rip the baby out of her arms. She owned her secret fantasy that the child had somehow survived, admitted searching the faces of children the age her daughter would have been in school yards and shopping malls. She described her shock at seeing Maggie Mae on the stretcher in the ambulance, the image of Moriah she'd been carrying around in her head, and raged at the reality that Maggie Mae Davis had been killed by marijuana.

Her editorial was as blunt as her column had been vulnerable.

Here's the truth still in the husk, Callison County. Marijuana just got a little girl killed. She wasn't my little girl but she could have been yours. And when Commonwealth's Attorney Simon Henry went before a grand jury to indict the dope-grower her killer worked for, twelve of your friends and neighbors let him walk.

If you ask them why, they'll tell you they didn't believe his accuser. That, folks, is a pile of the warm, sticky substance you find on the south side of a horse going north. The truth is the grand jury wouldn't indict him because he and all the other dopers don't just run this county, they own it.

But not for long.

Local law enforcement has finally had enough. They're fed up with making arrests on revolving-door dope growers who barely stay in jail long enough to get the bench in their cells warm.

It stops here, now.

On Monday, Circuit Judge Earl Compton dissolved the county's jury pool and ordered the clerk's office to compile another one, to randomly pick another 300 names. From that list, a new grand jury will be selected and it will convene August 25. Those 12 people—you, your friends, your neighbors—will determine who owns this county, the dopers or its citizens.

But be forewarned. If this jury pool rolls over and plays dead for the marijuana growers just like the last one did— game over. The law enforcement officers who have sworn to protect this county will declare judicial martial law. They'll turn their cases over to federal marshals and the U.S. District Court in Louisville will prosecute.

If federal charges, a federal grand jury and federal trials are what it takes to clean up this county, to protect all the other innocent Maggie Mae Davises who live here, then that's the way it's going to go down.

It's up to you, Callison County. Don't let it come to that.

Around midnight, somebody threw a brick though the picture window of the newspaper office. Chief Cochran called Sarabeth and told her about it. She went to the office, duct-taped cardboard over the hole and swept up the mess. When she went back out to get into her car, all four tires had been slashed. So had the tires on the *Trib's* delivery van. She walked the three blocks back to her house and fell into the bed exhausted. Shortly before dawn, after the third prank call, Sarabeth rolled over, took the receiver off the hook, stuck it into the top drawer of the nightstand and closed the drawer.

Sonny had invited Ben and Sarabeth to go to church with him Sunday morning. They'd planned to go but decided instead to stay home and clean off the obscenities somebody had spray-painted on the sidewalk in front of their house.

All of that paled, however, in comparison to what happened in the second floor, corner cell in the Callison County Jail sometime Sunday night.

Ben had just come out of the darkroom Monday morning when Jonas burst in the front door of the newspaper office.

"Your police scanner workin'?"

Sarabeth glanced at the black box that lived on top of the filing cabinet. All the lights were dark. She'd forgotten to turn it on when she got into the office that morning.

"You need to get your butt over to the jail," Jonas said. "I just passed by there and something's going on."

She grabbed her camera and ran the two blocks to the jail with Ben on her heels. Somehow she knew, even before she got there, she knew. After she shoved her way through the crowd, an officer waved her past the police perimeter. Detective Hayes had just stepped aside to let an ambulance crew and two rescue squad members pass by when he saw her.

"What happened?"

"Doodlebug's dead. Hanged himself in his cell last night."

"Hanged himself? How?"

"Used his belt."

"He had a belt? A depressed guy who's been telling anybody who'd listen that he wants to die had a *belt?*"

"Jailer swore Doodlebug wasn't wearing one." Hayes' voice was tight and controlled. "Said he'd have confiscated it if he'd had one." The tall, thin detective squinted into the morning sun and laughed mirthlessly. "But the jailer didn't actually watch Doodlebug change into the clean clothes his uncle brought him when he first got busted. Now, he's saying Doodlebug's belly hung down over the top of his pants so far he couldn't tell if he had on a belt or not."

The jailer saw Sarabeth talking to the detective and marched over indignantly.

"You tell that nosey newspaper lady the way it really was? Don't you make it sound like this was my fault! You was in here last night talking to him; did *you* see a belt?"

Hayes didn't answer, just reached up and brushed his flaxen hair off his brow. But the jailer hammered away. "Did you? Come on now, could you see a belt on that man?"

Finally, the detective shook his head sadly. "No, I didn't see a belt on Doodlebug. I couldn't see the top of his pants at all."

"See!" The jailer fairly squealed in triumph. "See, I told you!" He sneered at Sarbeth, then turned to trumpet his vindication to the rest of the crowd. "I can't help it if a guy's so fat I can't tell if he's wearing a belt or not."

Sarabeth tuned out the rest of the jailer's rant and walked toward the first floor holding area. When she noticed that it was momentarily empty, she stepped inside, turned to Ben and put her finger to her lips. If she asked permission to be there, the jailer would most assuredly say no and she had no right of access without his approval. So she didn't ask. She just walked confidently up the steps to the second floor and around the back to Doodlebug's cell. It was the only functioning one on the second floor of the ancient, three-story facility. The barred doors of the other four cells had been piled against the wall so the cells could be upgraded to bring them into compliance with the ever-changing codes of the Kentucky Department of Corrections.

Doodlebug hung right in front of the cell door. The deputy jailer, two EMTs and two rescue squad members were so intent on figuring out how to get the big man down that they didn't notice Sarabeth standing quietly off to the side.

She slowly lifted her camera, wishing she had one of the newer "silent shutter" models that wouldn't announce her presence with an annoying "click-click." She'd just have to hope they were so far away they couldn't hear it.

Through the view finder of her wide-angle lens, she saw Doodlebug dangling above the floor beside an overturned chair. His face was black, his swollen tongue hanging out of his mouth. His belt was wrapped around his neck and then looped around a 6-inch metal pipe that ran crossways across the ceiling of his cell.

The belt was barely long enough to reach over the pipe and around the big man's neck. Unless he snapped his neck when he stepped off the chair, and it didn't look like he fell far enough to do that, Doodlebug must have strangled to death.

Three men took hold of Doodlebug's body and grunted as they lifted it up a few inches to take the weight off the belt so the EMT could unfasten it from around the pipe. Sarabeth fired frame after frame. Most of what she shot was too gruesome to use, but she was on autopilot: shoot it all and figure out later what you can actually publish.

One of the EMTs had dragged the cell's other chair over to the dangling body, and was standing on it on his tiptoes to reach up above the pipe where the belt was buckled. There was only a couple of inches of clearance between the ceiling and the pipe, and he struggled to fit his fingers into the small space to unfasten the clasp.

His grunting and complaining kept everyone's attention focused away from Sarabeth. She quietly slipped the 30 mm wide-angle off the camera and replaced it with a 120mm close-up lens. But she only fired a couple of frames, got the EMT and the grimace of effort on his face—that was a shot she could use—when the deputy jailer spotted her standing there. He gave her a hostile look and cocked his thumb toward the door in a get-out gesture.

As she walked down the street with Ben, she rewound the film and handed him the cassette.

"Process this as soon as we get back to the office. I know the shot I want you to print. The rest are … "

She didn't say, "Doodlebug, dead." She also didn't say, "As dead as the indictment against Bubba Jamison."

• • • • •

Bubba held *The Callison County Tribune* out a little further from his face to get the print into focus; the big man wasn't about to admit he needed glasses.

Those 300 Callison County residents will determine who owns this county—the dopers or its citizens.

He read the words again, the editorial written by that meddling newspaper editor who was turning out to be even more trouble-some than her father. What she'd written made Bubba so angry he wanted to tear the newspaper page into little pieces. But he didn't do that. He wanted to tear Sarabeth Bingham into little pieces, too, and he didn't do that either. He couldn't.

If the nosey editor turned up dead, all hell would break loose in Callison County, and the last thing he needed was a martyr for the cause, somebody the bleeding hearts could point to and scare the county into believing that dope-growing really was dangerous, that maybe they better do something about it.

He didn't need Sarabeth dead. What he needed was Sarabeth distracted. He needed her discredited. He needed to make sure folks didn't start listening to her. And he needed to teach her a lesson.

He put the newspaper down on the table, picked up the pistol and hollered for Jake.

When Jake heard his father call his name, his skin crawled.

He quickly slid the pamphlets he was reading under the mattress of his bed, pasted a smile on his face and went downstairs. His father was seated at the big kitchen table made of rough-hewn wood to match the hand-made cabinets. He had a gun in his hand. Bubba loved guns, any kind, had dozens of them around the house, in drawers or in gun cases. But this one was different. It was a small revolver with a broken handle. A pile of used duct tape that Bubba'd obviously just removed from the handle lay on the table and he was struggling to fit the broken pieces together and wind black electrician's tape around them.

Bubba gestured for Jake to sit down, then placed the gun in the boy's hands. "Hold this right here and push them two pieces together."

Jake lined up the edges of the broken handle pieces.

"Yeah, like that, don't let it slip, now."

Jake held firm; Bubba ripped off a piece of tape and began to wrap it slowly around the handle.

"Saw Coach Morgan in the bank this morning, said the team sure wasn't gonna be the same this fall 'thout you and Ben out there makin' plays—hold it still, dang it! I'm trying to tape it!"

Jake concentrated on holding the two pieces of broken handle tight together. Were his hands shaking?

"Said he sure was gonna miss you two." Bubba paused, then continued in the same casual tone. "You didn't tell me you'd decided not to play football at UK this fall. Didn't even mention it. Now, why is that?"

Jake was profoundly grateful he had something to focus on so he didn't have to look his father in the eye.

"I didn't think you cared one way or the other about football, Daddy. I wasn't keeping nothing from you, just didn't think it mattered, that's all."

Bubba's voice was as smooth and cold as the barrel of the gun in Jake's hand.

"Everything you do matters to me, son. You understand that? Everything. Now you tell me what happened, and don't leave out nothing."

Jake swallowed hard.

"There's not a whole lot to tell, Daddy. I just decided I was tired of it. Football was fun in high school. Ben and me … it was like he could read my mind, knew just when to break, so he'd be a step ahead of the defense when I threw. But going off and playing somewhere else, with a bunch of strangers … "

"Where's he going again?"

"University of Southern California. Full-ride academic scholarship. He couldn't afford to go to school without a scholarship. Even though his father was a coach there, he's not going out for the team either, not his freshman year 'cause—"

"You're not plannin' on goin' off to California with him, now are you? 'Cause you can think again if you are."

"No, no, Daddy. I don't want to go way off somewhere. UK's just right up the road. That's good enough for me. I just don't want to play ball there, that's all."

The answer seemed to satisfy Bubba because he shifted gears. He took the gun out of Jake's hand and continued to wind tape carefully around the hand grip.

"I'm gonna need you and Ben tomorrow. I'm short-handed, so I'm paying time-and-a-half."

Jake and Ben had worked as farm hands for Bubba all summer— setting tobacco in the spring, weeding it, taking care of his livestock, cutting hay and most recently housing tobacco. Jake only did it because Ben needed the money. Legitimate work for fair wages; Bubba'd never let Jake near his marijuana business.

"Time-and-a-half? Sure! Ben can use the extra money and he doesn't have much time left to work. We'll both be gone in a couple of weeks." Jake hoped his voice didn't betray the absolute delight those words kindled in his heart. "You need us to finish up that field off Landry Road?"

"Nope. It's a smaller field, barn's kinda hard to get to. You can ride out there with the rest of the crew. Go by and get Ben and meet Skeeter Rogers at Squire Boone's Tavern at noon."

"At noon? Why so late? By noon, it'll be hotter than a firecracker lit at both ends."

Jake never even saw it coming. One minute he was sitting in the chair, the next minute he was on his back on the floor, the whole left side of his face an explosion of pain.

"Don't you question me, boy," Bubba said with quiet menace. He'd slammed his fist into his son's face without even getting out of his chair. When Bubba got angry, his thick brows knit together in a deep crease at the bridge of his nose and unfathomable depths of cruelty glowed like twin red coals in eyes as black as midnight. Bubba Jamison mad was a thundering menace no man had ever faced down. "Don't you *ever* question me, hear. You think you're all grown up. Think you know mor'n your Daddy knows. Well, you're wrong, son. Way wrong."

Jake got slowly to his feet, his cheek throbbing, his eye swelling like a little kid with a wad of gum blowing a bubble.

"I didn't mean nothing by it, Daddy." The movement of speech made his face hurt worse. "I'm sorry. Squire Boone's at noon. I got it."

Bubba merely nodded, so Jake turned and started out the door.

"You need to know I been thinkin' about you goin' off to college." Jake stopped, frozen, his back to his father. "I ain't made up my mind 'bout that yet. Just so you know."

Then Bubba returned his attention to the gun. Even with his back turned, Jake felt the connection break and somehow managed to walk out of the room in spite of the gigantic hole that had opened up in his midsection, a void so vast he could actually feel a chill wind whistle in one side and out the other.

• • • • •

Home Grown

Kelsey Reynolds stood in the doorway of the loft bedroom, slowly, mechanically buttoning her blouse as she looked down on the back-to-school party below. The music was loud. Billy Ocean wailed "Get out of my dreams, get into my car," and the rhythm beat in time with the hammering of her headache.

She watched the two dozen teenagers talking and dancing, smoking weed, drinking beer and sniffing coke. It was like looking at colorful tropical fish swimming in a tank, in a world totally separate from hers, a place so alien she couldn't survive there, a universe where she couldn't breathe.

Raucous laughter drifted up to her from first one group of kids and then another and she wondered enviously what was so funny.

Kelsey wasn't altogether certain whose fishing cabin this was. Robbie's maybe, or Jason's. She may have known at one time, but she couldn't remember anymore.

She remembered leaving her house that night, though, running out the door with her father's voice in her ears, shouting at her to come back, that he wanted to talk to her.

Yeah, right, Daddy. Let's talk.

She'd been getting ready, piling her spiral-curled hair high on her head and fitting her shoulder-length earrings in her ears when he'd come into her bedroom to question where she was going, who she was going with. Then he'd launched into his favorite sermonette about having the "right kind of friends" and not "growing up too fast."

"I'm in a hurry, Daddy. Could we just cut to the chase? Is this the you-tell-me-how-to-live-my-life part or the I-pretend-I'm-listening part?"

He had looked so hurt that for a moment, she'd wanted him to smile and put his arms around her and make her giggle with silly noises and funny faces. But the little girl who knew how to laugh didn't exist anymore.

When Kelsey was 13, she had become achingly, painfully shy. Overnight, the outgoing child had turned into a scared, insecure adolescent.

The teenagers around her seemed to have it all together and they'd cut a path around suddenly-shy Kelsey wide enough to drive a sperm whale through. And then she'd figured out the secret and everything changed. Everyone liked her. Everyone wanted to be her friend. Everyone invited her to their parties and their raft trips and their ski weekends.

Oh, but Kelsey—bring drugs! If you don't bring drugs, don't come.

Oh, and Kelsey—put out. Take your clothes off and let the boys put their hands all over you and hurt you in ways and places no one ever told you about.

That's when she began to seek the savage embrace of sharp razor blades. Their sweet release was the only way she could cope with the pressure.

She didn't even know on a conscious level how furious she was that when she so desperately needed her father, Daddy had been cruising along in his Dope Mobile, throwing money on all the bumps in the road like those thin little bills could actually soften the blows when you slammed down into ruts and bounced up over jagged rocks. He had let money so blind him he couldn't see his own daughter, and Mama had let drugs so blind her she couldn't see anything at all. Kelsey didn't know that repressed rage was the mother of depression. But she did know that at age 15 she didn't care anymore whether she lived or died.

"You don't need to bother buttoning that up," whispered the boy standing behind her. He was tucking in his shirt as he came out of the bedroom, the tangle of sheets on the bed behind him still damp from their sweat. He cocked his head toward the bottom of the stairs. Another boy was standing there grinning, starting to come up.

Kelsey stopped buttoning her blouse. The other boy blew by her and into the bedroom and was sitting on the bed taking his shoes off when she turned around. So she merely unbuttoned the buttons she'd already fastened, stepped into the room and closed the door behind her.

Chapter 18

Billy Ocean wailed from the stereo and dancing teenagers gyrated around her. Jennifer Jamison wasn't dancing. She sat on the couch, looking up at the loft, watching Kelsey Reynolds walk into the bedroom where Jason was waiting for her.

She'd caught the look on Kelsey's face when the two boys met on the stairs. Jennifer had never seen that look from the outside, on someone's face, but she'd felt it from the inside every day that she could remember.

She sighed and shook her head. Then she pulled her long, black hair back from her face, leaned over, put the straw to the end of the line of coke and sniffed heaven into her nose. Between one heartbeat and the next, reality morphed into a new thing. The outer edges of her vision grew soft and faded, but every other image stood out as crystal clear as the sparkle on a soap bubble.

All of a sudden, she was happy, charming and beautiful. The people around her were her cherished friends who would take a bullet for her as willingly as she would take one for them. Life was good!

Outside her coke-induced delusion, none of that was true, of course.

The people around her were hardly her cherished friends. They were users. Jennifer knew that and accepted the exchange of goods and services for social acceptance as the price of admission to life. She provided drugs, the hard stuff, way beyond baby-steps weed. Meth. LSD. PCP. Heroin. Even the new drug that was all the rage in the city—crack cocaine. Name it and she had it or could get it.

Jennifer wasn't beautiful, either, and she certainly wasn't happy or charming. Ask anybody and they'd tell you: Jennifer Jamison was just weird.

The disintegration of her soul began on a bright summer morning when she was 7 years old. She never thought about that time. If her mind got anywhere near the memory, she quickly got drunk or high or a delirious combination of both until the memory crawled back into the black pit of hell where it belonged.

It was the day her mother disappeared. One minute Darlene Jamison was there and the next she was gone. Vanished without a trace. No one had any idea what had happened to her.

But Jenny knew. Jenny saw.

Men in brown uniforms came to the house late that afternoon and talked to Daddy. Jake barricaded himself in his room, thinking nobody could hear him in there sobbing.

Until that day, Bubba Jamison had never participated in any way in the care of his children. Never held a baby, changed a diaper, read a story, played a game or hugged a child goodnight. But at bedtime, their father barked at Jake and Jennifer to put their pajamas on and brush their teeth.

Then he grunted, "Go to bed!" That was it, the extent of his tenderness for two motherless children, a preview of coming attractions from the movie of the rest of their lives.

Later that night, Jenny awakened in the grip of a horrible nightmare. She'd been curled in a fetal position sobbing when suddenly Daddy appeared at her bedside. He'd come into her room as silently as a moth on velvet.

"Don't you be crying for your mama, you hear me!" he told her, an edge of menace in his rumbling voice. The look in his deep, dark eyes was as sharp as a broken bottle. "Daddy'll take good care of his little girl."

In that moment, a different kind of nightmare—one called "real life"—began to gobble the child up, slowly ripping her apart with its jagged teeth.

A series of housekeepers had orbited in and out of the house over the years, cooking and cleaning and looking after the children. Then they'd do something Daddy didn't like and he'd fire them. Jenny learned quickly not to become attached to anybody. Eventually, everybody vanished.

In her whole life, Jennifer Jamison had never had a friend.

The teenagers began leaving, singly or in groups until the cabin was empty. Kelsey came down the stairs disoriented. She was coming off a high, too, so Jennifer understood.

"I rode out here with Brandon. Did he leave without me?" she asked.

"If you need a ride home, I can take you."

Kelsey sighed. "Sure, whatever."

Jennifer's head snapped up. "Hey, don't give me a 'tude, Sweetheart, or you can walk your skinny butt five miles to Crawford!"

"I ... sure, I want a ride, thanks." Kelsey looked around at the mess. "This your cabin?"

"It's my father's." Jennifer got up, went into the kitchenette, opened the cabinet under the sink and took out a roll of trash bags. "He'll beat the crap out of me if I leave it like this." She peeled a bag off the roll and struggled with the thin plastic, trying to get it open.

Kelsey stood and held out her hand for a bag. "With two of us, it won't take long."

They threw beer cans, ashes, the remains of joints, soft-drink cans, assorted loose pills, liquor bottles and dirty paper plates into the bags. Half an hour later, the place was presentable. It wasn't clean by any stretch—beer and food had been spilled everywhere and there was a vomit mess to clean up in the downstairs bath that neither girl was willing to touch. But Jennifer would get their housekeeper to come out and finish up the rest.

"Your daddy's Bubba Jamison, isn't he?" Kelsey was a year younger than Jennifer, and though the two had been to several of the same parties, they'd never been alone together until now.

"Yeah, and ... ?"

"My daddy works for him; Mama said so." The girls stood for a moment looking at each other.

"Sucks, doesn't it." Jennifer's voice was tired and defeated.

Kelsey set her full trash bag on the floor and plopped down on the sofa. "It sucks big-time."

Jennifer curled up in the overstuffed chair across from Kelsey and the two girls started to talk. After an hour of pouring out the raw sewage of their lives, Jennifer dropped the conversation-stopper.

"I'm pregnant."

"My mother took me to a doctor in Bardstown last year and got me on the pill or I'm sure I'd be knocked up, too," Kelsey said. "What are you going to do?"

"I'll tell you what I'm *not* going to do. I'm *not* going to have it!" She suddenly felt sick at her stomach, so she leaned back in the chair and closed her eyes. When she opened them, she sat for a moment, studying Kelsey. Why not? It looked like this girl needed rescuing as much as she did.

"I'm getting out of here." Jennifer's voice was quiet and intense. "I'm not living like this anymore; I'm bailing." She looked hard at Kelsey. "I'll take you with me if you want to come."

"I'm listening."

• • • • •

Sarabeth opened her front door and found Sonny Tackett standing on her porch. She'd been baking Ben's favorite pineapple upside-down cake from scratch. She'd embarked on this culinary adventure because in a little over a week, Ben would be gone to California to college. And that was going to hurt. He'd come into her life when she so desperately needed someone to focus all that mothering instinct on that had had no outlet after Moriah died. But even more than that, he'd been companionship, he'd been there so she didn't get lonely and end up in a bad relationship with some random guy just to have somebody to talk to. Ben had made so much that was difficult in her life easier, and it'd be one of the hardest things she'd ever have to do to let him go.

"What are you doing here, in uniform on a Sunday?" She unlatched the screen door and held it out for him. "Tell me you didn't preach this morning with a gun strapped to your hip!"

The Sherman tank of a man stepped inside with his hat in his hand. He didn't smile and he had that official air about him that told her instantly this wasn't a social call.

"Did you find out something? You said you were going to open the investigation again—did something turn up already?"

The sheriff had reported to the Brewster City Police Department and the Kentucky State Police what Joe Fogerty had said as he lay dying on the riverbank. Such a "deathbed statement" was considered undisputed truth, even admissible in court. Joe Fogerty didn't gun Jim Bingham down in front of the newspaper office more than a year ago, which meant somebody else did.

Since the crime was committed inside the city limits of Brewster, the local police had been the primary investigating agency. But there'd been precious little investigating done after the sheriff found Fogerty lying by a dumpster just outside town with the murder weapon in his pocket and the victim's hat on his head. Now it was clear Fogerty had been set up. Somebody knew the old man had threatened Bingham and figured they'd get him drunk and dump him somewhere with the gun and the hat and the police wouldn't likely waste their time running down any other rabbit trails. And they hadn't. Now all those rabbit trails were stone cold.

Sarabeth held out her hand for Sonny's hat. "Have a seat and tell me all about it. Just don't let me forget I've got a cake to get out of the oven in 15 minutes."

The sheriff didn't give her his hat and he made no move to sit down. Sarabeth looked at him, and a sick dread gripped the pit of her stomach, pinched it tight with the instant nausea of a stomach virus. Police officers never came to your door with good news.

"What's wrong?"

"I'm not here about your father. I'm here about Ben."

All the color drained out of her face.

"Is he hurt?"

"No, he's not hurt."

She let out a huge whoosh of air; relief flooded over her in a warm tide.

"Sonny, you just about scared me to death!"

"Ben's in jail. The state police busted him and three other boys in a dope barn the other side of Crawford."

She blurted out a little hiccup of relieved laughter. That was ridiculous! It was somebody else, somebody with the same name or who looked like him. It wasn't Ben!

"Oh come on, Sonny, you know better than that! I slept in this morning and found a note on the kitchen table from Ben saying he'd be home in time for dinner. I don't know where he is, but—"

"He won't be home in time for dinner, Sarabeth. They're booking him right now."

Sonny might as well have told her that a herd of dancing purple aardvarks were in her back yard planting tulips. That the sun had fallen out of the sky and landed in the Pacific Ocean with a gigantic *pusssttt* sound. She sat down on the arm of the chair and stared at Sonny with wide, uncomprehending eyes.

"I know this is hard. I didn't believe it either. When I saw the arrest report, I actually thought it was funny that they'd busted somebody with the same name as your brother. Then I looked in the holding cell ..." his voice got quiet. " ... and saw the red hair."

Sarabeth groaned, a wounded-animal sound.

"I wanted you to hear it from me. It won't be long before the whole town knows, so I came right over. I'm going back to the jail now to make sure they're done processing him so I can go talk to the judge, see if I can get him to release Ben into my custody. But it may take me a little while to find Judge Compton. On Sunday afternoons, Earl usually goes fishing."

Sarabeth dropped the towel she'd been unconsciously winding into a knot in her hands. "I'll just be a minute." She turned toward the kitchen.

"You're not coming with me."

"Oh, yes I am."

He reached out and took her hand. "Don't do that to yourself, Sarabeth." He locked his eyes on hers and held firm, his voice full of compassion. "Don't go down there to get him. Don't do that to Ben, see him like that. Soon's I get the paperwork done, I'll bring him home."

She sat there in the quiet house after Sonny was gone while the pineapple upside down cake in the oven burned to a crisp.

• • • • •

Not for one minute did Jake believe it! It was no coincidence that the ugly guy with the broken nose had called him over after they'd been working for about an hour and told him he needed a roll of twine, a big one. He'd pressed $10 into Jake's hand and told him to high tail it into Brewster and get back with it quick.

Jake had asked why he couldn't get the twine in Crawford. It was five miles closer. But the man had squinted at him and told him that the twine he wanted was in Brewster, in the hardware store, open one to five on Sundays. Just ask the clerk, the dopey-looking guy with the thick glasses and he'd see Jake got the right kind, one of the big rolls wrapped in plastic.

Jake went over to pick up his hat and tell Ben where he was going. Shoot, by the time he got back, they'd probably be finished. There'd been hardly any tobacco to house, just a couple of wagon loads in the front half of the barn. The whole back side of the barn was closed off. Ben had wiped the sweat out of his eyes and teased him about always getting the cush job.

And Jake had left.

He'd been barreling down KY 32 to get back to the barn when a Kentucky State Police cruiser blew by him like he was standing still. And then another one. Then two more.

Jake floored the accelerator on his Jeep Wrangler, not caring if the road was swarming with cops, not caring if he got a dozen speeding tickets.

He passed the convoy of cops coming back toward town before he ever got to the barn, though. Saw figures in the back seats of the cruisers. He was sure one of them had red hair.

And he *knew* then it had been a set-up. His father had lied. He'd told Jake to make friends with Ben, then used that friendship to get Ben busted. And Jake had been too stupid to see what was going on until it was too late.

Now Ben was in jail. And there wasn't a single dang thing Jake could do about it.

• • • • •

It was among the worst two hours Sarabeth had ever lived though, sitting in the living room of her father's house, with the sheriff and Detective Hayes trying to get Ben to tell the truth.

When he got out of Sonny's car and came walking up the sidewalk, she had raced out the door, down the steps and thrown her arms around him. Hugging him fiercely, protectively, she'd started to cry. Then Ben started crying. Standing there on the front sidewalk, not caring that all the neighbors were watching, they just sobbed.

She couldn't stop staring at him. The whole time he was talking she had trouble concentrating on what he said because she was looking at him so hard. She tried to look into his head, into his soul. Tried to understand. At first, it was almost like he was a stranger, a clone of the Ben she knew and loved, and she kept looking for the difference, the chink, the little detail that was wrong.

The sound of his voice, so tender and vulnerable and young-sounding, broke her heart. The look on his face, shame and utter despair, and the pain in his eyes made her want to hold him in her lap like she did right after his parents died, and rock him, telling him everything would be alright.

Trouble was, everything wouldn't be alright. She knew it and so did Ben. In fact, it could just be that nothing would ever be alright again.

The sheriff's questions were kind, but firm and no-nonsense. Detective Hayes' inquiries almost sounded academic. But when it came down to it, they both wanted to know the same thing: who had hired him to work in the barn? And Ben wouldn't say.

At one point, Sarabeth had lost it briefly, shouted at him that he was crazy to protect someone who had totally ruined his life, told him to stop acting like the star of his own movie and grow up. Be a man. Tell the truth.

Ben wouldn't budge.

Of course, she knew why. It didn't take a Rhode's Scholar to figure out who'd talked Ben into working in that barn.

"It was Jake Jamison, wasn't it, son?" Sonny asked.

"No sir, Jake didn't have anything to do with it!"

"Come on, Ben, I know Jake's your best friend and his father's the biggest doper around."

Ben lifted his head and fixed the sheriff with a burning gaze from red-rimmed, swollen eyes. "Jake's not like his father! Not anything like his father. If you knew him, you'd know he'd rather die than get mixed up in dope!"

And so it went, back and forth, over and over. The sheriff and Detective Hayes pressed; Ben remained tight-lipped and silent. Again and again the same questions and the same answers. Finally, Ben got to his feet, and in that moment something shifted. The boy standing tall and defiant in front of Sarabeth wasn't a boy any longer. He was a man.

"I have the right to remain silent and I'm invoking that right. I'm done talking. You want to take me back to jail, go ahead, but I'm not saying anything else."

Sonny sighed and shook his head.

"Nobody's taking you to jail, Ben. Go to bed. It's been a long day. You're worn out. We'll talk more tomorrow."

Without a word, Ben turned and headed up the stairs. As soon as he was out of earshot, Sarabeth asked, "What's going to happen to him?"

Sonny and Hayes exchanged a glance, then both of them looked at Sarabeth.

"He was caught in a dope barn," Sonny said. "The whole back side, floor to ceiling, was full of it. That's a manufacturing marijuana charge and the penalty for a Class B felony is—"

"I know the penalty for a Class B felony." At least 10 but not more than 20 years. In *prison!* Even with a minimum sentence, Ben's life would be ruined. Her precious little brother would grow to manhood in a cage. Just like Jesse Lee.

Sonny leaned forward and put his forearms on his knees. "You know what's going to happen, Sarabeth—all the bricks are going to come tumbling down on Ben's head because of you."

She knew that. She'd thought of little else as she sat staring out the window waiting for Sonny to bring Ben home. Sarabeth Bingham, the newspaper editor, had stood up on a soapbox and screamed about the evils of marijuana. She'd insulted the county, taunted the jury pool, dared them to have the guts to stand up to dopers—even threatened to call in federal authorities if they didn't. So what, pray tell, were those good people going to do when the newspaper editor's brother was standing before them on a dope charge? They'd chuck him in a cell somewhere and throw away the key.

Sarabeth put her head in her hands, afraid she was going to start crying again. And there was a buzzing, a ringing in her ears that had started as soon as Sonny told her about Ben. It had been getting louder and louder in the hours since. Now, the jet-engine roar was so distracting she almost missed what the sheriff said. His voice was quiet, intense.

"You've been set up. You know that, don't you? Both of you have been set up."

Sarabeth raised her head and stared at him.

"Say you want to get the newspaper off your back. Name me a

better way to do it than to discredit the editor, make everything she says suspect. And how could you do that?"

"Get her brother arrested on marijuana charges." Sarabeth said in dawning understanding. Of course! "It's Bubba Jamison, isn't it. Somehow, he used Jake to set us up."

Sonny nodded, his lips pressed tight together.

"Makes sense to me," Detective Hayes said.

Sarabeth felt that airy hole open up in her belly again and she sucked in a little gasp. But then the hole closed back up all on its own. Rage had slammed the door shut on it. If Bubba Jamison thought he could scare her into submission, believed he could intimidate the press …

"Ben's not going to prison!" She ground the words out through clenched teeth. "That monster in a human being suit is not going to get away with it. He's not going to bully me or my brother … or my newspaper!"

Sonny looked at her and almost smiled. "You sound just like your father," he said.

Chapter 19

Some days, Jennifer Jamison just cried. She certainly had every reason to cry, but that didn't have anything to do with why she did it. Crying just happened to her, like rain happened to you every now and then if you stood outside long enough. You couldn't stop the rain. You just had to stand there and get wet until an invisible wind blew the clouds away.

She woke up the morning after the back-to-school cabin party and crying happened. She cried for hours, went from whimpering to great, heaving sobs, until she was limp and all her muscles ached and the only thing in the world she wanted was to stop crying.

That's how Jake found her when he came home after he'd gotten his best friend arrested. He could hear her sobbing through the closed door of her room.

He'd never had a close relationship with his sister and he'd studied Ben and Sarabeth the way you wallow an equation around in your head, not just looking for the answer but trying to figure out how to work the problem. He sat with them on their front porch in the evenings as they talked—about MC Hammer and whether rap really was music. About love and honor and God, how to keep raspberries from turning muffin batter pink, and what it meant to stand up for what you believed in. He watched them chuck pieces of popcorn at each other during *Cheers* and *The Cosby Show,* saw Ben tiptoe into his sister's darkened room with hot tea and dry toast on a tray when she had one of her headaches.

But no matter how hard he tried, there was no way Jake could interpret that kind of relationship in the context of his world. Jennifer was weird, with a desperate, wild look in her eyes most of the time that was just plain creepy.

Jake wanted to ignore his sister's tears. He had enough to think about. But he had already bailed on one person in his life today; he couldn't bail on another.

She was lying on the bed with her back to him and didn't hear him knock.

"Jennifer?"

His voice startled her and she leapt to her feet with that cornered-animal look in her eyes. When she saw it was Jake, she sank back down on the bed.

"What do you want?"

"Are you all right?"

She stopped sniffling and looked at him.

"Why in the world would you care if I'm all right?"

That hurt.

"You were crying, and I just wondered—"

"Wondered what? Wondered if something was wrong? Oh, *please.*"

She picked up a t-shirt off the bed to dry her face, her tears reduced to hiccupping sniffles, the hangover of a severe crying jag.

"Excuse me for asking. You're obviously having a great time. I'm sorry I crashed your party."

He turned to go and she blurted out two words.

"I'm pregnant."

Jake froze. Then he turned slowly back around. When he lashed out at her, she almost seemed relieved, like he'd confirmed her view of the nature of reality.

"You're pregnant! Do you have any idea how many guys I've decked over the years for making filthy remarks about you?"

Jennifer studied him like she was looking at an ant farm.

"Who's the father?"

"Oh, I have no idea. But I'd say it's a safe bet you owe an apology to just about every male human being in the county above the age of puberty. I got to as many of them as I could."

Jake stepped back, stunned. "You've been ... you were *trying* ... ?" His mind wouldn't go there. "Why?"

Between one heartbeat and the next, Jennifer went from serene to wild-eyed, shrieking rage.

"*Daddy!*" Her fury clothed his name in a thousand layers of loathing. "As soon as I was old enough to know what the word *slut* meant, that's what I wanted to be. Because Daddy *hated* it! Called Mama a slut over and over again ... *while he was strangling her.*"

Jennifer's words hit Jake in the chest like a wrecking ball.

"What?"

"You heard me! I said Daddy killed Mama." Her voice sounded like a wild animal, a cheetah or a cougar, with its paw caught in a trap. "I saw him. He put his big hands around her neck, held her out with her feet dangling above the floor and choked her to death."

Her voice changed abruptly and she became a little girl, narrating the scene playing on the movie screen of her memory.

"Mommy cried. She said, 'No, I didn't! It's not true!'" Jennifer shook her head back and forth, her wide eyes staring into empty space. "She begged, fought him, but he wouldn't let go, just kept squeezing her neck. Squeezing and *squeezing* until she hung there limp as a doll."

Jake gaped at his sister, his mind scrambling to process. Nothing made any sense and suddenly everything made perfect sense, both at the same time.

"And he'd kill me, too," she said in the scared-little-girl voice, "if he knew I was a slut like Mommy."

As quickly as Jennifer had become a cowering child, her terror was transformed into rage again.

"But he's not going to find out! I'm going to get rid of it long before there's anything for Daddy to see. *He's not going to do to me what he did to Mama!*"

Jake was stupefied. He took a step toward her, reached out. "Jennifer, I—"

She turned on him. "Get out of here!" The power of her wrath stopped him in his tracks. "Don't you think it's a little *late* to be all sweet and snuggly and worried about me? Where have you been my whole life?"

She leapt off the bed, shoved him backward into the hallway and banged the door shut in his face.

Jake stood rooted to the spot for a few seconds, then he turned and staggered toward the bathroom. He barely made it before he threw up.

● ● ● ● ●

The pull-off from KY 44 about half way between Brewster and Hoperton was a little hard to find unless you knew what to look for, knew it was the first turn into the woods after the vandalized, torn-in-half road sign that promised "Hope" was only nine miles farther down the road.

Jennifer always sneered when she passed that sign.

A two-tire track led through the trees for a quarter of a mile and then out to a sandbar formed by a large loop in the Rolling Fork River. There was a rock embankment on the other side and the river had chiseled out a deep cleft beneath it 50 feet wide and 70 feet long where the water flowed dark, smooth and deep. Old Joe's Hole.

The spot was a favorite hangout for teenagers on the weekend. Beer bottles, soft drink cans, and the other assorted flotsam and jetsam of picnics and parties littered a riverbank freckled with charred circles where kids had made fires to cook hot dogs or roast marshmallows for S'mores.

Though Old Joe's Hole was a densely populated piece of teenage real estate Friday night through Sunday, it was as silent and empty as a tomb at just after dawn on Monday morning. That's why Jennifer Jamison had selected this spot. She drove Bubba's black Ford Bronco across the smooth sand to the river's edge so she could look both ways down the Rolling Fork, where the morning mist floated like tattered lace on the water.

She put the truck into park, turned off the ignition and it was quiet. All you could hear was the river sound, not rapids, just moving water that sang a soft, soothing melody. The wind tiptoed through the leaves in the trees and a solitary lark chirped in a nearby dogwood.

Jennifer turned to Kelsey. "You like this place?"

"Yeah, it's nice."

Kelsey had said little after Jennifer picked her up in the predawn dark on the side of the road down from the drive leading to her parents' "estate." Just told Jennifer that she'd stuffed a couple of pillows under the covers in her bed and stopped briefly to look in on Bethany before she sneaked out the back door.

She'd told her father before she went to bed that she didn't want to go on the class field trip the next morning, that she wanted to sleep in, so it would be hours before anybody missed her. She said it was entirely possible, in fact, that they might never notice she was gone at all.

Jennifer knew for lead pipe certain she'd be missed! Soon as Daddy realized she'd taken his truck, the fire of his rage would light up the sky like the explosion of the Challenger.

"I like this place because the flowers smell so good here," Jennifer said.

Kelsey glanced at the rolled-up windows on the truck and surveyed the riverbank. "There aren't any flowers here. And even if there were, you couldn't—"

"You don't smell them?" Jennifer's was the voice of a small, frightened child.

"I … I can't smell anything. I've got a cold."

Jennifer leaned past Kelsey, opened the glove box and took

out the .22 pistol. She knew nothing about firearms, had merely grabbed the easiest one of Daddy's guns to steal. She'd watched enough television to figure out that it was loaded.

She placed the pistol on the dash board, reached into the Brewster Market sack at Kelsey's feet, pulled out two beers and handed one to Kelsey.

"You want something stronger, I got it. There's—"

"No, thank you."

"*No thank you?* Do you think I invited you out here to some kind of garden party—white gloves and mint juleps?"

Jennifer unscrewed the cap on the beer bottle and chugged half of it down in one long gulp. "I'm checking out. You don't want to go, that's fine and dandy with me. Nobody's twisting your arm, Sweetheart."

When Kelsey still didn't respond, Jennifer screamed at her. "Say *something!* Or you can haul your fuzzy butt out of my truck and go home!"

"No! I'm not gonna go home. *Ever.*"

"Then what is your problem?"

"What do you want from me?" Now Kelsey was screaming. "What do you want me to do? To say? I don't know how I'm supposed to act. *I've never done anything like this before.*"

It took a couple of seconds for the words to register, then they both burst out laughing.

"Neither have I, baby sister," Jennifer chuckled. "We'll just have to figure it out as we go along."

She took another big swig of beer and motioned for Kelsey to take a drink. Kelsey turned her beer up and chugged three or four swallows, let out a very impolite burp and fixed her electric blue eyes on Jennifer.

"The problem is, I'm scared," she said, then quickly rushed on. "That doesn't mean I don't want to do it. I *do.*" She spoke the next words softly with an intensity that shouted. "I want *them* to see how it feels to have a hole in the pit of your stomach so big you can't eat, or swallow or even stand up straight." The rage-fueled energy left her voice and the flat, lifelessness returned. "It's not that I don't want to. It's just, I don't think I *can*. I don't think I can actually pull the trigger."

Jennifer studied the pale blond girl sitting next to her. Without the heavy makeup she always wore, the black eyeliner and thick mascara, Kelsey looked pure and innocent, like an angel. It didn't matter how perfect she looked on the outside, of course. All that mattered was what lay on the inside, and sometimes Jennifer could see that, could look into people. She never looked directly into her father's eyes, because when she did, she could see the rot inside him, worms, maggots, hairy-legged spiders and dung beetles in a writhing, tangled pile.

She tried to look into Kelsey now, but she couldn't see anything. Maybe that was it, though. Maybe she *was* seeing into Kelsey and there just wasn't anything inside her to see.

"Do you want me to do it? Do you want me to pull the trigger for you?"

Kelsey stared into Jennifer's pale green eyes for a long time. A lifetime of communication passed between them in that look. Then she nodded her head slowly.

Jennifer turned, stared out at the river and inhaled deeply. "I love the smell of flowers." Then she turned back to Kelsey. "Ok, let's do what we came here to do."

She lifted the beer to her lips and finished most of it, then with an odd little smile slowly poured the rest of the beer out on the seat. She dropped the beer bottle in the floor and picked up the gun off the dashboard. She'd never fired a gun before.

"Will it hurt?"

"I don't think so. How could it? And even if it does, it won't hurt for long."

"You think there's a God?"

"There couldn't be." Jennifer's voice was tired, defeated. "It's just over." She pulled the hammer back with her thumb—she'd seen that on cowboy movies—until it clicked. "You ready?"

There was a wild, panicked look in Kelsey's eyes for a moment. Then it was gone and something like peace took its place. "Yeah, I'm ready." Her voice was determined and strong, then it faltered and she sounded like a little kid who didn't want to see the vaccination needle. "But I can't look."

She wadded her hands up into fists in her lap, held her breath, tensed and squeezed her eyes shut. "Just do it!"

Jennifer put the gun to Kelsey's temple and pulled the trigger.

The shot reverberated like a cannon in the truck cab. When the cold gun barrel touched her skin, Kelsey instinctively pulled away, jerked her head, and the force of the bullet knocked her the direction she was already falling, sideways into the door. Then her limp body collapsed forward, slid down into the floorboard on her knees. Like she was praying.

Jennifer was surprised there was so little blood, and mildly disappointed. That's why she'd taken her father's truck. She wanted him to have to clean up the mess of her death, and she intended to make a big one! She cocked the gun again and felt a grand rush of triumph.

One more breath.

She sucked in the sweet scent of flowers and thought about her mother.

"I'm free now, Mommy," she whispered in a ragged half sob. "Just like you." Then she put the gun barrel up to the side of her neck, tight against the carotid artery she'd learned about in health class, and pulled the trigger.

The second bang startled the lark that had been chirping in a nearby dogwood tree and it fluttered away. Then the silence was broken only by a gurgling, gasping noise coming from the truck cab that went on for three or four minutes. When it finally stopped, there was no sound but the quiet rush of the river.

Chapter 20

Seth sat behind the big cherry desk in his office at Double Springs. It was just after seven o'clock; he'd been up since four. He always came in before everybody else, particularly on a Monday morning, got half a day's work done before the rest of the staff showed up.

There was no reason to come in early today though. A crack in the gigantic cypress vat that held "distiller's beer" on its way to becoming Double Springs bourbon had shut the whole operation down Friday afternoon. Seth had given his whole staff a week off. It would take at least that long to replace the vat.

But he'd still shown up early this morning, turned his rescue squad pager off, determined to get some work done. It wasn't happening, though. He'd done absolutely nothing since he sat down in his big, high-backed chair but stare at the whiskey bottle covered with chicken feathers that sat by his phone, and think about Sarabeth.

Seth had heard about Ben's arrest. It was big news; the brother of the crusading newspaper editor busted in a marijuana barn. That was rich!

What in the world had that boy been thinking! He might as well have written on his chest in black Magic Marker: "Send me to prison forever!" Sarabeth must be scared to death. He ached to call her.

He reflexively followed that painful tug of emotion, sucked on a single strand of spaghetti and quickly pulled up short in front of the whole, tangled pile.

Fiddle-dee foo!

That's what Granny Walker would have said. She'd have crossed her skinny arms across her flat chest, cocked her head to one side and spit out the plain truth—reality in long johns with the butt flap down.

"You're sweet on that gal ain't ya ... well, ain't ya?" That's what she'd have said. And he'd have replied that every time he tried to get close to the beautiful red-head, she pushed him away. Still, the truth was—

The phone rang and Seth jumped, hoping against all reason it might be Sarabeth. The caller was John Cassidy, a whiskey distributor in Tulsa who had known Seth's father.

"John? What in the world are you doing up at this hour? Are the chickens even awake in Oklahoma?"

"Funny, McAllister, very funny. I like to get in early to get a jump on the day, that's all. I was going to leave you a message, but since you're there ... just looked at the orders for Double Springs that came in last week. What have you been doing, my friend? They're near double what they were six months ago."

What had he been doing? *Work.* Just roll-your-sleeves-up, hard work. That's all he had done for ... for more than a year now. Had it been that long? Had he actually done nothing but work—18, 20 hours a day—for a whole year?

"This much volume, I need a shipment by mid-week. You handle that?"

"Consider it done, John. We're not bottling, leak in the cypress vat, but we're shipping. I'll see to it there's a truck leaving Callison County headed your way by noon today."

"Callison County? That's where Double Springs is, in Callison County, Kentucky?"

"Well, it says Brewster on the label, but Brewster's in Callison County. Why?"

"Nothing, just that's the second time I've heard of Callison County, Kentucky in the last 24 hours."

"To what does my fair homeland owe its notoriety? Didn't have anything to do with moonshine, did it? That or the Derby are Kentucky's chief claims to fame—and the Louisville Slugger. But we don't have horses or baseball bats in Callison County."

"It didn't have anything to do with moonshine, but it was just as illegal."

"Marijuana." There was no expression whatsoever in Seth's voice.

"Yep, dope. Joe never told me he ran a distillery in the marijuana-growing capital of North America."

Seth felt sick. "How did you hear about dope-growing in Callison County all the way out there on the prairie?"

"The dope I'm talking about wasn't growing in Callison County. It was growing here."

"You lost me, John."

"Oh, you hear now and then about somebody getting busted for growing dope here. Some guy raising it to sell to his friends, college kids growing some out behind the dorm. Just small-time stuff. Until last week. It was all over the news."

Cassidy's brother, a deputy sheriff in Muskogee County, southeast of Tulsa, had told him all about it.

"I know you're not going to believe this, Seth, but he said they found a barn that had apparently been completely *full* of dope, full of it! The whole barn, can you imagine that!

Seth didn't have any trouble at all imagining that, but he kept his mouth shut, just listened.

"This guy who lived down around Lawton rented the farm out. He called to tell the man who'd rented it that he was coming by to pick up a plow head he'd left in the barn, and when he showed up, the place was empty. Nobody in the house, and pieces of dry marijuana plants all over the barn. Checked the field and looks like they must have grown a couple of acres of it!"

"Thanks so much for the entertaining Story Hour with John Cassidy," Seth laughed. "But I fail to see what any of this has to do with Callison County."

"Just this, my brother was telling me that when they were going through the house, they found a year-old newspaper that the dope growers left behind. It was a copy of the *Callison County Times or Tribune* or something like that. Had this story about how dopers—that's what the story called them, *dopers*—had just about taken over the whole county. Talked about farmers making a fortune who never worked, and hung juries, dogs with their throats cut—I didn't get that part—and police helicopters looking for a particular shade of—"

"Marijuana green. I remember the story."

"I'm just saying, maybe one of your *dopers* decided to come out here to grow his crop." He laughed. "Can't say I blame him. Farmland in Oklahoma's way better than anything you've got in Kentucky."

Seth hung up the phone and shook his head.

There'd been a time when the dopers could grow marijuana by the acre in Callison County, too. He remembered reading about the busts, but that was years ago. Now, it was a few plants here, and a few there, high-octane, super dope that sold by the ounce like gold.

He glanced out the window at the bright sparkle of dew on the begonias that lined the walkway outside his office.

What if some enterprising Callison County doper had decided to grow super-dope someplace else, somewhere the cops wouldn't give him such a hard time? How much money could you make on *an acre* of sensemilla? Shoot, maybe they'd all figure out they could make more money raising it somewhere else. Callison County certainly had enough know-how and expertise to export all over America. Pretty soon, it wouldn't just be Sarabeth railing about dopers in the newspaper. It would ... *make national headlines.*

Seth froze. The day Sarabeth had come to Double Springs, she'd talked about her father. Now he heard her speak inside his head as clearly as if she were sitting beside him. "The last time I heard my father's voice, he sounded so alive. He said he was working on an important story that would *make national headlines.*"

Could this have been Jim Bingham's big story? Maybe it wasn't just some random Callison County doper growing pot in Oklahoma. Maybe some local doper really *had* decided to expand his empire outside the county. Outside the state. What if Jim Bingham had figured that out? Sarabeth had described Joe Fogerty's death-bed statement in her story about his capture. The old drunk hadn't killed Jim Bingham ... so maybe somebody murdered the editor of the newspaper to shut him up.

Seth's heart began to pound. He squeezed the arm rests on his chair, clamped down tight with both hands in an effort to grab hold of his racing emotions. If Granny Walker had told him once, she'd told him a thousand times, "Now Seth-boy, one robin don't make it spring."

All Seth had was one robin, a lone feathered creature that might, in reality, turn out to be nothing more than a sparrow or a crow. And even if there were, indeed, a whole flock of robins out there somewhere, how could anybody possibly find it?

Well, he'd found the first bird, hadn't he? And Double Springs had half a dozen to a dozen distributors in every state.

I can't call them all!

Why not? His WATS line had no limit on the number of long distance calls he could make. And with the distillery shut down for a week, he certainly had the time.

But what were the odds that he could find somebody who just *happened* to know, oh by the way, if the police in that particular community just *happened* to find acres of marijuana growing out in a field somewhere—that just *happened* to be rented to somebody from Callison County, Kentucky?

This is crazy. Certifiably crazy!

He picked up the phone and dialed his assistant's extension.

"Martha, I gave you a week off, but I know you're checking your messages. You always do. Daddy left you a message once on Christmas Day and you called him back five minutes later. So call me. I'm in the office. I need you to tell me where you keep the complete list of the names and phone numbers of Double Springs' distributors, every one of them, anywhere in America. I have most of it, but I don't want to miss anybody. And no, I'm *not* going to tell you why I want it. Don't ask."

He started to hang up, then added, "And don't you dare come into the office to find it for me! Just call and tell me where to look." He began flipping through the A section of his Roll-A-Dex, looking for the names of distributors in predominantly agricultural areas—nothing in New York City, Boston, Philadelphia. He was looking for people in the Eastern Time Zone, who might be awake.

• • • • •

Not so much as a pin prick of light shown in the black ditch of absolute darkness that shrouded Kelsey Reynolds, like there'd been a power failure in the universe.

She was on her knees, slumped sideways against a wall. When she tried to straighten up, the motion shoved an agonizing ice pick of pain into her head. She gasped and stopped moving, concentrated on breathing.

Where was she and why was it so dark here?

There was something fabric against her back, something smooth and cold, like metal, in front of her. On the right, there was a handle or lever on the wall. She grasped it, used it to try to pull herself up off her knees and—

Without warning, the wall moved and she was falling. Before she could cry out, she landed on something soft—sand, cool sand, pebbles and rocks. She rolled over carefully from her side to her back. She could feel warmth on her face and a cool breeze, and she could hear birds singing and another sound, a rushing sound, water maybe.

"Hello," she said quietly, just as a test, and she could hear it, so she wasn't dreaming. She struggled to think but her head hurt so

243

bad it made her sick. She lifted the heels of both hands up to massage her temples where the headache pain throbbed, and there was something sticky all over her face.

Why was she lying in the sand in the dark with sticky stuff on her face?

All at once, her slowly dawning awareness was out-distanced by a faster growing terror. In a lightening bolt of realization she grasped that the darkness all around her was not just the absence of light. It wasn't a negative "not-light." It was a positive, a real thing, an entity.

It was Dark, brooding, malevolent and silent.

And Dark was a shape-changer. Like the beserkers of Norse mythology could transform themselves into bears and wolves, Dark could change into anything, everything or nothing at all. So Dark could become liquid and pour into her, through her ears and eyes and nose, and fill her up, drown her, put out all the lights, make her dark inside, dark and cold and dead.

"Mommy," she whimpered. "Daddy! I'm scared."

Kelsey started to cry quietly and the tiny shaking movement of her sniffles hammered in her temples and made her dizzy. Then even Dark went away, reality dissolved, and she floated off into nothingness.

When she came to again, she lay quiet, trying with all her strength to open her eyes! But it was like her eye-lids were nailed shut. She finally reached a trembling hand up to her face to see what was holding her eyes closed, but what she felt with her fingers made no sense. Her eyes *were* open! She could feel it, touch her eyeballs. But if her eyes were open, why was it so dark?

She rolled slowly over onto her stomach and pushed herself carefully up to her hands and knees. Then she lurched to her feet, sobbing, and somehow managed to stay upright. She staggered around, grasping at empty air, felt water on her foot and then lost her balance and fell face forward into the river. Struggling, disoriented, Kelsey tried to come up for air but which way was up? She tried to scream, but her mouth was full of water. She gasped and sucked in water with the air, choked, gagged and somehow managed to wail, "Help me, help!"

Two old fishermen in a johnboat heard her cry and saw Kelsey struggling to stand in the waist-deep water. They beached the boat and raced toward her.

The bald man, Buford, got to her first and tried to take her arm. "It's not deep, you can stand up." She lurched at him and almost knocked him down, grabbed hold of his arm and held on so tight she almost pulled him under.

Harry, Buford's fishing buddy for 35 years, was a step behind and he took her other arm to get her out of the water. She was a little bitty thing, just a kid, looked like. He half lifted, half dragged her to the shore and collapsed on the sand with her.

"Don't leave me, please!" Kelsey begged.

"Honey, we ain't 'bout to leave you here all by yourself!" Harry tried to comfort her. "Everything's gonna be just fine. Ain't nothing gonna hurt you."

Her long blond hair was wet and tangled, with blood in it around her face. Looked like she'd whacked both sides of her head on something and blood was oozing down over her ears. Not gushing; the wounds weren't very big.

Buford had been standing nearby looking at her and he tapped Harry on the shoulder, pointed to his own eyes and then to hers, and mouthed *she can't see*. Harry waved his hand in front of her face and she didn't respond.

"Now Honey, I need to know your name and what happened to you, can you tell me that?" Harry asked, but the girl was incoherent, kept babbling about the dark coming to get her.

Buford cocked his head toward the black Ford Bronco parked next to the river with the passenger door open, Harry nodded and Buford turned and crunched down the riverbank toward the truck. That was obviously how the kid got here, but who drove her? She sure didn't drive herself! So where was the driver and why'd he leave a blind girl here all by—

Buford suddenly hollered, a strangled cry of surprise and horror, stumbled backward from the open truck door, tripped and landed on his butt in the sand. He turned toward Harry; shock had drained all the color out of his face.

"There's a girl in there! And blood, blood all over, blood everywhere." He swallowed hard a couple of times to keep from throwing up. He hadn't seen anything like that, or smelled the copper stench of so much blood, since he'd led a platoon of grunts into the jungle on Iwo Jima almost half a century ago. "She's dead!"

"You sure?"

"Dang right I'm sure! I'm goin' for help."

Buford lurched to his feet and took off at something that approximated a run up the trail to the road to flag down a car. He wasn't just running for help, though. He was running to get away from the truck and what he'd seen in it.

There was a bloody pistol in the lap of the girl slumped behind the steering wheel. With so much blood on her, he couldn't tell where she'd been shot, but the thing was, the blood wasn't just on the girl. It was *everywhere*—on the window beside her, on the steering wheel and the dashboard, on the seat and on the roof above her head. It wasn't splattered blood. It was *smeared* blood. It'd been wiped on all those surfaces; you could see the hand prints plain as day. And not just smeared prints—*words*.

Buford fell, buggered up his knee, and staggered on, his mind reeling. The girl who'd been driving had shot herself and smeared blood all over the truck cab while she was dying. And then she'd written on the windshield in her own blood!

No, couldn't be!

Buford kept on running.

Chapter 21

Harmony Pruitt called out from the front office, "I'm locking up now, Sarabeth, you sure you don't need anything?"

"I'm sure, Harmony. Thanks. See you in the morning."

She heard the door close and Harmony's key in the lock and the sudden silence that followed was the first real quiet, the first chance to take a deep breath since ...

Her mind jack-knifed like an 18-wheeler on a freeway, returned to a moment frozen in time—her fingers sticky with cake batter as she reached to open the front door. The last sane, good moment before her life had been dumped into a blender set for puree.

She actually moaned, and pushed her father's—*her!*—leather chair back from the typewriter, leaned her head forward and tenderly massaged the back of her neck where the muscles were as taut as cables on a suspension bridge. She was tired, way the other side of exhausted.

The police scanner that lived on her mantle had started squalling before seven o'clock, exploding with calls. Police! Rescue squad! Ambulance! She'd been fully dressed, had finally dozed off on the couch just before sunrise, so she was like a fireman—into her shoes and out the door with her camera bag slung over her shoulder in less than a minute.

That's how she'd managed to make it to the swimming hole in the Rolling Fork River before the ambulance had Kelsey loaded for transport. She shivered at the memory of the pale child lying on the stretcher—blind.

Sarabeth sighed and stopped rubbing her neck. Her fingers were getting sore and the muscles were still as hard as an anvil. And she couldn't help waiting for the other shoe to drop. Would her fatigue make her legs go numb? Or stab a dagger into her ear? Or maybe … nothing at all. Maybe she'd get a pass from the MS slot machine this time.

Impulsively, she reached over, picked up the receiver off the phone on her desk and dialed her home number. Ben answered on the second ring. His voice sounded a little hoarse. Had he been crying?

"I just wanted to check in on you, see how you're doing."

"I didn't say it last night, but I just want you to know—"

"Not now, Ben!" She hadn't meant for it to come out harsh, but his instant silence told her she'd wounded him. "I'm on overload. Let's not go there right now. There'll be plenty of time later."

"I understand." He hesitated. "I don't like dumping one more thing in your lap, but …"

"But what?" Her mouth went dry.

"Sarabeth, Jake's *gone.* Nobody can find him. The sheriff called here to ask if I knew where he was, but I haven't talked to him since—" The heartbeat of silence spoke volumes. "I mean, his sister's *dead!* Killed herself, and Jake doesn't even … nobody can find him to tell him."

Sarabeth hadn't been able to get her arms around how to feel about Jake yet. Ben was facing prison because Jake had … well, Jake had done *something*, was mixed up in it somehow. But she absolutely could not go there right now.

Ben's voice was full of pain. "I just wish he didn't have to hear it from his father, that he could find out some other way."

Sarabeth had talked to the Kentucky State Police troopers who had driven out to Bubba's house earlier that day to give him the news. They said he'd been as cold as a flagpole in a blizzard. They'd told him, straight out, what had happened. His daughter had been found dead in his truck on the riverbank at Old Joe's Hole. She'd been shot, a self-inflicted wound.

Bubba'd taken a step backward, didn't exactly stagger, but it looked like he'd been pushed. The corner of his mouth had twitched, but other than that, his expression never changed.

"You're sure it's my Jenny?"

They'd nodded.

"And she's dead." That wasn't a question, but they'd nodded just the same. Then he told them he'd be in town later to make arrangements, actually thanked them. Before they made it back to their cruiser, they heard a crash from inside the house, like something huge, a china cabinet or a book case, had hit the floor. And they heard a cry come from the house, almost like a howl, that raised the hair on their arms.

Ben was right, Sarabeth thought. It'd be better for Jake to hear about it from somebody—anybody!—other than his father.

"Call me if you hear from him," she told him. Then it occurred to her that if he chose not to call her, there was nothing she could do about it. She had no control over him anymore. Truth was, every parent's sense of control over any child above the age of 6 months was illusory at best. "I mean it, Ben, call me! I want to help."

"I'll call." And maybe he would.

She heard a rap-rap-rap on the locked front office door and looked at the clock—exactly 5:30. That would be Callison County Sheriff Sonny Tackett. She'd called him earlier in the afternoon and asked him to stop by.

He greeted her with a smile. "How you holdin' up?"

Sarabeth scratched around inside herself for a return smile, but couldn't locate one anywhere. "There was a man at the funeral home when Daddy died, a guy who looked like a turtle. He expressed it pretty well, said, 'When the good Lord sends you tribulations, he intends for you to tribulate.'"

Sonny followed her into her office.

249

"The reason I asked you to come by is … I mean …" She couldn't get the words out.

When the idea had first struck her, it had seemed brilliant. And the plan that followed had just sort of blossomed out of nowhere. But now, hours later, so utterly tired, she feared she wouldn't be able to summon the energy to make sense of it for Sonny.

"You don't need a reason," he said and sat down on the couch. "If you just need somebody to talk to, I'm in. Says right there on the side of my cruiser: 'To protect and to serve.' And the 'serve' part, that's in my other job description, too. It's called multi-tasking."

Then she did smile.

"How do you manage it?" she asked. "Do what you do, see what you see every day without becoming cynical or callous?"

"There's this thing about power made perfect in weakness, but now's probably not be the best time for that conversation. Just remember what I told you about right and wrong, good and evil. It's not a fair fight. I know who wins in the end."

She looked into his steady gaze, took a breath and exhaled slowly. And when she started talking, she felt calmer. "I've got a plan to save Ben and catch Bubba Jamison."

Sonny sat up straight. "That's some plan! Where'd it come from?"

"It's sort of like Tecumseh." She watched that blow right by him. "The Indian Chief Tecumseh claimed he wasn't born, said he'd burst full-grown from an oak tree. That's the way this idea came to me."

"I'm listening."

"Jennifer Jamison and Kelsey Reynolds. Why do you think they were together out there on the riverbank this morning?"

"Whoa! You might want to announce: 'new topic, no transition,' so I could keep up with what you're talking about. How did we get *there*?"

"It's not a new topic. I've talked to a lot of people about those girls today." She'd gone to the high school after classes let out, hung out at band practice, watched cheerleader try-outs, sat in the stands while the drill team warmed up. It hadn't been hard to gather information. Every kid had a story they were eager to tell her.

"They were loners, outcasts. They had no friends—including each other. No one had ever seen the two of them have a conversation."

"So what's your point?"

"I could only find one thing Jennifer and Kelsey had in common."

Finally, the light bulb blinked on above Sonny's head.

"Both their fathers are dopers."

"Right. Now here's the part that's a stretch. There are ... well, according to your estimates, there are *hundreds* of dopers in Callison County."

"I never said hundreds."

"Dozens, then. So how did the daughters of two of them hook up unless—I said this was a stretch—maybe their fathers worked together. That would have been a bond they shared that nobody else knew about."

"Not 'together.' If Bubba Jamison was involved, he was in charge."

"That's what I figured. So maybe Billy Joe works for Bubba."

"For the sake of discussion, I'll buy it. I still don't see what this has to do with saving Ben and catching our friend Mr. Jamison?"

"I think I could talk Billy Joe into turning on Bubba."

Sonny almost choked. "Earth to Sarabeth! Listen to yourself. Why would Billy Joe Reynolds—?"

"Because he's B.J. He's Bije. You don't know him like I do." She lifted her hand before he could protest. "I know he's a doper. But underneath it all, he's a good man. And marijuana is destroying his family."

Sonny said nothing.

"Have you ever met his wife?"

"I've pulled Becky Reynolds over twice and Anderson Bertram got her off both times. She's a train wreck."

"And now Kelsey …" Sarabeth's voice quavered. Sonny reached over and patted her hand and she finished in a strangled whisper. "His whole life's coming apart!"

"I won't argue that part. But to turn Bubba in, Billy Joe would have to come clean, own up to being a doper, too. That admission will land him in the iron house. You really think he'd be willing to do that?"

"Wouldn't the state cut him some kind of deal in exchange for his testimony?"

"A deal, yes. Immunity from prosecution, not likely."

"His wife's a drug addict." Sarabeth hung her head and her red curls tumbled down and hid her face. "His teenage daughter just tried to kill herself and now she's blind. I think it's worth a try to—"

"And I agree."

Sarabeth's head snapped up. "You do?"

Sonny smiled. "I do. I'm not convinced it's going to work, but Tecumseh is worth a shot. What have we got to lose? Worst-case scenario—Billy Joe says no."

Actually, that wasn't the worst-case scenario. The worst thing that could happen was far more horrible than either of them could ever have imagined.

• • • • •

Seth had shown up on the courthouse steps Tuesday morning before the building was even unlocked and had way-laid the sheriff on his way to his office.

Now he felt exposed. Like those dreams you have about being in a public place naked.

But Seth didn't think Sonny Tackett would decide he was imagining little pink bunnies. He'd never had any dealings with the sheriff to speak of, had only chatted with him a time or two in the courthouse. He knew the man's character, though. Through fires, floods, wrecks—tragedy and danger—he'd seen how Sonny conducted himself. He was the real deal. Besides, Seth had sensed that Sarabeth trusted him. That was high praise.

On Sonny's part, he had to concentrate really hard to get past the fact that this big dark-haired dude was apparently the man in Sarabeth Bingham's life. Sonny had never asked, of course, but he was pretty good at reading body language. He'd seen them at house fires and car accidents, trying not to stare at each other. And the day they'd found Maggie Mae Davis' body. Sonny genuinely wanted to dislike the man, but he was having a rough go. What he had done was impressive. And if Seth McAllister was right ...

"Let's start over," Sonny said. The two men were sitting together in Sonny's cramped office. Its size made Seth seem even bigger than he was, and Sonny thought he was big enough already, thank you very much. "You're jumping ahead of me and I need to understand it from the beginning."

"I guess I was talking fast because I wanted to get it all out before you chucked me out of your office on my ear or had me carted off to the Kentucky Home for the Bewildered."

"Just tell it to me slow. I'm listening."

Seth started over, telling the sheriff about the owner of Cassidy and Sons Distributing Company in Tulsa, Oklahoma, and describing the conversation in which John had told him about the barn full of marijuana and the copy of *The Callison County Tribune*.

"That was in Muskogee County, right?" Sonny wrote it down. "Muskogee County Sheriff's Department?"

"That's what John told me. So I guess you'd be looking for Deputy Sheriff Cassidy, John's brother. That's who John said told him about the newspaper."

"And that's all he said, right?"

Seth nodded.

Sonny put his pen down and looked at Seth in wonder. "How in the Sam Hill did you get from a barn full of dope in Oklahoma to a national network of dope growers all over the country, masterminded by somebody here in Callison County?"

Seth stood up and would have paced back and forth as he talked if there'd been room to take more than two of his long strides before he had to turn around. "I had absolutely zero reason to believe that what John said meant anything. Shoot, it didn't even prove the dopers in Oklahoma were from Callison County, let alone that they were a part of some grand conspiracy. Maybe somebody from Brewster sends the hometown newspaper to Uncle Bob in Tulsa. It could be as simple as that."

"You didn't think it was, though."

"No, I didn't, but you need to understand that I had no *reason* to believe otherwise. It was just a hunch." Seth reached up and ran both hands through his black hair. "Sounds ridiculous, I know, but my father always told me to trust my gut."

"Our fathers must have been friends; my daddy told me the same thing." Sonny looked up at Seth's 6-feet 7-inch frame. "They were probably on the same basketball team."

Seth didn't drop a beat. "Your father play shooting guard, did he?"

"Nope. Center."

Sonny gestured toward the chair. "Sit down, you're blocking out so much light I'm gonna get Seasonal Affective Disorder."

Seth sat back down in Sonny's overstuffed armchair.

"So you figured, 'What the heck, I don't have anything else to do today, I'll just call 187—"

"No, 185."

"Excuse me, 185 of my close personal friends all over America and ask them a bunch of questions they can't answer. I got this right so far?"

"Yeah, but you left out the part about how these people are my customers and I'm grilling them for information about illegal drugs. That about covers it."

Sonny had to ask, though he knew the answer already. "Why?"

Seth paused. "Because I'm sick and tired of watching dope destroy people."

Sonny knew the specific "people" Seth was talking about, but let it slide.

"What exactly did you say?"

"Well, after about a dozen calls, I had a rap down. Told them marijuana-growing was a big problem in my community, said I was doing a little investigation of my own to see if I could find out if any Callison County dopers had taken their show on the road. Then I just went fishing. I asked what they knew about dope—busts, confiscations, anything—where they lived."

"And what did you find out?"

"Absolutely zero from 181 of them."

"And the remaining four?"

"They're the other robins that make it spring." He started to explain the bird analogy, but it was plain Sonny understood. Apparently, their grandmothers had played on the same basketball team, too.

Then Seth gave the sheriff a specific, detailed description of what the distributors in New York Mills, Minnesota; Aberdeen, Kansas; Tupelo, Mississippi and Amarillo, Texas had told him.

In all four locations, police had discovered the remains of huge marijuana-growing operations in places where there'd never been so much as a lone dope plant in the ground before. In all four cases, the dopers had signed crop-share leases for the land, which meant until their crops, supposedly soybeans or cotton, were sold, the landlords didn't get paid. So the dopers got to use free fields to grow acres of marijuana.

"In Texas, they made an arrest, a local guy, and based on what my distributor friend could remember of the story about it on TV, he wasn't saying much. But apparently he was some dumb cowboy and nobody could figure out how he suddenly knew so much about how to grow high-test marijuana.

"In Aberdeen, the police fingerprinted the house where the workers were living. Maybe they did in all the other places, too, I'm just telling you what my sources remembered about something they saw on the news or read in the paper. You can make some phone calls of your own to find out the details."

Sonny had been taking notes furiously the whole time Seth was talking. He looked up then, a little sheepish himself. "You know that big pile of dirt you had to walk around to come up the courthouse steps?"

Seth nodded.

"They dug up the sewer pipe yesterday leading to three clogged johns in the basement. Cut right through the courthouse's buried telephone cables. Patched it up for local calls only today. But you can bet your granny's sweet bippy I'll be calling all these places as soon as I can."

"You might want to call the folks in Aberdeen first."

"Because?"

"The Aberdeen police ran the fingerprints and got hits on two men with prior arrests for growing dope ..." Sonny burst into a grin that threatened to split his face open before Seth even completed the sentence. " ... in Kentucky."

"I'd give you a high five if I didn't have to climb up on a chair!" Sonny said.

Seth abruptly stopped smiling. "You know, if I figured this out, maybe somebody else did, too."

"Like who?"

"Like Jim Bingham."

Chapter 22

Billy Joe felt someone touch his shoulder and looked behind him. It was Bessie. He reached up and patted her hand and said nothing. What was there to say?

"How's Kelsey?" Her voice was quiet, sad.

Billy Joe had moved a waiting room chair over in front of the window and was sitting backward in it, straddling the seat, with his arms folded on top of the chair-back and his chin resting on them. His ever-present UK ball cap was cocked back on his head.

A handful of other people stood together in groups talking softly nearby. Squire Boone and his wife from Crawford were there, Billy Joe's neighbors from down the road, and a couple of his sisters and their husbands.

The view from the sixth floor of Norton Children's Hospital was spectacular. Tuesday morning rush-hour traffic bustled past on the busy streets below, and if you leaned way out and looked to the left, you could actually see a slice of the Ohio River.

But Billy Joe hadn't moved the chair for the view. He just had to look at something besides the baby-puke green walls of the waiting room or he'd start screaming and they'd have to haul him out of here in a straight jacket. They might yet.

How's Kelsey?

Billy Joe had absolutely no idea how Kelsey was. Oh, if you

were talking about her physical condition, he could speak to that. She was "stable." Given the nature of her injuries, that was remarkable. A bullet had entered her left temple about two inches in front of her ear and had exited the other side half an inch closer to her eye socket. There had been no significant bleeding, and the brain did not appear to be swelling from the trauma. Her face was swollen, though, blown up like a balloon so she was unrecognizable. Other than that, she was fine.

Except the bullet had ripped out both optic nerves on its way through. Kelsey would never see so much as a sliver of light again as long as she lived.

"Right now, she's got umpteen-dozen machines and gizmos attached all over her and she can only have visitors for five minutes once an hour," Billy Joe said.

"Can she talk?"

"They've got her heavily sedated. Her mother's in there with her."

And she's probably heavily sedated, too.

"If you need somebody to watch Bethany, I'd be glad to have her over."

"Mom and my sisters got that covered, but thanks."

Billy Joe was relatively sure Bethy didn't know what had happened to her older sister. She'd been asleep, they all had, when the police came knocking on the door yesterday morning with a ridiculous story about how Kelsey had been shot.

That was impossible, of course, because Kelsey was in bed in her room. Billy Joe had gone to answer the bang-bang-bang on the door with Becky in her nightgown behind him, and she'd turned when the officer mentioned Kelsey and run down the hall to the child's room.

"I'm sure sorry you had to come all this way for nothin'," Billy Joe'd said to the officers as they waited for Kelsey to stagger out of her room, her flaxen hair in a profound state of bed-head. "I can put on a pot of coffee right quick if you—"

A high-pitched wail had exploded out of Kelsey's room, so *desolate* it'd raised the hair on Billy Joe's neck. He'd found Becky standing beside the girl's bed. The covers had been turned back and two pillows were lying there where Kelsey should have been.

What had happened after that wasn't real clear in Billy Joe's head, but he knew that Bethany had slept through most of it.

"All Bethy knows is that Grandma came by to pick her up so she could spend a few days on the farm. I'm going back home late this afternoon to gather up some stuff for Becky and spend some time with Pumpkin. Somebody's got to tell her what happened to Kelsey, but I swear I don't know what to say or how."

Sarabeth leaned over and spoke softly into his ear. "And how are *you*, Bije?"

That was a fair question, but Billy Joe was still one behind. He hadn't answered the how's-Kelsey question yet.

Truth was, he didn't have any idea how Kelsey was. Because if he'd known that she was so miserably unhappy she didn't even want to live anymore, he'd have done something about it. He didn't know what, but he'd have done *something!*

A little sob stitched his breathing and Sarabeth squeezed his shoulders.

"Police said they believe there was a suicide pact. Said she went out there yesterday morning with Bubba Jamison's daughter and they were both gonna kill themselves." He turned around then and faced Sarabeth. "They were going to *kill* themselves. Fifteen years old and you want to die! Oh, Bessie, what happened to my baby girl?"

Sarabeth pulled him to her and he held on, his arms around her waist, crying in silent, heaving sobs. She cradled him, patted him on the back and cried with him.

Billy Joe sat opposite Sarabeth in the hospital cafeteria. She shoved a cup of coffee and a sausage biscuit at him but he just shook his head.

"Eat, Billy Joe. I know you haven't had a thing today and I bet you didn't eat yesterday either, did you?"

"I don't remember."

"Just for the sake of argument, let's assume you didn't. So you're due to drop over from dehydration or low blood sugar in … " she looked at her watch " … I'd say 30 minutes, an hour max. Maybe Becky can get them to put you in a bed next to Kelsey so it's not so hard on her to look after you both."

He reached down, picked up the biscuit and took a bite, chewing like he had a mouthful of Styrofoam packing worms.

"You're going home this afternoon, didn't you say?" she asked.

"I'll come back to Louisville Wednesday morning and bring Becky a change of clothes, a toothbrush, that kind of thing. The doctors say Kelsey might wake up tomorrow. And then … "

"Cross that bridge when you get to it."

"Right." He took another bite of the breakfast sandwich.

Sarabeth glanced around the room. When she was sure she and Billy Joe were alone in the deserted cafeteria, she reached up, put her hands above her head, fingertips touching, elbows out, and said, "Ok, Bije, Umbrella of Mercy."

Umbrella of Mercy was their code for: "I'm about to say something totally off the wall, but you can't laugh and you have to give serious consideration to whatever it is." They'd used it all the time when they were kids.

The ghost of a smile appeared on Billy Joe's face. "Haven't heard that phrase in a hundred years."

Sarabeth kept her hands in the air in the umbrella position. "Come on, I'm serious, B.J. Will you grant me an Umbrella of Mercy?"

"Sure, Bess. Whatever you want."

Sarabeth lowered her arms and took a deep breath.

"You know what happened to Ben Sunday." It wasn't even a question. She knew he knew.

"Yeah, and I'm real sorry."

"He didn't do it, Bije. He didn't know there was dope in that barn, he couldn't have. He was set up. Bubba Jamison got him busted to shut me up."

Billy Joe's eyes widened.

"Unless I do something, an innocent boy's life is going to be ruined." She reached out, grabbed his hand and squeezed tight. Her voice was low and intense. "You understand better than anybody else on the planet right now how it feels to watch somebody you love be destroyed. I need *help*, Billy Joe!"

"I'm sorry Bessie, but I don't know what I can do."

There was a beat of silence, then she just said it, flat out. "I want you to help me and the police bust Bubba Jamison." Billy Joe's head snapped back like she'd clocked him in the jaw. She concentrated hard, studying his face when she hit him with the second blow in the one-two punch: "I know you work for him."

In the little crack of time between one heartbeat and the next, shock rendered him totally transparent. Surprise froze his features. *But there was no denial. No outrage!*

Billy Joe quickly rearranged his face, slammed the doors and locked the windows. She'd seen, though. She'd *seen*.

"Sarabeth Bingham!" he sputtered. "Why on earth would you say a thing like that?"

She spoke with quiet intensity. "Because Ben's best friend is Jake *Jamison*. He practically lives at our house. And we talk!"

All the air went out of Billy Joe and he sank back in his chair. It had been a bluff, of course; Jake had never said a word about his father or his father's business dealings to Sarabeth.

"You need to remember who you're talking to, Bije," she said gently. "I was always the one who delivered the cock-and-bull stories to our parents when we were kids." She reached out, patted his hand and continued quietly. "You were a lousy liar then and you're a lousy liar now."

Billy Joe made a motion that might have been an effort to stand up, but he couldn't pull it off. Sarabeth kept at him. She couldn't let him off the hook. Too much was at stake.

"You work for Bubba Jamison and he's out to get me, through Ben. Unless you help us, my little brother is going to spend at least a decade of his life in prison. He'll come out the other side as wounded as that little girl of yours lying in a bed upstairs hooked up to machines. Both innocents. Both of them destroyed by dope!"

"I ... I don't know what you're talking about. I barely know Bubba Jamison."

"I talked to probably two dozen teenagers yesterday about Kelsey. None of those kids were her friends. They just used her to get drugs and ... " She dropped her voice to barely a whisper. "They used *her*, Billy Joe, the boys did. Abused that girl in every possible way."

He shook his head back and forth, his wide eyes full of anguished tears.

"I hate to have to tell you this stuff, Bije. I know it hurts you, but you said you didn't have any idea why Kelsey would do what she did. Well, *I* know why!" Her voice grew louder. "Your little girl tried to kill herself because dope money destroyed her family! How many people does the marijuana industry have to kill—Maggie Mae Davis, Lester Burkett, Donnie Scruggs, Jennifer Jamison—before—?"

She realized she was shouting and stopped in mid-sentence, watching tears pour down Billy Joe's face. When she spoke again, her voice was quiet and controlled.

"Billy Joe, you've got another little girl at home. Do you want her to grow up in the same world Kelsey grew up in?"

She reached across the table and covered his hand with hers. "I know you love your family and never intended to hurt them. But you did, Bije. Don't you see ... ?" She stopped, let out a long breath.

"I can't make you own up to what's happened to your life. I can't force you to help Ben. So I'm going to shut up and leave you alone. Just one question. Answer it for yourself, not for me."

She leaned close, spoke quietly for a few moments, then patted his hand and rose to her feet.

"Bije, I love you." Her voice was thick. Tears filled her eyes and overflowed down her cheeks and she made no effort to wipe them away. "No matter what you decide, you know I'll always love you." She leaned over and kissed him on the forehead, then turned and walked away without looking back, her shoes click-click-clicking on the tile floor in the empty cafeteria.

● ● ● ● ●

The world was wrapped in a layer of Saran Wrap so thick Sarabeth could barely see through it to drive the 70 miles of winding farm roads from Louisville back home to Brewster. The pinky and ring fingers on her left hand had gone completely numb while she was talking to Billy Joe. And the dull pain of twin ear aches thudded with every heartbeat. Stress. Rhymes with MS. Well, sort of.

She left work early, after spending a few hours holed up in her office, went home and found Ben holed up, too. He was locked in his room and wouldn't talk to her. Never before in their relationship had he completely shut her out, and she felt lost and powerless.

The phone rang for the third time in half an hour as she sat in the porch swing trying to relax, and she almost didn't answer it. The first two had been anonymous callers who'd gloated about Ben's arrest and then hung up. If this was another heckler ...

It was Billy Joe.

"Can you come over tonight?" His voice was hoarse, like he'd been crying. "You and ... the police. Just to talk, that's all. I need to know what you want me to do."

She said she'd be there.

Sonny wasn't in his office when she called him, so she left a message with his secretary.

"Tell him Tecumseh just hit one out of the ballpark. Tell him to meet me at 7:30 tonight at Billy Joe Reynolds' house, and to bring Darrell Hayes."

Billy Joe opened the door for Sarabeth before the chime of his doorbell completed its elaborate song.

"Everybody else is already here," he told her. She put her arms around him and pulled him close but it was like hugging a tent pole. Then he turned and ushered her into the huge living room that swept across the whole front side of his house. The room was lit by a crystal chandelier, had a grand piano by the door and a marble fireplace on the far wall.

Detective Hayes sat in a big, overstuffed chair beside a leather couch.

Sonny sat on the couch next to Seth McAllister! The sheriff must have caught the look of shock Sarabeth's face registered when she saw Seth.

"I asked him to come," Sonny said.

"What for?" Her voice croaked like a pond frog. Of course, she'd never asked Sonny. She'd wanted to so often, almost got the words out a time or two. But she'd never managed to summon the proper casual tone to inquire, "Oh, by the way, Sonny, that list of known dopers—it wouldn't happen to have Seth McAllister's name on it, would it?"

Truth was, she'd been afraid to ask, too, because she feared Seth's name wasn't on the list—and by asking, she'd tip Sonny off that it *should be*. The man was obviously subsidizing his distillery's finances with money from somewhere.

"Seth has information that bears on what we came here to talk about tonight," Sonny told her. "Have a seat, Sarabeth, and hear him out." She sank down into a chair opposite Hayes and stared unblinking at Seth.

Sonny turned to him. "You're on, pal."

"Your newspaper certainly gets around, Sarabeth" Seth said, and then he told all of them his story. Everyone in the room was riveted by his account. As he described marijuana operations in Mississippi, Minnesota, Kansas and Texas, the realization that she might have been mistaken about him was totally eclipsed by the enormity of what he had discovered.

"Who else knows about this?" Hayes asked Sonny as soon as Seth finished. "Have you talked to the U.S. Attorney's office or the DEA?"

"Thanks to three clogged-up crappers, I haven't had a chance to talk to anybody, including the officers involved in these busts," Sonny said. "Soon as I've got long distance service back, I'll find out the specifics of these cases. I'm going to make sure this is what it looks like it is before I call in the feds."

"It *is* what it looks like it is," Billy Joe said softly. It was the first time he had spoken and all the others turned and looked at him. He sat on the piano bench by the door, silently drumming his fingers on the shiny black wood.

They couldn't see it, of course, but Billy Joe could. It was blue, bright blue, the electric blue of Kelsey's eyes, and it divided the room right smack down the middle. He was on one side of it; everyone else was on the other side.

The line.

He remembered the question Sarabeth had asked him in the hospital cafeteria that morning. He had thought about nothing else all day.

"What if you'd said no?"

There had to be a time, she'd told him, when someone—maybe it was Bubba Jamison—talked you into growing dope. And you said yes. How would your life be different now if you'd said no?

Time to cross the line.

His next words would put him permanently out of the marijuana business. Likely sign him up to be a guest of the state for a few years as well, maybe for longer than a few years. And Billy Joe had no illusions about what Bubba Jamison would do to him if he found out Billy Joe had gone belly-up.

He glanced around the room. Looked at his *stuff*. And it meant nothing to him. It almost seemed transparent somehow, like dawn haze on the river before the sun cleared the top of the knob and burned it all away.

Billy Joe stood and walked slowly across the room. He paused for a moment before he put his foot across what the others couldn't see. Then he took a single step.

"That national organization thing, it explains a lot," he said. "I could give you the names of a lot of the people involved in it. I know, 'cause I trained 'em for Bubba."

He took another couple of steps and settled himself on the fat arm of the chair where Sarabeth sat. She reached out and patted his knee as he spoke. "It started for me one night after I found cardboard in Kelsey's shoes." He looked down at Sarabeth and his voice got thick. "That's when I decided to say yes."

Into the silence that followed, Billy Joe turned his life wrong side out. He told it all, vomited the whole story out like a dog chucking up bad meat. He described how Bubba had stopped him in the parking lot of Squire Boone's Tavern that night, and outlined his rise through the ranks of the big man's organization since. It was a fascinating look into an amazingly complex world, and both the law enforcement officers were stunned by the wealth of information he was providing.

"I never could figure out why Bubba needed so many farm hands," Billy Joe said. "And it struck me odd at the time that several of those fellas kept asking questions 'bout raising dope by the acre. Shoot, we haven't been able to do that in this county for years." He smiled a rueful smile at the two officers. "Thanks to you guys."

When Billy Joe finished his story, there was absolute silence.

Then Sonny turned to Seth. "I guess it's time to connect some dots," he said.

"Yeah, I guess it is." Seth looked at Sarabeth but before he could speak she gasped.

"Daddy's national story!" Her eyes were huge. "Daddy said the story would bring the press here from *all over the country!*"

She looked at Sonny. "He found out, didn't he? Somehow, Daddy found out what Bubba Jamison was doing and—"

"Bubba killed him to shut him up." Sonny finished for her. Sarabeth looked like he'd slapped her.

Billy Joe felt sick. Uncle Jim! He reached over and put his arm around his cousin's shoulders.

"He murdered my father to kill Daddy's story," she said slowly. "He's trying to send my brother to prison to shut *me* up." Then Billy Joe watched her anguish morph into a defiant rage he'd never seen in Sarabeth before. "Well, it won't work. He won't silence *me*. He's *not* going to get away with it!"

"No, he isn't." Billy Joe said. He squeezed Sarabeth's shoulders. "The answer's yes, I'll help. No more bodies. It stops here, now. Tell me what you want me to do."

"Testify against Bubba in federal court," Sonny said. "I can't speak for the U.S. Attorney's office, of course, but I'm sure they'd be willing to work out some kind of immunity for you in exchange for your cooperation."

"What good does it do *Ben* to take Bubba down for running some massive national dope ring?" Sarabeth leaned toward Sonny. "And what evidence is there to link Bubba to my father's murder? There's got to be more to it than just B.J.'s testimony."

Detective Hayes spoke for the first time. The pale detective used one finger to push his wire-rimmed glasses up on his nose, and asked Billy Joe matter-of-factly, "Would you be willing to wear a wire?"

"You mean a recording thing, to ...?" Billy Joe hesitated, then looked into Sarabeth's upturned face. "If that's what you need me to do, I'll do it."

"I'll have to set it up with the state police lab in Frankfort, maybe work with the DEA. I'll need a little while to plan out the logistics. But what I'm thinking is we rig Billy Joe with a wire, then he gets Bubba to talk about Ben and Jim Bingham."

"How am I supposed to do *that*?" Billy Joe looked from Hayes to Sonny and back to Hayes. "Sounds to me like neither one of you ever met Bubba Jamison. 'Cause if you had, you'd know he's not exactly ... chatty."

Sonny looked dubious, but Hayes was determined.

"I'll coach you. There are ways to initiate the kinds of conversations we need ..." He stopped. "Look, we can talk about the *how* later on. Right now we just need to stack hands on the *what*."

He looked at Billy Joe. "You in?"

"Yeah, I'm in." Billy Joe tried to sound more confident than he felt. "I'll wear the wire and do my best to get Bubba to say something we can hang him with."

Hayes sat back with a satisfied smile and addressed the others. "One more thing—it's going to take me a few days to set all this up, so what was said in this room tonight has to stay in this room, agreed?" He looked pointedly at Sarabeth, Seth and Billy Joe. They each nodded.

Then he turned to Sonny. "Can you hold off until the first of next week calling those officers to verify what Seth found out?"

"I can."

"Good," Hayes said. "'Cause the last thing we need is for Bubba Jamison to get wind we're on to him."

Chapter 23

Sarabeth had just left for work the morning after the meeting at Billy Joe's house when Ben heard a knock at the front door. He hadn't been up very long, had hardly slept at all. He was definitely *not* in the mood to make nice with some starched-shirt Jehovah's Witness.

When he swung the door open, there stood Jake Jamison. He was dirty, unshaven and smelled of campfire smoke.

"Can I come in?"

Ben reached out and unhooked the screen. When Jake stepped past him into the house, Ben grimaced. "I was going to ask if you wanted a bowl of cereal, but maybe you'd like to take a shower first. You smell worse than the sock hamper in the gym locker room."

"Ben, don't." Jake halted just inside the door. "Stop pretending everything's fine and dandy between us. It's not. I know it's my fault and I came here to make it right."

"Came here from … ?"

"The mountains, the Smokies. I bailed that night after what happened at the barn. I went out into the woods, had to be by myself to think. It wasn't just about you, either. Jennifer said something, told me something."

He doesn't know!

"You haven't been home, have you?"

"Do I look like I've been home? Do I smell like it? I came straight here because I wanted you to know you're not in trouble anymore. Neither one of us is."

"Let's sit down and talk," Ben said.

Jake plopped on the couch and Ben sat next to him.

"Jake, you need to know—the police asked who hired me to work in the barn and I wouldn't tell them. I never mentioned your name; you're in the clear."

Jake actually smiled, a sad, tired smile. "Well, you don't have to keep your mouth shut anymore. You don't have anybody to protect. I'm going to the police and tell them exactly what happened."

"And that was?"

"My father wanted you busted in a dope barn." Jake's voice was deep and rumbling. Ben could hear the rage in it. "He tricked me into getting you there. When I dared to question what he wanted, he cold-cocked me."

"That shiner. You didn't run into a cabinet door."

"And I believed him." Jake hung his head, leaned forward and rested his elbows on his knees. "I never should have trusted a word out of his mouth."

"He's your father. Hard to get your mind around a man who'd use his own son."

"You lie to yourself because the truth is too hard to look at." His voice was soft. "You pretend you don't see. You live with so much deception that after awhile you believe it's reality." He turned and looked into Ben's eyes and his voice was ragged. "But I swear, I *swear* I didn't *know!*"

Ben wasn't sure exactly what it was Jake didn't know.

"Some things you can't do anything about, though, can't go back and do it all over again different." Jake sat up and squared his shoulders. "But some things you can fix, and you have to be a man and fix those."

He turned to Ben. "I'm going to the police. I'm going to tell them what Daddy did to you, how he tricked both of us. I'm going to tell them everything I know about my father." Jake paused. "*Everything!*" He leaned toward Ben and continued in a low, urgent voice. "There's more than you know, more than you could ever imagine!"

He smiled. "And his empire's going down with him. Daddy keeps meticulous records—names, dates, places, money—about all his business dealings, both legal and illegal. I've seen the secret books. I know where they're locked up and I know where he keeps the key."

"Jake, you can't do that! If you turned your father in, Bubba would—"

Kill you.

Jennifer.

"Jake, I've got something to tell you."

"What?" Jake sounded exasperated. What could possibly be more important to talk about?

"It's about your sister, something Jennifer did Monday morning."

"Monday? So soon?" Jake looked confused. "And how would you know anything about that?"

Now Ben was confused. "About what?"

"About the abortion."

"Abortion?"

"Jennifer was pregnant." Jake looked away. "She told me about it Sunday night and I couldn't deal with ... what she said. She wasn't going to have the baby, already had it all planned out. But I didn't know she was going to get an abortion *the next day!*"

Jake stopped abruptly and looked at Ben. "How could you possibly know about Jennifer's abortion?"

Ben was shook. There was no easy way to say it.

"Jake, Jennifer didn't get an abortion." He paused for a beat, then said as gently as he knew how. "She killed herself."

Jake's face went pale. He looked like Ben had slugged him in the belly. "No." Just the one word. A whisper. Then he shook his head to match the word. "No! See, she told me she wasn't going to have the baby, that she had a plan ..." he said the next words slowly, in dawning understanding " ... to get rid of it."

"Jake, I'm so sorry."

Jake was dizzy. Sick. Dark, ugly thoughts he could see but couldn't manage to think fluttered around in his head like angry bats.

"*No!*" This time he roared the word. "You're wrong, it's not true!" He leapt to his feet. "She was fine when I saw her Sunday night."

No, she wasn't! She wasn't fine at all. She hadn't been fine in years. How could she be? And he had just skated through life right next to her without bothering to look over and notice she was bleeding.

"Killed herself?" he whispered.

"She and Kelsey Reynolds drove down to Old Joe's Hole early Monday morning and shot themselves. Kelsey survived. But Jennifer ... "

"Jennifer's dead."

Ben nodded.

Jake collapsed onto the couch, put his head in his hands but didn't cry, just let it sink in, the reality that he wasn't going to be able to make it all up to her like he'd planned.

Jake had spent hours staring into a flickering campfire. He'd have sworn the dancing light had altered the pattern of synapses in his brain somehow, had rearranged the electrical current so he wasn't just emotionally or psychologically changed but actually *physically* transformed, a completely different human being on a fundamental, cellular level.

"I was going to sit her down, talk to her," he said. Not to Ben. He was barely aware of Ben's presence. "Oh, she was hard to talk to, but I was going to get through to her. Convince her I understood *why* ... I was going to tell her my plan."

He turned to Ben.

"I'm not going to UK in a couple of weeks. I joined the Marines."

Ben sat back in surprise.

"Daddy thinks he's in charge, that he gets to decide where I go to college and whether I play ball there." The rage he felt was so huge it threatened to explode out his chest in a fireball that would consume him and Ben, too. "Well, my father doesn't make the rules for me anymore! That's over. *Forever!* I'm 18 years old. I don't need anybody's permission to enlist. I signed the papers at the recruiting center in Elizabethtown yesterday. I report to boot camp in two weeks."

He threw his head back and barked out a sound that was half laugh, half anguished wail. "Bubba Jamison can't cow *the United States Marine Corps!*"

Then the triumph drained out of him.

"I was going to take her away," he whispered. "Soon as I got out of basic, I was going to send for her. I was going to get her away from here, away from him, help her start over somewhere fresh."

He looked at Ben and his voice broke. "Now she's dead, and it's Daddy's fault, because he—"

He couldn't go *there*. Couldn't tell Ben what Jennifer had seen and what the seeing had done to her. Not now. Not yet.

He started to cry, great heaving sobs that shook his body like seizures. Time slid off the tracks and lay on its side in the ditch. He didn't know when Sarabeth showed up. Jake sat between her and Ben on the couch, felt their comforting arms around him, and cried until he was empty and exhausted.

When he was done, Ben handed him a dish towel to wipe his face.

"I went high up in the mountains," he said, his voice hoarse from crying. "Walked for hours. At night, the stars were so bright you could reach out and pluck a bouquet of them. And I understood things there, looked some things in the eye."

He turned to Sarabeth. "I'm going to fix it for Ben."

He loved watching relief flood her face when he told her what had happened with Ben and the barn, and how he planned to explain it all to the police. They'd believe him, too, when he gave them chapter and verse about his father's dope operation, and gave them proof.

"Visitation for Jennifer is at Beddingfield's Funeral Home, starting this morning at 10," Sarabeth said. "Ben will go with you; I'll stay as long as I can. And you'll be eating with us and sleeping here tonight."

Jake started to speak but she cut him off.

"You're not going to spend another night in that house with that man ever again!" She reached out and took his hand. "There are things I can't talk about. But this is going to get ugly real soon. Just know that we're in it with you. You're family, Thing Two. We're all going to get through this together."

Sarabeth had to get back to work, and as soon as she was gone, Jake turned to Ben. "I'm going home," he said, and raised his hand to ward off Ben's protest. "For a little while. I didn't want to upset Sarabeth, but I have to gather up some things. And I need to take a shower and get cleaned up for the … "

"If you're going out there, I'm going with you," Ben said.

• • • • •

The phone rang as Billy Joe was rounding up the last of what Becky had said she needed. By the time the state police arrived at their house Monday morning to tell them about Kelsey, the girl had already been airlifted to Norton Hospital. They'd thrown on clothes and gone barreling up to Louisville.

It was Wednesday morning now and he hadn't slept more than a couple of hours here and a couple there since Sunday night. He tried to concentrate, wished he'd written down what Becky wanted. Besides a change of clothes, she'd said she needed—

The phone interrupted his thought. It was probably Becky, knowing he wouldn't get it right, calling to remind him what she'd said. It wasn't Becky. It was Bubba Jamison.

All the air went out of Billy Joe when he heard the big man's rumbling voice, and he sat down hard on the arm of the couch.

"Billy Joe? That you, boy? I need to see you. Now, this morning."

"Bubba, I'm on my way to Louisville. Kelsey's in ... " Then he thought about Jennifer. His daughter was still alive; Bubba's wasn't. "Hey, Bubba, I'm sorry 'bout Jennifer. I don't understand why they would—"

"That's what I want to see you about. Jennifer left a note. I just found it this morning and I thought you'd want to see it."

"Does she say why, does it explain what they—?"

"It says a lot of things, and a bunch of it is about your little girl." Billy Joe stifled a gasp. "It's somthin' you need to see, Billy Joe. My Jenny's dead," Billy Joe could have sworn the big man's voice broke, "but your little girl's still got a chance. It ain't gonna be easy for you to read this, but if I was you, I'd want to know."

"I'm coming right over," Billy Joe said, hung up the phone and headed out the door.

Bubba put the receiver back on the cradle and smiled at the man seated across from him.

"He's on his way," Bubba said.

Billy Joe knew something was wrong as soon as Bubba opened the door. He had seen that look on the big man's face before, that sort of amused, evil look that said he knew something you didn't, and when you found out what it was you weren't gonna like it.

"Why, come on in Billy Joe."

When Billy Joe stepped past him into the house, Bubba shut the door with a resounding thump, turned and headed for his living room.

Billy Joe's mouth went dry. "I gotta get on up to Louisville to take some things to Becky, so if I could just see that note."

Bubba sat down in his big leather chair, picked up a pistol off the coffee table in front of him, and a cloth, and began slowly wiping the barrel with it.

"What note?"

The bottom fell out of Billy Joe's stomach. He tried to sound casual, but he couldn't. His voice trembled. "You said you found a note that Jennifer left."

"There ain't no note, Billy Joe." Bubba continued to wipe down the gun in his hand.

"Then why'd you tell me there was?"

"I wanted you to come over here without a fuss. 'Cause you and me, we got business to discuss, important business."

"You could have just told me you wanted to talk." Billy Joe hated the false good humor he could hear in his own voice. "You know I'd a'come right over."

"Yeah, but I wanted to talk to you without you being all wired up with recording equipment to take down everythin' I say."

Billy Joe couldn't breathe. "I don't know what you're—"

"My friend here tells me you're all set to turn me in."

Bubba cocked his head toward the kitchen door and Billy Joe turned. Leaning against the door jam, with his arms crossed and a smirk on his face, was Kentucky State Police Detective Darrell Hayes.

Billy Joe went white.

"Darrell says you and that newspaper editor, Seth McAllister and Sheriff Tackett got it all figured out that I'm running some kind of national marijuana business, that right, Darrell?"

Billy Joe looked from one to the other of them, his eyes huge.

Hayes said nothing, just nodded.

"And the four of you come to the conclusion that I killed Jim Bingham 'cause he found out about it, that the way it was, Darrell?"

"That's the way it was, Bubba," Hayes said.

"And you know what, B.J.?" Bubba paused and looked dead into Billy Joe's eyes. "You was right on both counts! I got me a national organization like nothing you ever dreamed of." He dropped the cloth on the table. "And I put a bullet in Jim Bingham, too."

He suddenly pointed the gun at Billy Joe's chest.

"Bang!" he said. "Just like that."

"Bubba, I never—"

"Never what?" Bubba roared. The cat-and-mouse game was over. "Don't you tell me you never! I know what you done, you and the rest of 'em, and I know what you're gonna do now. You're gonna help me fix it so don't none of your schemes work out like you planned."

Bubba stood up. "Git goin'." He gestured with the gun toward the front door. "We got some serious talking to do and this ain't the place to do it."

• • • • •

The dogs started barking and Bubba froze. He was in the workshop in the garage with Hayes and Billy Joe, who was tied to a chair with duct tape. The big man held his breath, listening. In a few seconds, he could hear the sound of a vehicle coming up the driveway.

Bubba went to the window and watched his son drive up in front of the house. Ben Malone was with him, and a big smile spread over Bubba's face when he saw him.

The two boys got out of the Jeep. Even though the red-headed kid had been to the house often enough that the dogs knew him, each gave him a good sniff before wandering away.

"If they come out toward the garage, I'll head 'em off," Bubba told Hayes. "But they won't." As far as the boys could tell, nobody was home. Hayes always left his cruiser deep in the woods whenever he paid a visit, and he had stashed Billy Joe's Chevy Silverado in one of the empty bays in the garage.

Bubba didn't have a truck. Not anymore.

The image instantly filled up the big man's mind. Between one eye-blink and the next, the sight appeared crisp and clear before him—more real than the rough wood walls of the workshop. The copper smell of blood was stronger than the aroma of sawdust in the workshop, too.

Bubba had gone down to Ole Joe's Hole Monday afternoon. There had still been a good-sized crowd of gawkers there, a couple of troopers, too, keeping folks away from the area cordoned off with yellow Police Line tape. One of them recognized Bubba and nodded. Bubba ignored him and everybody else, ducked under the tape and walked up to his black Ford Bronco parked on the river-bank. Both doors stood open. As soon as he got near it, he could see blood. So much blood. Smeared …

He moved the final few steps to the truck like a man in a trance. Stunned. Stood transfixed, staring in the driver's side door at the blood. And the *words* on the windshield! Vomit rose up in his throat and the struggle to keep from throwing up was so intense it brought tears to his eyes. He swallowed once, twice. Then he whirled around and hollered out at the crowd.

"Anybody want a truck?"

Everyone turned to look at him, but nobody responded.

"I'm serious. This here's my truck. Anybody want it?"

Several voices called out tentatively.

"Yeah, I want it!"

"Sure, I'll take it."

Bubba reached into his pocket for his keys and fairly yanked the spare off his keychain. The on-lookers realized he meant it then and everybody started hollering. He picked out a farmer in bib overalls with a shiny bald head and a plug of snuff lying like a banana under his bottom lip. Bubba marched over to him and held out the key.

"You serious?" the farmer asked.

"I'll be in the clerk's office next Monday morning at nine o'clock to sign it over to you," Bubba told the man and dropped the key into his outstretched hand. "Be there."

Then he'd turned and walked away.

Bubba squeezed his eyes shut and shook his head violently, like he'd done to get the sweat off his face the day he'd set Daisy on the squirrel hunter. When he opened his eyes, the images from the riverbank were gone. He breathed in—nothing but the smell of sawdust.

He turned back to the window in time to watch Ben and Jake disappear into the house. He hadn't seen Jake since Saturday night and had no idea where the boy had been. But he'd find out. Yes siree, he would most certainly find out.

About half an hour later, the boys emerged. Jake was dressed in a suit and tie. They got into Jake's Jeep and drove away. As soon as the automatic gate closed behind them, Bubba left the window and went to stand in front of Billy Joe.

"I got to go see to my little girl now," he said. "And you're gonna wait here for me. When I get back, I'm gonna throw a little party for some mutual friends."

Billy Joe just looked up at him, eyes big, like a doe waiting to get shot. Bubba loved to see that look on a man's face!

"I need for you to make sure all my guests show up, so you're going to call that cousin of yours, that Bingham woman. I'll tell you what I want you to say."

"I'm not getting Sarabeth all messed up in this," Billy Joe said.

"Oh, but she already is. She done stuck her nose in where it don't belong." He cocked his head toward Hayes. "Darrell here's gonna stay and keep you company, make sure you don't get lonesome 'til I get back."

"You really don't want to make this any harder on yourself than you have to, Billy Joe," Hayes said and pushed his glasses up on his nose. "Nobody's going to get out of this, not you, Sarabeth, Seth McAllister or Sonny Tackett."

"You don't really think you can get away with killing the sheriff, the editor of the newspaper, and the owner of Double Springs, do you?"

"And you," Hayes put in.

"And me. That's insane."

"Now, Billy Joe, don't you be calling me crazy," Bubba said

casually. Then he slammed the back of his hand into Billy Joe's face. Blood instantly spurted from his smashed nose and split lip. "I ain't crazy. But *you are* if you don't do what I tell you to do."

Bubba leaned over Billy Joe, so close he could smell the fear sweat. "While I'm gone, you need to think about being hurt. Not just a bloody nose. I'm talking about pain that makes a man scream and beg. You cooperate with me and you die easy; you don't and I'll make you plead with me to kill you."

Chapter 24

When Jake and Ben got to the funeral home before the doors were opened for the visitation, Mr. Saunders told them that Bubba had come down the day before.

"Your daddy said he wanted the best casket I had, didn't care what it cost," Saunders said. "He picked out the most expensive one in the building. Paid cash for it, too."

The casket was not like the dignified silver one Sarabeth had selected for her father. Jennifer's casket looked like a sarcophagus fit for an Egyptian princess, with gaudy gold trim, and hand-painted detail on the sides that Ben thought looked like racing stripes. He wasn't sure, but he didn't think Jake much liked the casket.

Jake hated the casket; it was *obscene.*

Think if you put her in a pretty gold box that'll fix everything? An expensive casket for your little girl's dead body will make up for what you did, for what you turned her into?

Jake's rage was a ferocious beast that paced back and forth in his guts, roaring and growling, threatening to take over his soul as well as his mind and heart.

The only thing that saved him from the beast was overload. All his circuits were fried. Grief, shock, despair, hatred, regret—all tumbled around inside him like clothes in a dryer as he sat in the uncomfortable, too-small chair beside Jennifer's casket.

He actually sensed it when his father came into the room. It was like there was a power, an intimidation in the bulk of his presence that sent out ripples in the air. Jake looked up and Bubba was standing in the big double doorway, looking at him.

Bubba just stood there, apparently expecting Jake to come to him. When Jake didn't, he came to Jake, crossed the room and stopped in front of where Jake was seated.

"Where you been, boy?" It was a simple question, no emotion.

Jake didn't rise, just looked up at his father. "I was in the mountains, the Smokies. I got back this morning."

"You know what happened to your sister?" Again, a simple question.

"I know she killed herself." Jake heard the hard edge of anger in his voice and knew his father could hear it there, too. And he didn't care! With a instant, incredible elation, he realized he wasn't afraid! "And I know *why* she killed herself, too."

Bubba just looked at him, his eyes so dark and deep it was impossible to read his reaction. If Jake'd had to guess, he'd have said his father was probably confused.

"Then you know more'n I know." Bubba paused, waited for Jake to reply. "You gonna tell me, or not?" And for the first time, there was the familiar rumble of disapproval, like a low-power electric shock, in his words.

"Yeah, Daddy, I'll tell you," Jake said, and he felt Ben stiffen at the venom in his words. "Not here and not now, but I absolutely *will* tell you."

"Fair 'nough."

Bubba turned and walked away.

Ben let out a breath he'd obviously been holding and whispered, "Poke a tiger with a stick once too often and it'll bite your hand off."

Jake was barely able to keep his own voice a whisper. "He ever lays a hand on me, ever touches me again, and I'll kill him."

He turned to Ben, looked him in the eye. "Believe this, Ben—if you ever believed anything I've ever said, believe this—I will *kill* him."

"I believe you, Jake. I just don't want him to kill you first."

For most of the morning, there were only a handful of people at the visitation at any given time. Lots of kids from the high school came in the beginning. After all, Jake was a big football star, even if his father was a doper.

Sarabeth came in alone on her lunch break and sat down beside Ben. She nodded toward Bubba.

"That man is a cobra," she said quietly, "and he's looking at us like we're mice."

Bubba had an odd, unpleasant half-smile on his face. Then he turned abruptly and walked out of the room. It wasn't even noon, and the visitation wasn't set to be over until 2:30.

As soon as Bubba left, Sarabeth got up and knelt in front of Jake. She took both his hands in hers. "How you doing, Thing Two, you going to be alright?"

"Yeah, I'll be fine."

Jake saw Ben and Sarabeth exchange a glance.

"I need to get back to the office now, but I'll see you boys at supper tonight. Ok?" She stood and patted Jake's shoulder.

Ben and Jake watched her walk away and then sat there, just the two of them, the room almost empty, waiting for the ordeal to be over, waiting because it was the respectful thing to do for Jennifer.

"What was it like in jail?" Jake asked. His was more than a simple curiosity. Though he was operating under the assumption that if he told the police the truth, they'd believe him, there was always the chance they wouldn't. Something could go south. If he admitted he'd been in that barn with Ben, he just might end up in jail, too.

"It sucked. Smelled like pee. Roaches the size of chipmunks. The six hours I spent in that cell felt like three days."

"What did you do?"

"I cried."

Jake groaned. "Hey, man, I'm sorry."

Ben looked like he was embarrassed he'd blurted that out. He cleared his throat and shifted directions. "Most of the time I was sitting there trying to figure out how that guy hung himself in that cell."

"What guy?"

"One of the men who kidnapped the little Davis girl, the one Sarabeth said was going to testify against ... " Ben stopped. "He was going to tell who he and his buddies worked for."

"And it was my father, right?"

Ben nodded, then told Jake what Sarabeth had told him about Doodlebug, described how he had gone to the jail that morning with Sarabeth, processed the film and printed the picture of the EMT for the front page.

"I saw the pictures that didn't run in the newspaper, too, the ones that nobody else saw. Pictures of him hanging there. And something about them just didn't look right. Anyway, I didn't have anything better to do for six hours, so I sat there on the bunk trying to figure out how he did it."

"And did you?"

"No. I tried, but I couldn't come up with any way it could have worked. There were two chairs in the room, both the same size. I stood on one of them and I could barely reach up high enough to put something over that pipe. Doodlebug was a short dude, like 5 feet 5, so how did *he* do it?"

"Well, he must have come up with a way, 'cause he's dead." Jake said.

"Yep, he's dead, and now he can't test ..."

Jake finished for him. "Testify against my father."

Then they were silent. A few people came; others left. The room emptied out.

Jake stood up. He was done, finished. He couldn't sit there another minute.

"I gotta get out of here." His voice was edgy, almost frantic.

"I'll tell Mr. Saunders to close up, that the visitation's over early," Ben said. "We'll go to my house and—"

"I don't want to go to your house.

"Jake, we've already been over this, you can't go home."

"I want to go to the newspaper office."

"What for?"

"To look at those pictures of the guy who hanged himself."

"Why?"

"Because I … oh, I don't have a reason. I just do, Ok? Humor me."

Jake was scrambling for something to occupy his mind, anything to keep from thinking about …

Ben must have picked up on the edge of desperation in Jake's voice because he merely shrugged and said, "Let's do it."

When the boys got to the *Trib* office, Sarabeth wasn't there and Harmony only knew that she'd gotten a phone call and rushed out of the building saying she'd be back before five o'clock.

The boys went into the darkroom and as Ben thumbed through the pile of old contact sheets, he explained the process to Jake. "A cassette holds about 36 inches of film. After I develop it, I cut the negatives into strips of six frames each, lay four or five strips down side-by-side on a piece of photographic paper and make a contact sheet of negative-sized pictures. Then Sarabeth looks at it and picks out which frames she wants me to print into photographs to use in the newspaper."

"So most of what she shoots is never actually made into a full-sized photograph?"

"That's right." Ben found the contact sheet he'd been looking for with the negatives in a paper sleeve stapled to it. He pointed to a tiny picture of an EMT's face, grimacing with effort. "Sarabeth knew this was the shot she was going to use. She barely glanced at the rest of them."

Jake studied the sheet of tiny pictures. "So what didn't look right about these?"

285

"I don't know, exactly. You know how something's just wrong, but you can't quite put your finger on what it is?"

"Why don't you make full-sized prints of all these negatives? Maybe we could figure it out if we could see them bigger."

He saw Ben start to protest, then relax. "Sure. Why not?"

Half an hour later, the boys were looking at the 15 shots Sarabeth had taken in the jail that day. Some were wide-angle shots that showed everything, including Doodlebug's body, the chair and the EMTs trying to get him down. Two were horrific close-ups of the man's face with the belt cutting into his neck. Another couple showed the EMTs trying to unfasten the belt with the buckle between the pipe and the ceiling.

Nothing struck Jake as odd about any of them.

"You said you stood on the chair," he mused out loud, "and you could barely reach up over the ceiling pipe?"

Ben nodded. He was staring intently at the pictures.

"But I guess you wouldn't have to reach all the way up. You could shove the belt through from below and fasten it, then scoot it so the buckle was on top of the pipe. But why would you bother to do that?"

"How long would you say that belt is?" Ben said, pointing to a full-body shot of Doodlebug hanging from the pipe.

"I don't know, but it's barely long enough to go around his fat neck and up over the pipe."

"Doodlebug's waist was huge! His belt would have been long—45, 50 inches—maybe longer," Ben said. "That can't be Doodlebug's belt; it's too short!"

"Well, if it's not his belt, whose is it? And how did he get it to kill himself with?"

In the greenish glow of the safe light, Jake could see Ben's eyes open wide with growing excitement.

"Somebody gave him that belt. Somebody helped him rig it up and fastened it at the top because he wasn't tall enough to do it. Somebody helped him commit suicide."

Jake thought of something that turned his skin cold.

"Tell me again about going to the jail that day with your sister."

So Ben told the whole story again. "… and the jailer didn't want to be blamed for Doodlebug's suicide so he made Detective Hayes admit he couldn't see whether Doodlebug had on a belt or not when he'd been in Doodlebug's cell the night before."

"Detective Hayes is that albino-looking guy, tall and skinny, right?"

Ben's response was quiet. "With a thin little waist."

Their eyes met.

"Ok, reality check. Are we saying a Kentucky State Police detective helped a prisoner commit suicide so he couldn't testify against your father?"

"Yeah, that's what we're saying." Jake's voice was hard and cold.

"That's nuts."

"You got that right! It's nuts. But what other explanation is there?"

Ben was silent. When he spoke, his voice sounded hard, too. "Soon as these pictures dry, we'll take them to my house and see what Sarabeth says about them when she comes home to supper. Maybe there's a perfectly reasonable explanation we didn't think of."

But Ben's sister didn't come home to supper that night.

● ● ● ● ●

Billy Joe had sounded funny. Sarabeth couldn't put her finger on exactly what wasn't right, but there was something. He'd assured her that he was fine, but she wasn't convinced.

His call had come in about an hour after she'd gotten back to her office from the funeral home.

"Sarabeth, it's Billy Joe," said the voice on the other end of the line when she picked up the receiver. He sounded breathy, and why'd he identify himself? Like she wouldn't recognize his voice.

"I found something at Bubba's."

"You went to *Bubba's?* What for?"

"He called me, said he'd found Jennifer's suicide note and that it talked about Kelsey."

"What did it say?"

"We can talk about that later. That's not why I called. While I was at Bubba's, I found something you and the sheriff have to see."

"What?"

"I can't talk about it over the phone. I had to book it out of there before he realized I'd found it, went out the back way and over the knob. I'm at Double Springs now with Seth. You need to get out here as soon as you can. I'll explain everything when I see you."

Then the line went dead.

Sarabeth had grabbed her purse and camera, told Harmony she'd be back before closing time, and ran to her car. It was cooler outside. A storm was moving in from the west and the wind whipped her hair into her face as she ran.

As she drove the winding roads out to the distillery, she held on tight to her growing excitement, wouldn't let it sweep her away. Instead, she mulled over what Billy Joe had said, tried to put her finger on what it was about it that didn't fit.

He'd just sounded … odd. Like he had a cold and his nose was stopped up. He hadn't had a cold when she saw him last night, at least she didn't remember that he had. And his voice was hoarse and breathy. Of course, if he'd just run all the way from Bubba's over the knob to Double Springs, that would certainly explain being out of breath.

But his voice had sounded tight, too. The pinched way you talk when you just slammed the car door on your thumb. That was it, Billy Joe had sounded like he was in pain. An uneasy chill ran down her spine. He'd just come from Bubba's and he sounded like he was in pain.

That could be explained reasonably, too, though. The run up the knob would put a stitch in your side, for sure. Or maybe he fell, skinned his knee or something.

Her car rumbled across the covered bridge over the Rolling Fork and onto the distillery property. Right away, she noticed that the grounds were empty, the parking lots open and vacant. Then she remembered Seth mentioning that he'd given his staff a week off while he waited for delivery of a new cypress vat. She drove up the steep incline to the distillery on top of the knob. When she pulled into a space in front of the office building beside a beat-up old Chevy pickup truck, she saw Sonny Tackett's cruiser parked next to Detective Hayes' car. She let out a breath and relaxed. The sheriff and the state police were already here.

It wasn't until that moment that she realized how tense she had become. As she walked through the empty reception area, she tried to smooth down her windblown curls. It didn't have anything to do with seeing Seth, of course. The door to Seth's office was closed, so she knocked and turned the knob at the same time.

Seth was seated at his desk. Detective Hayes was perched on the corner of it with his back to her. When he turned around, there was a gun in his hand.

"Welcome to the party, Miss Bingham," said a voice from beside the big bookcase to her left. The world cranked down into slow motion and she turned to face Bubba Jamison. His gun was even bigger than the one Hayes held. Sonny Tackett sat in a nearby chair, with his hands cuffed behind his back. Billy Joe was curled up on the floor beside Sonny's chair. His face was bruised and bloody, his eyes black, his lips and nose smashed. He'd suffered a fierce beating. Then she saw his hands! They were *crushed*, like he'd gotten them caught in some piece of mechanical equipment that had mangled them.

She turned on Bubba,

"What have you done to him?"

As casually as swatting a fly, Bubba stepped forward and backhanded Sarabeth. His huge paw caught her on the side of the face and knocked her against the wall. She hit it with a thud and slid down it to the floor as the world spun around and around like the Tilt-A-Whirl at the state fair.

Through a fog, she watched Seth leap to his feet, saw Hayes shove the barrel of his pistol in Seth's belly.

"Sit down, or your die right here, right now!" Hayes' voice was muffled by the ringing in Sarabeth's ears.

Seth slowly returned to his seat, his eyes blazing holes in Bubba's back.

She struggled to sit up. As soon as she righted herself, her hearing cleared, but she could feel her left eye swelling. Her hand went to her cheek. It was more than just tender. The skin was burning from the slap and there was an ice pick of pain deep in her face, an agony that brought tears to her eyes that gushed down to drip off her chin. She suspected that Bubba Jamison had broken her cheek bone.

Chapter 25

Things were moving along exactly as Bubba had planned.

It had taken awhile to break the Reynolds boy, longer than Bubba had expected. Hayes had beaten him mercilessly before Bubba got back from the visitation, but he still refused to make the call to Sarabeth. Then Bubba'd taken the sledge hammer to him. He'd duct-taped the boy's left hand to the top of an anvil and started smashing his fingers one by one. His screams had echoed in the woodshop, but there was nobody to hear him cry.

When Bubba'd finally crushed his whole hand with one blow, Billy Joe blubbered that he'd do anything Bubba wanted him to do, say anything Bubba wanted him to say. Bubba had strapped his right hand to the anvil then and promised to crush it, too, if he gave even the slightest hint to Sarabeth or the sheriff that they were walking into a trap.

Billy Joe had done fine, just fine. Was totally convincing; neither of them suspected a thing. Then Bubba'd slammed the sledge hammer down on his right hand with all his strength anyway.

Hayes had gotten them in to see Seth with ease. And they'd been waiting there for the sheriff when Sonny showed up half an hour later.

With the nosey newspaper editor in hand, the stage was set and Bubba realized just how much he had been looking forward to killing them.

"I want to thank ya'll for coming to my little surprise party," he said. "I promise you will have the time of your life. The *last* time of your life."

"You don't really think you can get away with this!" Seth was incredulous. "You think you can kill the sheriff and the newspaper editor, Billy Joe Reynolds and me and nobody will notice? You're crazier than everybody says you are."

Bubba almost laughed out loud. "You know, that's exactly what Billy Joe said. Right before he said he'd never call Sarabeth and get her all messed up in this. But as you can see, he was persuaded to make the call."

He casually kicked Billy Joe right in the face, knocking out one of the man's front teeth. Sarabeth screamed, but Billy Joe only groaned. He'd been sliding in and out of consciousness for more than an hour, was likely going into shock.

He turned to Seth. "No, I don't think I can kill all you fine people and nobody will notice. For starters, *I'm* not going to kill anybody." He paused for effect. *"Jimmy Dan Puckett is."*

He crossed to Seth in two huge steps, like a rhinoceros charging. Seth didn't flinch.

"And somebody's gonna notice, all right. Everybody's gonna notice. Your deaths will be the biggest, most-watched event in Callison County history. It will be a spectacle you can see for miles in every direction."

He turned to Sarabeth, sitting silently on the floor, her face swelling so fast you could watch it.

"The big city media's gonna be all over what's about to happen here today. You won't be around to write it, of course, but somebody's gonna have quite a tale to tell."

He turned to Detective Hayes.

"Darrell, why don't you describe for these folks what's gonna show up tomorrow morning on the front page of every newspaper in Kentucky—the sad story of the deaths of three of Callison County's most well-known citizens."

Home Grown

The pale blond detective smiled and began to talk. Bubba watched Sarabeth's face, saw her connect the dots about the scholarly police officer. Her stunned surprise was testimony to how good a job Hayes had done at keeping his cover all these years, being a mole for Bubba, letting him know when and where the busts were going to go down. A man in Bubba's position needed a state police detective on a chain. Not for long, though. Hayes knew too much now. Soon as this business was over, Bubba would get rid of him. An accident, a car wreck, maybe. No, a drowning; the man liked to fish. When he had the time, Bubba would put his mind to it and come up with something credible. The state police detective wouldn't live to see another Christmas.

"A little while ago, I radioed dispatch in Columbia and told them I was going to stop by Double Springs Distillery on my way home," Hayes said. "I said somebody out here claimed they'd seen Jimmy Dan Puckett, the man who shot that poor little Davis girl. It wasn't likely, but I was going to check it out anyway. I said I'd radio back if I found anything." He paused. "But you know how these knobs are." He shrugged his shoulders. "Sometimes you have radio coverage and sometimes you don't."

The normally taciturn Hayes began to warm to the story, waving a pistol in the air when he gestured. It was a small handgun with black electrician's tape covering the handle.

"And when the television news crews shove a microphone in my face, I'll get all choked up talking about it. I'll explain how I came out here, just to check things out, came into the office, but nobody was here. Which struck me as odd, Seth not being in his office and the door unlocked and all."

"So I went over to his house up by the woods. Nobody was there, either. But I did find Sarabeth's car parked in front of it. And I found this."

He reached down and picked up Sarabeth's purse where she had dropped it when Bubba back-handed her.

"And this … "

He used his toe to scoot Sarabeth's camera bag away from her out into the middle of the floor. " ... sitting on the kitchen table." He shoved the bag up next to Seth's desk and placed her purse on top of it.

Then he looked at Seth and smiled. "You'll like this part of the story." He turned back and addressed the others.

"So I called out. 'Seth! Sarabeth!' Nobody answered. I searched the house then, and back in the master bedroom I found the bed all messed up, and these ..."

He pointed to Sarabeth's shoes. "Take them off."

She just looked at him.

He cocked the gun and aimed it at her head and said softly. "You heard me, I said take your shoes off."

Sarabeth reached down, removed her shoes and lifted them up to him. He gestured to the spot where her purse and camera bag leaned against Seth's desk. "Over there."

She tossed the shoes toward her purse. One landed on top, the other beside her camera case.

"Now, being the astute detective that I am, I put it together that Mr. Seth McAllister and Miss Sarabeth Bingham must have been up at his house playing a little game of bump and tickle while the distillery was shut down and nobody was around." He glanced at Seth. "The way you look at her, it's obvious you wish you had been. You should have moved faster, pal. You snooze, you lose."

Then he continued his narrative.

"So if Seth and Sarabeth had been getting it on, where were they? Why'd she leave her purse and shoes and go wandering off somewhere? I get concerned. Sarabeth's a fine, crusading journalist, after all, and a close personal friend and I'm beginning to get worried about her."

He turned to Sonny, who sat as silent as a stone statue, his hands cuffed behind his back. "You're just waiting for a chance to jump me, aren't you, Sonny?" He took a step away from the sheriff as he spoke instead of toward him. "Don't bother. You may be strong, but you're not quick. You'll be dead before you stand all the way up."

He picked up the thread of the story where he left off, now including Sonny in his tale.

"I'm so worried then that I pick up the phone and call my good friend Sheriff Sonny Tackett. I explain the situation. He says he'll be right over. I search the house and the office while I'm waiting, and pretty soon, the sheriff pulls up out front."

He stopped. "You did follow the instructions Billy Joe gave you when he called, right? You didn't tell anybody where you were going or why." The sheriff said nothing, but it was obvious he'd done as he was told.

"The two of us set out to search the rest of the premises. I've got my pistol, the sheriff gets the shotgun out of his cruiser. We check the bottling room and the print shop. Nothing. The barrel warehouses are next and we start on the old ones up here by the office, the Family Five. And we see the catch is undone on the door of the middle one, Flying Ebony. Sonny slides the door open and goes in. I get to the door and then a terrible thing happens. Jimmy Dan Puckett opens fire on us."

Hayes held up the gun in his hand, the one with the taped handle. "With this. And the slugs we dig out of the door on my cruiser where he missed ..." He turned and said coldly to Sonny "... along with the slug we dig out of the sheriff when he *didn't* miss, will match the slug the coroner pulled out of poor little Maggie Mae Davis.

"Jimmy Dan must have broken into Seth's house and interrupted the big man and his girlfriend in the act. He's been on the run, hiding out for more than a week. He had to need money. Maybe he broke in to get something to eat, too. I guess we'll never know for sure why he did it, will we Bubba?"

Bubba took up the story.

"Nope. Nobody will ever know why Jimmy Dan Puckett showed up here today and kidnapped Seth McAllister and Sarabeth Bingham. " His voice was as cold as a stone on the desert floor at night. "Because the only three people who know the whole story—Seth, Sarabeth and Jimmy Dan—won't be around to tell it."

Bubba looked back at Hayes.

"So, suddenly gunshots are flying at us. And that's when my good friend, Sheriff Sonny Tackett, becomes a hero. Yes siree, that's how he'll be remembered. There'll be cops from all over the country at the ceremony. Cops show up at the funerals of other officers killed in the line of duty, you know. And I'll stand up and tell them all what a fine man he was, what a hero he was, how he gave his life to save the life of a fellow officer, died trying—in vain—to save two poor hostages whose only crime was making whoopie in the wrong place at the wrong time.

"You see, when Jimmy Dan starts shooting at us, Sonny turns and shoves me back out the door, out of the line of fire. And that's when he takes a bullet. Drops him right there in the doorway. I reach in and grab him, drag him out, carry him back to my cruiser. Just as I get there, Jimmy Dan starts firing at us both from the warehouse doorway, and when he runs out of bullets with this ..." He waggled the gun with the taped handle. "... he picks up the shotgun the sheriff dropped and starts shooting at us with that."

"And I call out to him, try to get him to give himself up, you see, but he won't listen. Says he killed a kid and he'll get the death penalty. Him holding hostages and all, I can't very well return his fire. I mean, the man's in a warehouse full of *alcohol*. I can't very well shoot into it! I get my car door open and call for backup. But dang it! You know how hit and miss the coverage is. The signal just won't go through. So I do the only thing I can do. I get the sheriff into my cruiser, hunker down low behind the wheel and I drive away to get help." He sighed. "But, unfortunately, Sonny doesn't make it."

Bubba took up the story then, his face alive and animated. "But when Detective Hayes does what he has to do to save the life of the poor, injured sheriff, he leaves Jimmy Dan behind in the warehouse with his two hostages."

Hayes smiled. "And as I'm driving down the hill, I hear gunfire from inside Flying Ebony. Don't know what's happening. Maybe

Seth's trying to get the shotgun. Maybe he and Sarabeth are making a run for it. Or maybe Jimmy Dan's just executing his hostages. No way to tell—"

"Because all that shooting with the sheriff's shotgun ... " Bubba leaned over toward Seth and watched his face when he whispered the words. " ... *starts a fire!*"

Bubba relished the wave of horror that washed over Seth's face.

"And the fire burns so hot there's not a trace left of Jimmy Dan Puckett, Seth McAllister or Sarabeth Bingham. Or of another body that'll just vanish." Bubba caught Hayes' eye and winked. "Why, people'll probably wonder out loud about it for years. 'Ain't it odd,' they'll say, 'that Billy Joe Reynolds disappeared and was never heard from or seen again on the very same day ...'" he paused, and hissed out the rest in a rush of triumph "'... the historic Double Springs Distillery burned all the way down to the ground.'"

Chapter 26

Hayes and Bubba herded the hostages out of Seth's office at gunpoint, with Seth carrying Billy Joe.

Sarabeth expected that they'd all be marched down the road to the huge barrel warehouse for the mythical gunfight with the equally mythical kidnapper. Where was Jimmy Dan Puckett, anyway? How had Hayes gotten his gun?

But they weren't taken to the warehouse. Bubba motioned with his gun for Seth to dump Billy Joe's unconscious body into the back of the beat-up Chevy pickup parked next to Sarabeth's car. Then he told Seth and Sonny to climb up into the back of the pickup with Billy Joe. Seth had to help Sonny balance because his hands were cuffed behind him.

Bubba turned to Sarabeth and gestured toward the driver's side door. "Get in. You're driving." The wind whipped her hair into her face and even that slight tickling on her cheek was excruciating. She pushed her curls back behind her ears and wordlessly climbed in.

The seat had been adjusted for Bubba's girth and legs. Sarabeth's feet didn't touch the accelerator or the break.

Bubba stomped over to her, leaned in, pushed the lever and shoved the seat forward.

"Put on your seatbelt, Sweetheart," he purred in her ear. "Safety first."

Then he turned to Seth and Sonny in the back of the truck.

"You boys remember that I'm gonna have this gun trained on your little red-headed friend. Make the slightest move and I will blow her brains all over the cab."

Then he went around to the other side of the truck and got in on the passenger side.

"Follow Darrell," he said. She turned the key in the ignition and when the cruiser pulled out and started back down the road leading toward the highway, she pulled in after him.

"Where are you taking us?" She didn't mean for her voice to tremble, but it did and she couldn't stop it.

"You'll see."

Hayes drove slowly down the road leading to the covered bridge spanning the Rolling Fork River, but didn't cross it. Instead, he turned off on the side road that lead to the Quart House and parked in the gravel lot beside it.

Sitting at the bottom of the hill below the Family Five, the Quart House was just inside the 6-foot-tall rock fence that ran alongside the Rolling Fork River and encircled the distillery property. A museum and gift shop, Seth had told Sarabeth about it the day she'd come to interview him for the story about Double Springs.

Tears sprang to her eyes that had nothing to do with the roaring pain in her face. She'd thought Seth was a doper that day, believed he was subsidizing his business with marijuana money. She'd been so certain, had held that certainty against him in the months since; used it to build a wall between them. And she'd been so wrong! If only she could tell him she was sorry, tell him that maybe things would have been different if ...

But there was no time for that now. It was too late for everything, now.

Seth watched the big man in the front seat wave the gun around at Sarabeth and clenched his hands into fists. The image of Bubba slapping her up against a wall was still playing on a movie screen in his mind.

Seth had spent a good portion of his life wondering if he could be brave. His father certainly hadn't thought so. Joe McAllister believed all the bravery in the McAllister clan had died when Seth's brother had thrown himself on a live grenade in a steamy jungle on a June night in 1969.

Seth had been 16 at the time.

"Your brother's gone," his father had said. Just like that. No preamble. Seth had been brushing his dog, trying to get the briars out of the beautiful golden retriever's coat, when his father walked out onto the porch and announced that life as he had always known it would never be the same again. "Caleb's dead."

Seth had been stunned by the look on the old man's face, a look he would see there every day for the rest of his father's life. Absolute defeat had been etched on his features. Defeat and despair. Everything in his father that was good and courageous, strong, vibrant and full of life had vanished. In its place stood the empty husk of a man who merely kept on living because his heart was beating.

Billy Joe groaned. Seth looked down at his destroyed hands. What kind of man could do a thing like that? The man sitting in the pickup cab with a gun trained on the woman he loved.

It just popped out. The woman he loved. Time to admit the truth. And the big ugly man who'd slapped her intended to do far worse than hit her. He intended to kill her. And all the rest of them, too.

Could Seth stop him? He didn't know. But he did know he intended to die trying.

Sonny was preparing himself to die. He probably had a more accurate view of their chance of survival than the other captives. And he knew they didn't have one. He'd already weighed every possible option, tried to formulate some plan. But he and Seth were no match for the heavily armed Bubba and Hayes. And handcuffed, he'd be no help at all.

He knew that as soon as a police officer lost his weapon, he was doomed. A man takes a cop's gun, he's more or less obligated to shoot him with it. He'd given up his gun in Seth's office when Bubba stepped up behind him and placed the barrel of a .38 caliber pistol at the base of his skull.

And he'd never suspected a thing. Looking back, he could see now that Billy Joe had sounded a little strained on the phone. But he had been convincing. Sonny had bought it, and had come running out here to Seth's office right into a trap.

He glanced over at Billy Joe, at his destroyed hands, and decided that he'd probably have said whatever Bubba told him to say if Bubba had done that to him, too. He didn't blame Billy Joe; he pitied him. What he felt mostly now was an overwhelming sadness. He didn't want to die! He didn't want to leave his daughter. Gracie'd already lost her mother, how could she possibly survive losing him, too? Mary's mother would be there for her, sure—but she was so little, so innocent and fragile.

And he wasn't the only person who was going to die here today. Sarabeth! He'd been running from his feelings for her for more than a year now, but there was nowhere to run anymore. And no time. Oh, it was obvious she and Seth had something going, but it wasn't a done deal, the fat lady hadn't sung yet. He still had a chance. Or he would have if any of them were going to live more than another fifteen minutes.

He closed his eyes.

Lord, I've said since I was 9 years old that I believed in you, based my life and who I am on your promises. Guess I'm about to find out if they're true.

He took a deep breath and let it slowly back out.

And if this is the way it's supposed to end, if this is what you want, then I'm Ok with it. But please, just a couple of things. Please, Lord, don't let Sarabeth die, too. I'm not asking for my life, but I am asking for hers. I'm begging for hers! Take me, but don't take her. Please. All I ask for me is—get it over with quick. Don't let it go on and on. And help me die like ... I just want you to be proud of the way I step out of this world and into the next.

When Sarabeth pulled to a stop in the Quart House parking lot, Hayes was standing beside his car with the back, passenger-side door open. He had Jimmy Dan Puckett's gun drawn.

"Get out," Bubba told Sarabeth, and she opened the door and stepped down onto the ground beside Hayes.

The detective stepped back so he could cover all of them and Bubba said to Seth. "You sit right there where you are. Don't move."

Then Bubba reached into the back of the pickup and hauled Sonny out, pulled him by the arm the few steps to Hayes' car and shoved him through the open door into the back seat. He fell in face first and couldn't right himself because his hands were cuffed together in the back. So he lay there on his belly with his feet hanging out the door.

Hayes pointed the gun at the car door and fired three rounds into it.

"Three bullets to match to the one that killed the little Davis girl," he said to nobody in particular. "One more round in the chamber."

He turned to Bubba then, and gestured toward Sonny. "Roll him over. It needs to be a gut-shot, lots of blood."

Bubba reached into the car, grabbed Sonny's arm, flipped him onto his side, then set him upright in the seat with his feet in the floorboard.

Then he stepped back and said to Hayes, "Kill him."

"No!" Sarabeth screamed, a strangled, anguished cry. Sonny heard her. She did care. *She did!*

Hayes lifted the pistol. "Any last requests?"

Sonny had time to think—*here it comes; game over*—before he looked Hayes square in the eye and spoke in a clear voice, didn't falter even though his heart was hammering like the pistons in a run-away train. Just three words and then Hayes fired.

Sarabeth screamed, really screamed then, a high piercing, horrified wail. Sonny merely grunted. A bright red stain appeared on his brown shirt just above his belt. He looked down at it, almost surprised. Then he began to slide slowly over onto the seat until he was lying on his side. Blood quickly soaked his shirt and began to pool on the seat.

Hayes leaned in and rolled the sheriff over enough so he could get to his hands and unfasten the handcuffs.

"Wouldn't want to leave any marks," he said to Bubba.

Sonny couldn't see her, but he could hear Sarabeth sobbing. He felt no pain, just a profound, whole-body weakness. And dizzy, the world was spinning. He could hear people talking, but their words were as hollow as voices shouted through a drainage pipe.

"A gut-shot will bleed a long time; I need to be covered in his blood from where I carried him to the car after Jimmy Dan shot him."

Sonny was exhausted, more utterly spent than he'd ever been. Had not the strength even to move his hands where they'd been bound behind him. His face was on the seat of the cruiser. He could smell the warm vinyl. And *honeysuckle!* He could smell honeysuckle. Just like he used to smell when he was a boy and he stood on the back porch beside the honeysuckle trellis. He'd pull off the little yellow-and-white flowers and a tiny drop of liquid nectar would drip out the hole in the bottom onto his finger. And he'd smell it, then put his tongue to it and taste the sweetness. He wondered if there'd be honeysuckle in Heaven. Maybe there was. Maybe that's where he was smelling it!

He smiled and sighed out a long breath.

Bubba leaned in the back door and looked at him. "So much for bleeding a long time," he said as he straightened up. "The sheriff's dead."

Sarabeth sobbed harder. Hayes shoved past Bubba to see for himself, then let fly a string of expletives.

"It should have taken him 10 minutes to bleed out!" he roared. "Shoot, there's barely enough blood here to get my shirt wet!" He spewed out a few more curses, then let out a resigned sigh. "Well, it is what it is. Guess something just stopped his heart."

From where he was sitting, Seth could only see the back of the sheriff's head when Hayes shot him, watched it slide sideways as he fell over.

At the sound of the shot, Seth's mouth went dry. In a heartbeat, he had no spit, couldn't have licked a postage stamp and gotten it wet. He shook his head violently to orient himself, to get his bearings again. Hayes had pointed the gun at Sonny and shot him. Just shot him! There was no room anywhere for denial. These men had killed Sonny and they intended to kill the rest of them, too.

Bubba stepped over to his truck and motioned for Seth to climb out. "And bring him with you." He pointed to the unconscious Billy Joe.

Then Bubba moved back, out of range of Seth's long arms.

Seth climbed out, reached in and dragged Billy Joe out behind him. Billy Joe opened his eyes briefly, then blacked out again. Seth had to maneuver him out of the back of the truck and up onto his shoulder. B.J. was dead weight, and Seth staggered toward Bubba.

"Don't even think about it!" Bubba growled as he moved with astonishing quickness out of Seth's way. "You think I don't know you're aiming to jump me. Well, if that's the way you want to die, suit yourself. But I'd think you'd want to keep your lady friend company, be a shame to make her die alone."

Hayes slammed his car door shut, turned to Sarabeth and motioned toward the Quart House. "In there."

A stonework fence about 2 feet wide and 3 feet tall encircled the little building. Begonias had been planted in shallow dirt on the top of it and a manicured lawn stretched out between it and the building. An ornate wrought-iron gate with a National Historic Landmark insignia was set in the fence between the parking lot and the stepping-stone path leading to the porch, but the gate was blocked by a pile of dirt where the grounds crew had stopped work Friday on a small fishpond they were digging.

Hayes and Bubba stepped over the wall, then stood back while Sarabeth eased over it barefoot and Seth climbed over with Billy Joe thrown across his shoulder.

When they got to the porch, Bubba held out his hand to Seth. "Gimme the key."

"I don't have a key. You think I carry a key to every building on this property around with me?"

Hayes spotted a large rock in the flower bed beside the building. He used it to smash out one of the panels of glass in the front door, reached in and unlocked it. Sarabeth stepped inside, careful to avoid the broken glass. Seth followed, carrying Billy Joe.

"Put him down," Bubba said, "over by that barrel." A whiskey barrel rested beside one of three huge posts that rose like tree trunks out of the floor of the building to hold up the ancient roof. Seth laid the injured man gently down on the floor.

"Guess you're wondering what we're doing here since I told you I was planning to burn you with the distillery."

Neither Seth nor Sarabeth spoke.

"What, not the least bit curious? Well, I'll tell you anyway." Bubba leaned close. "You're going to burn all right. But it ain't going to be quick. You're gonna die inside while you watch death come at ya."

"Get over there to that post," Hayes said. For the first time, Seth noticed that Hayes carried a roll of duct tape in the hand that wasn't holding Jimmy Dan's gun. "Stand up against it and put your hands behind you around the post."

This was it, Seth's last chance. Once he was tied up, it was over. He took a step toward the post, then whirled around and launched himself at the tall, thin detective, slammed all the force of his huge height and weight into the smaller man in a full body tackle.

Hayes crashed backward, hit the wall and went down on his back with a grunt. Seth grabbed for the gun.

And the world went black.

Bubba leapt with the quickness of a cat. As soon as Seth turned toward Hayes, Bubba knew what was coming. He could have shot Seth, but that would have spoiled his fun. Instead, he slammed the gun down on the back of Seth's head.

Bubba had invested a lot of time and emotional energy into figuring out the best way to kill his prisoners. He'd have liked for the sheriff to have joined in the festivities he'd arranged for the others, but they needed his body to substantiate Hayes' story about what had happened. Bubba would have to settle for Seth and Sarabeth. And Billy Joe, too, if he woke up. They'd be enough, though. They'd be plenty.

The big man understood death. He understood pain and terror, too, reveled in the whole process on a tactile, visceral level. He recognized that suffering and dying were, after all, the ultimate human act, the ultimate art form, and the most delicious element of that art lay in the *knowing*.

When a creature knew it was going to die, knew but couldn't do anything about it, ahh, that was the most exquisite death of all. Bubba'd killed hundreds of animals in his life—from squirrels to deer—and he had made each one of them suffer in the end. Always made them wait for an inexorable, inescapable death. He'd killed more than a few human beings, as well. Whenever he could, he made them watch death come for them, too.

And every time he killed, he re-lived the supreme death experience of his life. The Vietnamese villagers, the ones who'd been tied to posts when the rivers of napalm streamed down the hillside toward them. He'd watched their faces, stayed behind until he dang near got burned up with them. They'd screamed, wailed, writhed in agony long before the first tongue of fire ever reached out for them. Watching them die, seeing the door of their souls open up to the Night Stalker, had been a high the sadist in him had never been able to equal.

Until now.

Oh, he wouldn't get to watch this time. Watch them writhe in terror as death flowed down to burn the flesh off their bones. But he could imagine it. He could watch the fire and imagine it. That would have to be good enough.

Hayes shoved Seth's limp body off onto the floor and stood up, sputtering and cursing.

"Why didn't you shoot him?"

Hayes had made it clear he didn't like the way Bubba planned to kill the newspaper editor and the distillery owner. Why not just shoot them and be done with it? Just put them in the warehouse and burn it down on top of them. Bubba hadn't even bothered to explain. Hayes wasn't the kind of man who could appreciate the fine art of jagged-edge terror. He wasn't smart enough.

"He could have killed me!"

For a moment, Bubba thought that might not have been a bad idea. But no, not now. He still needed Hayes to make this plan work. Later, there'd be time for that later. And then the skinny albino would understand why Bubba's plan had been an infinitely more fitting way to die. He'd get it then, when the death terror was clawing around in his own belly. Yes, that was something to look forward to. Indeed, it was.

"You're all right. He didn't hurt you. Drag him over to the post."

Bubba kept his gun on Sarabeth, not that he expected the newspaper editor to put up a fight. Still, you never knew. She'd shown more guts all along than he'd expected.

Hayes dragged Seth's limp body over to the post nearest the door, hauling him up to his knees with his back to the post and his feet on either side of it. Bubba grabbed a handful of Seth's hair and held his body in place while Hayes duct-taped his hands together behind the post. Then the detective wound tape around and around Seth's body and the post, starting at his shoulders, all the way down to his waist. It was a silver prison; he'd never wiggle free.

"You, over here," Bubba said to Sarabeth. She stepped up to the post next to Seth's and obediently put her hands behind it. Hayes wrapped them in duct tape, then enshrouded her in a cocoon of it from her neck to below her hips.

Bubba cast a glance at the still-unconscious Seth and shook his head. "He may not wake up in time for the party," he said to Sarabeth. "In which case, you're going to have to enjoy it all by yourself."

He could see fear and confusion in her eyes and it excited him.

"You're going to die, Sweetheart. Think about that. You might die here all by yourself, with two," he indicated Seth and the unconscious Billy Joe on the floor, "deadbeats who can't even offer you company or comfort."

He leaned closer. "You think about it, think about it real hard. *You're going to die.* You're going to *burn! Burn to death.*"

He gestured to the huge picture window in the front wall of the building, pointed up at the Family Five at the top of the hill you could see clearly through the window. "And you're going to watch death come for you. Watch it stream down the hill at you—fire coming to burn the meat off your bones!"

He grabbed a handful of her red curls. "Your hair on fire, burning off your head. And there won't be anybody around to hear your screams."

He cocked his head to one side, studying her. "You do favor your daddy, missy, and that's a fact. Got the same look in your eye right now he had in his when I shot him."

She gasped and Bubba's predatory smile grew wider.

"Yes, sir, Jim Bingham was scared to death soon as he saw my face, never even noticed the gun in my hand. He wasn't scared long, though."

He leaned in and added in a ragged whisper. "But you're gonna suffer enough for the both of you. Payback the Binghams get for messing with Bubba Jamison."

The two men turned, walked out the door and slammed it shut behind them.

Chapter 27

The call came in to the Callison County Fire Department at 4:39 p.m. Fire Chief Jedediah Craddock was at the fire house playing Rook with the four on-duty firefighters and he made the dispatcher repeat what she'd said to be sure he'd heard it right.

He swallowed hard and a cold chill ran all the way down his spine.

Fire at Double Springs Distillery.

He reached over and grabbed the big red handle on the wall that set off the claxon cry of the fire alarm and yanked down on it hard. Then he bolted out the door, yelling over his shoulder at the dispatcher to put out an emergency-assist call to every volunteer fire department in a 50-mile radius.

"Fifty miles?"

"No," he yelled back. "Make it 75!"

By the time he and his men roared up to the covered bridge spanning the Rolling Fork River at the base of the distillery grounds 14 minutes later, it looked like hell itself had opened up its back door and was having a cook-out right there on the top of the knob. Fire leaped 150 feet into the afternoon sky above a blazing inferno.

There were already dozens of cars parked on the side of the road, maybe 100 gawkers, folks who lived nearby and had seen the column of black smoke that was visible from just outside Brewster, 11 miles away. There was a big blue car sitting crossways, blocking the entrance to the bridge, but the driver saw the fire truck coming and moved it out of the way. When Craddock got closer, he could see the car was an unmarked Kentucky State Police cruiser, and as the fire truck roared past and over the bridge, Craddock saw Detective Darrell Hayes get out of it. He had something all over the front of his shirt, something red. Looked like blood.

As the big pumper truck pounded up the winding road, leading a train of two other pumpers, two ladder trucks—100-foot and 50-foot—and two tankers, Craddock surveyed the scene and formulated his strategy, such as it was. There was no sense trying to fight the fire. He'd figured that out 30 seconds after the truck rounded the last corner and he could see what was burning, what lay at the base of the column of smoke that turned the blue sky black over the whole knob.

When he saw it, he thought for a minute he was going to be sick. It was the 54-year-old career fireman's worst nightmare. He'd worked at Double Springs on the grounds crew when he was a kid. He knew the layout. As the truck had raced down the winding roads toward the mounting mountain of smoke, Craddock had prayed that the distillery itself was burning.

Lord, let it be the fermenting rooms, where the big vats of mash are brewed, the bottling plant, the print shop, anywhere but—

And then they'd rounded that corner and he'd seen. A barrel warehouse. Not just any warehouse, either, but one of the Family Five, Flying Ebony, the big one in the middle. If somebody'd set the fire deliberately—and maybe somebody had, that'd be for the fellows from the Bureau of Alcohol, Tobacco and Firearms to figure out—they'd picked the perfect spot.

The five warehouses were spaced out like the number 5 on dice, with Flying Ebony as the center dot. They were set 300 feet apart, but the fire was so huge in the middle one that flames were dangerously close to the other four. Each warehouse was 100 feet wide and 200 feet long, built out of wood—old and dry now—that had been covered over with metal siding.

The four smaller buildings were seven stories tall; Flying Ebony

was eight. They all had tar roofs. He figured there had to be 15,000
to 18,000 barrels in the warehouse that was burning with 50 gallons of whiskey to a barrel. It was ludicrous to believe he could
pump enough water to extinguish more than half a million gallons
of flaming bourbon—alcohol burned hotter than gasoline!

What he had to do was contain the fire, keep it from spreading
to the other warehouses around it. Each of the smaller ones probably held 12,000 barrels. Craddock was good at math; altogether,
the Family Five held more than 3.25 million gallons of whiskey. If
they all went up...

A fire that size was absolutely incomprehensible.

And on the other side of the road from the Family Five on the
hilltop, stretching all the way across the top of the knob, was the
distillery itself, and eight more warehouses, far bigger warehouses,
back in the woods behind it.

Jedediah Craddock shook his head. He couldn't go there. His
math wasn't *that* good. And he did have one thing going for him—
the wind. Must be blowing 40 miles an hour, left to right across the
hillside and *away* from the distillery buildings.

Before the fire fighters even got to the top of the hill, the heat hit
them like a fiery fist. The burning building was a furnace, belching blistered air 250 feet out in every direction. They could smell
it, too, the pungent odor of flaming booze, and fear slithered into
their bellies.

Sarabeth couldn't feel her fingers. She was wiggling them. She
thought she was wiggling them, but she couldn't feel them moving.
Hayes had wrapped the duct tape so tight around her hands that
he'd cut off the circulation.

And without circulation, her hands could—

She didn't finish the thought. Why was she worried about the
circulation in her hands when the panoramic view out the big window on the front of the Quart House showed the most spectacular
fire she'd ever seen straight up the hillside above her! Flying Ebony

was burning. She could see it between the two front warehouses, the flames leaping high above them, yellow and red turning into soot black smoke in the sky.

She tried again to rouse Seth.

"Seth! Seth, can you hear me? Answer me. Seth. *Seth!*"

Nothing. His head dangled on his neck, limp. The blood from the wound in his hair streamed down the sides of his face and dripped off the cleft in his chin onto the front of the silver straight jacket of duct tape across his chest.

Billy Joe moaned. He was lying on his side on the floor where Seth had placed him, next to the whiskey barrel beside the front door.

"Bije, Bije! Listen to me. Open your eyes."

Correction—eye. His right eye was completely swollen shut. And so was Sarabeth's left eye. Between the two of them, they only had one functioning set. She almost laughed; hysteria, first cousin to panic.

And panic was crawling around inside her, a rat gobbling up her guts. She realized she was crying. Tears were streaming down her face, even out of her swollen eye, and her body was shaking. But she wasn't making a sound. The silent tears themselves terrified her and she began to scream.

"Help! Help me! Please, somebody. Help us!"

Who was there to hear? On the little bit of road she could see from her vantage point, she'd watched the train of fire trucks barrel up the hillside. Everybody was focused on the fire. No one would pay any attention to the Quart House. Why would they? It was the distillery that was burning.

And somehow, that fire was going to come for her. Bubba'd said so. Bubba, the man who'd *murdered* her father. Bubba'd said the fire would burn her alive. How it was to happen, she couldn't figure out. There was only grass on the hillside stretching up to the warehouse. Did he expect a grass fire to catch the stone-walled Quart house on fire? Even she could see the wind was blowing the other way, across the hill, not down it.

But Bubba Jamison had promised, and she was certain he wasn't the kind of man who'd break a promise like that.

Darrell Hayes waved off the EMT's effort to bandage his left arm where he'd been grazed by one of Jimmy Dan's bullets in the gunfight.

An ambulance crew had already taken the sheriff's body back into Brewster, but two other ambulances, one from Brewster and another from Bardstown were hanging around in case some of the firemen needed assistance. It was an EMT from Bardstown who noticed his arm was bleeding, but the last thing Hayes wanted was a tidy white bandage on it. He wanted the bloody wound to show! He'd held Bubba's pistol up beside his left shoulder and fired, meant to barely graze himself but the bullet had plowed a furrow half an inch deep across the top of his arm. It *hurt!* He wanted people to see it.

There were cops everywhere now, must have called in half the troopers out of the Columbia State Police post's 11-county area. Some of them were from the Elizabethtown post, too. All the Sheriff's Department deputies were there as well, but they weren't doing a lot of policing and nobody expected them to. They were all too torn up over the death of Sonny Tackett.

After Hayes moved Sarabeth's car, he and Bubba got the fire going good, with a gallon of gasoline poured on the old wood floor of Flying Ebony. Then Bubba drove away and left Hayes on the side of the road next to the covered bridge where he finally got radio coverage—you know how it is in the knobs!—to call for assistance. The fire had spread so fast the smoke was attracting gawkers like a hound dog attracts fleas 15 minutes after they'd pushed the warehouse door closed.

Deputy Jude Tyler had been the first law enforcement officer to respond to Hayes' desperate radio call. He lived only a few miles away and he'd come roaring up with lights flashing and siren wailing. That's how you responded to a Code 10-99—*officer needs as-sistance*. He'd taken the sheriff's death hard, real hard. When he got over the shock, he'd bawled like a baby. Hayes had put his arm around the big man's shoulders and had to fight to keep from crying himself.

He'd already told his story three times. To Tyler and to a second deputy when he showed up a little while later. And to the first trooper on the scene. He'd have to tell it a whole lot more times, of course, but he had it down. The story was sound.

And that story was going to cost Bubba Jamison a king's ransom! Hayes intended to demand $500,000 for his contribution to Bubba's master plan. Deposited in his name in an offshore account he'd set up years ago to stash the money he made as a mole. He had his own plan all worked out. Soon as things died down, he was going to take early retirement from the state police, tell folks he just couldn't do it anymore, not after his good friend Sonny Tackett had died in his arms and all. They'd understand. Truth was, he'd always hated the holier-than-thou sheriff, was glad he was the one who got to put a bullet in him.

Hayes hadn't made up his mind where he'd retire. Somewhere warm, with beaches and good fishing. Just give him a bucket of sunscreen, a straw hat and sunglasses and he'd be set to live the rest of his life in luxury.

The other officers had the scene under control. They'd blocked the road half a mile up in both directions. Of course, people just left their cars parked along the roadside, got out and walked. No way could you keep people away from this pyrotechnics display.

The crowd probably numbered 300 or 400 people now. But crowd control was not an issue. The only access to the distillery grounds was across the covered bridge. The Rolling Fork River, plus the 6-foot rock fence on the distillery side of it all the way around the property, kept the gawkers in check. People just stood on the road in front of the bridge, looked up the hill and watched the show. They'd be telling their grandchildren about seeing it. The biggest event in Callison County history—that's what Bubba'd called it.

It was Craddock's job to contain the fire to the warehouse where it started. Simple task; tall order. Two other warehouses sat on each side of Flying Ebony. Lt. Gibson and Black Gold on the uphill side; Citation and Black Star on the downhill side. All four were at risk, but the two closest to the road were Craddock's primary concern—keep the fire out of Citation and Lt. Gibson and it wouldn't spread to the distillery. And to the other eight warehouses.

The wind had shifted slightly, was no longer blowing due east—left to right across the hillside. It was tapering a little south now, downhill, which put Citation and Black Star in greater danger. Craddock decided to concentrate his limited resources and manpower on Citation.

He turned and shouted to the men he'd set in position with hoses trained and ready. "Wet it down!"

Streams of water shot up into the sky and down onto the tar roof of Citation, already so hot the water turned instantly into steam.

The heat was more fierce than any blaze the firemen had ever fought. The air was so superheated it scorched their noses and mouths every time they inhaled. In their double-layered Kevlar jackets, the firefighters felt like baking potatoes popped into the oven for supper.

Assistant fire chief Harold Baxter reached up to adjust his helmet.

"Jeeze!" he whispered under his breath, "Jeeze, Louise!" He concentrated on what the chief was saying, refused to think about his helmet, which was warping in the heat.

"Harold, take a dozen men and hose down the inside," Craddock said.

The man nodded and gestured for the other firefighters to follow. They dragged hoses from the hydrant next to the distillery office through the big door on the front of Citation. Half the 12-man crew went down the center aisle of the warehouse to the back wall, spraying the racks of barrels as they went; the other half stood near the doorway and fired water up at the ceiling.

The assistant chief and his men had only been in the warehouse a couple of minutes though, when the metal siding on Flying Ebony suddenly disintegrated, shooting a wall of fire 60 feet into the air. Even with the wind bending the flames the other direction, fire leapt across the space between the two buildings and ignited the tar roof on Citation.

"Get out of there, Harold!" Craddock shouted through a megaphone so hot the metal burned his lips. "Get your men—" The megaphone in his hands squealed and went dead.

The men inside the warehouse had not heard Craddock's frantic command, but they saw smoke suddenly billow down from above. An edge of flames licked through the old wood ceiling and they didn't need to hear the fire chief's warning to know they were in danger.

"Out, *now!*" Baxter yelled.

The men dropped hoses and nozzles, abandoned $17,000 worth of equipment and raced for the door as the building filled with thick, black smoke that reeked of burning tar. The firemen barely escaped with their lives.

Within minutes, Black Star's roof caught, too.

All of a sudden, Flying Ebony collapsed. With a mighty roar that launched whiskey barrels and flaming debris hundreds of feet into the air, Flying Ebony imploded. The sides fell in, the roof crashed down and the crushed whiskey barrels inside squirted burning alcohol in every direction, hundreds of thousands of gallons of liquid flames spewing out toward all four of the other warehouses. And toward the firemen, scrambling to move their defense line back.

The walls on Citation burst into flames and doubled the size of the fire. Black Star quickly tripled it. Flames shot 20 stories up into the sky.

The flaming alcohol that gushed out of the inferno of Flying Ebony morphed like dragon's breath into rivers of fire, molten lava that flowed toward the other two burning buildings. Flowed around them, downhill from the dying warehouse. Toward the Quart House below.

Seth opened his eyes. The world was all wrong so he closed them again. He was having trouble catching his breath; there was something tight around his chest. And that smell. Something was burning.

His eyes popped open and he jerked his head up. The pain in the back of his skull hit him so hard he couldn't suck in the next breath. The thoughts in his mind were in a blender and he chased madly after first one and then another, trying to catch one of them long enough to think it.

He groaned.

"Seth!" A voice near him spoke his name. Sarabeth!

"Can you hear me? Listen to me, Seth. Stay with me! Don't pass out again."

He turned toward the sound. The movement slammed a baseball bat into the back of his head and he felt sick. Dizzy. He used every bit of the will he could summon to fight the darkness on the edge of his vision, a black mat framing a picture that threatened to close up around him

"Talk to me, Seth!"

"Sarabeth." That was all he could manage, just the one word. But it was enough. Just saying her name focused and centered him. The spinning world slowed down, the blackness receded and light flooded his sight and his mind.

"Can you see me? Look at me."

As soon as he did, it all came back to him. Detective Hayes in his office pulling a gun and Seth thinking at first it was a joke. Bubba. He hit Sarabeth!

Sonny!

The memory of the gunshot, of Sonny's head disappearing as he slid down out of Seth's sight, was a blow that took so much breath out of him he almost blacked out again.

He'd lunged at Hayes. The world was blank after that.

But it was blank no longer. A two-second survey of his surroundings brought another groan. Look at her, taped up to a post.

"Seth McAllister, if you don't say something I'm going to scream."

"Don't do that." His voice was weak and breathy. "You wouldn't want to upset the neighbors and have them call the police."

"Seth. Double Springs ... *look.*"

Then he focused for the first time on the view out the big picture window on the front of the Quart House and he stopped breathing altogether.

A nightmare inferno had taken over the hillside above them. Flying Ebony was a ball of flames that stretched as tall as the building itself up into the sky, belching out a cloud of black smoke that rose up beyond his vision.

The roofs on Citation and Black Star were burning, too.

Then with a sudden, thunderous crash, Flying Ebony collapsed. The implosion shot flames in every direction, hurled fireballs into the sky and squirted out geysers of flaming bourbon. It looked like a blow torch had been turned on Citation and Black Star. Within seconds, they went from flaming roofs to writhing fireballs.

Seth watched rivers of flaming bourbon from Flying Ebony edge around the other burning warehouses, ooze into the space between them and around the ends of them, encircling them in fire.

And the lava of burning bourbon, three streams of it, began to flow down the hillside.

"Seth?"

It was all he could do to drag his eyes away from the conflagration to look at her. The slight movement of his head made him dizzy and the world spun.

"Bubba told me what was going to happen but I didn't understand." She nodded toward the window. "He said we'd get to watch death come for us. That's why he tied us up here like this. He wanted us to see the fire coming down the hill to burn us alive."

She stopped, took a couple of breaths, but still could only manage a hoarse whisper. "We're going to die."

He wanted to comfort her, to tell her it wasn't so, that something would happen, that somebody would come. But he didn't believe it and neither would she if he said it.

"Seth, I'm scared."

It wasn't a very manly thing to say, but it was reality. "I'm scared, too." Their eyes met and locked; they drew strength from each other, two stands of wire wrapped together.

Chapter 28

Ben wasn't really surprised when Sarabeth was late to supper. She was often late. When you were a newspaper editor stuff just came up. News happens, she always said. She was probably off covering a car wreck somewhere.

Supper was usually at five o'clock. She was an hour late. The boys sat in the living room of the big, quiet house, waiting. They tried to carry on normal conversation, tried to talk about college. Ben really would be going, once Jake told the police his story. And Jake was on his way to the Marines! But neither could keep his mind on chit-chat for long and soon the room grew silent.

Another hour passed before Jake finally said what Ben was thinking.

"You think something's wrong? She's not here and she hasn't called."

Ben looked at the dark police scanner on the mantle. He hated the thing, always kept it turned off unless Sarabeth was home. It squalled and squeaked and made all manner of weird noises. Then sudden bursts of static would interrupt voices in garbled police-speak dispatching unit this and that to code something and something else. It was massively annoying. But he stepped to it now and switched it on, thinking maybe it would give a hint to Sarabeth's whereabouts.

It gave more than a hint. Within seconds, it was clear where every police officer, fire fighter and rescue squad member in a 10-county area was located. Double Springs was burning. No wonder Sarabeth was late to supper!

Jake and Ben dashed to the front porch. The northern sky was dark, like a storm was moving in. That couldn't possibly be smoke!

"Come on!" Ben said. "And bring those pictures of Doodlebug with you. I want to know if Sarabeth sees the same thing in them we do."

The boys hopped into Jake's Jeep Wrangler and tore through town toward Ballard Springs Road. Ben was excited. He'd only once gone with his sister to cover a fire. It had been a simple house fire, but it had been amazing and sobering. He'd stood with the other on-lookers behind the fire line, looking at hell through the front window, flames eating the room, devouring the curtains and the couch and the pictures on the wall.

As soon as they cleared the last street and headed out of town, they could see a gigantic black pall hanging over the knobs around Cade's Crossing. It rose thousands of feet into the air, like a mushroom cloud after a nuclear detonation.

They quickly discovered they weren't the only ones rushing to see the fire. Traffic was as thick as a crowd on their way to a football game. A half mile from the distillery, a Kentucky State Police trooper stood in the road turning cars around and sending them back the way they came. Most people simply drove back down the road until they could find a place to park on the roadside, got out and started walking. Ben and Jake pulled over before they reached the trooper and joined the throng.

Above them, helicopters hung in the air like dragon flies, swooping down as low as they dared so the news cameramen inside could film the scene. Ben wouldn't have wanted to be up in one of those choppers in this wind.

It was impossible to judge the size of the crowd when Ben and Jake turned the final bend in the road and could see the fire on the hillside. There must have been thousands of people. Like the other onlookers, they stopped in their tracks when they could finally see the fire itself. It was an sight neither of them would ever forget.

Sweat dripped into Chief Craddock's eyes and made them water. He thought about his wife, peeling onions.

"I might as well think of something sad," Betty'd always tell him, "'cause I'm already crying. No sense wasting a good cry."

Maybe he ought to go ahead and cry, too.

Stretched out before him as far as he could see was an inferno that defied description. The Family Five were ablaze, belching flames 35 stories high and smoke thousands of feet into the air. The TV news helicopters were reporting that you could see a black smudge on the horizon from 40 miles out.

The gigantic writhing fireball of burning alcohol on the hilltop produced tornadoes of flames that danced in the air above it. When walls and roofs collapsed, the crushed barrels shot out geysers of whiskey that squirted up into the sky until they hit a pocket of oxygen, then ignited in explosions of red-orange flames.

The furnace heat of the blaze radiated out 300 yards in every direction. Blistering, unbreathable air bubbled the paint on the pumper truck they'd had to abandon, and exploded the tires.

All they could do was fall back in the face of the flames' advance. They couldn't fight such a monster. Even with almost 100 firefighters at his disposal, from 20 different departments, Craddock had been unable to save a single warehouse. They'd just gone up one after another—all five of them had burned.

The distillery was still standing, though he couldn't take any credit for that. The 40-mph wind had blown the flames the other direction. Oh, he'd kept all the buildings hosed down, drenched the office, the bottling room and print shop, kept the fire out of the trees that surrounded Seth McAllister's house.

But if the wind shifted, there'd be no stopping it.

He'd sent crews around to the far side of the knob where the flaming warehouses had ignited the nearby woods, with instructions to let the fire burn down to the river and stop it there.

All Craddock could do was let the fire burn itself out. The whole hillside in front of the warehouse was ablaze, with burning bourbon flowing like volcanic lava down toward the Quart House and the Rolling Fork. He'd just have to let the fire burn itself out there, too.

"I bet Sarabeth's up there somewhere close," Ben said. "She has a press pass to get through police lines. If we can find her, maybe she could get us up close, too."

The boys shoved their way toward the front. The police had cordoned off an area directly in front of the covered bridge half the size of a football field. Yellow Police Line tape stretched across the road on both ends of the area and half a dozen troopers stood watch there. Several ambulances and rescue squad trucks were parked on the roadside in that spot, along with three white behemoths—mobile television broadcasting trucks with WHAS 11 News, WLKY Channel 32, and WAVE 3 News First emblazoned on their sides.

Officers up and down the road had kept the crowds of onlookers out of the lanes of traffic so they'd be clear for equipment, though it looked like every fire truck in central Kentucky was already at the scene. The whole hillside left of the road leading up to the distillery was littered with them, like cattle grazing on a field.

There was no equipment on the right side of the road, though. That's where burning bourbon flowed down the hill like lava.

When they finally managed to elbow their way to the front of the crowd, they could feel the heat of the fire and smell the barbecue sauce stench of burning bourbon. Ben looked around for Sarabeth. Maybe she was talking to officers somewhere in the cleared-out area. But it was much more likely she was up there where the action was, up on the hill, firing away as the firemen fought the most incredible conflagration anybody in Callison County had ever seen.

Ben spotted a trooper he'd run into a time or two in Sarabeth's office. The guy was dish-faced—looked like something had smashed in the front of his head so the tip of his nose barely stuck out further than his forehead and chin. He was talking to an EMT and pointing toward the bridge.

Ben called out to him. The gray-uniformed officer turned, searching the crowd, looking for the person who had called his name. When the trooper spotted Ben, saw it was some teenage boy, he started to turn back around.

"It's Ben Malone, sir, Sarabeth Bingham's brother." He felt silly shouting out like that. People all around turned to look at him. But the trooper said something to the EMT, who looked briefly Ben's way, then he walked over to where Ben and Jake were standing just outside the yellow Police Line tape.

"Son, you need to come with me," he said and lifted up the tape. Ben shot a look at Jake.

"Bring your friend. This way."

The trooper turned and started off toward the covered bridge with Ben and Jake in tow.

"Have you seen Sarabeth? I know she's—"

"You need to talk to Detective Hayes about that."

Ben and Jake exchanged a glance. Detective Hayes was here? If there was anybody on the planet Ben didn't want to see right now, it was Kentucky State Police Detective Darrell Hayes. Lying on the seat of Jake's Jeep down the road were pictures of a guy hanging in a jail cell, a guy who'd died with the skinny state police detective's belt wrapped around his neck.

As soon as he got the chance, he planned to show the pictures to Sarabeth, see if she saw in them what he and Jake had seen. How could he stand around and make nice with Hayes when he suspected he'd killed a guy?

But he had no choice. There was Hayes, leaned up against the hood of a cruiser, talking to a television reporter. Standing behind the reporter, a cameraman balanced a camera on his shoulder.

The trooper stopped with the boys to avoid interrupting the interview.

Ben thought Hayes looked enormously self-important, puffed up like a bullfrog. Though his tie was neatly knotted and hung down straight, the rest of him was a mess. His thin, flaxen hair was blowing wildly—like everybody else's. There was a stain on the front of his shirt—a bloodstain!—and a wound on his left arm had left his shirt sleeve torn and bloody.

Hayes was talking animatedly until he happened to glance Ben's way. He stopped abruptly, leaned over and said something to the reporter and gestured toward Ben. She turned, looked at him and nodded, said something to the cameraman, who lifted the camera off his shoulder and moved with her away from Hayes.

Ben's stomach tied in a knot.

Hayes gestured to the trooper, who walked with Jake and Ben to where he was standing.

"You know who this is—Sarabeth Bingham's brother," the trooper said, though it was obvious he knew Hayes had recognized Ben. Hayes nodded and the two officers had an odd moment that Ben didn't like one bit. Something was going on.

The trooper turned and left the boys alone with Hayes.

"Your name's Ben, isn't it, son?" Hayes said. He put out his hand, "I'm Darrell Hayes." Ben shook his hand, even though he didn't want to touch the man. Hayes ignored Jake.

"I know who you are. I was with Sarabeth that day at the jail, the day Doodlebug—" Why had that popped out? He could have said a dozen things and not mentioned that!

"Ben, I have something to tell you about your sister."

A sudden ache took up residence in his gut, an ache that hurt worse than being blind-sided by an unblocked safety. His throat seemed to close so he had trouble speaking.

"What about her?" His voice was shaking. How could his voice instantly start shaking like that?

"Son, there's no easy way to say this, so I'm just going to say it flat out. I'm sorry to tell you, but she's dead."

"Dead?" He felt Jake's hand on his shoulder. "That's not possible."

Ben lost his voice, as if he'd been running, all out, and slammed into a brick wall at full speed. He wanted to talk, to explain that this guy had it all wrong. Sarabeth couldn't be dead. But he didn't have the breath to speak. The world was airless, a vacuum inside a vacuum. He just stood there and looked questioningly at Hayes and didn't say a thing.

Jake felt like somebody had just slapped him. But instead of sending him into shock like the news did Ben, it snapped him out of it. He'd been in a daze, following along with Ben, momentarily engaged when he could get his mind to concentrate on something, like the mystery of Doodlebug's pictures. But mostly he was in some kind of stupor, trying to get his arms around his own loss. Jennifer had killed herself because what she'd seen as a 7-year-old child had driven her mad.

Now he was instantly hyper-alert, his nerves tuned so tight they almost sang. He felt like someone had tossed a bucket of ice water in his face.

He squeezed Ben's shoulder.

"What happened?" he asked Hayes.

"We don't know for sure."

Then the guy was silent. Like they were going to be content with an answer like that!

"What do you mean you don't know?"

"There are a couple of ways it could have gone down. Maybe she died in the fire. Maybe she was dead before the fire started." Hayes reached up and pushed his smudged spectacles to the bridge of his nose, his pasty face as emotionless as a crash dummy.

Jake felt anger fill up a huge empty space inside him. *Hayes was enjoying this!* Jake could tell. He liked being the guy with the bad news, the guy who knew the inside scoop, making you drag it out of him in little pieces. Made him feel powerful and in charge. Hayes wasn't engaged with Ben, wasn't concerned about Ben. He was performing.

"Stop dancing around and tell us what happened. In more than one or two sentences. We want the whole story, now!" There was a razor-sharp edge of rage in Jake's voice.

Hayes' face closed like somebody'd slammed a door. Jake could tell he didn't like being talked to like that. But Jake didn't give a rip what he liked.

"She and Seth McAllister were in the warehouse when it caught fire. The fire could have killed them." Killed *them*? Seth McAllister was dead, too? "Or Jimmy Dan could have shot them. Maybe that's how the fire started."

He paused again, but saw the dark look on Jake's face and was somehow cowed by it. Jake could look amazingly like his father when he was mad. And he was mad now.

"Ok, here's everything I know about it."

Hayes told his story, starting with a description of the call about the Jimmy Dan sighting, then coming to the distillery and finding Sarabeth's purse and shoes, and she and Seth gone.

Ben was frozen, so pale the freckles stood out on his face like pepper on a fried egg. He didn't even flinch when Hayes insinuated Sarabeth and Seth were sleeping together. Jake reacted, though Hayes didn't see him clench his jaw so the veins stood out on his neck. He'd spent his life defending Jennifer's reputation, beat up half the boys in the county. And she'd had no reputation to defend. But Sarabeth! And Hayes liked telling that part. Jake saw the look in his gray eyes. Something was wrong here. Something was very, very wrong.

When Hayes described the gunfight and the sheriff's death, Ben actually groaned. Jake knew how kind the sheriff had been to him, how he'd treated him with dignity when he got busted.

All at once, the enormity of the loss hit Jake, too. Sarabeth wouldn't be there to see Ben cleared. She was gone.

Jake's throat tightened with unshed tears, but he still listened to Hayes, with a laser-beam focus on every word. And not just to the words, but to his tone of voice when he said them.

Then Hayes talked about loading the sheriff into his cruiser and driving hunched over in a hail of gunfire.

"As I was driving away, he stopped using this," Hayes said, pulling Jimmy Dan Puckett's gun out from where he'd shoved it down under his belt, "and started using the sheriff's shotgun, the one Sonny dropped in the doorway when he went down. After I was out of range, I could hear the shotgun go off again inside the warehouse. I heard three shots, but there could have been more after I got down here to the covered bridge where I could radio for help. A few minutes later, I looked back up the hill and I saw smoke."

He was explaining how the shots could have been Jimmy Dan murdering his hostages or just shooting random. He gestured up the hill and pointed out that with a shotgun like that firing in a warehouse full of whiskey...

Jake couldn't hear him anymore. In an instant, the world went totally silent. Hayes was standing there, his lips moving but there wasn't a sound. In fact, he seemed to be moving in slow motion, too, waving the gun around in the air. *A gun with a broken plate on the grip wrapped with black electrician's tape!*

Jake recognized the gun he'd helped his father tape together the night before Ben got busted in the dope barn. The night daddy'd said he wasn't sure he was going to allow Jake to go off to college after all.

But if it was Jimmy Dan Puckett's gun, how had Daddy gotten it from him? And how did it get here? Jake froze. Good question: how did it get *here*?

"Nobody will ever know for sure why Jimmy Dan showed up at Double Springs today," he heard Detective Hayes say, "or why he kidnapped Seth and Sara—"

"How'd you get the gun?" Jake cut him off. "If Jimmy Dan was shooting at you with it, how did *you* get it?"

Bubba Jamison's boy was glaring at him with a look on his face that made Hayes want to punch him. But he was a big kid, strong, not anybody you'd want to cross. Besides, he was Bubba Jamison's son. Good thing, too, because if he'd been anybody else, Hayes would have been screwed!

The gun! *He'd forgotten to get rid of the gun!* How stupid was that? Setting the fire, then dashing down here to call for help, talking to the other officers, the press ... he'd just forgotten all about it. He'd gotten so caught up in telling the story, making it good for Sarabeth's little brother, that he'd just whipped it out.

He hadn't before. The other times he'd told what happened, he'd stuck to the script.

"You didn't answer my question. I said 'how'd you get the gun?'"

"Son, you need to learn to *listen*," Hayes hissed. He paused and looked pointedly into Jake's eyes. "Get *your Daddy* to teach you how to pay attention. I said Jimmy Dan used a small gun *like* this one. And as I was saying"—back to the script now—"when they pull the bullets out of the door of my car, and out of the sheriff, ballistics will show they came from the same gun that shot little Maggie Mae Davis."

There was a sudden boom behind him and they all turned. A fireball of flaming bourbon had exploded 100 feet in the air above the blaze, shooting streams of orange and red in every direction. Everyone gasped, oohing and aahing like a crowd watching a fireworks display on the Fourth of July.

Hayes turned back and looked at Ben, not Jake. The kid was shattered, his face a mask of shock and confusion. He hadn't caught Hayes' blunder. He probably hadn't tuned in to a word Hayes said after he told him his sister was dead.

The knot in Hayes' stomach began to uncoil. He'd dodged a bullet, that's for sure! Bubba's boy was still snarling at his heels, but he'd let Bubba handle him.

He reached out his hand and put it on Ben's shoulder. The boy didn't even look up.

"I'm sorry, son, I really am. A lot of good people died here today."

And before Jake could say another word, Hayes motioned to the television reporter. She scurried back, cameraman in tow as he shoved the gun into his belt and pulled his shirt out over it to cover it up.

Lights were blinking on and off in Jake's mind like a pinball machine on Tilt. Hayes turned away and Jake put his arm around Ben's shoulder.

"Come on Ben, let's go."

"She's dead." Ben's voice sounded like a wind-up toy. "Sarabeth's gone."

Jake could tell Ben was about to lose it, so he took him by the arm and led him around behind a rescue squad truck, then into a 4-foot gap between two ambulances. It was as private a place as he could find.

Ben leaned up against the side of the ambulance, bowed his head and covered his face with his hands. But he didn't cry, just stood there like that, shaking his head back and forth.

Jake wanted to be comforting, to say something to help. But his head was spinning. Words, phrases, thoughts jetted through his mind, random and nonsensical.

Hayes said that gun was Jimmy Dan Puckett's gun, said the bullets would match the one they'd found in Maggie Mae Davis. But Daddy had had that same gun just a few days ago. Jake had held it in his hands while Daddy taped the broken handle. There was no way for Hayes to get that gun unless Daddy gave it to him, which meant Daddy was mixed up in all this somehow.

And if Daddy was involved in it, he was in charge. Bubba Jamison didn't *follow* orders, he *gave* them. Hayes was the hired help, not Daddy. Hayes must be on Daddy's payroll, which would explain why he'd helped Doodlebug commit suicide! Hayes had been taking orders then and he was taking orders now. Whatever had happened here today, Daddy had orchestrated.

And no matter how it had really gone down, Sarabeth, Sonny and Seth had been murdered!

Jake sucked in a breath as the reality of it hit him. Daddy had killed her. He'd wanted Sarabeth out of the way. He'd forced Jake to make friends with Ben to get at her. He'd set Ben up to discredit her. He must have decided discrediting wasn't good enough, so he'd lured her out here somehow and then he'd set the fire to cover it up.

Ben began to cry. Jake couldn't hear anything, but he could see his friend's chest shaking. Not knowing what else to do, he put his arm around Ben's shoulder. Now wasn't the time to tell him. But Jake knew, as certain as he'd ever known anything in his life, that his father had killed Sarabeth Bingham, the sheriff and Seth McAllister, too.

"Wow, would you look at *that!*"

Jake jumped. He hadn't realized anybody was sitting in the ambulance he was leaning against. A woman's nasal voice came from the passenger side window a few feet away. "That burning whiskey's flowing down that hill like syrup dripping down a pancake!"

"Flaming syrup," the man in the driver's seat said. "Check out the Quart House down by the fence." The man grunted. "Glad that ain't *my* house down hill from those warehouses. How'd you like to be a'sittin' in your living room watching *L.A. Law* and look up and see rivers of fire coming right at you!"

Jake could only see a narrow band of the hillside from where he stood. Framed between the ambulances was a slice of the field. At the base of the hill, inside the stone fence that encircled the distillery property, sat the Quart House gift shop. And above it, flaming bourbon lava flowed down from a volcano.

Suddenly, Jake was 14 years old again.

"We had four gooks tied to posts at the bottom of the hill and there were rivers of fire flowing down, coming right at them. It was like lava from a volcano."

His father's story about the time in Vietnam when the Air Force had laid down a swath of napalm on a hillside above the village where he and his platoon had been questioning prisoners.

"Seeing death come for you, that's worse suffering than dying. Watching it, and all you can do is scream."

The day they'd stood over the helpless body of a wounded doe, Daddy'd said, "The best part's seeing it in their eyes. They know they're gonna die but they can't do nothin' about it."

Daddy never killed anything outright. Not a deer, not a rabbit. Not a Vietnamese prisoner. And he wouldn't kill Sarabeth outright either. He'd want her to see death coming. Watch the rivers of fire flowing at her.

Jake grabbed Ben's arm.

"Come on! We've got to go. *Now!*"

"Where?"

"Just come on!" He pulled on Ben's arm. Ben yanked it free.

"Leave me alone. What's the matter with you? Don't you get it? Sarabeth's dead!"

"No, she's not!"

Over Ben's shoulder, Jake could see the burning whiskey begin to pool around the Quart House. Dammed up by the slave fence in front of the river, the liquid now formed a flaming moat all the way around the raised rock flower beds that encircled the building. There wasn't much time!

He grabbed Ben's shoulders and got right in his face, almost nose to nose.

"Do you trust me?" He said each word individually, like plunking four pebbles into a creek one at a time.

Did Ben trust him? He had, after all, gotten him arrested, charged with a Class D felony, looking at prison time.

Tears streamed down Ben's face, but he met Jake's gaze. "Yeah, I trust you."

"Then come on. I can't explain, it would take too long. We might be able to get to Sarabeth, but we have to go *right now!*"

Jake turned and tore out toward the woods on the riverbank across from the Quart House with Ben at his side, running as fast as they'd ever run toward the goal line with a football.

Chapter 29

Sarabeth was panting like a dog trying to cool off. Her soaking-wet hair dangled in her face dripping, the way it did when she stepped out of the shower.

And she couldn't feel her hands at all, nothing below her elbows, though she had stopped worrying about that altogether. She had bigger fish to fry.

She let out a little hiccup of hysterical laughter. Fry. She had fish to fry alright. No, more like bake, and not a fish either. Swathed in a cocoon of duct tape from her shoulders to her waist, she was a Christmas turkey, trussed up in aluminum foil and set in an oven on low.

But as the wall of heat and flame drew closer and closer, the burner on the oven was turned higher and higher.

Billy Joe hadn't made a sound in a long time, not since he opened his eyes briefly when Black Gold exploded. He just lay there, not moving. She could see he was still breathing or she'd have thought he was dead.

Seth slid in and out of consciousness. He obviously had a concussion. He fought to stay awake and aware, but there were times she knew he didn't really know what was going on around him.

His eyes were open now, staring out the window at the spectacular panorama of flames. She was certain this would be their last conversation.

"I thought you were a doper," she said. Inhibition certainly served no purpose now. "Until you started talking about making all those phone calls, trying to track down—"

He didn't let her finish. "I know what you thought. The day you came to do the story on Double Springs, you figured that's how I'd managed not to lay anybody off, that I was using dope money."

She was surprised she'd been so easy to read.

"But if you weren't using dope money, how were you keeping the distillery afloat?"

"Mortgage. If I couldn't pay it back in 18 months, the bank would own Double Springs. Instead of handing it free and clear to the sixth generation in McAllister lineage, I'd sign the title over to Farmers State Bank."

"And that would have been the end of the world because … ?"

He looked up at her with his dark hair plastered in a wet widow's peak above his eyebrows. The effort of moving planted a grimace of pain on his sweaty face.

"If I had a week, I could explain it to you."

"But we don't have a week."

"No, we don't."

"How long? How long do you think?"

Fear as real as a gust of wind passed between them. His dark eyes grabbed hers and held on fiercely. "Half an hour. Maybe."

Half an hour to live. The prospect of imminent death certainly put a whole new spin on life.

Losing the distillery really would have been the end of the world—*then*. But now?

Now, Seth couldn't manage to muster a thimbleful of concern about whether or not his dead father might be proud of him.

The old man never would have been, some voice inside him confided gently. No matter what you did. You could have brought home the gold medal in the bourbon-making Olympics and he wouldn't even have noticed. Joe McAllister didn't notice anything after Caleb died. The world went on, the sun came up, the sun went down but the old man was just marking time. His reason for living was gone.

Why? Caleb had been a good guy but he wasn't *that* special. He got drunk a lot when he was in the academy in Bardstown. He made good grades, but not great. Seth's were better. Caleb was funny and charming—a real ladies' man. Seth even wondered sometimes, given Caleb's way with women, if the sixth generation of McAllister lineage was already out there, growing up somewhere in Bardstown or Elizabethtown, even in Brewster. But no matter how he worried it around in his head, Seth could come up with nothing about his older brother that would inspire the kind of consummate, almost fanatical devotion their father had for him. Seth always hoped that someday, when he had a son of his own, he'd be granted a peek in the window of his father's soul.

He cut his eyes to Sarabeth, without moving. It hurt too bad to shift the position of his head, even a little bit, made him dizzy. Sarabeth had lost a child. She understood. And he'd let his mind play out fantasies now and then. That the two of them might some-day ... maybe he ought to tell her about that.

Jake and Ben raced down the shoulder of the road that ran alongside the river, ducking around the gawkers like dodging tack-les. No one paid them any heed. All eyes were fixed on the once-in-a-lifetime light and pyrotechnics show on the hilltop. When the road curved away from the riverbank, they plunged into the woods, hanging close to the water, stumbling over tree roots, crashing through thistles and thorn bushes that grabbed their shirts and tore dozens of tiny wounds in their arms and faces.

The heat hit them as soon as they drew even with the Quart House on the opposite riverbank, an island in the center of a flam-ing sea. Jake wondered what it must be like for Sarabeth inside the building, and he was certain that's where she was. What must the heat be like in there? Could anybody survive that?

Sarabeth shook her head, tried to get the sweat off her face that was dripping into her eyes. She had to *see*. So little time left, she didn't want to squint at the final sights of her life.

They both spoke at once. Sarabeth reloaded first. "I have MS, Multiple Sclerosis. It was diagnosed right before Daddy died, right before I moved here."

"What does it do to you?"

"It's the mystery disease. No cause, no cure. I could live a perfectly normal life or I could be in a wheelchair in a month."

She wouldn't live long enough to be in a wheelchair! She wouldn't live long enough to have a normal life either. It was over, now, today. In just a few minutes. All that worry about the future—for what? As it turned out, she didn't have one.

"Guess I don't have to care anymore about not being a burden on somebody." She started to cry. She didn't mean to; there'd been no warning. The tears had come like the wind. You didn't see it before you felt it blow your hair into your face. Oh, how she'd like to feel a cool breeze, just one more.

"I'm sorry. I want to be strong. It's just I don't want to die!"

"Neither do I." His voice was gruff, gravelly.

The heat grew more intense with every breath as they watched the flame moat that encircled the Quart House rise higher and higher. The rock wall topped with fried begonias would be breached soon. But they wouldn't likely last that long. A tree outside the wall was burning like a torch and any second the flames would leap to the roof of the building.

Though the walls were stone, the roof was covered in cedar shingles, and Sarabeth could smell the odor of hot cedar. If they weren't already on fire, they soon would be. That's what would get them, she supposed. The burning roof would collapse on them. They certainly wouldn't live long enough for the barrels of whiskey around them to explode, like they'd done in the warehouses on the hill. But when they did, the whole Quart House would vaporize. And all trace of them, all physical trace that there'd ever been three people in that room, panting in the heat, would vanish.

"Will it hurt? Dying? Do you think?" She supposed she was still crying. It sounded like it when she talked and she was shaking. But the rivers of sweat running down her face made it impossible to tell if there were tears. too. "Will we know we're burning?"

Jake led the way past the Quart House to a spot about 75 yards downstream where the river was narrower.

"You think she's in there, don't you, in the Quart House?" Ben gasped.

"I'm sure she is." He hadn't been *sure* before, but he was now. The certainty had been growing on him as he ran, his mind racing faster than his body. The more he'd thought about it, the more convinced he'd become. He believed Sarabeth Bingham was across the river in the Quart House, and maybe Seth McAllister was there, too.

"How do you know?"

"Trust me."

Then Jake waded out into the water, Ben right behind him.

Seth's heart broke for Sarabeth. He would gladly have given his life to get her out of here. He didn't feel afraid, not for himself. But he ached to hold her and comfort her, yearned to protect her.

"I wish I could put my arms around you. There are so many things I should have told you and now there's no time. Sarabeth, you have to know—that day at Elsie Bingo, when you turned down my barbecued chicken. That's when it started. That's when I began to fall in love with you."

The boys started swimming when the cool water was chest high. The current wasn't strong, but still it washed them downstream, farther away from the Quart House. Jake grabbed an overhanging branch to slow his progress and tried to pull his feet under him. The water was still too deep. He let go, swam another couple of strokes and tried again, and then he could feel the muddy bottom. He turned, reached out to Ben, dragged him in and the two of them slogged their way out of the deep water toward the riverbank.

But they didn't climb out of the river. Brush, bushes and briars had grown up on the riverbank so dense it would be impossible to get through. As quickly as they could, they made their way upstream in the shallow water to a slice of riverbank that connected to a dirt and rock embankment about 8 feet tall. The rock fence that surrounded the distillery was built on top of the embankment.

"How are we going to get through these bushes?" Ben asked as they sloshed through the water. "And once we get to the rock fence and climb it, how are we going to get through 10 feet of flaming alcohol?"

"We're not going to climb the fence."

"Then how—?"

"We're not going over it; we're going under it."

Sarabeth was so surprised by Seth's words that she wondered if maybe she'd misunderstood him. He loved her? Oh, she had sensed something, or thought she had. She'd felt an attraction, like a magnet drawing her. But he'd been a doper and she couldn't let herself get involved with him. Dopers were the enemy. Besides, she had MS.

"I love you, too."

There was silence then. What was there left to say? The truth was out there, and it was truth, too. Deathbed statements were even admissible in court. She looked into his dark eyes. You could drown in the depths of those eyes. It was such a shame...

Smoke!

They both smelled it in the same breath. Cedar smoke. The roof was on fire.

If Jake had had time, he'd have explained to Ben how he used to play in these woods as a boy. His house was on the other side of the knob, and he'd spend all day in the woods in the summertime, just being by himself. Anything to keep from going home. As soon as the sun was up in the morning, Jake was gone. He came home as late as possible, ate supper and went to bed. He forged an entire life built around maintaining as little contact with his father as possible.

And that meant he'd had almost no contact with Jennifer either. A bolt of pain shot through him so fierce he almost gasped. She had been in that house all those hours he'd been outdoors, or playing baseball or football or running track. In that house, slowly losing her mind.

The ache of regret and longing was so intense he almost missed it. But there it was, a break in the thickness of the bushes, a small opening. He'd been afraid he might not be able to find it after all these years, but he had. And on the other side of the bushes, indented into the dirt wall was the grate, the rusty old grate he'd first discovered when he was 12 years old.

He'd been fishing in the shade of the covered bridge when his baseball cap blew off in a sudden gust of wind. It landed in the water and floated like a paper boat downstream. He'd dropped his rod and chased it, wading along in the shallow water, reluctant to get his jeans completely wet. But the hat stayed just beyond his reach, a carrot on a stick in front of a donkey. He finally made a lunge, got wet all the way up to his knees, and grabbed it. He straightened up and fit it on his head, turned to go back to the bridge, and that's when he saw what looked like sort of an opening in the bushes on the riverbank. From the far shore, the thicket seemed absolutely impenetrable. But from here … He stepped out of the water, pushed branches and limbs out of his way, burrowed back into the undergrowth. And there on the embankment wall in front of him, totally hidden from view, was a metal grate.

The grate was old, industrial-strength old. About 4 feet tall and probably 3 across. It was set in an iron casement that had been chiseled into the rock. The grate was iron, too, worn and pitted. It swung inward on hinges that had rusted solid 100 years ago. The latch had rusted solid, too. He'd tried that day to get the grate open so he could explore inside, because he'd understood immediately what this was. This was the opening run-away slaves had used to get in and out of the refuge under the Quart House that was one of the stops in the Underground Railroad.

"This leads to a room under the Quart House," he told Ben. At least he assumed it did. He'd never actually seen for himself. The day he found the grate, he'd spent the whole rest of the afternoon trying to get it open. But it wouldn't budge. It was possible the way was blocked now, possible that even if they got into the tunnel, it no longer connected to an opening in the Quart House cellar.

"How are we going to get this thing open?" Ben asked.

"I have no idea."

Sarabeth began to cough. A white cloud settled into the room and burned her eyes, too, made her squint. The smoke hadn't gotten to Seth yet, on his knees beside her.

"Do you believe in God?" she coughed out the words, then tried not to breathe so deeply.

"Absolutely!" Seth hadn't realized until he heard the word come out his mouth how firmly convinced he was that there was a God. It had been that sense of God, of right and wrong, that was the primary reason he had turned down the opportunities to get out of his financial difficulties with a little seven-pointed green leaf. He'd been propositioned by a former schoolmate, offered a ridiculously large sum of money to set up transport of a barrel full of dope along with the other used barrels hauled away from the distillery to greenhouses and wineries all over the country. But Seth turned him down, told the guy to get off Double Springs' property and never come back.

There was an order to the universe. God had established it and maintained it. An understanding of right and wrong, the triumph of good over evil—that was all from God.

"When you die, do you think you—?"

"You go to Heaven." Then Seth began to cough, too.

"Sonny knew that." She was coughing hard now. It was almost impossible to speak. "Before Hayes shot him ... " She gasped.

Coughing stole her words away. Sarabeth dragged in a breath of smoke-filled air and her head began to swim. "Sonny told him, *'I forgive you.'*"

"You don't know how to get this thing open?" Ben was incredulous, almost crying with frustration.

Jake's voice was fierce. "We'll rip it off with our bare hands if we have to!"

He turned to find a piece of wood to use as a pry bar. Ben kicked at the gate in anger and it moved.

"Jake, lay down! Come here and lay down, like this."

Ben dropped to his back on the ground with his head toward the river. He put his feet on the grate and scooted up so his knees were bent. Jake did the same.

"On the count of three, rear back and kick it." Ben said. "One, two, *three!*"

Both boys pulled back and slammed their feet into the grate with all the strength in their legs. Bam!

The rusty clasp snapped with a popping sound and the grate scraped inward a couple of inches.

"Again! One, two, *three!*"

Bam!

Another few inches.

Bam! Bam! Bam!

After half a dozen blows, the grate was open wide enough to squeeze through and Jake plunged into the darkness beyond it.

Sarabeth felt herself beginning to pass out. And she didn't fight it. It was a good thing. She didn't want to know when the fire gobbled her up. Maybe she'd already be dead when it got to her; at the very least she'd be unconscious. Wouldn't feel the flames. Wouldn't know the pain.

Oh Ben, poor Ben! His face swam in front of her eyes and she'd have cried if she'd had enough air. What would he do without her?

He needed her and she wouldn't be there for him. How she ached to see him one more time! Tell him how much she loved him. She could hear the sound of his voice, hear him calling her name.

"Sarabeth! Sarabeth, can you hear me? *Sarabeth!*" The smoke was so thick Ben could barely catch his breath. He lifted his sister's head and shouted into her pale, sweaty face with its swollen black eye. But there was no response.

Jake reached into his pocket and pulled out his Swiss Army knife. The best knife money could buy. Daddy'd given it to him for Christmas. He whipped open the longest blade, stepped behind the post Sarabeth was taped to and sliced down the duct tape until he reached her arms. He and Ben each grabbed a side of the jacket of sliced tape and ripped if off her. Ben produced a knife then, not a Swiss Army knife, but it would do, and began to cut the tape off her wrists while Jake sliced the tape off the post behind where Seth McAllister hung limp, his head dangling.

And there was a body lying on the floor beside a whiskey barrel. Neither of them knew who it was.

Both boys were coughing and choking. Ben let Sarabeth down onto the floor and dropped beside her. The air was a little fresher there. Then he began to drag her to the trap door in the floor that led to the cellar and the tunnel. He got to the steps, picked her up and carried her to the bottom and placed her gently on the cellar floor before racing up to help Jake with the other two.

As Ben dragged his sister's limp body through the tunnel to the glow of twilight sky at the entrance, he prayed, prayed as he had never prayed before. He didn't know if she was alive or dead. He just prayed she'd breathe.

• • • • •

Darrell Hayes was on a roll. This was his third televised interview and he had the story down so pat now he could embellish it, add little touches like, "Sonny grabbed my hand, told me to tell his little girl goodbye, that he loved her."

He said that into the camera, so sincere the cutie-pie reporter from WHAS 11 News in Louisville hung on his every word. "You knew he had a daughter, didn't you?" he said to her. "His wife drowned and he was raising her all by himself—a Down's Syndrome child."

Even though the sun had set, the roaring fire on the hillside provided plenty of light for the television crews to film their stories for the 11 o'clock news. Hayes knew his face would be on every channel. Well, maybe not Channel 32. That interview had been interrupted by the explosion of the Quart House a little while ago.

What a spectacle that had been! And all Bubba's and Hayes' problems had gone sky high with the blast. It had been a glorious sight. A few minutes after the roof fell in, the building exploded, blew up with a thunderous roar. It was the combination of the whiskey barrels inside and those stone walls. But the most spectacular part was the hole the explosion blew in the rock fence behind the Quart House, like somebody'd shot a Howitzer through it. And then all the burning bourbon that had pooled around the Quart House had flowed out through the hole into the river, and set the Rolling Fork on fire. The firemen had been scrambling then!

Chief Craddock had come tearing down the hill in a pumper truck and took off around the knob. Probably planned to intercept the blaze at St. Stephen's Bridge, try to hold it there. Though how he intended to put out burning bourbon on top of water ... well, that'd be a challenge. And, of course, the fire in the river had set both the riverbanks on fire, too.

The news crews had gotten all carried away with that for quite awhile, but the choppers were getting video coverage now and Hayes was back as the center of attention again.

"I looked into Sonny's face and I promised him, I said, 'Sonny, I swear on my badge that I'll take care of your baby girl.'"

There was a commotion of some kind among the gawkers off to his left and Hayes turned to see what it was. And all at once, he couldn't breathe. His jaw literally dropped open. Coming toward him, staggering out of the crowd on her brother's arm was Sarabeth Bingham!

Her hair was wet, tangled and matted, her clothes were muddy and torn, and one eye was swollen shut.

But her face! The look of naked hatred and blind rage there hit him like a fist in the gut and he literally staggered back two steps. The news anchor wannabe stopped her report in mid-glib and turned to see what he was staring at. The cameraman turned, too, and caught Sarabeth live.

That was the story that was on every channel's 11 o'clock news that night. The footage of Sarabeth Bingham advancing on Darrell Hayes like death walking.

"Murderer!" she growled, her voice contorted by rage and damaged by smoke inhalation into a gravelly bark. "Murderer! You killed him, you shot Sonny Tackett in cold blood."

She let go of Ben's arm, turned and searched the crowd for a sheriff's deputy.

Spotting Jude Tyler, she cried, "Arrest him, Jude. He killed Sonny, shot him. I watched him."

Tyler was stunned, looked confused and undecided.

Then Seth appeared at Sarabeth's side. Jake was gone. The boy had helped Seth stumble through the woods after he and Ben had dragged the three injured people across the river.

The river, *ahhh,* how good that water had felt! Ben had been holding her up as they crossed and it scared him when she abruptly went under. She'd just wanted to get her head wet, she explained, wanted the feel of the cool water on her face.

Jake had sent some gawkers back to see to Billy Joe where they'd left him propped up against a tree, and Seth had leaned on the boy's broad shoulders as they elbowed their way through the crowd. But Seth was standing tall on his own now.

"I saw him, too," Seth said, and the low rumble in his voice was pure loathing, not smoke damage. "He killed Sonny Tackett, shot him down and watched him die. And he tried to kill us, too!"

Then Seth lunged at Hayes. Before anyone could stop him, he drew back his fist and slammed it into the state police detective's jaw, knocked him backwards so hard his glasses went flying and he crashed on top of the hood of his cruiser and then tumbled off onto the ground.

When he rolled over, a gun fell out in the dirt—a gun with black electrician's tape wrapped around the handle.

"That's the gun he shot Sonny with!" Sarabeth said. "It's Jimmy Dan Puckett's gun, the one he used to kill Maggie Mae Davis."

Tyler acted then. Reaching down, he grabbed Hayes and yanked him to his feet. Then he slammed him down on the car hood, yanked his hands behind his back and locked handcuffs around his wrists.

"You're under arrest for the murder of Sonny Tackett," he growled. "You have the right to remain ..."

Seth swayed. Sarabeth reached out and took his arm to support him, though she didn't feel all that steady herself. She turned to her brother ... but he wasn't there.

"Where's Ben?"

Ben was gone.

Chapter 30

"**D**addy."

Bubba whirled around, almost fell out of his chair. Nobody sneaked up on Bubba Jamison! But there stood Jake in the doorway of the house, looking like an earthquake survivor.

Bubba had been sitting on the back deck watching the flames light up the sky above the knob. It was an amazing sight, even more extraordinary at night. The fire turned the top of the knob into a glowing fireball that sent exploding flares up into the black cloud of impenetrable smoke with resounding booms he could hear clearly here, almost three miles away.

He could smell the stink here, too. A sticky-sweet stench that reminded Bubba of barbecue sauce.

He would have liked to have seen the fire from a front-row seat on the other side of the knob, but it was better to stay away, keep a low profile. He wasn't going to be allowed the pleasure of seeing Sarabeth, Seth and Billy Joe die, anyway, wouldn't be able to watch their faces as death bore down on them. He could only imagine it, and he could imagine it sitting on his own deck as well as he could standing around with a crowd of rubber-neckers in the road.

What was obvious even from this side of the knob was that the whole distillery hadn't burned. Nothing he could do about that. Blame it on the wind. With a 40-mile-per-hour wind blowing the flames away from the other buildings, Double Springs had survived. Probably best in the long run that it had. If the whole distillery had gone up—and the eight barrel warehouses in the woods—the fire would surely have swept all the way down this side of the knob and burned his house, too.

Wouldn't that have been a kick! Bubba wouldn't have cared, of course. He'd just build another house. It was only money. And the next time, he'd build something totally to his own tastes, wouldn't have to factor in what suited some woman.

He'd been considering that very thought, in fact, when Jake had startled him. His kneejerk response was rage. But the anger didn't have time to form because everything about the boy was profoundly wrong.

His clothes were wet and muddy. Dress clothes, too, what he'd worn this morning to Jennifer's visitation.

Jennifer. Bubba slammed that door as soon as it opened. He wouldn't let himself think about that, walled it off like it never happened.

"Where'd you come from?" he growled.

"I know what you did, and you didn't get away with it this time," Jake snarled. He stepped out of the shadows into the light from the big lanterns that stood on posts all around the railing of the deck.

Jake's shirt was torn, his hair wild.

But what was wilder still was the look in his eye. Bubba had never seen anything quite like it before in his whole life. No human being had ever looked at Bubba Jamison like that.

And the boy was holding a gun.

Any other man would have been frightened, at the very least unnerved by the visage of Jake standing there, dripping dirty water into a puddle on the floor. Bubba was merely curious.

"What are you talking about?" he asked, and lifted his massive girth out of the chair with an ease that always surprised people not used to a big man who moved as gracefully as a cat.

"You tried to kill Sarabeth Bingham, Seth McAllister and Billy Joe Reynolds, but you blew it, Daddy. Your own sick perversion ruined your plan. You wanted them to watch death come for them. Well, it didn't. Ben and I got them out of the Quart House about a minute before the roof collapsed."

Bubba went pale and took a step backwards, the wind knocked out of him. Not only by the information—they were still alive!—but by the demeanor of his son. The sheer magnitude of the boy's rage and loathing was so powerful it was a physical force as solid as a blow from a wrecking ball.

"It's over, Daddy. *Over*. You're through. You're through ruining people's lives, maiming and murdering. You're never going to hurt another living soul. It stops here. Tonight."

Jake lifted the .357 magnum he had removed from his father's gun rack moments earlier and pointed it at the big man's chest.

Bubba didn't back down.

"You ain't got the guts to shoot me, you snot-nosed little brat." He spat out the words with contempt. "I should have choked the life out of you the day I strangled your mama."

Jake recoiled with the same horror he'd felt when he saw that the brutally beaten man they'd hauled out of the Quart House was Billy Joe Reynolds.

Panting on the riverbank, gasping for air, Jake had watched Ben give mouth-to-mouth to Sarabeth. Then she began to cough. And Ben began to cry, just reached down, gathered her up into his arms, hugged her close and cried.

Jake pulled himself out from under Seth McAllister, who'd rolled over on him after they all collapsed just outside the grate. Billy Joe lay beside Seth, where Jake had dragged him out and dropped him. And there in the fading twilight, Jake realized who he was—and saw the mangled ruins at the ends of his arms! For a moment, he thought he was going to be sick.

Daddy. Daddy had done that. Had done *that!*

The horror never ended. It just went on and on and on. It never would stop as long as Bubba Jamison continued to draw breath.

Bubba was judging the distance between him and Jake. The boy was a little too far away, just barely out of his lunging grasp. He needed to buy a few more seconds to edge a little closer.

"I killed Darlene 'cause she was runnin' around on me. Your mama was a *slut!*"

He expected the boy to react. But instead of getting rattled, he seemed to settle, relax. Focus.

"Jennifer was pregnant." Jake said.

"No! My Jenny wasn't like that. She was a *good* girl!"

"She didn't even know who the father of her baby was! Jennifer slept with any guy who had a zipper to pull down." Jake's voice was cold and quiet. "Because of *you!*"

"Me?"

"You took more than one life the day you murdered Mama. You destroyed the 7-year-old girl who *watched you!*"

Bubba sucked in a breath. That's what it meant, what Jenny wrote in her own blood on the windshield of his truck. The words made sense now: *I SAW!*

He glared at Jake.

"You expect me to say I'm sorry? Well, I ain't. I gave Darlene what she deserved!"

"And I intend to return the favor," Jake growled. He pulled back the hammer, cocked the gun with a loud click. "Goodbye, Daddy. Tell Satan I said hello."

Bubba tensed.

Ben suddenly stepped out of the shadows into the light. He was wet, too, as muddy and ragged as Jake. He barely had enough air to speak. Not because he'd run all the way from Double Springs but because of what he'd just overheard.

"Don't," he gasped. "Don't shoot him, Jake. He's not worth it!"

Jake half turned.

Bubba lunged.

Ben's vision cranked down into slow motion.

The big man pounced like a lion. He actually roared, made this awful, guttural noise that wasn't even human as he flew through the air, his huge paws out, grabbing for the gun. He landed on Jake with the blunt force of a sledge hammer.

BAM!

The gunshot sounded like a bomb. Louder than the roaring crash when the roof of the Quart House caved in, belching fried air and smoke down into the cellar and out the tunnel.

Jake settled slowly backwards onto the floor with Bubba on top of him. The boy made a little grunting sound, then he was still and it was quiet.

"Jake?"

Ben took two steps toward him.

Bubba slowly lifted himself up off Jake's body. Ben's stomach rolled as he watched; vomit rose in the back of his throat. The big man sat up and turned toward him. The wild hatred in his black eyes was the most frightening sight Ben had ever seen.

But the boy couldn't even run, just stood rooted to the spot. Couldn't move, couldn't breathe.

Then Bubba fell over on his side, made a *whump* sound when his body connected with the deck floor. A bright, red smear of blood stained the left side of his shirt. His eyes stared sightlessly up into the black shroud of smoke that hid the stars in the summer night. He was dead.

When Deputy Sheriff Jude Tyler, another deputy and a trooper came crashing into the house with guns drawn a little while later, Jake and Ben were sitting together on the lawn sofa on the deck. The gun lay beside Bubba's body where Jake had dropped it.

"I killed him," Jake said, his voice hollow.

"But it was an accident," Ben put in. "Jake was holding the gun and Bubba jumped him. The gun just went off."

Tyler holstered his weapon, went to the body, reached down and felt for a pulse on the big man's neck. He straightened and asked the trooper to go out to his cruiser and call for a hearse. Then he turned and said to the other deputy, "I need a few minutes alone with these boys."

The deputy nodded, went into the house and closed the door behind him.

As soon as he was gone, Tyler said to Jake, "So you had a pistol pointed at your father, trying to hold him until the police got here, and he jumped you and the gun went off—that right?"

Jake lifted his dark eyes and met the deputy's gaze.

"My father strangled my mother, choked her to death in front of my little sister a decade ago. Jennifer told me about it the night before she ... committed suicide." The shrapnel-sharp edge of rage was there again in Jake's voice. "So, I wasn't trying to keep Daddy from running away. I was going to kill him! And I *would have*, too, but he jumped me before I had a chance to pull the trigger."

The deputy looked down at Jake and spoke slowly, grinding out each word, his throat tight with suppressed emotion. "Your daddy ordered the murder of Sonny Tackett this afternoon, had him shot down in cold blood. And if Bubba Jamison hadn't been laying there dead when I got here, I'd ... " He stopped, took a deep breath and let it out in a long, slow stream. "So here's what happened, son. You were holding your father at gunpoint, waiting for the police, when he grabbed the gun and it went off."

Jake opened his mouth to protest but Tyler held up his hand. "Listen to me, boy. That's what I'm going to write in my report. *That's how it went down!*"

Ben reached out and put his hand on Jake's knee. When Jake turned to him, Ben nodded. Jake looked up at Tyler, their eyes met and locked and understanding passed between them.

Then Tyler stepped back and said, "That's the end of it."

Chapter 31

The lead story in *The Callison County Tribune* the week of Thanksgiving, 1989, ran six columns across the front page above the fold: "Federal Grand Jury Hands Down 56 Indictments in Largest Domestic Marijuana Cooperative in U.S. History."

It was the story Jim Bingham had given his life for.

Using the records Jake had dug out of his father's secret safe, federal marshals had arrested the Callison County men who worked for Bubba in five states. They'd confiscated 182 tons of marijuana, too, with a street value of $400 million. The feds had dubbed Bubba Jamison's organization the "Cornbread Mafia."

But that wasn't the story that interested Sarabeth. She'd written a smaller story that ran below the fold and she was reading it when a voice asked from her office doorway, "What are you smiling about?"

Seth. Just hearing his voice planted chill bumps on her arms.

"I was reading about our good friend Darrell Hayes."

She turned to Seth and read out loud. "At a sentencing hearing Friday, Circuit Judge Earl Compton handed out the first death penalty in Callison County history to former Kentucky State Police Detective Darrell Eugene Hayes for what Compton called the 'ruthless, soulless execution' of Callison County Sheriff Sonny Tackett."

The smile faded from her face as the memory bloomed full blown in her mind. Seth crossed the room in two steps, pulled her to her feet and put his arms around her.

"Sonny was in love with you," he said into her hair.

She pulled out of his arms and looked up at him. "How do you know that?"

"I just know."

She did, too.

"He had good taste in women."

She watched Seth try to smile but he couldn't quite pull it off, either. So he cleared his throat and said, "Thing One and Thing Two are outside." He did smile, then. Ben was home on Thanksgiving break from USC; Jake had just completed basic training. "And the Marine standing out by my car is a *beast!* Right now he's a hungry beast and that's a dangerous combination, so I offered to take the two of them and my best girl to lunch. You interested?"

"Now? It's only 11 o'clock."

"I have to get back to Double Springs early. They're putting in the foundation on the new warehouse this afternoon."

She loved the irony of it. In order to get a mortgage on the distillery, Seth had been forced to take out ridiculously expensive insurance on the property. When Bubba burned the warehouses, Seth collected enough to pay off the loan and build back. Just one warehouse, though, not five. But Seth didn't waste time anymore worrying about how he *ought* to do things. Neither did Sarabeth.

She reached out and took his hand. "Let's eat."

$$\bullet \ \bullet \ \bullet \ \bullet \ \bullet$$

Billy Joe could see the trailer house sitting on the riverbank on the other side of the walking bridge. It had a flower garden out front and a vegetable garden out back with a nearby clothes line where Becky always left a pair of his old overalls hanging to flap in the wind. She said it helped keep the birds and the deer out of the garden.

He could see Becky, too, beautiful, wholesome—like her picture belonged on the front of a cereal box, her hair curled around her chipmunk cheeks and those eyes big and brown and framed by lashes so long and thick they looked artificial. She was standing at the sink beneath the window with red chintz curtains, washing dishes and he'd been staring at her.

She turned around and asked, "What? What are you staring at?"

And he said "I'm staring at you 'cause you're so da-gone pretty, that's wha—"

"*Billy Joe.*"

He opened his eyes. It was the jailer standing outside his cell.

"It's time to go now. You ready?"

"Ready as I'll ever be."

He stood and turned to pick up his UK ball cap off the bunk. It wasn't standard orange-jumpsuit-prison garb, but the jailer had urged him to keep it all the same, said maybe they wouldn't take it away.

The jailer had been good to him the past few months. Let Sarabeth sneak him burgers and fries from the new McDonalds that opened up in October. She'd promised to bring Billy Joe a Big Mac every week for the next five years, but he wouldn't hold her to that. The maximum security prison in Eddyville was a long drive from Brewster.

The jailer had hand-delivered the note from Becky, too. Billy Joe had it in his shirt pocket, close to his heart. He sure hoped they'd let him keep *that* where he was going. But it didn't matter if they took it. He had it memorized.

> *Billy Joe,*
>
> *Me and the girls are living in a trailer Seth McAllister got for us. He put it on a piece of land by the distillery where the fire cleared the woods away from the river. It's real nice, like the one we used to have ~~before~~ Like the other one, you know, only nicer.*
>
> *Bethany's fine. Kelsey don't say much. Just sits. But I take her outside some and she likes the sunshine on her face.*
>
> *I got me a job waiting tables for Squire Boone at the tavern*

and folks are real nice to me there.

I will write to you when you get settled.

Becky

He reached out and clasped his hat between his hands like you'd pick it up if you were wearing boxing gloves. And he might as well have been. His fingers didn't work anymore. They were so torn up and mangled they just hung useless. But he could use his right thumb, so he could grasp things. He was learning how to get along with that.

The jailer unlocked the cell door and held it open so Billy Joe could cross in front of him.

"I'm sure gonna miss your hospitality," Billy Joe said.

Then he smiled that dimpled smile of his. It had a gap in it now where Bubba'd kicked out one of his front teeth. But it still was a smile that'd break your heart.